With Love's Light Wings

by

Jann Rowland

One Good Sonnet Publishing
Publishers of Fine Romance
and Fantasy Fiction

By Jann Rowland

Published by One Good Sonnet Publishing:

PRIDE AND PREJUDICE VARIATIONS

With Love's Light Wings
Mistletoe and Mischief: A Pride and Prejudice Christmas Anthology
Another Proposal
A Matchmaking Mother
The Challenge of Entail
The Impulse of the Moment
Mr. Bennet Takes Charge
A Gift for Elizabeth

This is a work of fiction based on the works of Jane Austen. All the characters and events portrayed in this novel are products of Jane Austen's original novel or the authors' imaginations.

WITH LOVE'S LIGHT WINGS

Cover Design by Jann Rowland

Published by One Good Sonnet Publishing

ISBN: 1989212174
ISBN-13: 9781989212172

To my family who have, as always, shown
their unconditional love and encouragement.

CHAPTER I

*P*emberley, in Derbyshire, was a tranquil estate. Situated in a long valley, its fields were fertile and eager to yield their bounty to a patient hand, the whole of it surrounded by lush woods, providing ideal acreage for sheep and cattle, its wealth seeming unlimited. With such a pastoral setting, there was little expectation of any noise, other than the daily working of a farm, a tenant hailing another or the sounds of cattle lowing, or perhaps the raps of lumberjack's axes against trees.

Which was why the sounds of arguing were so incongruent one day in the early spring, and surprising as one combatant was known as a reticent man. He was tall, dark wavy hair framing a handsome face, dark eyes filled with intensity, and he was dressed in fine clothes as befitted his station. The other man in the dispute was not as tall or handsome, but would be called pleasantly featured by most, and was considered to be congenial by all, and easily led by the more cynical. In the present argument, however, he was not giving an inch.

"What is this madness?" demanded the taller man of the other. "I can hardly comprehend what you are saying, for it makes little sense?"

"Why should it make little sense? Since my father's death, I have appreciated your guidance, Darcy, but if you think to direct me, you shall be disappointed."

"Bingley," replied Darcy with exaggerated patience, "I have no wish to direct you, for you are my friend, not my subordinate."

"Then why do you take offense? Is it not my choice to pursue and — yes — even marry whom I wish?"

"Of course, it is," growled a frustrated Darcy. "In this instance, however, I must think you are at the mercy of some witchcraft, for you are making little sense."

"If witchcraft it is, then I am content to be caught in its grasp," averred Bingley. "For I know no such exquisite torture as being in love with a worthy woman."

"Infatuation, you mean," snapped Darcy.

"Do you think I do not know my own heart?"

"I believe the organ can be misled by your senses, that infatuation may be mistaken for deep and abiding love. Tell me, Bingley, what virtues does Miss Bennet possess that other ladies do not?"

"A beautiful countenance and a beautiful soul," rejoined Bingley. "Even you, who is so particular about those with whom you associate and will not give consequence to *any* young woman must acknowledge she is an exceptionally lovely woman."

"A lovely woman with a black heart."

Bingley's countenance became stony and he turned to march from the room without a word. Regretting his outburst the instant he uttered it, Darcy followed his friend, ignoring the thought it had always been Bingley following him, rather than the reverse.

"I apologize, Bingley," said he as he chased his friend. "My words were ill-judged."

"At least you confess it," said Bingley, stopping and whirling about, one finger jabbing in Darcy's direction. "I am surprised at you, Darcy. Though this fool disagreement between your family and the Bennets has persisted for longer than anyone can remember, I had never thought *you*, of all people, would dismiss a young woman because she is a member of a family you dislike."

"It is her membership in that family which fills me with disquiet! The Bennets, Bingley, are not to be trusted — I cannot imagine this Miss Bennet differs from any of the rest of them."

"Do you know her? Have you exchanged even two words with her? Has your family's misplaced pride allowed you to believe, even for a single moment, that she is not the blackguard you have always assumed she was?"

"I know nothing of her —"

"That is the point."

Bingley paused and calmed himself, taking several deep breaths. His friend, Darcy knew, was a man who disliked conflict, and would go to great lengths to avoid it. This was why Darcy was shocked their conversation had devolved to this state so quickly, for Bingley was more apt to laugh off that which he did not like, to evade unpleasantness instead of confronting it.

"Darcy, please listen to me, as a friend," said Bingley at length. "Our friendship has been a great strength to me over the years—I appreciate your assistance and that of your father more than I can ever say. When my father passed away, I would have been lost if you and Mr. Darcy had not guided me, and I am not insensible of my debt to you.

"With respect to *my life*, however, I will accept no interference, will allow no dissent. My reason for informing you of my intentions was nothing more than the desire to avoid shocking you at the assembly tomorrow. I shall open the dancing with Miss Bennet and it is my intention to pay her the compliment of my attentions in as fervent a manner as I can muster. When the time comes, I shall ask her to be my wife, and I expect no less than her acceptance, for she has made her sentiments clear.

"Do not denigrate her feelings, my friend," interrupted Bingley when Darcy opened his mouth to do just that. "It will not be beneficial for our friendship if you say any unkind word about Miss Bennet, for I will not tolerate it."

For a moment, the friends stared at each other, Darcy surprised, for he was not certain he even knew this Bingley. On Bingley's part, he stood and watched Darcy, not a hint of his feelings showing on his face. This, in itself, was unusual for Bingley, who was more akin to an open book than one closed tight.

"Please, Darcy," said Bingley, "I urge you to accept my choice. For our friendship to remain, I require your acceptance. While your regard for her is unnecessary, I will brook no criticism, none of the Darcy disdain. Though I hope you will remain a friend, I will end our connection if you cannot find it within yourself to abide by these strictures."

Then with a bow, Bingley turned and walked down the hall—within moments, the sound of Pemberley's front door closing reached Darcy's ears. Darcy wondered if he would ever speak to his friend again.

The genesis of the dispute between the Bennet family of Longbourn, and the Darcy family of Pemberley was a matter of much speculation, for no one living could remember how it had come about. It may have been a dispute over water rights or the exact location of the border between the two estates, or it might have been as innocuous as an ill-timed slight or misspoken word. There were even whispers that it might have been an argument between two young men over the affections of a woman, though many scoffed at such silly notions. Whatever it was, the two families, while they did not descend to open warfare, had little good to say about the other, and were never inclined to deal with the other with any civility.

It was fortunate the border between the two estates was a low hill rising between two valleys, otherwise the dispute might have escalated to greater bitterness. As it was, there was little value in the hill, other than providing a fine view of both estates, and previous masters had been content to ensure the fence between them was in good repair and attempted to forget the proximity of the other family. England was a civilized place and had been for many years, and the crown would not tolerate open warfare in an otherwise peaceful location.

As it was, few in Derbyshire were not aware of the quarrel between the two families. The Bennets were the higher in society, as the current master of Longbourn was descended from a long line of the barons of Arundel and possessed connections to many others of similar stature—and higher—in society. The Darcy family, by contrast, were naught but gentlemen farmers, albeit with a long and distinguished history, lengthier than their more highly ranked neighbors could boast. There had been Darcys at Pemberley from time immemorial, some said back to the days of William the Conqueror, and while the Darcys were untitled themselves, they possessed many connections to those who were, including the late Mrs. Darcy, who was the daughter of an earl. Some of society called the Darcy family proud and arrogant, but not one of them could deny the family's right to feel that way if they chose. It was nothing less than simple fact that previous Darcy masters had refused to accept titles, and the family was known to disdain those who did accept them. That they did not stint in showing this contempt to their titled neighbors was another bone of contention between them.

While those of a sensible nature might argue that a forgotten grievance was a poor reason to carry on a dispute, neither family had seen any need to attempt to reconcile with the other. The other families of the neighborhood fell into one of three categories—they sided with the Bennets, sided with the Darcys, or opted to remain neutral and clear of any argument. Most chose this final approach, though there were some who chose another because of friendship, connection, or as an attempt to curry favor.

Regardless of whatever others thought of the dispute, it was generally acknowledged that the absence of any violent tendencies between the two camps was a blessing. Instead, they tended more toward ignoring each other than arguing. And for that, most were grateful.

The day after his argument with Bingley Darcy attended the assembly Bingley had referenced only the day before. Dancing was not one of Darcy's favorite pastimes—it would be more correct to say he detested the activity. On that occasion, Darcy found he detested it more than he could ever remember. It took no great intelligence to understand the reason.

As the strains of the first set wafted over the gathering, Bingley stood across the aisle from his newest angel, his eyes fixed on her in a manner Darcy had seen many times before. While it was comforting to think this infatuation might not last any longer than the others, there was something in Bingley's countenance which suggested this time would be different.

As the steps began, Darcy found himself unable to watch, and he glanced around the hall, attempting to discover some other sight to hold his attention. Were the entire Darcy family to attend, Darcy knew they would take up a position in one corner, while the Bennets would claim the other across the hall—no Darcy would ask a Bennet to dance, and there would be little mingling between the camps. While there might be occasions when members of the two families might come together due to the steps of the dance, they would affect ignorance of the other's presence and exchange no words.

On this occasion, however, Darcy was the only member of his family present. Mr. Robert Darcy, his father, was even less inclined to society than Darcy was himself, and Georgiana was suffering from an indisposition which prevented her attendance—though Georgiana was only seventeen, she had begun attending certain events of the neighborhood to prepare for her eventual coming out. And as Alexander, his younger brother, was away from home, Darcy found himself enduring the evening alone.

"I see you continue to stand about in this stupid manner," said a gentleman of the neighborhood by the name of Fordham, when the first sets ended. Fordham laughed at his own jest. "I understand your reticence, but surely you could set it aside for tonight. There are no ladies in attendance tonight who are desperate to attach themselves to you."

"There are few pastimes I detest more than dancing," responded Darcy. Fordham was a good sort, but Darcy did not consider him a close friend, and he wished the man would retreat and leave him be.

"I cannot understand why," said Fordham. "Are there not many uncommonly pretty young ladies in attendance tonight? Take the Bennets, for example."

Darcy did not dignify Fordham's words with a response, though he was forced to agree with him. Though Darcy had no care for the Bennet family, the five daughters were exceptionally pretty, from the first to the last. The eldest, who had caught Bingley's attention, was one of the most beautiful women on whom Darcy had ever laid eyes.

"Can you deny it?"

Pulled from his thoughts, Darcy shrugged. "I suppose you are correct, though I have no care for them."

"Ah, yes, the infamous feud between the Bennets and the Darcys," replied Fordham with a shaken head. "Still, would a man not foreswear even enmity of longstanding to gain the regard of such an exquisite creature as Miss Elizabeth?"

Darcy's eyes found the second-eldest Bennet in response to the other man's words, though he refused to respond. Fordham, unfortunately, needed no encouragement.

"And Miss Mary, though of an overly religious bent, is not devoid of beauty. Even Miss Kitty and Miss Lydia, though still young, are acceptable, though I find Miss Lydia a little too calculating for my tastes. And then there is Jane Bennet."

Fordham paused for a moment, looking between Darcy and the eldest Bennet—not to mention Bingley, who stood close to her side. As Darcy might have predicted in advance, his next words concerned Darcy's friend.

"Miss Bennet is a beautiful lady, but I find myself interested in your friend, for it appears dear Bingley has slipped his leash. Unless I am mistaken, I suspect you are not happy about it either."

The full force of his glare Darcy turned on Fordham, which the man noted in an instant. Darcy's displeasure had been known to quell more courageous tongues than Fordham possessed, but in this instance, he chuckled and shook his head.

"Do not mistake me, Darcy," said Fordham, still laughing to himself. "Bingley is a good man, but he has been attached to your coattails for at least these past four or five years. This sudden interest in the eldest Bennet daughter cannot be to your liking."

"Bingley may do as he pleases," was Darcy's short reply. "I neither direct him nor give my approval to his amorous interests. It would be best if you do not say such things where others might overhear, for I would have no one misled by jests which are untrue and in poor taste."

"Your friendship is well known in the neighborhood, Darcy. It is this sudden distance between you which will excite the interest of the gossips. That and his attachment to the eldest Bennet, which, I might add, has escaped the notice of us all, will only throw fuel on the fire."

"As I said," replied Darcy with a shrug, "Bingley may do as he pleases. There is nothing I or anyone else can do to turn him from his course if he decides he wishes to align himself with her."

"Even his sister?"

It was difficult, but somehow Darcy avoided grimacing at the mention of the woman. The eldest Bingley sibling, Louisa, had married a man by the name of Hurst two years before and had produced an heir of late. Darcy doubted she would return to the district until at least the summer. Bingley's mother had recently returned from Norfolk where she had been assisting her daughter. The younger sister, however, was a different matter.

Caroline Bingley was a tall, willowy woman, not ill-favored, but more striking than beautiful. As the Bingleys were wealthy, she also possessed a handsome dowry, though the family's lingering connection to trade—Bingley's grandfather had purchased Netherfield Park, their estate—was still recent enough to engender an unwelcome stench to many in society. Miss Bingley, however, had decided from an early age that she was the perfect future mistress of Pemberley and was not subtle in the business of being noticed by Pemberley's heir. There was no intention on Darcy's part of ever making her an offer, a truth he had shared with his friend, but still she persisted. Even now, when she was dancing with Mr. Smallwood, her eyes often sought Darcy, her gaze hungry and predatory.

"Though I would imagine Miss Bingley is not pleased with her brother," said Darcy at length, "she has never had as much influence over him as she believes. Her displeasure is all because she *thinks* her brother's defection will make it more difficult to achieve her designs."

"Will it?"

Darcy turned a scowl on Fordham, but though his displeasure

would often cow the other man, that day he possessed the temerity to laugh. "I believe I have my answer, my friend. While Miss Bingley possesses a handsome dowry, you do not require it, and I believe the benefit of her fortune is offset by certain . . . disadvantages of the lady's temper."

Try as he might, Darcy could not find it within him to disagree. "I cannot say you are incorrect. The lady is a drawback I have endured to maintain Bingley's friendship."

"That is understandable. But consider the bright side of Bingley's actions—if he joins his fate to the Bennets' you may cut his sister with no consequences." Fordham paused, full of mirth yet again. "Unless you *are* considering paying her the highest of compliments."

"Given what I have just said about her?"

Fordham laugh. "I suppose not. It is likely for the best, for I doubt your father would approve of such a connection, regardless—he married the daughter of an earl, as I recall."

"Yes, he did," replied Darcy. "But he married her for affection, not because of her status."

"I am sure her status did not hurt."

The sound of feminine laughter reached them and they turned as one, noticing that Lady Margaret Bennet was holding court with some of the other women of the neighborhood. With her were most of the principal gentlemen's wives, none of whom were her equal in society, though Lady Charlotte Lucas, the daughter of an earl and betrothed to Darcy's cousin was present that evening. Lady Margaret had never been one to modulate her voice, and as such, her words floated through the air, easy to understand even with the musician's efforts filling the room.

"My Jane is the most beautiful girl in the room, is she not? I am not surprised she has captured the attention of a man as handsome and amiable as Mr. Bingley. Lord Arundel and I would have preferred our daughter to favor a gentleman of our stature, but it seems he has captured her heart."

With a scowl, Darcy turned away, an action noted by his companion. "It is difficult to blame them for espousing such wishes, Darcy. There are many their like in society."

"Well do I know it," replied Darcy, hoping his shortness of tone would induce Fordham to leave. When he did not, Darcy added: "You did not hear her at the last assembly, crowing to all her cronies of how her daughter would catch Lord Winchester."

Fordham laughed and exclaimed: "I do not know what you saw,

Darcy, but in my view, Miss Bennet had already *captured* Lord Winchester, and I do not blame the woman for an instant for throwing him back. Though he is a viscount and a future earl, Winchester is a dullard. I dare say if his valet did not lay his boots out the night before, he would not know which foot goes into which when he rose in the morning."

Though improper, the remark set Darcy to laughing, for it was nothing less than the truth. "Did she refuse him? Given how her mother was speaking, it seemed inevitable there would be an announcement before long."

"I do not know if Winchester ever offered for her," replied Fordham. "All I can say is the lady did not appear happy with the man's attentions. You must own the family at least allows the daughters to marry where they will — otherwise, Lord Arundel would not have accepted Bingley, nor would he have allowed her to refuse that mewling milksop Winchester."

Though Darcy nodded, he declined to respond. This lack of response indicated to Fordham he was not in the mood for conversation, for the man excused himself soon thereafter. Darcy wished to be left alone, but it was not to be.

"For your information, since you seem to have some interest, Jane did *not* favor Lord Winchester, nor would my father force her to marry against her inclinations."

Turning, Darcy noted the presence of the second Bennet daughter. She was standing close behind him, looking at him with suppressed mirth, tinged with asperity. The most diminutive of the Bennet daughters, Miss Elizabeth was also the darkest in coloring, her fine mahogany hair pinned behind her head, Darcy suspected, would reach the middle of her back if unbound. She was neither so beautiful as her elder sister nor ill-favored, but to Darcy's judgmental eye, there were several imperfections about her face and form, and a satirical look about her, the sight of which provoked him to a painful clenching of his teeth. Her one feature which could be called beautiful — her eyes — were fixed upon him, fire burning in their depths.

"I assure you, Miss Elizabeth, that I do not concern myself with the doings of your family."

"That is interesting, considering your recent conversation with Mr. Fordham. And to you, I am The Honorable Miss Elizabeth Bennet."

Darcy ignored her baiting in favor of focusing on her comments concerning his previous conversation. "If you recall, it was Fordham who spoke on the matter — not I."

The woman before him cocked her head to the side. "It takes two to converse, Mr. Darcy."

"It does, indeed."

"Then I suppose you must repine Mr. Bingley's ability to direct his own affairs. Your distance this evening speaks volumes as to your opinion of his interest in my eldest sister, though I wonder that anyone could have any objections, for Jane is an angel."

"Bingley may do what he wishes," said Darcy curtly. "As I told Fordham, I neither direct him nor am I his nursemaid."

"Perhaps not, but I am certain you wish you were." The woman gave him a thin smile. "For you cannot approve of a man having an interest in a Bennet, though we are his superiors in society.

"I must own, however," continued she, not allowing Darcy to insert a comment, "I wonder what you *do* wish for him. Though I know you would never settle for less than a princess—you would consider her your due—your friend does not have more than two gentlemen in his family history."

"Then I wonder why you Bennets would wish him to join your family," replied Darcy. "Is your father not a peer?"

"He is, and he is so conscious of his position that he rarely mentions it," replied Miss Elizabeth. "Of much more importance is my sister's feelings—my father would never do anything to interfere with that."

"Then I applaud him," replied Darcy. "If you think my father is any different, you are mistaken."

The impish grin with which she fixed him somehow irritated Darcy. "Mr. Bingley is a good man to follow his heart, Mr. Darcy. I hope you can find it within you to congratulate him."

"Whatever he chooses," replied Darcy. "I only hope he does not know disappointment because of his choice. It is unlikely he will remain unaware of your family's true colors."

"I should hope he already sees our true colors," replied Miss Elizabeth.

Then she fixed him with a smirk and turned away. But before she had gone more than a few steps, she turned back and glared at him. "As for my mother, know that she also wishes for her daughter's happiness. She may speak without thinking occasionally, such as on the subject you mentioned. But she would never act in any way other than to ensure her daughters' happiness."

Having said those final words, Miss Elizabeth departed, leaving Darcy to watch her retreating form. It was, he decided, a more cordial interaction between members of the two families than he could remember for some time, a particular incident which occurred the previous summer being the most obvious example of the discord between them. That event did not bear consideration, and he pushed it from his mind. Instead, he returned to his contemplation of Bingley and Miss Bennet, wondering if his observation would reveal something he could take to his friend. The Bennets were grasping and artful, and he would not have Bingley caught up in their web.

CHAPTER II

$\mathcal{A}$s feuds went, the disagreement between the Bennet and Darcy families was mild. There were no open conflicts among them, their servants were not at war, and while there had been an incident the previous summer, an excess of drink had been the culprit, drunken insults leading to other foolishness. The matter had been resolved with little difficulty, though hard feelings had persisted for some weeks after.

Having said that, there was little congress between the two camps and those who supported them. While the Darcys had no close family in the area—the closest family to them was that of Mr. Darcy's late wife, Lady Anne Darcy, who lived some thirty miles distant—the Bennets had several other relations in the neighborhood, though those were also, similar to the Darcy family, relations of Lady Margaret rather than the baron. Of their close supporters, it could be said there was a little more fraternization, but that was often a matter of necessity, where business and estate concerns intersected, rather than friendship or a desire to socialize.

Mr. Charles Bingley was, therefore, an anomaly. The Bingley family had moved to the neighborhood during the time of the present Mr. Bingley's grandfather, who had purchased the estate with funds obtained through generations engaged in a family business. At the time the family had been, as was the practice of those established as gentry, considered new money, and as such, while most were friendly, the Bingleys' status, regardless of their wealth, was decidedly low. That had changed over the years as others forgot their origins or discounted them as the family became more gentrified. With their newness to the neighborhood, neither side of the dispute at the time took much notice of them.

That all changed when the heir of Pemberley met the heir of Netherfield at university. Darcy, being two years older than Bingley, had been starting his third year when the man's father spoke to his own father, requesting guidance for his son, who was about to start his first year. The two young men, though not unknown to each other, grew to become excellent friends within days. This remained unchanged through the elder Bingley's death, the subsequent inheritance of the son, and the ensuing years.

To an observant viewer, however, cracks had begun to form in their friendship, not sufficient to make either wish to forswear their mutual connection, but those suggesting a change in the dynamic between the two men. Fitzwilliam Darcy was a confident individual, one of a high position in society and intelligence which served him well in anything he chose to do. While Bingley was not deficient, he was of a more retiring nature, one which delighted in friendship, laughter, and kindness to all. Darcy was a leader and Bingley his eager follower. Over time, however, Bingley gained confidence in himself as a master and landowner, and it was inevitable the relationship between them would alter. These changes in their friendship culminated in Bingley's admiration of Miss Jane Bennet.

In fact, Darcy had not been blind to Bingley's growth over the years. As a young man entering university for the first time, Bingley had been eager to please, though not always certain how to go about doing it. His first years in university had been characterized by a tendency to become enamored with a pretty face—this had happened more times than Darcy could count, and it did not seem to matter the level of society the young woman inhabited. This had stopped, however, some time around Bingley's last year of education, which coincided with his father's passing.

Though Darcy had not seen Bingley's interest and growing feelings for Longbourn's eldest daughter, there were others who had. Among those who had noticed it first was Miss Elizabeth Bennet, Miss Bennet's next younger sister, and her closest confidant.

While the day after an assembly was reserved as a time for the young ladies of the neighborhood to gather and discuss the night's events, of late Mr. Bingley had been a fixture at the estate, and that morning was no exception. Elizabeth, who had liked the young man since she had been introduced to him, had seen his interested glances and, later, his longing looks at her elder sister. It was nothing more than the natural progression of his interest that he should show it more openly.

"Was Jane not admired last night, Mr. Bingley?" asked Lady Margaret as they visited that morning. "I have rarely seen her looking better than she did; I am sure you will agree." Lady Margaret had ever been one to praise her daughters, her love for them showing in her pride in their beauty and accomplishments.

"How could I not?" asked Mr. Bingley, showing Jane an eager grin. "Then again, I think your daughter looks lovely in burlap and ashes, so I noticed no great improvement over the last time I saw her."

Jane, as was her wont, reacted with a pretty blush at the praise, but then again, Jane never expected it. The sight of Mr. Bingley, his heart in his eyes, pleased Elizabeth, for she knew Mr. Bingley would make her sister happy. There were many men of Lord Arundel's position in the world who would have thrown Mr. Bingley out on his ear for having the temerity to express interest in his daughter, but Lord Arundel loved his daughters and did not much appreciate society. His attendance in parliament was sporadic, and his forays into London society only made under duress applied by his wife.

"It is interesting to hear you say it, Mr. Bingley," said Elizabeth, laughing at the gentleman's words. "For, unless I am very much mistaken, I do not believe you have ever *seen* my sister in burlap and ashes."

"Perhaps not," said Mr. Bingley, his grin not dimming a jot. "But I am certain she would be no less than lovely in them."

It was a surprise to no one that Jane's cheeks took on the appearance of a ripe tomato, though she threw a glare at Elizabeth. Having too much enjoyment to pay attention to her entreaties to cease teasing, however, Elizabeth continued to speak with her sister's suitor.

"Then the next time there is an assembly, I shall induce Jane to test the theory."

"And I shall be happy to dance with her."

"Oh, how you do carry on, Lizzy," said Lady Margaret. "I know not how I raised such a teasing daughter, for none of your sisters tease as you do."

"Except Lydia, of course," said Elizabeth, smiling at her younger sister. "Kitty can hold her own too when she puts her mind to it."

"I would prefer you did not dominate my sitting-room with talk of teasing if you please," said Lady Margaret with a sniff. Then she turned back to Mr. Bingley and said: "How is your mother, Mr. Bingley?"

"Mother is very well," replied Mr. Bingley.

"And your sister? I understand she has had her confinement—are she and the babe both well?"

"Exceptionally so, I thank you," replied Mr. Bingley. "Hurst is beside himself with joy at the birth of an heir, and my sister has recovered without difficulty."

"That is well," replied Lady Margaret. "A woman's lying in is a time when so many things can go wrong—this news of your family pleases me. Inform your mother I shall visit her tomorrow."

"I shall do so, your ladyship."

Lady Margaret nodded and favored the gentleman with a gracious nod. Then her look turned pensive and she peered at Mr. Bingley for a few moments, the gentleman bearing up well under her scrutiny. After a few moments, she spoke again, saying:

"I must say, Mr. Bingley, that learning of your interest in my eldest daughter was a surprise, for I had seen nothing of it."

"You did not?" asked Elizabeth. "It was obvious before Jane even turned eighteen—my only question was when Mr. Bingley would act on his obvious interest."

Lady Margaret's eyes swung to Elizabeth, a hint of censure contained within. Elizabeth, however, had never been cowed by her mother, and she grinned back, prompting a shake of her head.

"Once again, you are allowing your impertinence to show, Daughter."

"Perhaps I am," replied Elizabeth with suppressed laughter. "But you still love me, regardless."

A laugh escaped her mother's lips and she touched Elizabeth's hand. "Yes, I suppose I do, though I will own that sometimes you vex me exceedingly! Now, hush so I may speak to Mr. Bingley."

"Miss Elizabeth is correct," said Mr. Bingley. "Long have I admired your daughter, but I thought it would be best to restrain my ardor, for at the same time I was struggling to assume my father's role on the estate."

"That is understandable," replied Lady Margaret. She paused and considered Mr. Bingley, and added: "Jane seems happy with you, so I approve. I can only think you have made a fortunate escape, given your past association with young Master Darcy."

"If you excuse my saying so, nothing could be further from the truth."

The raised eyebrow with which Lady Margaret regarded Mr. Bingley did nothing to cow the man—the opposite seemed to be true, for he was not hesitant to explain himself.

"When my father passed away, I might have been lost if it were not for Darcy and his father. Their advice and assistance have been invaluable, for I was in no way prepared to assume the burden.

"Furthermore, Darcy has been a good friend to me all the years I have known him. He is, perhaps, not the most voluble of men, and at times he can be downright taciturn, but he is a good man—the best I have ever known."

Lady Margaret regarded Mr. Bingley for a moment before saying: "No doubt he offered help and friendship to bring you under his control. These Darcys are all that is arrogant and condescending— there are many in the neighborhood under their thrall."

"I know little of the difficulties between your family and the Darcy family," said Mr. Bingley, his tone slow and hesitant, as it to ensure he was not giving offense, "but I know Darcy and he is not all you say. There is no firmer friend than Fitzwilliam Darcy, and I have ever benefited from his society."

"And yet he stands about at assemblies and refuses to give consequence to those he does not consider his equal," said Elizabeth, her tone challenging.

Mr. Bingley laughed in response. "It is amusing to hear you say it, Miss Elizabeth, for that is something I might have said to Darcy myself."

"It comes from something I overheard last night, Mr. Bingley."

With a shaken head, Mr. Bingley said: "Though it is unfortunate, it is true Darcy is not at his best in a social situation. But I stand by my words concerning his character."

"Did he not disapprove of your interest in my daughter?" challenged Lady Margaret.

"It is unfortunate, but he did," replied Mr. Bingley. "Given the situation between your two families, it is not surprising." Mr. Bingley eyed Lady Margaret and asked: "May ask as to the origin of the dispute between you? I have asked Darcy, but he did not wish to speak of it."

Lady Margaret was silent for a moment, and then she spoke with hesitation like the words were being pulled from her lips. "I do not know the origin of the dispute, Mr. Bingley."

"And you would find no one who does," said Lord Arundel, speaking for the first time. "Though some of the eldest members of the community might remember, I do not myself, for the enmity was already established when I was a young man."

"If you will forgive me saying it," said Mr. Bingley, "is it not silly to continue to despise the Darcys if no one remembers the reason?"

"When you put it that way," replied Lord Arundel, "perhaps it is silly. But then again, we Bennets have had dealings with the Darcy family over many years, and we know them to be inherently untrustworthy."

Though Mr. Bingley opened his mouth to speak, Lord Arundel waved him to silence. "I know what you will say young man, and it is to your credit that you defend your friend. It does no good for me to continue to inform you of the evil of the Darcy family, for I do not believe they are. Any reconciliation, however, is many years in the future, if it is a possibility at all.

"Of more importance," continued Lord Arundel, "Is the status of your friendship with the Darcy heir. Your own words tell me you disagreed with your friend, but you have said nothing of the current state of your friendship. Do you mean to maintain it?"

Mr. Bingley was silent for a moment, considering the question, but when he opened his mouth, it was with a curious mix of hesitance and determination. "Will you deny me the opportunity to court your daughter if I tell you I have every intention of keeping the connection?"

A laugh was Lord Arundel's response. "Well said, young man. It seems to me you *have* grown these years, for when you were a young man of eighteen, I know you would have given me an answer designed to appease me."

Lord Arundel, still chuckling and shaking his head, turned his attention to his daughter, noting how Jane appeared unmoved. Jane, Elizabeth knew, was incapable of seeing in anyone anything other than the best, and this talk of continued friendship between Mr. Darcy and Mr. Bingley would not alter her opinion of either man.

"What I will expect," said Lord Arundel, coming to the correct conclusion, "is that your loyalty will be to my daughter first. I will not require you to give up your friendship, but I wish my daughter's suitor to protect her."

"That is easy to promise, Mr. Bennet," said Mr. Bingley. "If I were not prepared to give my first loyalty to Miss Bennet, I would not bother her with my attentions."

"Well said, young man. Well said, indeed. Then I believe you may proceed at your leisure and as long as Jane welcomes you."

Pleased, Mr. Bingley turned his attention to Jane, and could not be moved from her side for the rest of his visit. Elizabeth watched, once again happy her sister had such an ardent and devoted admirer. Even more than this, Elizabeth felt more than a hint of relief that he had shown such an assurance of purpose, for as her father said, she well remembered when the young man's character had been described as more complying than firm. With such a protector, Elizabeth knew her dearest sister could not help but attain her happiness.

With these thoughts, Elizabeth's mind turned to the difficulties with the Darcy family. Though she had not thought of it much before, she could not help but suppose Mr. Bingley had made an excellent point. Not knowing the origin of the dispute, was it worth it to continue to hate each other? It all seemed so silly.

While Mr. Bingley was visiting his lady, another visit was in progress, though the situation was reversed from the visit occurring at Longbourn. For one, Darcy would have cheerfully dispensed with this visitor, for he had no interest in the Lady in his family's sitting-room with his sister. For another, the lady's intelligence of her brother's visit to Longbourn that morning brought to mind again his stated intention to woo Longbourn's eldest daughter, setting Darcy to brooding again.

"Charles is foolish—very foolish," said Miss Bingley, for perhaps the fifth time. "Though Jane Bennet *is* beautiful, I cannot but think he will regret this reckless decision to throw his lot in with them."

Though Darcy could not but agree, he did not make any response, as he had not the last time she had made this same statement. As for Georgiana, her youth was such that she was little aware of such matters which prevented her own response.

"I tried to counsel against it, but he will not listen to me." Miss Bingley made a sound of annoyance, which served to annoy Darcy. "There was a time when Charles was eager to please and willing to listen to my advice, but of late he has grown hard-headed and recalcitrant. I cannot talk to him any longer."

As Miss Bingley droned on, Darcy allowed his mind to wander. Her purpose, he knew, was to inform them of her loyalty and continued support, all while intending to procure his good opinion in the hope he would offer for her. Darcy had never considered favoring her with his addresses regardless of her brother's folly or any other stratagem she might attempt. He did not find her interesting, let alone possessed any feelings for her which were not tinted by disdain for her mercenary ways.

"I assure you I have no intention of committing such a betrayal," said Miss Bingley, drawing Darcy's attention back to her continual blathering. "You will never have a firmer friend than me, Miss Darcy, for those awful Bennets will not lure me into their webs."

"It is my hope your brother will be happy in his choice," ventured Georgiana in a hesitant tone. "Though I have never spoken to Miss Bennet, she has always seemed like a lovely woman."

"Of course, she seems that way," replied Miss Bingley in a tone which was all that was condescending. "The entire family excels at appearing respectable. But underneath, they are everything to be despised, true wolves and sheep's clothing."

"And yet, they are a family respected by society," said Darcy, drawing Miss Bingley's eyes back to him.

"Has your opinion of them softened, Mr. Darcy?" asked she. While Miss Bingley exuded confidence, underneath, Darcy detected a note of insecurity.

"The Darcys and the Bennets have never gotten on, Miss Bingley," replied Darcy. "But that does not mean I refuse to see any worth in them. In particular, it would be best if you recalled that the Bennets *are* of the peerage—Lord Arundel is a baron. It would not do at all to offend him by speaking in such a fashion. Should it reach his ears, he would be displeased, and rightly so."

"But I am among friends," said Miss Bingley with a smile which carried a hint of uncertainty. "I am sure neither you nor your lovely sister will bear tales to the baron."

"No, we shall do no such thing. Speaking in such a manner, however, can become habit, and may result in something imprudent being said when in a position of being overheard. Thus, it is better to avoid the subject altogether."

For an instant, Miss Bingley regarded Darcy, attempting to discern whether there was some hidden meaning in his words. There was not, but Darcy was more than happy to allow the woman to continue in uncertainty and silence. She came to the correct conclusion, though she did not appear to be any more certain of herself than she had been before.

"Thank you for your advice, Mr. Darcy. I shall accept it in the manner you offered it."

For the rest of the visit, Miss Bingley concentrated on his sister, leaving Darcy in peace. Though he knew Georgiana was not enamored of her, she spoke politely, and Darcy knew she did not begrudge him the lack of his own share of Miss Bingley's attentions. When the time for the visit elapsed, Miss Bingley rose and departed, albeit with obvious reluctance.

"What do you think of Mr. Bingley's attentions to Miss Bennet?" asked Georgiana when Miss Bingley had departed.

It was all Darcy could do to suppress a grimace. "Bingley is his own man," said he with what had become his default response, and if his reply was a little short, he did not think Georgiana noticed.

"I know he is," said Georgiana, impatience coloring her voice. "I was asking what *you* think of it. You would not begrudge him his happiness because you do not approve of the Bennets."

"As I informed Miss Bingley," replied Darcy, "it is not my place to approve or disapprove of the Bennets. Lord Arundel *is* of the peerage—speaking rashly against any man of his position cannot end well."

"But we are connected to several lines of the peerage."

"That is part of the reason the Bennets have never used their advantage in society against us."

"Do you think they would have if we were simple gentleman farmers?"

Darcy paused and shook his head. "The current Lord Arundel does not strike me as a man who uses his position in such a manner, though I might be incorrect. I can say nothing of his predecessors. You must understand, Georgiana, that in our society, the peerage can often obtain what they want because of the position they hold."

"But Uncle Hugh does not do such things," said she of Lord Matlock, their late mother's brother.

"Uncle Hugh is a man who, while he is well aware of his position, he considers such abuse of power immoral, and I cannot disagree with him."

Georgiana did not speak for a moment, and when she did, her voice was quiet. "To be honest, Brother, I consider this whole mess to be more than a little silly. Should we not forgive and forget, especially since so many years have passed?"

"Our parson would agree with you," replied Darcy, fixing his sister with a smile. "Old grievances die hard, however, and there are newer grievances at play."

"I am concerned for our brother," replied Georgiana. "How will the neighborhood and the Bennets, in particular, receive him when he returns?"

"Mr. Gardiner does not seem to be a man who holds a grudge, and what happened was an accident—or at least an unfortunate event in which he was as much at fault as Alexander. If Alexander behaves himself, all should be well. I also do not expect Alexander to return for some time—by the time he is called home all should be well."

"But will he behave himself?" countered Georgiana.

Darcy chuckled and put an arm around his sister's shoulders. "I shall do my best to ensure he does. All will be well, Georgiana. You will see."

CHAPTER III

"What can you be thinking, Charles? What can Miss Bennet possibly have that would tempt you into betraying a man who has been your friend for many years?"

"Miss Bennet is everything I could ever wish for in a wife," replied Bingley, maintaining a calm demeanor in the face of his sister's provocation. "And before you say anything further, you should remember she is the daughter of a baron, and as such, outranks you by several degrees."

"I do not speak of her position in society," growled Caroline in reply. "For those who care for such things, I am sure the Bennets are acceptable. This has nothing to do with their position, and everything to do with your friendship with Mr. Darcy."

"If Darcy cannot accept my choice, then he is no true friend."

"Perhaps it would be best—" attempted Mrs. Bingley, but Caroline was not to be denied.

"A true friend would not descend to such betrayal."

"How is it a betrayal to follow my heart? There is a fallacy in your thinking, Caroline, for Darcy is a friend, and has been a good friend for many years, but in the matter of my happiness, *I* am the only one who may judge what is best for me."

A cry of dismay escaped Caroline's lips and she stepped away, pacing the floor in her agitation, wringing her hands together as her slippers glided over the tiles. Mrs. Bingley sat on a nearby chair, watching the confrontation with increasing alarm, though when she looked to Bingley, he shook his head to inform her it would be best for her to remain silent. Caroline felt she had the moral high ground in this situation, and Bingley knew she would have her say. It was better to do so now rather than allow her to continue to believe she had any power to change his mind.

"A fine judge you have shown yourself to be," said Caroline at length, venom dripping from her tone. "There are many acceptable ladies in society, some of whom live in this very neighborhood. Can you not aim for one of them? If none of them strikes your fancy, then turn your attention to some other woman of society."

"None of them hold my heart, Caroline," replied Bingley, proud of how his tone stayed reasonable in the face of her provocation.

"I am sure you would fall in love with another woman if you only allowed yourself to do so."

"There is no need to look elsewhere—I have found the perfect woman for me."

"Then what of our friendship with the Darcys? Do you mean to throw that all aside? I assure you, I will not."

"Nor would I expect you to," said Bingley, unable to keep the wry note from his tone. "And I have not either. Darcy was surprised but I have hope he will not prove unreasonable."

"Is that what you call me?" demanded Caroline, turning to him, fury shooting from her eyes.

"In this instance, yes," replied Bingley.

"This situation *does* concern me," said Mrs. Bingley, when Caroline proved incapable of responding through her anger. "This quarrel between the Darcys and the Bennets was old when I married your father and came to the neighborhood, and it has not abated with time. I would not wish my children to be courting opposite sides of the dispute."

"Courting!" exclaimed Caroline, spearing Bingley with a look. "That is exactly it, though it is not as if my brother is the one doing the courting. That Jane Bennet has sunk her claws into you and drawn you in—if anyone is courting another, it is she!"

"Please," said Bingley, shaking his head in disgust. "Why would Miss Bennet target *me* in particular? She is the daughter of a baron and cannot be in want of suitors."

"Those Bennet girls are artful," was his sister's dismissive reply. "Who knows why they do what they do?"

"In other words," replied Bingley, his resentment growing, "you cannot answer my question. There is no 'drawing in' of anyone because it makes no sense for her to turn to *me* if she *was* inclined to such behavior."

"You do not know that," snapped Caroline.

"I know one thing, Sister dearest," replied Bingley. "Any *courting* is all on my side, for there will never be anything on *yours*. Darcy will not offer for you, no matter how much you flatter him or his sister — you are wasting your time."

"My marital prospects are not at issue here!"

"No, they are not, for you have none with Darcy. But I well know that your objection to Miss Bennet is because of your desire to elicit a proposal from Darcy, and I can tell you that will never happen. Darcy does not consider you a potential wife — he does not even like you."

A cry of frustration once again escaped Caroline's throat, and she threw her hands into the air and stalked from the room, her voice floating back to then. "You will regret throwing over Mr. Darcy's friendship!"

"Charles," said Mrs. Bingley, her tone faintly chiding, "that was no kind thing to say to your sister."

"Perhaps it was not," replied Bingley, "but she is deserving of it. It is also the truth — Caroline is lying to herself if she thinks to provoke a proposal from Darcy."

Mrs. Bingley paused, doubt etched upon her features. "Caroline has been so certain she will be Mr. Darcy's wife."

A snort conveyed Bingley's feelings on the subject of Caroline's confidence. "When does Caroline ever see anything other than what she wishes to see? It is unfortunate father coddled her so as the youngest, for he taught her to believe that whatever she wished was hers by right.

"Darcy has no interest in Caroline, Mother — he tolerates her for the sake of our friendship. It would be best if you would take Caroline to London for the season and concentrate on finding her a husband, for I cannot expect my future wife to endure her in my home, given her virulent opposition."

"You know Caroline will not agree to go to London," replied his mother.

"Then she will continue to waste her time.'

Mrs. Bingley regarded him for several moments before speaking again. "Are you certain of this?"

"I have had it from the man's own mouth. The Darcys are a prominent family, one with connections to many in higher society. Darcy's father married the daughter of an earl, and Darcy himself is expected to make an excellent match. Though we are gentlefolk, we are not so far removed from our roots to render Caroline acceptable."

"Yet you aspire to the daughter of a baron," challenged Mrs. Bingley.

"Had you not noticed, Mother?" asked Bingley, overflowing with amusement, "the Bennets are not high and mighty like the Darcys. Though Darcy is my friend, I am not blind to his character, and the family *is* a rather proud lot. Was Lord Arundel any other man than he is, I might have found myself forbidden from speaking to his daughter."

"Are you certain of Miss Bennet, Charles? I know you believe yourself in love with the girl, and I have no complaints against her. But Caroline is correct in one respect—you *have* been Mr. Darcy's friend for many years."

"And if Darcy is willing to be reasonable, I shall be his friend for many more." Bingley did not need to inform his mother of his firmness of purpose, for he felt it was clear in his stance, his carriage, and the way he spoke without hesitation. It seemed his mother recognized it, for she sighed and nodded.

"Then I will support you, though you do not need my blessing."

"But I should like to have it all the same, Mother," replied Bingley, favoring her with a smile.

"You have it," replied she. "Only take care. I would not end like the Darcys and the Bennets." When Bingley nodded, she turned the subject back to Caroline. "You know Caroline will not consent to go to London, nor can we bend her to our will."

"Caroline is of age," acknowledged Bingley, "but she is yet a daughter of this house and depends on me for her allowance and the roof over her head. If she proves impervious to reason we can establish her own residence, paid for by her dowry, and she can do as she pleases."

"Oh, Charles," said Mrs. Bingley. "I do not wish to throw her off."

"Then she will learn for herself of Darcy's disinterest, perhaps when he marries. Regardless, I will not have her making trouble for me with Miss Bennet—of that I can assure you."

Mrs. Bingley nodded and rose, pressing a kiss to Bingley's cheek. "I shall do my best to open her eyes. You have made me proud, Charles, for you have grown into a man firm of purpose. I believe your father would have been as proud as I am."

Then his mother left the room to search for her daughter, her final words still echoing in Bingley's ears. As his father had been a good and industrious man, no words could be a greater compliment.

"That Mr. Bingley is such a pleasant man," said Lady Margaret that evening as the family was sitting together after dinner. "One might expect him to be the opposite, given his descent, though I suppose the family *has* owned their estate long enough to have shed some of the traits of the lower classes."

Elizabeth shared a look with her elder sister and shook her head, to Jane's amusement. Their mother's background was that of the daughter of a landowner, and they knew she was not a supercilious woman, though her elevation to the wife of a peer sometimes led her to speak as if she was.

"And yet, he appears smitten by our Jane," said Lord Arundel with a smile at Jane. "Though some might wish for more for their daughters than the scion of tradesmen, I believe we can all agree it is important for her to find happiness in her life."

"I thank you, Papa," said Jane. "As you know, I care nothing for the opinions of society, nor do I wish to marry a man who considers me to be nothing more than a bauble to adorn his arm."

"As you proved when you rejected Lord Winchester." The mirth in Lord Arundel's eyes made its way to his mouth, for he burst into laughter, his hilarity forcing him to remove his spectacles and wipe at his eyes. "I never saw someone so surprised. That dandy actually thought he would impress you and could not understand why I would not insist upon your marrying him."

"That is exactly it, Father," said Jane, retaining her serenity. "Lord Winchester, as Elizabeth would say, is everything I despise in a man."

"He *is* all that is contemptible," agreed Elizabeth. "Even so, I am grateful he did not attempt to press his perceived advantage as a future earl to compel Jane to comply."

"It would not matter if he *had*," replied her father. "Though perhaps I am not as high in society as Winchester, I am not friendless."

"Oh, Jane could not have married Lord Winchester," said their mother, "for I quite detest the man. Mr. Bingley is not so high in society, but he is much more pleasant. He is an excellent suitor for my dear daughter; I give you leave to like him, Jane, for he is all a man should be."

"Thank you, Mama," said Jane, her tone brimming with amusement.

"It is also beneficial for Mr. Bingley," added Lady Margaret, "for it removes him from the influence of those awful Darcys. How he must feel fortunate at his escape!"

"Given how he spoke of the younger Darcy when he was here," said Lord Arundel in a dry tone, "I cannot but imagine the opposite. It seemed to me he defended his friend with unusual verve and eloquence."

"I cannot imagine why. And I believe he will come to appreciate our society rather than the Darcys."

"Perhaps he will, my dear. But I, for one, will not ask him to make that choice. The Darcys have been our enemies for many years, but it is a man's right to choose his own friends, and I shall not gainsay Mr. Bingley that right."

"Even if your own daughter will be brought into the Darcys' influence?"

"Even then," was her husband's response. "Given the manner in which he defended his friend, Mr. Bingley should prove no less protective of a wife. Should Darcy attempt to mistreat Jane, *that* is how their friendship will end. Thus, I feel no compunction in allowing Mr. Bingley to choose his friends, and to throw them off should it become necessary."

With those words, Lord Arundel excused himself and left the sitting-room, likely to seek peace and quiet and his beloved books in the sanctuary of his study. It could not be said that Lord Arundel was a slothful man, but neither was he a diligent one. Books were his greatest love, and he sought their company whenever possible, although his family was always welcome to join him, for he loved to debate. He gave his daughters guidance but allowed them to go their own way which had resulted in the youngest being perhaps more lively than they should be. But their governess made up for any lack in Lord Arundel's parenting style, and all the girls were well-mannered, though again, Kitty and Lydia possessed high spirits.

Once her husband had left the room, Lady Margaret again began to speak of the Darcys and the untrustworthy nature of the family, and this time she spoke for some time, as there was no one to gainsay her. Whether any of the facts she related were in any way the truth Elizabeth could not determine, though she had heard many of these same complaints before. Elizabeth tried to ignore her mother's constant stream of words, and speak quietly with Jane, for they could do little to silence her.

After a time of this, her mother fell silent on the subject, as her youngest daughters drew her into other subjects. Elizabeth nodded at Lydia in thanks, which the girl returned with a pert grin. Jane, Elizabeth, and Mary were as yet the only Bennet sisters introduced to London society, in slight contravention of the established norm, which was to wait until the elder sisters married before presenting the younger. Jane's unacknowledged courtship with Mr. Bingley would remove any impediment to Kitty and Lydia's eventual presentation, as would the expected match Mary would make. As yet, no man had caught Elizabeth's fancy.

"Lizzy?"

Turning, Elizabeth noted her youngest sibling looking at her. Thomas was ten years of age and precocious, the long-awaited heir of her father's barony. He was also intelligent, active after the manner of boys his age, and close with Elizabeth who indulged him by playing with him in his youthful games.

"Yes, Thomas?" asked she, noting he was frowning in confusion.

"I do not understand. Why does Mama dislike our neighbors so?"

"It is a mystery to me too," replied Elizabeth, seating him nearby so she could attempt to explain in a fashion he would understand. "The Bennets have long considered the Darcy family to be untrustworthy."

"Why?" demanded her brother. "Did they harm us?"

"I do not know, Brother. The dispute has persisted longer than I have been alive. Papa does not even remember how it began."

"Then why should it continue? If the offense is no longer known, should it not be forgotten?"

In Elizabeth's mind, her brother showed impressive perception. "One would think, would they not? Unfortunately, it does not always work that way in our world. Sometimes people do not get on with each other for reasons no one can understand."

"Well, that is silly," insisted Thomas. "You may be certain that when *I* am Lord Arundel, I shall not continue such an absurd feud. I will end it and make peace with Mr. Darcy."

"Then I wish you success, Thomas," said Elizabeth, holding him close to her side. "It is laudable to wish to mend our relationship with the Darcy family. Perhaps you may succeed where the rest of us are too steeped in resentment to have any hope of success."

Thomas gave her a brilliant smile and retreated to his toy soldier collection which had held his interest most of the evening. On another night, Elizabeth might have joined him—much to her mother's chagrin—but tonight there were more important matters afoot. Her brother's startling perception notwithstanding, there was enough bad blood between the Bennets and the Darcys that Elizabeth wished to ensure her sister knew what she was undertaking by accepting Mr. Bingley's overtures.

"Jane," said Elizabeth, drawing her sister's attention. "Are you sure of Mr. Bingley, and your willingness to be drawn into the Darcys' sphere?"

"I had not thought you would champion distrust of the Darcy family, Lizzy," said Jane.

"You know I do no such thing," replied Elizabeth. "Mr. Bingley has been a close friend of Mr. Darcy for many years, and as Papa says, he shows no signs of wishing to give up the acquaintance. How will you manage, being near the gentleman, given the discord between us?"

"The same way I manage any other situation, Lizzy," replied Jane. "With patience and understanding. As Papa suggested, I do not think Mr. Bingley would allow Mr. Darcy to mistreat me."

"Nor do I think Mr. Darcy would do something so overt." Elizabeth paused, thinking of what she knew of the gentleman. "Mr. Darcy has always struck me as a stern man, a man who demands the best in himself and others. I know we Bennets think the Darcys possess no redeeming qualities, but people are more complex than that—any attempt to stuff them into a box and label it is doomed to failure."

"Then why do you ask?"

"Because I wish to assure myself that you know what you are about with Mr. Bingley. No, I do not expect Mr. Darcy to mistreat you, but he *is* our family's enemy. Furthermore, Mr. Bingley has always seemed to be under his influence, though I will own he has shown some firmness of purpose since his attentions to you began. The most important factor, however, is how you feel about Mr. Bingley. Do you love him as a woman ought for the man she is considering as a future husband?"

"Have we not always vowed we will marry for love?" asked Jane, her tone slightly chiding. "I thought you knew me better than to suspect I would allow a man to approach me when I do not love him."

"I have always thought I did," said Elizabeth. "But you are maddeningly difficult to understand at times, Jane, and I am uncertain."

"Then let your mind be at peace. I love Mr. Bingley as much as I should, and I would like nothing more than to be his wife. Any matter of Mr. Darcy I may consider when it becomes necessary, and not before. And I should also inform you, Lizzy, that had I any concerns about Mr. Bingley's firmness of purpose, I would not have allowed him to proceed even as far as he has."

Elizabeth regarded her sister, relieved at last to know Jane's innermost thoughts. "Then I wish you every happiness, Jane. I have always thought Mr. Bingley was an excellent man, and I know you shall be the making of him. Moreover, happiness shall be yours with your extended family, for Miss Bingley will be the most perfect sister a woman could ever have!"

Jane shook her head and laughed along with Elizabeth, for both women had known of Miss Bingley's limitations for many years. Neither held any illusions she would welcome Jane with open arms, despite her being the daughter of a peer.

"In truth, I pity Miss Bingley."

"Aye, she is a woman to be pitied. The way she throws herself at Mr. Darcy is only made more pitiable by Mr. Darcy's restraint and Miss Bingley's inability to see it for anything other than the contemptuous indifference it is. Then again, as her brother's wife, perhaps can explain it to her in such a way that she will see the truth and fix her mercenary attention on some other poor unsuspecting gentleman."

"Caroline is not *that* bad, Lizzy."

"Yes, she is, Sister dearest," replied Elizabeth, rising to her feet. "As much, for your sake, as I wish it was untrue, Miss Bingley *is* that bad, and perhaps worse. Though I worried about Mr. Darcy, and with good reason, I believe Miss Bingley to be the greater threat. Do not trust her, for you may find a dagger in your back if you do."

Then Elizabeth wished her family good night and sought her bed and the good book she had waiting on her nightstand. With Jane's words, she was now content with her sister's choice.

CHAPTER IV

*T*here was nothing the Honorable Miss Elizabeth Bennet liked
better than to walk the paths of her father's estate. Secondary
to that, however, was the enjoyment she received in riding her
mare, Midnight.

Having been taught from a young age, the same as her sisters,
Elizabeth accounted herself an expert horsewoman, and as she
engaged in it more often than any of them, her skills were superior.
Midnight was a young mare, only three years of age, which her father
had purchased for her after the old mare she used to use, Petal, was
sent out to pasture. She was a handsome animal, the deepest black, as
her name would suggest, but with a crescent-shaped white patch on
her forehead, which Elizabeth thought made her a pretty animal,
indeed. In addition, Midnight was also a gentle creature, friendly and
eager to please, yet hardy, possessing an ability to run like the wind.
Elizabeth had always thought they were well-matched, not only in
temperament but also in their love of the outdoors.

One fine spring morning, Elizabeth saddled her beloved friend and
rode away from Longbourn, enjoying the chirping of birds, whistling
of the winds through the trees, only just waking from their long rest.
The winter previous had been a harsh one in which Elizabeth's only

escape was to visit Midnight and commiserate with her over the stinging snowstorms which had swept through the county. When February waned and March arrived, however, it was as if a fire had been lit in a hearth, for warmth flooded the area and the snows began to melt. Even now there were still large drifts of hard-packed snow dotting the landscape, and the grounds within the woods were thick with it, but the melting had begun in earnest, leaving the local landowners fearful of torrential waters flooding their lands. That possibility, however, was still far distant, and Elizabeth had no thought for it other than to stay away from the swiftly rising streams.

Unlike many mornings in which she set out on horseback, today she had a destination in mind—the village of Lambton something more than three miles distant. While her father's estate was a large one, with many paths Elizabeth had come to know as well as she knew the halls of her home, the Bennet sisters often found themselves drawn to Lambton, in particular the younger, eager as they were for the society of friends. The road she followed was an undulating track leading through the rolling hills of Derbyshire. Midnight could cover the distance in a matter of minutes, if Elizabeth felt she was up to it, though on this morning, Elizabeth contented herself with allowing her mare a slow canter, while she reveled in the world waking from its long winter sleep.

Lambton was a jewel among market towns, nestled in the hills, some distance to the north and east, not far from the shared border between Pemberley and Longbourn. The town had no major thoroughfare, as the roads wound up and down the hills in which it sat, giving it the charm of a Swiss valley town. The thought provoked Elizabeth to laugh, for she had never been to Switzerland—she had only read about it in her father's copious collection of books.

As soon as Midnight set foot on the cobbled streets, a gaggle of girls she loved gathered around her. They called their greetings and romped about Midnight's feet, and soon Elizabeth felt it necessary to dismount, lest one of them stray too close.

"Miss Elizabeth!" cried one of them in greeting, echoed by her friends.

"Shall we have sweets today?" called another.

"Jenny!" disproved one of the older girls.

Elizabeth laughed, however, and gathered little Jenny to her. "Have you behaved yourself of late? Have you been attending your mother?"

"Yes, Miss," replied the little girl. "My mother claims I am her favorite daughter."

"That is only because you are her *only* daughter!" exclaimed the eldest girl, Jillian.

The other girls broke into laughter, though Jenny pouted. Elizabeth could not refrain from laughing herself, though she gathered Jenny to her in a gentle embrace. "Then you shall have a sugar stick since you have been so well-behaved."

The girls laughed and cheered at their good fortune, leading Elizabeth down the street to the confectioners. Though Elizabeth had been cautioned by the mothers not to treat their daughters too often—and Elizabeth was careful of the need for restraint—it had been the previous autumn since she had last indulged them. The morning was bright and cheery enough, and their manners so fine, that Elizabeth felt an indulgence was permitted.

The sweet shop owner hailed her and took each girl's request for their favorite candy, and soon they each had a sticky treat, though Elizabeth reminded them to wash their hands clean when they had finished. The girls followed Elizabeth for a few more moments, chattering in their charming ways until they ran off to eat their treats and play their games. Elizabeth watched them go, her heart full of fondness for them, hoping that she, too, would one day have a little girl of her own to spoil. Then she caught sight of her aunt and led Midnight to where she was standing outside the church, bussing her cheek in greeting.

"You spoil those girls so, Lizzy," said Mrs. Gardiner, though without rancor.

"If I do, it is nothing less than they deserve," replied Elizabeth. "They are such dear girls. I am surprised, however, that I did not see Abigail amongst their number."

"Abigail has caught a little cold," replied Mrs. Gardiner. "It is nothing serious, but I felt it would be best if she stayed indoors for a few days until it receded."

"Then perhaps this will raise her spirits," said Elizabeth, holding up a peppermint stick, Abigail's favorite flavor.

Mrs. Gardiner laughed and embraced Elizabeth. "You are too good. The girls adore you, and not only for the way you indulge them."

"And I adore them. Now, shall we look in on Abigail? Perhaps a visit from her favorite cousin will cheer her."

Mrs. Gardiner laughed and linked her arm with Elizabeth. "I am sure she would love to see you, Lizzy."

Abigail was the eldest of the Gardiners' four children; it pleased Elizabeth to find her in better spirits than she might have supposed.

The girl sniffled and sneezed because of the effects of her cold, but she was a good girl, and exclaimed when Elizabeth presented her and her siblings with the treat she had purchased for them. Elizabeth sat with them for some thirty minutes, reading with them and hearing the tales of their recent childish exploits. Some time later she departed with the assurance that Abigail would soon be outside frolicking with the other children.

"How is Uncle?" asked Elizabeth as she was readying herself to depart.

"Edward is well," replied Mrs. Gardiner. "Today he left early to visit Mrs. Dunbar and call on the Miss Wrights."

"Is old Mrs. Dunbar ill again?"

A smile flitted about her aunt's face. "You know her—everything is an ague which will see her on her deathbed. The woman is healthier than many half her age."

"Aye, that she is," said Elizabeth with a laugh.

After a few more words, Elizabeth kissed her aunt's cheek and departed. It was a blessing to have her aunt and uncle installed in Lambton's parsonage, for they were her favorite relations. Uncle Gardiner had considered a career in London running his own business and his family had been supportive, but when he attended university, he found the call of the seminary was too strong. The incumbent in the Lambton rectory had passed on unexpectedly about five years earlier, leaving the position vacant, and allowing her father, who held the power of its gift, to give it to his wife's brother.

Pushing thoughts of her family to the side, Elizabeth visited the bookstore, which had been her primary reason for coming to Lambton that day, greeting the proprietor with a cheery salutation. With a welcoming smile, the man produced a half dozen books that had been delivered to his shop for them. Most were her father's, but Elizabeth had been waiting for a certain new volume of poetry by Mr. Blake and was eager to immerse herself in its pages.

There was a meadow just west of the road to Lambton hidden in the trees which Elizabeth had discovered by accident two years earlier. Its location was such that it sat on the far edges of both Longbourn and Pemberley estates, and as the ground was rather rocky, great boulders thrust up from the ground in various places, it was of little value, which was why, she suspected, neither family had ever claimed it. The sun was bright that morning, and while it gave off only a hint of the warmth it would provide in the summer months, the air was calm and invigorating, and Elizabeth thought it the perfect time to sit on her favorite rock and read.

It was while she was in this attitude that she was interrupted.

The feeling of being out of sorts had plagued Darcy for some days — if he was honest with himself, since his friend had defied all claims of friendship and focused his attention on the eldest Bennet. While Darcy knew no harm of the girl — it was said she was sweet, kind, and calm — he could not put the thought of those scheming Bennets from his mind.

An additional source of annoyance for the gentleman was the imminent return of his younger brother.

"Alexander is to return?" Darcy had asked, frowning at the news his father had just dropped. "Is that prudent?"

"Enough time has passed," had been his father's reply, thumbing his way through a sheaf of papers on the top of his desk. "As far as I can tell, there are no lingering hard feelings on the matter. It was an accident."

"I understand that, Father. But matters between us have not improved at all. It would be best, I should think, if Alexander was to stay away for another sixmonth."

At last, his father looked up from his desk. "One might think it is for the best, but I have a specific reason to call for your brother's return. Thorndell, as you know, has been under your management since you came of age."

"Yes, I know it," replied Darcy. "Alexander has never taken an interest in what is, after all, his inheritance."

"It is time he began to take an interest," was Robert Darcy's short reply. "While I am still in good health, that will not always be true — I wish you to take on more of Pemberley's responsibility, and Thorndell will be a distraction. Once you gain enough experience, it will not be a problem, but until you gain that experience, I would prefer you turn your focus here rather than thirty miles away."

Darcy could not help but frown at his father. "Are you ill?"

"No," replied Mr. Darcy, shaking his head. "However, I am attaining the age where I would like to enjoy something of retirement before I become infirm. Pemberley, as you know, is a very large and complex estate. Your brother is now five and twenty, and it is high time he put away the revelries of youth and fixed his attention on his duties. I hope you will guide him when he returns, show him Thorndell's estate books, and ease him into his future as a landowner."

"Very well, Father," said Darcy. "I shall do my best."

Family was an important part of Darcy's life. The close relationship he had always had with his father, his mother — before her passing — and his sister brought great joy. His younger brother had, however, always provoked mixed feelings. Alexander was not a morally deficient character, but he tended toward gambling and occasional heavy drink, not to mention his exploits with the ladies. More than once during the two years where their studies at overlapped at Cambridge Darcy had been forced to help his brother out of a sticky situation. Then there was the trouble with the Bennets and their relations . . . .

Not wishing to think on the matter, and knowing he would worry over it like a dog with a bone, Darcy had his horse saddled and rode out that morning, no destination in mind but to run the beast until their exertions took his mind from the worries that beset him. Riding had always proved soothing to Darcy, and for a time it helped him forget his troubles. Then he found *her.*

It was a place he only visited occasionally, for the meadow was not somewhere he could ride his horse and not risk damaging a hoof or breaking a leg. When Darcy studied the haphazardly strewn rocks, he thought he could see the remains of human excavation, the straight line of rocks suggesting the foundation of some building of days long past. Darcy did not know why he directed his mount there that day, but when he arrived, he found it was already occupied.

Given the situation between the two families, it would have been better had Darcy ridden on, ignoring her presence. The moment he drew close and caught sight of her, however, she lifted her head. Had she not seen him, he may have continued on and avoided her. But the look of challenge on her face provoked him, and he found he could not turn away.

"Mr. Darcy," said she, a faint mocking undertone in her voice, "I see you have found my favorite place to read. If you have brought a book with you, there is more than enough room on this or any other rock."

"*Your* favorite place?" asked Darcy in spite of himself. "By my reckoning, this is more properly a part of Pemberley than Longbourn."

An impertinent eyebrow rose at his statement. "By my account, no one has claimed this spot, for it does not seem to have much value except as a retreat for those bent on solitude. Are you warning me off?"

"Nothing of the sort," replied Darcy, deciding it was unwise to argue the point with her. "What are you doing here?"

Miss Elizabeth lifted her book, displaying it as if it should be obvious; which it was, of course — Darcy had spoken out of a sense of obligation, rather than interest. Then he looked at the book in her hand.

"*Songs of Innocence and of Experience?*" asked Darcy, feeling a hint of surprise. "Is that suitable material for a young lady?"

"Are you my father?" jibed she. "For your information, Mr. Darcy, Lord Arundel does not direct my reading. Rather, he trusts my intelligence and education to lead me to proper choices—I need no guidance from you or anyone else."

Insolence, it appeared, was a characteristic of the Bennet family. As the heir to a large estate, Darcy was accustomed to young ladies seeking to curry favor with him, intending to provoke his approval and, eventually, a proposal. Even the daughter of a baron should find his position in life, extensive wealth, and connections to the higher nobility tempting. This woman disturbed Darcy's equilibrium, for she did not act as he expected.

"Far be it for me to approve or disapprove of your reading material, Miss Elizabeth," said he. "I only repeat what is commonly understood about the education of a young lady."

"Oh, so you are one of those who believes a woman should concern herself with embroidery and music, netting purses and painting tables, and other such activities?"

"Many would claim those are the mark of an accomplished woman."

Miss Elizabeth released a most unladylike snort. "If you will pardon me, I am not one of them. While I have some proficiency in some of those disciplines, I prefer to know something of the world in which I live, and I love the outdoors. Is it not incumbent upon every young woman to broaden their minds with extensive reading?"

"That is a claim I cannot dispute, Miss Elizabeth, for I have often thought so myself."

Once again that maddening eyebrow rose to tease him. "Then it seems we *do* agree on this, at least. However, if you will pardon me, I believe I must return to Longbourn."

The woman rose from her seat and went to her mount, a dark mare Darcy thought was of a splendid breed, and stowing her book in the saddlebag, prepared to depart. Though Darcy had no intention of speaking of the matter, on an impulse, he raised the subject of his friend.

"What of your sister drawing Bingley in?"

Miss Elizabeth froze, and when she turned to regard him, she wore a look of such fierceness as he never would have expected to see from a gentle young woman. "The way you speak," said she, her voice low and hard, "one might think it is *Mr. Bingley* who is the higher in society, rather than my family who, after all, is headed by a peer. Is that what you suggest, sir?"

When Darcy did not respond, Miss Elizabeth sniffed with disdain. "Regardless, you are incorrect. If there has been any drawing in, Mr. Bingley has accomplished it, not my sister. Though Jane is happy with his attention and is in a fair way of being in love with him, it was Mr. Bingley who pursued her—not the reverse. If you believe I am lying, I suggest you speak to your friend."

The woman paused as if to turn away, then she delivered a final barb. "I hope Jane will find happiness with Mr. Bingley, for I believe him to be a good man. It is also my hope you will have the same with Miss Bingley since it is obvious she means to be your wife. The only unfortunate part of the matter is that Jane will have such a sister, and even worse, such a brother. But I am confident Mr. Bingley will accept no criticism, as I am sure you and your wife will be eager to dispense."

With those final words, Miss Elizabeth turned away, mounted her horse, and rode away, all without looking back. There was something in Darcy which was strangely moved, though he was uncertain what it was. The reproof she had hurled his way Darcy thought he deserved to a certain extent—no, he was not happy with Bingley's intention to offer for Miss Bennet, but he knew the woman was unassailable where propriety was concerned.

For a moment, Darcy considered going after Miss Elizabeth to inform her . . . Of what? Darcy did not know himself, for though he might have spoken in a manner he should not, the very notion of apologizing to a Bennet was galling. After thinking about it for a moment, he decided against it and turned his horse toward his distant home. Just because he did not go after her, it did not mean he did not think of her. Thoughts of Miss Elizabeth plagued Darcy for the rest of the day.

When Elizabeth returned to Longbourn, she had not thought to betray any mention of her brief encounter with Mr. Darcy. Though Elizabeth thought her father was, on the whole, level-headed about the affair, there were still times when he was known to make choice comments about the Darcy family. In addition, her uncle, David Gardiner, was visiting when Elizabeth arrived home, and given the trouble between him and the younger Darcy brother, perhaps it may have been best to stay silent.

"And how is his demeanor when among company?" her uncle was

asking Jane as Elizabeth entered the room. Mr. Gardiner smiled at Elizabeth but did not pull his attention from Jane.

"There is nothing the matter with Mr. Bingley in any situation," replied Jane. "He has been a perfect gentleman."

"And his connection to the Darcy family?"

"Is this inquisition required, Gardiner?" asked Mr. Bennet. "I have satisfied myself as to Mr. Bingley's intentions and his character."

"What of his friendship with the Darcy heir?"

"I shall not dictate who Mr. Bingley can and cannot have as a friend," declared Jane.

"Nor did I think you would," replied her uncle. "It is not my intention to cast shade on the Darcy family, for I do not think they would be so crass as to impose themselves on Mr. Bingley's family. However, Mr. Bingley's reliance on Mr. Darcy's advice is an established fact. Shall you marry a man who will forever look to another for instruction?"

"You are hard on young Mr. Bingley," said Lord Arundel.

Jane, at the same time, showed a little spirit and anger, a glare slipping through her calm demeanor. "I have every confidence in Mr. Bingley's ability to live his own life without reference to Mr. Darcy or anyone else. Much of the advice Mr. Bingley received from the Darcy family concerned the management of his estate, for he was not prepared to become master when his father passed."

When Mr. Gardiner paused, Elizabeth felt it necessary to speak up. "I dare say Mr. Darcy is not as bad as we might all like to believe."

Three sets of eyes found Elizabeth, her father and sister with curiosity, while Mr. Gardiner's expression was intent. "What do you mean?"

"I met him on my ride this morning," said Elizabeth, speaking as if it was nothing out of the ordinary.

"Just so we are clear, Mr. Darcy the heir?"

"Yes," replied Elizabeth. "Though I will not suggest our conversation was in any way an exchange of pleasantries, he was gentlemanly, and I never felt the man was intent upon imposing himself upon me."

The two men, in particular, regarded her, eyes searching, while Jane sat, her serene countenance restored. After a moment of this, Mr. Gardiner turned to her father, his expression questioning. The sour look Lord Arundel returned spoke to his displeasure.

"I suppose the elder son is less of a problem than the younger. It has always been my observation that he is a quiet, reflective sort of man." Lord Arundel then turned a searching gaze on her again. "Was the meeting coincidental?"

"Entirely," said Elizabeth. "I had gone into Lambton to receive the books we ordered and had stopped on the return to read. Mr. Darcy appeared to have been out riding; our meeting was not intentional."

Lord Arundel brightened at the mention of books but continued to ask about Mr. Darcy. "You did not feel threatened by him."

"No," was Elizabeth's reply. "Mr. Darcy had much to say on the subject of Jane and Mr. Bingley, but there was never any hint of a threat."

When Elizabeth noted Jane looking at her, a hint of concern in her manner, she added: "It seems to me Mr. Darcy's influence with Mr. Bingley is less than it was. Though the gentleman is not happy his closest friend is pursuing a Bennet daughter, I dare say there is nothing he can do about it."

"Then I suppose we may forget about the matter," said her father. "Should the young man become a problem, you will inform me, Lizzy. Darcy may have connections to the nobility, but I am a baron, and will not allow him to behave inappropriately."

"As I said," replied Elizabeth, "I cannot see Mr. Darcy becoming a problem."

"Very well," replied Lord Arundel. "Then if you will excuse me, I shall return to my study. Thank you for visiting, Gardiner."

The gentleman nodded and Lord Arundel departed, leaving Mr. Gardiner alone with his two nieces. For a moment no one spoke, and their uncle regarded them, deep in contemplation. It was an established fact that Lord Arundel was not the most proactive man, and at times he appeared more interested in laughing at the world than living in it. If serious matters arose, he was not hesitant to act but most of the time, he was content to let matters pass him by.

In a real sense, Mr. Gardiner had become the girls' protector, especially in the past few years since his eldest nieces had come out. It was Mr. Gardiner who attended every assembly with them, watched over them like a hawk watches over newly hatched chicks, assisted with overeager suitors. It had also been Mr. Gardiner who had shepherded them through their first and subsequent seasons, as Lord Arundel's distaste for town was legendary. The Bennet girls were fond of their uncle and the man was close to them and to his sister. It was an excellent arrangement for them all.

"Are you certain of this man, Bingley?" asked he at length of Jane.

"I am, Uncle," replied Jane. "There is no better man than Mr.

Bingley; I have no doubts of his affection, his ability to be his own man, or his ability to fend off well-meaning friends, or dare I say, even a sister who wishes he would focus his attention in another direction."

Mr. Gardiner snorted, for there was no one in the district who misunderstood Miss Bingley's interest in the heir of Pemberley. The lady's desire that Mr. Bingley connect himself to young Georgiana Darcy, who was still only seventeen, was not as well understood, that being the province of the more observant of society. Mr. Gardiner was among those who could see the way the wind blew with ease.

"Then I shall support you," said Mr. Gardiner. "Perhaps, however, we should attempt to assist Mr. Bingley ourselves. Should we offer our assistance, he will not be so dependent upon Pemberley."

"Mr. Bingley can manage his own affairs," replied Jane. "But I cannot think such an offer would be amiss, should the occasion arise."

"Then I shall do so when the opportunity presents itself," said Mr. Gardiner. "Until then, I shall only wish you every happiness with Mr. Bingley, Jane. There is no one who deserves happiness more than you."

"Amen," was Elizabeth's soft but fervent reply. With that statement, she could not agree more.

CHAPTER V

*I*t was a curious fact of the family at Longbourn that there were no close relations bearing the name Bennet. While there were some distant cousins, descendants of this aunt, or that cousin, they were all descended from female lines, and while the current Lord Arundel had two younger brothers, both had perished before their tenth birthdays. Thus, the only members of the family bearing the name Bennet all lived at Longbourn.

What they lacked in closeness with Lord Arundel's side of the family was more than made up for with respect to Lady Margaret Bennet's relations, of whom there were many. It is not the purpose of this work to detail in great length the branches of Lady Margaret's family tree. Of more importance to the matter at hand was the members of her close relations, which comprised two brothers, one of whom had his own family.

The eldest brother, Mr. David Gardiner, was the master of Shambling Hall, which, though it may not have possessed the most distinguished of names, was a large estate of about eight thousand pounds per annum—or equal in size to Longbourn—and boasted a large and respectable manor house. Mr. Gardiner, though now five and thirty years of age, was yet unmarried, and had lived alone at the manor since his mother's passing two years earlier, his father having passed some ten years before.

The younger brother, Mr. Edward Gardiner, was the parson at Lambton. Mr. Gardiner, unlike his brother, was three and thirty and had been married the past eight years to Madeline Plumber, the younger daughter of a gentleman of more modest means of the neighborhood. Together, the Gardiners had produced four children, the eldest, Abigail, and her two younger brothers, James and Benjamin, and an infant girl, Sophie.

The Gardiner brothers were similar men, both in stature, the dark hair which curled about their heads, their dark brown eyes and upright bearing. Their characters were also alike, though, being a parson, the younger was more pious, while the elder possessed more of a temper. But both were excellent men, and the Bennets were very fond of them.

It was the custom of the family to gather often—at least once a week on Sundays—to partake of a large family dinner. The location of this dinner alternated between Shambling Hall and Longbourn, as the parsonage was too small to accommodate them all. On the evening in question, Longbourn was the site for their usual weekly family dinner.

Given the composition of those gathered together and the presence of five young women, conversation was always lively at the dinner table. That evening it consisted of various subjects, but after a time, turned to one not palatable for Elizabeth's taste.

"You have had no further meetings with Mr. Darcy?" asked her Uncle Gardiner of Elizabeth. To avoid confusion when referring to the brothers, the Bennet sisters were in the habit of calling the younger brother Uncle Edward.

"No, Uncle," replied Elizabeth. "Nor would I have expected it. It was, as I informed you before, an accidental meeting, and one I do not think Mr. Darcy is eager to repeat."

"One can never be certain when it pertains to the Darcy family," said Lord Arundel.

It did not escape Elizabeth's attention that members of her family often made such statements of the Darcy family, but with little evidence, and with casual authority rather than conviction. The mention of the Darcy family, however, drew the attention of her younger uncle.

"This is the first I have heard of this. Which Mr. Darcy did you meet?"

"The younger," said Elizabeth, thinking it was obvious. Had the elder man come across her, Elizabeth thought it unlikely he would do anything other than sniff with disdain and ride away.

At her uncle's prompting, Elizabeth was obliged to repeat the story of the encounter, a matter which had been unknown to anyone other than her father, her elder uncle, and Jane. When she completed her tale, Elizabeth was quick to add:

"It was a minor matter altogether. Mr. Darcy and I did not speak much, and I soon left. The gentleman did not follow me when I left him."

"Using the term 'gentleman' may be a stretch for anyone bearing the Darcy name," said Lord Arundel. "Though they have the land and connections for the title, their behavior is anything but gentlemanly."

Elizabeth thought to protest, but her Uncle Edward spoke before she opened her mouth. "It has long been a matter of much curiosity and confusion to me that the Bennets and Darcys do not get on, and no one has ever explained the origin of the dispute to my satisfaction. Do you care to elaborate, Brother?"

Lord Arundel, to whom he had directed the question, shrugged. "I do not know the beginning of our antipathy. That does not change the fact that I have never known the Darcys to deal fairly with anyone."

Uncle Edward and his wife exchanged a glance. "It is interesting to hear you speak so, for I have often met the Darcys—the father *and* his sons—in Lambton and have never had so much as a cross word from any of them."

"Young Miss Darcy is a lovely and gentle creature," added Mrs. Gardiner. "She has often stopped in the street to speak with me, and she never gave the impression she thought herself proud or above her company."

"Oh, Georgiana Darcy is as far from the pride displayed by the rest of her family as hot is to cold," said Lydia.

Lord Arundel's eyes found his youngest daughter. "And have you met with Miss Darcy often enough to know her character? It was my understanding that Bennets spoke with Darcys but little, regardless of Lizzy's recent fraternizing with the elder son."

Elizabeth noted the grin with which her father favored her and knew he was teasing.

"No, I dare say I have not exchanged two words with Miss Darcy in my life," replied Lydia. "But one only has to see her to know she is reticent and shy."

"That she is, Lydia," said Mrs. Gardiner. "Whatever you may think of the other Darcys, Miss Darcy has no part in pride or unchristian tendencies you may attribute to the other members of the family."

"Again, I will assert I have seen nothing of such tendencies in the first place," pressed Uncle Edward.

"Do you forget the offense of the younger son?" asked his brother, his mild tone belied by his sharp look at his brother.

"By all accounts that was an accident, as much your fault as his," said Uncle Edward, meeting his brother's gaze with a pointed look of his own. "Do you still hold a grudge against the younger Darcy? If so, I hope you will release it, for by all accounts he is to return soon."

"He is?" asked Lord Arundel and Mr. Gardiner in unison.

Uncle Edward shrugged. "It is something that has been rumored in Lambton of late. There is some talk from the Pemberley servants that Mr. Darcy wishes his son to return home to complete his education in managing an estate. The younger Darcy does, if you recall, own an estate, but his elder brother has managed it for some years in his stead."

"Then I hope Mr. Darcy has some success in taming his son," said Lord Arundel. "While you may not put any stock in our opinions of the general characters of the family, the younger son has long been known to be wild."

"That I will not dispute," said Uncle Edward. "I will note that his character is tame compared to many other young men of his station, though he is too boisterous for my taste."

Lord Arundel nodded and returned his attention to his plate. The family was quiet for a few moments, and Elizabeth was relieved the discussion seemed to have wound to a close. However, her relief was soon revealed to be nothing more than wishful thinking.

"I do not carry a grudge," said Uncle Gardiner after a moment, "if that is what you are suggesting."

"That is well," said Uncle Edward. He directed a pointed look at his brother and added: "For a time after the event, you were contemplating calling him out if my memory is accurate."

"Aye, you were at that," said Lord Arundel. "In fact, I remember you hobbling about my sitting-room, muttering epithets about any and all Darcys."

"Yet that was a sixmonth ago," replied Mr. Gardiner. "The injury was not substantial and I have healed with no lasting effects."

"So you would still be angry with him if your injury was more substantial?" asked Uncle Edward.

"It seems to me that any man would be," rejoined his brother. "That is nothing more than human nature."

"That does not make it right. It has often been my opinion that a man who has not mastered his baser impulses is an enemy to God, and this only proves my supposition. Do the scriptures not say we must forgive *all* men, lest we receive no forgiveness for *our* sins?

"I would counsel you to forget old grievances, Brother, for allowing hatred and resentment to fester in your heart can only lead to ill ends."

"As I have said," replied Uncle Gardiner, his tone a warning his brother to cease harping on the subject, "I have no resentment for the younger Darcy. What may have been is not at issue, for I will never know what might have been.

"What I will say is I have often been uncertain of the Darcy family, though I will own I have no experiences which I can use to point to their dishonest characters. As you all know," said he, looking about the room, "the Darcys have a good name, not only in Derbyshire but also in town. Thus, I try to be careful near them, and I make no overt accusations."

"This sounds too much like a dispute," said Lady Margaret, glaring at her brothers. "Please avoid arguing at my table."

"I apologize if it seems like I was provoking an argument," said Uncle Edward, attempting to placate his sister. "As my brother has declared he holds no grudges, I shall leave the subject be. I hope a détente can be reached with the Darcy family, for it seems we have all perpetuated this dispute with no notion of why."

"You may be correct, Edward," replied Lord Arundel. "I will not go looking for trouble with the Darcy family, but I will retain my reserve until they can prove their goodness. I hope you will not fault me for determining to protect myself and my family."

"No man can be faulted for protecting his family. I only hope you do not attribute unchristian behavior to others without reason."

"Never that," murmured Lord Arundel. They all dropped the subject for other, more general matters.

As the days passed, Elizabeth's thoughts returned to that dinner conversation often, and she could not help but think in different ways, they were all correct. Given the longstanding enmity between the families, it was only prudent to remain watchful of the Darcys. That was also true for her Uncle Gardiner, who had sustained an injury at least in part because of a Darcy.

However, her Uncle Edward was also correct. The Bennets were a good Christian family, and by all accounts, the Darcys were the same, though Pemberley was a part of the Kympton parish, and as a result, the Darcys worshiped there. The Bible had never been ambiguous about the need to forgive others—Christ himself taught that one should forgive another seventy times seven times, which Elizabeth had always taken to mean one should extend forgiveness as many times as necessary.

Did that require the offended party to accept whatever abuse the perpetrator saw fit to unleash, all while forgiving without hope of relief? The question was one better asked of her Uncle Edward, but she did not think that was the purpose of the commandment, for it seemed to her the Bible said nothing of allowing persecution. Forgiveness itself was important, for not allowing oneself to forgive allowed anger to fester, ill-feelings to grow, which could bring great future pain.

It was Elizabeth's opinion that forgiveness between the Bennets and the Darcys both applied and did not apply to the situation. It applied because the commandment to forgive encompassed all, and the consequences of perpetuating the grudge between them carried the potential for future harm; her uncle had already been injured once. Who knew if it would happen again?

Where it did not apply was the fact that no one—not even the two patriarchs of the family—could remember the initial offense. Mr. Bingley's testimony of his friend's response when asked on the matter was evidence, albeit not proof, that the Darcy sire knew no more of the origins of the dispute than did her father. As there were no specific injuries to forgive, did that not make the continued dispute even more ridiculous?

There was no one in the family to whom she could speak unless she went to Lambton to counsel with her uncle. Mary would agree with her, Elizabeth knew, but she also possessed a moralizing streak, meaning anything Elizabeth said on the matter might provoke her younger sister to preach to the rest of the family, which she did not want. Jane would also agree with Elizabeth, but that was more a function of her inability to think poorly of anyone, while the youngest Bennets would laugh and turn the conversation to something else. Even Lord and Lady Margaret were not options, for her father did not concern himself much with the situation, and her mother, outside of a few occasional comments, had little interest in it.

Elizabeth could not determine why the matter seemed so important to her now, for she had thought little on it in the past. Somehow her uncle's words, coupled with her meeting with Mr. Darcy combined to make her wary of the situation. Whether Mr. Darcy had, in some manner, given her to understand he was not the man her family had always thought, even given the testiness of their exchange, Elizabeth could not say. But it was now a matter of some interest to her, leading to a desire to unravel the mystery and heal the breach.

Had Elizabeth been left to herself it is possible she may have worried to excess on the matter. It was fortunate that she was not allowed the opportunity for constant reflection, for Longbourn was a busy home with eight residents and the servants, the occasional visits of relations and friends to keep her company. In particular, there was one who often clamored for her attention in those days.

"Can we not go out of doors, Lizzy?" asked her younger brother, Thomas, more than once. "Are the frogs living along the river? I should like to catch some."

Though the Bennet siblings were affectionate with one another, Elizabeth had long been Thomas's favorite sister, because, Elizabeth thought, she was the one who indulged him and joined him in his games. Playing with toy soldiers was not a favorite, though Elizabeth often got down on the floor with him, leading to her mother's lamentations. While none of her sisters could countenance capturing frogs, her father had taught her the best ways to do it many years ago. Thus, Elizabeth thought it was her duty to pass her learning down to her youngest sibling.

The next day, when young Master Bennet was released from his studies, the two of them dressed in warm clothes and departed for the nearby river, though with Lord Arundel's admonishments concerning the danger of going near the waters ringing in their ears. The day was fine, though perhaps cooler than the weather had been of late. Elizabeth guided her young brother along, talking and laughing with him as she walked.

As it turned out, however, their efforts that day were in vain, for they could discover no hopping denizens anywhere nearby. They searched, for Thomas was not to be denied without an argument, but could find no sign of the amphibians he desired.

"It is not a surprise we found nothing today, Tommy," said Elizabeth, her affection for the boy prompting her to ruffle his hair. "Given the cold of the day, I would have been surprised if we had found any, and it *is* still early in the season."

"Where do the frogs go when there is snow?" asked the young boy, looking up at her with trust in his eyes.

"I do not quite know," replied Elizabeth with a straight face, unwilling to enter a conversation of the hibernation and mating habits of amphibians with her innocent brother. "Perhaps they find some warmth under the water which they find to their taste."

Thomas looked up at her, curiosity and concentration in his crinkled brow. "Do they not need to breathe?"

"I believe frogs may hold their breath for some time, but yes, they must breathe. When the spring becomes warmer and the snow is all gone, there is a greater chance of finding some. Then I shall teach you how to capture them."

The boy continued to give her a serious look. "I hope we may do it soon, for I long to hold one in my hands. Perhaps I shall give it to Lydia—she might appreciate it as much as you do."

With a laugh, Elizabeth shook her head. "It would be best if you refrained from giving her such gifts, my dear brother, for none of our sisters appreciate the finer points of a lively frog. If you are careful and do not allow her to catch you in the act, you may even be able to smuggle one into mother's bed!"

A grin appeared on the boy's face. "Mama does not like frogs at all, Lizzy. I saw her face when we talked about looking for frogs, so I do not believe she would appreciate finding one in her bed."

"No, I dare say she would not. If you do bring a frog into the house, remember not to inform me of it, for I should not like Mama to blame me."

"But if I do it myself, Mama would suspect *me*, and we could not have that!"

The siblings laughed together. "Father would not appreciate having his peace disrupted either," said Elizabeth. "It is best, then, that you content yourself with capturing them and admiring them near the river. Putting a frog in another's bed is a good joke, but those who do not appreciate them would be angry."

"What if I kept the frog in my bed?" asked the youngster.

Elizabeth laughed again. "Somehow, I doubt Mama would appreciate that either. Your mother would inform you frogs are meant to be outside, not in the house. In that, she would echo your grandmother, who, as I understand, found more than one amphibian present in the house courtesy of your uncles."

This prompted Thomas to ask after Elizabeth's meaning, and she shared some of the stories she had heard from her uncles with the eager boy. Though not misbehaving hellions, the Gardiner boys had gotten up to their fair share of mischief.

"Thank you for your stories," said Thomas as they drew close to the house. "When next I see Uncle Gardiner, I shall ask to hear more of his adventures. I wonder if he would consent to have adventures with me, as you do."

"It is possible," said Elizabeth.

"Then I shall speak to him."

"Do you not wish for a brother, given these stories of your uncles?" asked Elizabeth, curious of his introspection.

"Why should I wish for a brother when I have you?" asked Thomas, with clear confusion.

Elizabeth's heart melted at his honest answer, and she stepped close and embraced him. "Why, indeed? I am lucky to be a sister to the most wonderful boy in the world, Tommy."

With a grin, Thomas darted toward the house, calling over his shoulder: "If I am such a wonderful boy, you must come and play with my soldiers. I consider them a suitable substitute for frogs!"

Shaking her head, Elizabeth followed her brother into the house where a maid was taking his outerwear. The boy ran upstairs toward the nursery, calling for Elizabeth to follow him. It appeared there was little to do other than oblige him, and Elizabeth was about to do so when her mother entered the room.

"I hope you did not bring any frogs back, Lizzy."

"No, Mama, there were none in evidence. It is still early."

Lady Margaret nodded. "Please do not encourage him to bring such treasures to the house. Should I find a frog in my bed, I shall know Edward did not leave it."

Elizabeth laughed and embraced her mother. "We discussed it, and I believe I conveyed the drawbacks to any such pranks. There should be no unexpected presents left in any of our beds."

The voice of her brother calling out for her had Elizabeth exchanging a rueful glance with her mother before she turned to join him. It appeared great battles and deeds of heroism were in her immediate future, and she turned to them with a will.

CHAPTER VI

*R*eunions were almost universally acknowledged sweet after long separations. At present, however, Darcy would be lying to himself if he claimed he watched his brother's carriage approach with anything other than mixed emotions.

It was not that he did not love his brother, though sometimes love and exasperation were so intimately entwined that they were impossible to separate. The two brothers were not alike in any sense — quite the opposite. Whereas Darcy was serious-minded, his brother was frivolous; Darcy tended toward careful consideration, while his brother was impetuous; his brother was at ease in any society, whereas Darcy was awkward; and while Darcy was attentive to all his duties, his brother more often than not tried to avoid his.

Thus, as the carriage pulled up before the front door of the house, Darcy watched it, wondering if his brother's last six months spent in exile had changed him to any great extent. Then again, exile was a strong word, for, after only a week at his own estate, Alexander had found it too tame for his tastes, and had left for London — it was there he had spent his time, no doubt carousing with whatever friends were also present in the capital with him drinking more than he ought, gambling, wenching, and behaving in a manner no gentleman ought.

When the carriage came to a halt, Alexander did not wait for the footman—he grasped the handle himself instead and stepped down, his pleasure at seeing them all plain to see. While Darcy and his father greeted the younger member of their family with the soberness in keeping with their own characters, Georgiana squealed and threw herself at him, prompting him to pick her up and swing her in the air, laughing. Georgiana had always been close to them both, though for different reasons.

"Alexander," said Mr. Darcy, grasping his son's shoulders when he separated from his sister. "It is good to have you back with us."

"It is good to be back, Father," replied Alexander with a grin. "I do wonder at you summoning me now, however, for town was just becoming interesting. Shall the Darcys not attend the season this year?"

"Perhaps we shall later," replied Mr. Darcy. Alexander refrained from saying anything in response, for he knew his father and brother did not appreciate society. Then he turned to Darcy himself.

"Hello, Brother."

"Alexander," replied Darcy, laying a hand on his brother's arm. "Welcome home."

His brother favored him with a cocksure smile he often displayed when he was about to jest. "Are the final words you spoke to me before I left to be forgotten?"

"If you recall," replied Darcy, "I only suggested it was time for you to take life seriously."

"Yes, and it is time we all had a serious discussion," interjected their father. "Let us not argue the moment Alexander has alighted from the carriage. There will be time enough for disagreements later."

Darcy nodded, but his brother regarded him as if he were trying to understand. Soon, however, they entered the house, where Alexander took to his room to change. Darcy noted his father's stern look, warning him to avoid provoking a dispute. From what Darcy knew of his father's purpose, he doubted such a disagreement was anything other than inevitable, but he refrained from making any comment.

The afternoon in the company of his brother was characterized by lively conversation and stories, though the one member of the family possessed of an open disposition did most of the talking. Alexander had much to say, as he always did, though he did not tell any of his indelicate tales in the presence of his sister, for which Darcy was grateful. How much was the truth and what was fiction—or embellishment—Darcy could not determine; it was always impossible when it came to his brother's tales.

Alexander had always had a unique position within the family. As Lady Anne had been like her husband, elder son, and daughter in character, Alexander was the only one of the family of a more open disposition. Georgiana had always been close to him, as had Mr. Darcy, who enjoyed Alexander's engaging manners. Darcy could not say that his father preferred his brother to himself, but it was clear to Darcy that in such circumstances, his father enjoyed his brother's company more than Darcy's.

Though he had wondered, at times, if he should feel more offense because of it, Darcy had long ago decided there was no reason to do so. Alexander was a jovial man, his ease in company something Darcy could never duplicate. Darcy knew his father loved and esteemed him, his relationship with his father differed from what Alexander shared with the elder man; Darcy thought it was more meaningful in many ways. Mr. Darcy was always proper and showed no favorites, and thus, there was nothing to resent, even if Darcy had fancied in himself a resentful temper.

That night after dinner the elder Darcy raised the subject Darcy had been waiting for all day—the crux of the reason his father had called Alexander home. As Alexander was not unintelligent, Darcy thought his brother knew it himself, though he had not spoken on the subject.

"I know you would have preferred to stay in London for the season," said their father, opening the conversation, "but I have a specific reason for wishing you in Derbyshire again."

"Oh?" asked Alexander, his manner all insouciance. "I would never have guessed, Father. Shall you inform me of your reasons, or should I attempt to divine them for myself?"

The study in which they sat—Georgiana having retired—boasted the comfort of a roaring fire in the grate, the three men of the family having pulled three armchairs close so they could speak. With a glass of his father's fine brandy, Alexander sprawled in a chair, one foot resting on the table, while he took periodic sips of his drink.

"You are not as insensible as you sometimes attempt to portray yourself," said Mr. Darcy, resting a faint smile on his younger son. "And I am not deceived. You know why I have summoned you."

"Yes, I have some inkling of it," replied Alexander. "But I should like to hear your reasons all the same."

Mr. Darcy gave him a distracted nod before he said: "Very well. As you know, you have an estate of your own, which William has been managing in your stead. Though the lure of town and the amusements you may find there are compelling at your time of life, I believe for you to begin pursuing serious matters."

"And I thank you, William, for caring for Thorndell in my stead," said Alexander, lifting his glass in Darcy's direction. "It is a bother, though I know I must attend to it sooner or later. There is a good steward at Thorndell, however, so I do not know why I should have to concern myself with every detail."

"If you concerned yourself with *any* detail, I would be obliged," said Darcy. That he did not snap it in frustration Darcy thought was a display of his restraint, though his father gave him a look suggesting he should remain silent.

"Managing an estate is not a trivial matter, Alexander," said Mr. Darcy. "A man employs a good steward to relieve the burden of managing every little detail—no one is asking you to concern yourself with matters better left to the purview of a steward.

"However, in order for the enterprise to continue to operate as it should, the master's input is required for matters of larger significance. Your brother has been managing the estate since his majority, but the time has now come that you must take the burden on yourself."

Though Darcy had often known his brother to make a flippant response on such occasions, he toyed with his glass while he considered his response. After a moment of this, he drained it and set it on the nearby table.

"I would not have you believe I am unwilling, Father," said Alexander at length. Darcy knew that while he was not *unwilling*, he was not *willing* either. "It occurs to me to wonder why you raise this subject now."

"There are several reasons," replied Mr. Darcy without hesitation. "For one, you are now five and twenty and at the age when the frivolities of youth must give way to the responsibilities of being an adult." When Alexander made to respond Mr. Darcy added: "It is not my thought to curtail your fun, my son; life is drudgery if we do not enjoy it. Sometimes, however, you have focused too much on your amusements. It is time for you to become a dependable man of responsibility."

Such a harsh assessment was likely not what he had expected from his father, for Mr. Darcy had indulged him more often than not. Then again, Darcy knew his brother was not surprised, for their father had hinted his expectations for some time now, long before Alexander had departed for London.

"I suppose you are correct," replied he at length.

"There are other reasons," said Mr. Darcy. "For one, I would like William to take up more of Pemberley's management, and for that, he must be free of the cares of managing Thorndell."

Darcy might have expected his brother to state that many men managed more than one estate — including their father himself — but he refrained. Instead, he regarded Darcy for a few moments before speaking.

"Thorndell is but half the size of Pemberley."

"Less," replied Darcy. "With careful management, its yields can approach five thousand a year, but a prudent man would budget four thousand instead."

"Have there been any issues of which I am not aware?"

"Nothing of major importance," replied Darcy. "The tenants are cared for and all the buildings are sturdy. There was a bountiful harvest last autumn and the money from the rents has been added to your accounts, as I am certain you already know."

"I do," was Alexander's reply. "The majority remains in the accounts, for I did not find myself in need of funds."

Darcy, who had access to the accounts because of his management of the estate, knew this. It was one piece of evidence which had given him hope his brother was changing for the better, for in the past, while Alexander might not have gambled it all away, it would have been several hundred pounds less than it was.

"Then do you wish me to return to Thorndell at once?" asked Alexander, turning back to their father.

"Having just welcomed you back, I am not eager to give up your company again so soon," replied Mr. Darcy. "I thought, rather, you could assist William in some of his duties at Pemberley. Though I have trained you as well as I am able, it has been some time since you took an active interest. Working with your brother will allow you to become accustomed to it again."

It was an exaggeration — Darcy knew it and knew his brother and father did also. For all he was not without knowledge, Alexander had not taken *any* interest in estate matters in the past.

"And what of the other matter?" asked Alexander. "Shall my presence in the neighborhood not cause difficulties?"

"If it does, that is *their* problem," said Mr. Darcy shortly. "What happened was an accident. There is little gossip any longer, and to the best of my knowledge, Mr. Gardiner is well and does not hold a grudge."

"My return will *provoke* gossip," Alexander pointed out.

"And it will die down soon."

With a shrug, Alexander said: "Very well. I am at your disposal, Brother."

There was a glib undertone in Alexander's response Darcy could not like. But there seemed no reason to call him out on it. Instead, Darcy indicated his agreement and fell silent. The three men stayed in the study until early morning, speaking of that and other matters. How long estate business would hold Alexander's attention he could not say. He feared it would not be long at all.

It was the very next day when his brother's education began, and Darcy was at the same time optimistic and disheartened. There was something about the way Alexander went about his life which suggested a lack of seriousness, and it had always given him grief. Some of the conversations they exchanged gave him hope that this time would be different, but then Alexander would say or do something which contradicted his previous assurances, leaving Darcy exasperated.

As there was a tenant or two they needed to see, they left early that morning, though not as early as Darcy might have gone if he had been alone. Alexander was an excellent horseman, confident and easy in the saddle, his mount, which had languished in Pemberley's stables since the previous year, eager to run. They allowed their steeds to run for some moments before slowing and walking them toward Mr. Hearn's farm, located at some distance south from the house.

"You know," said Alexander when they were again at ease, "the problem is that you are much more suited to the role of being the master of an estate than I am."

Darcy turned a hard look on his brother. "In what way?" asked he, though in a tone which informed his brother he should take care of what he said. It was no surprise when Alexander did not heed the warning.

"Why, that I enjoy my life far too much to allow my mood to be ruined worrying over an estate."

Alexander spoke in jest but Darcy knew his words contained a kernel of truth—or what Alexander considered to be the truth. While Darcy knew it was likely pointless, he could not but glare at his brother, and when Alexander saw it, he was quick to put out his hands and laugh.

"I know, Brother. But you must own that it is correct. I do not intend for you to manage my estate forever, but you are much better suited to the task than I."

"It is my opinion," said Darcy, holding his glare on his brother, "that you are not incapable of doing what needs to be done. More than that, you do not take the trouble to apply yourself. If you did so, I believe you would discover you would do very well; moreover, you would also discover that the management of an estate, while it requires attention, is not an onerous task which occupies you from dawn until dusk, and has its own rewards."

"Yes, Brother, I know. As I said, I am grateful for your assistance, and I know I could not have done nearly so well with my estate as I am sure you have. I am only confessing the truth."

Deciding there was no reason to continue to belabor the matter, Darcy kicked his horse a little faster, pulling ahead and allowing Alexander to follow him. His brother's chuckle of amusement followed him as he rode, but Darcy decided it was best to ignore him.

When they arrived at the tenant farm they stopped to speak with Mr. Hearn regarding the business of his plot of land. The area Mr. Hearn farmed was toward the southeast of the estate, a location which required some ability to adapt, for the man both had a plot of land he farmed, and a flock of sheep which grazed on the rockier terrain toward the borders. Their primary concern with Mr. Hearn was to discuss some impending repairs to the tenant cottage, a matter on which they quickly came to an agreement. Then the farmer brought up another issue of which Darcy had not been aware.

"One of our sheep escaped to the meadow beyond the corner of the estate," said the man in his gruff voice. "I had Jonathan look at the fence, but he could not detect any openings in it."

"Jonathan is your son?" asked Alexander.

The farmer confirmed Alexander's question, though Darcy had not thought his brother acquainted enough with the tenants to know who he was. Then he did something even more surprising.

"Perhaps William and I could ride along the fence and inspect it for ourselves."

Farmer Hearn doffed his wide-brimmed hat in a gesture of respect. "If you could, I would be mighty grateful. Jonathan means well, but I doubt he looked too closely if you catch my meaning. He has other concerns to occupy him."

"It would be no trouble, Mr. Hearn," said Darcy, his brother echoing him. "We will ride in that direction, and if we discover anything, we will arrange to have it repaired."

"Thank you, good sirs. I appreciate the help."

After a few more words, the gentlemen took their leave and rode off to the south toward the border. As Darcy recalled, Mr. Hearn kept his sheep close to that area, and while some of it was wooded, it rose toward a small hill, the end of which contained the barrier between Longbourn and Pemberley.

They rode in silence for some few moments, and as they approached the fence, Darcy's mind kept returning to his brother's conduct with Farmer Hearn. Though Alexander had never shown much of an interest in the estate, his conduct confirmed Darcy's opinion that he was capable when he chose to be so. The matter of the Hearn son, however, provoked Darcy to curiosity, and after a time he determined to ask his brother on the subject.

"Jonathan is my age," replied Alexander to Darcy's question. "Though he is a tenant's son and I the son of the gentleman, sometimes we played together as boys. I have not seen him in some years, but I remember him." Alexander paused for a moment and asked: "What is this business to which Mr. Hearn alluded?"

"It is my understanding Jonathan is courting Mr. Peabody's oldest daughter."

"Little Betsy Peabody?" asked Alexander with a laugh. When Darcy replied in the affirmative, Alexander grinned and said: "I remember Jonathan was sweet on her when we were children. She was quite a handful, as I recall—I hope he understands what he is about."

Darcy nodded but did not reply. A few more minutes riding brought them close to the border, and they soon came across the fence. It was a good, solid barrier, built of the wood surrounding them, rising to about shoulder height on a man. Darcy's father had always ensured the fences were kept in good repair; they were inspected at least once every year, which was worrisome if there was a problem. The section where they arrived appeared to be in good order, and an experimental push on a post was met with little flex.

"Well, Brother?" asked Alexander, looking in both directions from where they stood. "As I recall, the fence runs to the northeast before turning due north, parallel to the Lambton road. If we turn the other direction, we must go southwest and then west. Shall we turn in that direction, or go toward the north?"

"Most of the meadow of which the farmer spoke is toward the south. Let us go in that direction."

"Very well," said Alexander, heeling his horse in the direction Darcy had indicated.

The country in this part of the estate was rough, undulating hills mixed with rocky outcrops rising from the earth. For the hardy and sure-footed sheep, it was no trouble, but for two men on horses, the rough terrain required them to go around obstacles or through woods of close, spindly trees. It was time-consuming and aggravating, but in the end, they discovered a board that had been knocked loose and left a hole in the fence large enough for a sheep to go through.

"Looks like we have found our culprit," observed Alexander as Darcy bent to put the piece of wood back in place. It was not perfect, but Darcy positioned it so that the wood provided at least a partial barrier. "Shall we return to Mr. Hearn and let him know what we have found?"

"We can send someone later," said Darcy, shaking his head. "It would be best if we continue and ensure there are no other issues with the fence."

Alexander fixed him with a dubious look. "You suspect other problems?"

"No," replied Darcy with a look at his brother. "Father had this fence examined just before the winter snows and declared it sound. But I would not wish for other issues to go undiscovered and lose livestock."

With a shrug, Alexander voiced his willingness, and the brothers mounted and set off. It was fortunate they found nothing, for everything else appeared to be in good order. Soon the land grew less rugged and they found themselves on a gradual upward slope, leading toward the hill between Pemberley and Longbourn, the land growing easier for them to navigate as they pressed forward. That was when they came across another sight Darcy had not expected to see.

"There is someone up ahead," said Alexander at about the same time that Darcy noticed the sound of voices.

A few moments later the brothers broke through a line of trees, and the bare slope of the hill rose before them, leading to a crown some distance ahead. There, on the other side of the fence with Longbourn, under a great, lone oak tree which had grown out of the top of the rocky hillock some distance from the fence, were several young women, accompanied by what appeared to be a young boy.

"The Bennets," said Darcy.

"They appear to be having a picnic," said Alexander as they rode up the hill. "Perhaps we should join them."

Darcy turned a glare on his brother and Alexander laughed. "Forgive me, Brother, but I forgot for the moment about the never-ending enmity between the Darcys and the Bennets. If you will forgive me, however, I shall not consider this lot to be a threat. The Bennet sisters are a comely brood of women, and the boy appears to be nothing more than a young boy his age, eager to run."

"I suppose you are correct," said Darcy, looking on the women with interest.

The boy, who was throwing a ball toward one of the young women holding a cricket bat in her hand, caught Darcy's interest. To Darcy's surprise, the young woman struck it, though not hard as there was no one to field it, bouncing it back to the boy. Darcy had never known any young lady to play cricket, so it was a surprise to see her, much less that she had struck the ball. Then the young boy with whom she was playing caught sight of them and pointed with excitement.

Then she turned to look at them, and Darcy could see for the first time it was Miss Elizabeth. The way the sun shone in the woman's hair made it appear as if a halo were hovering over her head, and the light of her dark brown eyes, which he could see were narrowed in challenge even from this distance, gave her the appearance of uncommon beauty. It was the first time Darcy had ever looked at her in such a fashion; the sudden wave of desire which swept through him startled him with its intensity.

Shocked by the improper feeling, Darcy turned his mount and urged it away from the scene, all thought of inspecting the fence forgotten. Though he did not notice it at once, his brother did not immediately follow him. After a moment he stopped and looked back, seeing Alexander making his leisurely way toward him, a wide grin at something only he found amusing.

"Did you see the sister who gave me a challenging look?" asked he when he rode close to Darcy. "If she were a man, I might have thought she would call me out for the temerity of riding on our side of the border!"

"Oh?" asked Darcy. "Which one?"

"How am I supposed to know?" asked Alexander. "I do not know one Bennet from another. The blonde beauty was sitting near her, though this one was just as comely, though darker of coloring. She was also younger unless I miss my guess."

"The blonde is the eldest, Miss Jane Bennet," replied Darcy with a hint of distaste. "The one you describe might be one of the youngest sisters—perhaps Lydia, who suffers from no lack of brashness, from what I understand."

Darcy grunted, eager to leave the subject behind. "It would not do to dwell on them, for they are an improper bunch."

"I would not call her manner improper," replied Alexander. "It was only daring me to . . . Well, I do not know—say something to her, though that is not it either.

"But I will own to curiosity. The way you spoke of the eldest suggests some disapproval of the woman, and yet she is quiet and proper from what I have heard. What have you to hold against her?"

Though Darcy had no desire to speak to his brother about Jane Bennet, he knew Alexander was capable of wheedling it out of him. Alexander was also friendly with Bingley, and as the matter was one acknowledged in the neighborhood, Darcy knew he would learn of it sooner rather than later. Thus, he decided there was little reason to keep it from him.

"Jane Bennet is Bingley's current amorous interest."

"Bingley?" demanded Alexander, a hint of hilarity in his tone. "I like Bingley well enough, but he has always depended on your advice. Might I assume you did not point him toward the eldest Bennet?"

"Bingley has changed since you last saw him," replied Darcy. "He is his own man and may choose for himself without reference to me, or anyone else."

"Oh ho!" exclaimed Alexander. "Then he *has*! I sense a tale here, Brother, one I cannot allow you to refrain from sharing with me."

A groan escaped Darcy's lips and he shook his head. Alexander, he knew, would not allow him to demur now, leading Darcy to wish he had just stayed silent. With no other choice, Darcy began relating the whole of the matter to his brother, wincing when Alexander laughed and cheered Bingley on. Though Darcy was still of two minds about it, he knew Alexander had the right of it. And though he still was uncertain about anyone named Bennet, Darcy acknowledged to himself that he could not wish Bingley anything but the best.

CHAPTER VII

$\mathcal{F}$ine spring days were in short supply in Derbyshire that year. Though spring had come early, leading to a melting of the winter's snows, the days had been characterized by an abundance of rain, leaving the landscape a sodden mass, unfit for man nor beast. Thus, when the weather permitted, it was no surprise that certain elements of the Bennet family were eager to be out of doors.

"Shall we not go out today, Lizzy?" pleaded the young Master Thomas Bennet to his sister. "It has been so long since we have had a proper outing."

Elizabeth laughed and drew her beloved brother close. "Was not our expedition to the river a proper outing?"

"But it was so muddy and short and we did not catch anything!" protested the boy.

With a laugh, Elizabeth looked toward Jane. "What do you think, Jane. Perhaps we shall have a picnic?"

"A picnic?" demanded their mother. "With all that mud, I am sure you will not find a place to lay your blankets!"

"Oh, I believe I know a place that might suit, Mama," said Elizabeth. "And I dare say the last two days of fairer weather has allowed it to dry."

The Bennet siblings all agreed that a picnic was a capital idea, and they prepared baskets of food and blankets, and a few games to play while they were out. Then, as the hour for luncheon approached, they departed from the manor, Lady Margaret's admonishments to refrain from dirtying themselves ringing in their ears.

The manor house of Longbourn was situated north of the center of the estate, and as such, the walk to the hill dividing Longbourn from Pemberley was an easy task, as it was no more than two miles away. Elizabeth, who was long accustomed to the exertion, led the way, Thomas swinging her hand in wide arcs as they walked, with the remaining sisters trailing behind. Though none of them were accustomed to the exercise as Elizabeth was, they were, in general, an active family, and there was little grumbling about the location she had chosen.

"This is lovely," said Jane as they broke through the trees and began climbing the hill. "I do not come here often, but every time I do, I am reminded of the beauty of the place in which we live."

"The hill provides a fine view of both Longbourn and Pemberley," said Elizabeth as they neared the crest.

"Is that not the estate of the Darcys?" asked Thomas, remembering the conversation about the two families' troubles.

"It is," said Elizabeth. "One cannot see the manor house from here, for I believe it is around a bend in the valley, but it is a fine prospect nonetheless."

And a fine prospect it was, one enjoyed by all. The fields of both estates lay before them, as the Bennet side of the barrier included the crest of the hill and a little further down on the other slope. Later in the spring, those fields would sprout with new life, the summer's harvest, providing the life's blood of the families' wealth. At the top of the hill stood one solitary tree, an old oak which had defied the rocky terrain and had stood sentinel on the Bennet lands for uncountable years. Elizabeth had whiled away many a pleasant hour under the protective boughs of that old tree, reading a book, or even taking shelter from the occasional storm. It was a beloved friend.

"Does this hill have a name?" asked Thomas, looking around as his sisters began to lay the blankets and set out their meal.

"If it does, I am not aware of it," replied Elizabeth.

Thomas frowned. "Should not all places such as this have a name? After all, it is quite a prominent feature, is it not?"

"I suppose it is," said Elizabeth with a laugh. "But not all places have names. If you should name every hill, every bit of rock which sticks up from the surrounding landscape, I should think we would eventually run out of names."

Though the boy considered this for a moment, he was not persuaded. "That may be so, Lizzy, but I am convinced this hill should have a name." Thomas gazed about for a moment, and, catching sight of the tree, said: "I believe I shall call it Oakham Mount."

Elizabeth could not help the bubble of laughter which welled up in her, joined by her sisters. It was Kitty who pointed out the obvious problem with his declaration.

"It seems to me to be a grandiose sort of name, Thomas. This little rise of land is not even a hill, let alone a mountain."

"Perhaps," said Thomas, undeterred. "But I believe the name suits it, with the oak tree sticking up in the center. Yes, I believe I shall call it Oakham Mount from now on."

"Then Oakham Mount it shall be," said Jane, drawing her brother into a soft embrace. "Now, if you are finished playing at being Sir Francis Drake, I believe we should sit down for our meal."

It might have been time to sit down for a meal but inducing Thomas to be still for any length of time proved difficult. His first visit to the hill, he was continually gazing about, exclaiming over this scene or that view, until his sisters were quite at their wits' end. When this had gone on for some time, Elizabeth proposed some exercise in the hope it would settle him.

"Yes, let us play cricket!" exclaimed the enthusiastic boy. "I shall bowl, and you will bat."

As it was best to allow him to have his way, Elizabeth agreed and rose with the aforementioned tools in hand. They set themselves up on the edge of their picnic site, with Thomas throwing the ball in such a way that if Elizabeth missed, their sisters would be in a position to catch it and toss it back to him. Though the boy was awkward in his attempts, his gangly arms flailing about as he ran forward to throw the ball, Elizabeth thought he was skilled for his age.

"Take care, Lizzy!" cried Mary with a laugh when Elizabeth missed one of her brother's bowls. It was, she thought in her defense, rather wide of the mark. "It would not do for the ball to end in the food."

"Perhaps it is best we put everything back in the baskets," said Jane.

"It was my thought to leave it out so Thomas could eat more when he tires of the game," replied Elizabeth.

"I am not hungry," declared Thomas. "Mary, throw the ball back!"

When he once again held the ball, Thomas resumed the game, throwing the ball again, though this time with more accuracy. They continued in this manner for a few more throws, until Elizabeth began to think about offering to exchange places. Then Thomas stopped and pointed in the distance past the border with Pemberley.

"Look!"

As one, the sisters turned in the direction of Thomas's outstretched arm, their gaze falling upon a pair of riders. The taller of the two was well-known to Elizabeth, for she had met him in the nearby meadow only a few days before. The other, though a little smaller of stature, looked much like the first, and though Elizabeth had not seen him for some time, she knew at once who he was.

Elizabeth looked once again at the other man, and she was struck by the handsome lines of Mr. Fitzwilliam Darcy's countenance, the way he sat on his horse with little overt effort, as if he were one with the beast, or perhaps *was* the beast—a centaur out of legend. Their eyes met for an instant and Elizabeth felt something pass between them though she could not have said what it was if pressed. And then the man broke the connection between them when he wheeled his horse and began cantering away.

There was no time to wonder what had just happened—or if it had happened *only* to her, for the second man caught her gaze again. He was watching them, a slight smirk adorning his features, his gaze locked with Lydia's. Lydia was giving as good as the gentleman, for her look in response spoke of challenge. The young gentleman then flipped them a jaunty salute and turned to follow his companion. Soon they were out of sight.

"So, it is true," said Elizabeth after a moment's pause.

"That was the rumor," agreed Jane, her manner a little worried. "I wonder how this will affect Uncle Gardiner."

"I should think it will not affect him at all," said Lydia. When her sisters turned to look at her, she shrugged and added: "Uncle Gardiner himself said he has no grudge to hold against the younger Darcy."

"Perhaps that is so," said Mary. "But I should hope the uneasy peace is not tested soon, for words may be spoken which may lead to threats, or even worse."

"I should hope Uncle Gardiner is better able to control himself than to descend to such behavior," replied Jane.

Mary shrugged, showing her agreement, and did not respond. Elizabeth took the opportunity to speak to her sister.

"It may be best to refrain from provoking them, Lydia."

Turning, languid and uncaring, Lydia replied: "Do you think them capable of attacking a group of undefended women?"

"What do you mean?" asked Thomas, puzzled. "They are gentlemen of quality—no gentleman would do such a cowardly thing."

"Gentlemanly they may appear," replied Lydia, "but their behavior may be suspect, I think. I believe I have found a new diversion, for I like to mock them."

The protests from her sisters were immediate and loud, not that their displeasure affected Lydia. She just sat there, a slight smile fixed on them all while they berated her for her behavior.

"Oh, do not be silly," said Lydia after a moment of enduring their combined displeasure. "There is nothing they can do, for though they are Darcys, they are not savages, nor do I believe they are stupid. It was just a little harmless fun."

This talk of mocking did not sit well with Elizabeth, but she decided there was no need to belabor the issue. It seemed the rest of her sisters agreed, for they said nothing more on the subject and they returned to their game. After a few moments, Lydia rose from where she sat on the blanket and joined them, taking her place behind Thomas and allowing Elizabeth to hit the ball with a little more force.

At length, they decided it was time to return to the house, and they packed the remaining food and the blankets away and began the walk back. Though Thomas was boisterous and eager to run on ahead on most occasions, this time he was quiet and introspective. When they had covered half the distance, Elizabeth discovered why.

"You do not think the gentleman would have done something reprehensible, do you, Lizzy?"

"Of course not," replied Elizabeth, trying to impart her surety through her tone. "The Darcys *are* gentlemen, despite audacities the Bennets may attempt to attribute to them."

"Then why did you scold Lydia?" asked Thomas.

"Because, Brother, it is not polite to behave so. Regardless of who it is, we should always strive to show respect to our fellow man. If the Darcy family thinks ill of the Bennet family, will such behavior not induce them to further suspect us of being untrustworthy?"

"I suppose you are correct," replied Thomas. "As I said, when I am master, I shall not continue this silly feud. Then they shall have no reason to suspect the Bennet family of any poor behavior."

Laughing, Elizabeth drew her brother to her as they walked. "I am sure you will make an excellent master, Thomas. It is my hope you succeed in mending the breach between our two families."

The living of Lambton parish had been in the Bennet family's possession since long before the family had been ennobled many generations before. The town was close to the manor at Longbourn — only two miles distant — and the glebe was just inside the border of the estate, an easy distance for the rector to see to the land which provided his support. When the previous parson at the estate had passed away, Mr. Edward Gardiner had been the obvious choice to succeed him.

Elizabeth enjoyed listening to her uncle preach every Sunday. It was somehow more personal, like the words of God were directed at her in particular when a close family member spoke them. Though Elizabeth was not as much of an adherent of the holy scripture as her sister, Mary, she thought her uncle's knowledge of the Bible excellent, and thought someday, likely in the not distant future, there were loftier positions in store for him, for Elizabeth was certain the church was watching him with an eye toward a position in a college. There might even be a bishopric in his future.

That Sunday, however, not all those in attendance appreciated Mr. Gardiner's lesson. When the first words rolled from her uncle's mouth and she heard the word "forgiveness" feature prominently among them, along with similar admonishments to deal fairly with one's neighbor, Elizabeth knew what her uncle had done. Lord Arundel kept his countenance, but to anyone who knew him well, it was clear he was quite displeased. It was fortunate her uncle could withstand his patron's displeasure.

"I do not appreciate your choice of a sermon today, Edward," said her father within Elizabeth's hearing soon after the service ended.

"Yet I believe it was what the congregation needed to hear today," replied Uncle Edward. Elizabeth knew it was a polite way of saying the Lord did not care what her father wished to hear on a Sunday.

Lord Arundel fixed his brother with an annoyed glare. "Perhaps, then, you should direct your comments to the *Darcys*. I doubt Robert Darcy's parson is lecturing him about the situation between our families."

"There you would be incorrect," replied Uncle Edward, his tone and grin amused. "Mr. Peters and I spoke on Wednesday, and we agreed both parishes needed the reminder of the Lord's commandment to forgive. I cannot say whether Mr. Darcy had any greater appetite for his parson's sermon, but I assure you, he heard much the same message today at Kympton."

The hard look with which Lord Arundel impaled his brother made no impression, and after a moment he turned away, muttering as he went. Uncle Edward did not seem affected at all by his patron's displeasure. In fact, he appeared more amused than anything.

"It may be best not to provoke him, Brother," said Uncle Gardiner, filling the space Lord Arundel had occupied only a moment before.

Uncle Edward just shrugged. "Do you think he did not need to hear it?" Then Uncle Edward's look turned pointed. "For that matter, I suspect *you* needed the message as much as Lord Arundel did. More, perhaps."

"You may be correct," replied Uncle Gardiner, a pensive quality in his tone and look. "But you know the subject of the Darcys is sensitive for our brother, whether warranted or no. It is laudable that you should attempt to soften the enmity between them. Small steps are required, I think."

Uncle Edward nodded his acknowledgment and then turned the subject, leaving Elizabeth to ponder what she had heard. Today's dinner was to be at Uncle Gardiner's estate, as it often was, despite his lack of a hostess. Her father might be a little out of sorts after exchanging words with Uncle Edward, but Elizabeth knew he would not hold a grudge. The matter of hating the Darcy family was more habit than conviction.

With the unpleasantness between her father and Uncle Edward at an end, Elizabeth concentrated on the others attending church that day. The Bingleys had, at times, attended in Kympton, but of late Mr. Bingley had ushered his family into the church in Lambton more often than not. It was no stretch to understand what brought him hither, and his eager attendance upon Jane proved the supposition.

Miss Bingley, who stood a little aloof, looking for all the world like she wished to be somewhere else — and Elizabeth was certain she did — was a contrast to her brother's openness. Being of a lower social stratum, given her grandfather's history in trade and purchase of the estate they now called home — Miss Bingley took care not to offend. But she did not attempt to deepen any acquaintance with the Bennet family, though Elizabeth knew there had been a time when she had been friendly with Jane.

Of more interest than a woman who wished to be in church with *another* family was the presence of another, the only woman in the room who outranked the Bennet sisters other than their mother. Lady Charlotte Lucas was the daughter of the Earl of Chesterfield, and was of an open, friendly disposition, though Elizabeth knew the woman was possessed of a haughtiness common to one of her social position. Her father was conversing with Lord Arundel, the only other peer in attendance, leaving Lady Charlotte to speak to Elizabeth.

"It seems Jane's courtship with Mr. Bingley is proceeding apace," observed the lady with a glance in the couple's direction. Lady Charlotte had long been Elizabeth's friend more than Jane's— Elizabeth accounted her as one of her closest friends, in fact.

"It does," said Elizabeth. "I may say without reserve that I do not think it will be long before the gentleman proposes to her."

Lady Charlotte turned a long look at Elizabeth before she said: "Since he has not forbidden it, I suppose your father is disposed to allow Mr. Bingley's suit?"

There was the hint of arrogance Elizabeth had always known Lady Charlotte possessed. At the same time, Elizabeth knew Lady Charlotte did not intend to disapprove of Mr. Bingley or insinuate anything negative. It was something anyone of her level of society—and even lower—would consider. It was also true; a woman of Jane's social status must be certain she wished to marry a man of Mr. Bingley's.

"Papa has told us he wishes us to be happy," replied Elizabeth. "He would not forbid Jane for any reason other than an unacceptable match.

"There are many who might view Mr. Bingley as unsuitable."

"Perhaps they are. But not my father."

"Then that is well," replied the lady. "Mr. Bingley has always struck me as a good sort of man. I wish Jane every happiness. Your mother and father giving their support will help smooth their way."

Again, Elizabeth knew Lady Charlotte was speaking the truth, but as the conversation was a little uncomfortable for Elizabeth, she wished to change it. It was fortunate that Lady Charlotte changed it first.

"It is only a month until our annual ball for the neighborhood. Might I count on your family's attendance?"

Elizabeth laughed. "I believe you can unless you plan to invite the Darcys."

"Lizzy!" scolded Lady Charlotte. When Elizabeth gave her an impertinent grin, Lady Charlotte fixed her with an exasperated glare, tinged with amusement. "For that, I believe I shall mandate that you open the ball with Mr. Darcy."

"Why should he dance with me?" asked Elizabeth, feigning innocence? "Surely he does not wish to take a wife so much younger than he."

"I know you have not misunderstood me," said Lady Charlotte, her lips twitching. The higher ranked lady often reprimanded Elizabeth for her quips, but Elizabeth knew her friend delighted in her impertinence.

"For my part," replied Elizabeth, taking pity on her friend, "I am all anticipation for your ball, regardless of the Darcy family's presence or absence, and I believe I would even dance with Mr. Darcy if it was necessary. My father, however, after the scolding he has endured from my uncle, might not be eager. He might suffer apoplexy should he see me dancing with the son of his mortal enemy."

"We should not wish to provoke him to expire in my father's ballroom," was Lady Charlotte's irreverent reply

"No, indeed," said Elizabeth with a grin. Then she changed the subject again. "I have not seen Colonel Fitzwilliam in the neighborhood of late. I hope he has not been sent to the continent."

Lady Charlotte beamed at the mention of her betrothed. "Anthony is in London tying up some loose ends regarding the sale of his commission. His last letter suggested he will return to the neighborhood before the ball."

"That is good news," said Elizabeth. "Though I do not know the colonel well, he has always struck me as a good man. Have you decided on a date yet for the wedding?"

"It will be this autumn," replied Lady Charlotte, "though we do not know the date. I am only relieved he has surrendered his position in the army, for I did not wish for the uncertainty of enduring his return to the continent."

"Then I wish you the best," replied Elizabeth sincerely. "It seems you will be very happy with him."

They stayed in the attitude of conversation for some time, though now it consisted of Lady Charlotte speaking of the virtues of her intended. It was fortunate for Elizabeth's sensibilities that she was interested in what Lady Charlotte was saying. As a young woman who had always been of a romantic turn of mind, hearing of such obvious affection was agreeable. Elizabeth hoped very much she could find the meeting of minds her sister and friend had. It was fortunate she was in a position that she need not accept the offer of any man who deigned to propose to her. Had she not possessed her own fortune her choices might have been limited.

CHAPTER VIII

*O*ne of the few living Bennet cousins who remained close to the family was Mr. William Collins. Though Elizabeth could not recall the intricacies of their connection, Mr. Collins was her father's cousin at least several times removed, and had, until Thomas's birth, been the heir to the Barony of Arundel. Though some might assume Mr. Collins would resent his young cousin for supplanting him, nothing could be further from the truth.

The day following Uncle Edward's bold sermon that had angered his patron, Mr. Collins arrived for a visit which had been anticipated for some weeks. "Good morning, Cousin," said he, greeting Lord Arundel, then turning to the baroness and each of the daughters in turn. Then he bent down and greeted young Thomas at eye level, something he often did. "How are your lessons, Thomas?"

"Very well, Mr. Collins," replied Thomas with perfect civility. "But I would much rather catch frogs, yet there are none to be found."

Mr. Collins laughed and ruffled the boy's hair. "No, I should think it much too early in the season. Should I be here long enough, I shall assist you, for I recall my father teaching me similar skills when I was a boy."

"Then we should love to have you," said Thomas. "Lizzy will come with us too, for she is a master frog-catcher."

While Elizabeth could feel her cheeks heat with embarrassment and she heard her mother give a huff, Mr. Collins only turned and regarded her with some interest. "I am not surprised Elizabeth would know of such things, Thomas. Then we shall make a party of it." Mr. Collins turned an amused eye on Elizabeth's sisters. "Shall any of your other sisters join us?"

The looks of revulsion he received from them all provoked a snort of laughter from her father. Thomas made a face and shook his head.

"In this, at least, Lizzy is much more fun than any of my other sisters. Unless we can persuade Papa or my uncles to join us, we must content ourselves with our party of three."

"I am sure that will be enough," replied Mr. Collins.

The gentlemen sequestered themselves in her father's study for some time, though Elizabeth was not certain what they were discussing. That day she busied herself with her usual daily tasks, having already walked out that morning. When Mr. Collins returned to their midst, particularly that night at dinner, Elizabeth was interested to see how he behaved.

Elizabeth had always been fond of her cousin, a man who had been close to them all his life because of his father's closeness with her father. Mr. Collins was rather tall and lean, possessed a dark head of messy hair, pleasant blue eyes and walked with a slight limp because of a fall from a horse when he was young. Though not handsome, Mr. Collins was pleasant and engaging, and while he could be a little pompous on occasion, he was a good man.

Mr. Thaddeus Collins—Mr. Collins's father—and Lord Arundel had been raised together after Mr. Collins's own father's early demise. Elizabeth's grandfather had taken the man into his house and provided for him, sending him to study in the church when he was old enough, after which he had taken a position in a parish in Bedfordshire. The son had followed his father into the church, but the unexpected passing of another relation and his son had left Mr. Collins the proprietor of a modest estate in Nottinghamshire. Not trained to become the master of an estate, Mr. Collins had found it difficult but with her father's aid, he had learned what he needed to know.

"How is Brownlee Park?" asked Lord Arundel of Mr. Collins's estate that night at dinner.

"Very well, Cousin," said Mr. Collins. "With the improvements I made last year based on your suggestions, I have no doubt yields will increase next harvest."

"And how do you like being a gentleman? It differs greatly from life as a parson, does it not?"

Mr. Collins paused in thought and chewed his food before responding. "Yes, it is different in many respects. As a parson one is responsible for the spiritual wellbeing of the parish. While a parson must also concern himself with the physical, a gentleman has a much greater responsibility—and influence—over those who live on his estate. I cannot say which I prefer, for they are both worthy vocations. In some respects, I suppose I appreciate being a gentleman as it gives me much more freedom than I possessed as a parson, though one never wishes to benefit from the misfortune of others."

"And yet," said Lord Arundel, "I cannot imagine those living on your estate are not happier with you as their master than they ever were with Standish. The man was never more than an indifferent master, and his son had turned out very wild."

"That is true," agreed Mr. Collins. "I have endeavored to be a better master than the man who preceded me. If we all approached such tasks with such determination in mind, I cannot help but think the world would be a better place."

"I intend to be a better master than my father," piped up Thomas from his place beside Elizabeth. "I have already determined to end the feud with the Darcy family."

The family smiled at their youngest member's youthful zeal, though Lord Arundel appeared pained by his reference to the Darcys. Mr. Collins looked on with interest.

"Does that matter still lie between you?"

"Nothing has changed," replied Lord Arundel, his tone informing them all he did not wish to speak further on the subject.

Mr. Collins, unfortunately, was often obtuse in times such as this. "As a former parson," said he, his occasional pomposity showing, "I cannot urge you in a manner strenuous enough that you should not carry on this dispute. As the Lord has counseled us, we should allow no disputations to lie between us, for to forgive is divine."

"Yes, holding a grudge is not praiseworthy," said Lord Arundel, his tone testy. He was not enjoying the experience of having his relations preach to him. "It is unfortunate the Darcy family has ever been untrustworthy. However, I shall follow your advice and not raise the dispute in such a way that will lead to further unpleasantness. I hope you understand my point of view."

It appeared, at last, Mr. Collins understood his cousin's annoyance, for he inclined his head and refrained from pursuing the matter further. "Perhaps that is the best we can expect."

"It is," replied Lord Arundel.

"Have you made any improvements to your house, Mr. Collins?" asked Lady Margaret, eager to introduce harmony back into their conversation.

"As you suggested," said Mr. Collins. "Though there was some mention of shelves in the closets from certain unsolicited quarters, I refrained, as I believe closets are best used to hang clothes, and such barriers would defeat the purpose. Your suggestions, however, were excellent, and I have implemented them."

"I should like to know who made such a nonsensical proposal, Mr. Collins," said Lady Margaret. "It sounds like a silly concept to me."

"The source of the suggestion is not pertinent, but I cannot disagree."

"Then that is well for the moment. In the future, you will wish to have a wife to manage your home and will defer to her judgment in such matters."

No one missed the significant look Lady Margaret leveled in Mary's direction, least of all Mary or Mr. Collins. Neither, it seemed, opposed the notion, though Mary was a reticent young lady and did not show her feelings openly.

"I believe you are correct, my lady," replied Mr. Collins. "It has often been said that a clergyman should take the lead in showing the example of matrimony in his parish, much as my late father did. Though I am no longer a member of that profession, I do not believe any less in the wisdom of such counsel. I intend to rectify the unfortunate fact of my single status before long, I assure you."

It seemed to Elizabeth that Mary's lips curved up ever so slightly at Mr. Collins's declaration, but she made no other sign. As the conversation turned to other matters around her, Elizabeth considered the subject of Mr. Collins and Mary. It had long been the opinion in the family that Mr. Collins admired Mary, and there was some indication Mary returned the sentiment. As yet, neither had said anything to confirm or deny the supposition. It *was* true Mr. Collins was often with Mary when visiting, which gave then all reason to further suspect some announcement may be forthcoming.

The thought that Mr. Collins might have been discussing his intentions toward Mary when he had disappeared with her father that afternoon entered Elizabeth's mind. As her father had asked after Brownlee park at dinner, the estate had not been the focus of their conversation, so the idea had some merit. If Mary was destined to be the wife of Mr. Collins, Elizabeth was happy for her. Mr. Collins did not interest Elizabeth as a potential husband, not that he had ever shown any desire to have her as a wife. She could see why his situation and person would appeal to a young lady of Mary's character.

The more she thought on the matter and watched her cousin and sister, the more Elizabeth became convinced there was something there. They were not overt in their admiration, for neither was disposed to be so, but the little looks which sometimes passed between lovers were clear if one cared to look. The only question which remained was whether Mr. Collins or Mr. Bingley would take the initiative and propose first. Though Elizabeth suspected Mr. Collins's admiration was of a longer duration, she would not wager against Mr. Bingley's impulsive tendencies.

The opportunity to observe the courting gentleman presented itself the following morning when Mr. Bingley called at Longbourn. Mr. Bingley was acquainted with Mr. Collins and the two men approved of each other. Being different sort of men, they would never be great friends, but the prospect of their being brothers did not seem onerous. Mr. Collins, however, was a man who took his responsibilities seriously, even when they were not *his*. He amply demonstrated that trait during that morning visit.

"Mr. Bingley," greeted Mr. Collins when the gentleman had been sitting with Jane for a few moments. "I had heard that you have been calling on my cousin of late."

"I have," replied Mr. Bingley, his cheerful demeanor on full display. "And who could blame me? Miss Bennet is everything a man could want."

The faint smile with which Mr. Collins met this declaration showed his agreement, but he was not about to allow Mr. Bingley to pull him into a discussion of his cousin's perfections, Mr. Bingley's favorite subject.

"I cannot agree more, sir," said Mr. Collins, nodding to Jane. "She is a jewel of the first order, but then again, so are all of my dear cousins. What I am more interested in is the level of your interest."

Mr. Bingley seemed rather bemused he was having this conversation with a man who was not Jane's father. For Jane's part, her look at her cousin seemed to suggest he should leave the subject be, but neither man seemed to notice her. Mr. Collins wished to know of Mr. Bingley's level of commitment, and Mr. Bingley was by no means reluctant to declare it.

"Whatever you suspect of my level of interest," said Mr. Bingley, "you may multiply it by a factor of ten. I am ready to pay Miss Bennet every compliment and eager to assume the responsibilities that gesture entails."

As a statement, it was more than a little pompous in Elizabeth's opinion. It was also the sort of unequivocal announcement which would appeal to Mr. Collins, a man who, as Elizabeth had noted before, was given to his share of pomposity. Whether Mr. Bingley knew this of Mr. Collins and responded accordingly Elizabeth was uncertain, but his words could not fail to garner Mr. Collins's support.

"Then it is well, sir. I hope you will forgive me for the presumptuous manner of my query and assure you that nothing less than my cousin's happiness would induce me to speak so."

"I am sure Mr. Bingley is not offended," said Lord Arundel as Mr. Bingley voiced the same. "However, I must wonder if this interest in my eldest daughter's suitor by all and sundry is a product of the belief that I am unable to provide for their protection."

It was clear Mr. Collins did not quite understand the full import of Lord Arundel's meaning, which was no surprise considering he had not been present during Mr. Gardiner's inquiry. The gentleman, however, understood well enough the gist of his cousin's words, for he was quick to respond.

"I believe, Cousin, you should instead see it as our sincere interest in the happiness of your excellent daughters. One has only to see you know that you cherish them enough to be their protector—my question to Mr. Bingley was nothing more nor less than it appeared."

Lord Arundel, to whom such dry humor was a delight, grinned at his cousin. "Then I thank you, Cousin, for your diligence. I hope I shall also expect your diligence in *another* matter of import to us all, and perhaps more personal to yourself?"

The significant look Lord Arundel directed at Mary did nothing to discompose her, and Mr. Collins knew at once to what his cousin referred. "You may be easy on that score, Cousin. Like our esteemed Mr. Bingley informed us, I am eager to perform those duties to which I find myself obliged."

It was not, perhaps, a grandiose statement of devotion. But Mr. Collins was not a man given to such displays, nor was Mary a girl to expect such things from a suitor if that was what Mr. Collins was. The gentleman gave the notion more weight when he turned his attention back to Mary and conversed with her for some time after. Lord Arundel, who caught Elizabeth's eye, winked and turned back to his newspaper.

Soon after, when her father left for his study to see to some estate business, the conversation among the young members of the party turned to their amusement for that morning. And soon, they decided a visit to Lambton would be just the thing, for they were all eager to go out for a time.

"Then be off with you," said Lady Margaret, shooing them from the room. "This morning, I am to visit with old Mrs. Caruthers, and I have a few other calls to make. Perhaps I shall meet you in Lambton so you may ride back to Longbourn with me."

Elizabeth decided against pointing out that seven, besides her mother, would never fit inside the Bennet carriage, spacious though it was. Lady Margaret departed soon after, leaving them to their own devices. They donned their outerwear for the walk to Lambton which, though it was two miles or more, was well within the range of their ability to walk.

It was a fine morning, still afflicted with the chill of the season, though the sun shone bright and warm down on the party. Kitty and Lydia, being the most eager, roamed on ahead, their paces swift as they swung their arms and laughed between them. Elizabeth followed the two couples providing some measure of chaperonage, not that they needed any on such an open road. A part of her wondered what was in store for her future, for she had met no man who excited her imagination as her sisters had.

The thought provoked the image of Mr. Darcy, sitting tall and proud on his mount, and she felt a hint of embarrassment creep into her thoughts. Why had such a thing occurred to her? Surely the relative situation between the two families would prevent even the notion of such an alliance from ever coming to pass. Besides, Mr. Darcy had shown himself to be a proud man, and not one Elizabeth could ever imagine stealing her heart.

It was fortunate for Elizabeth that she was walking at the back of the party, for no one noticed her sudden anxiety. They made good time, walking at a quick pace—perhaps too quick for the courting couples—and soon they reached the outskirts of the village.

Their arrival in town showed to any who cared to look the disparate characters of the five Bennet sisters. Kitty and Lydia were eager to see what they could of the latest fashions at the dressmakers, and Elizabeth could hear them chattering to themselves about visiting the haberdashery, and perhaps even the milliner. Jane, in Mr. Bingley's company, wandered near the sweet shop—Jane's sweet tooth was legendary—while Elizabeth and Mary took themselves to the bookstore with Mr. Collins escorting them.

There they spent an agreeable time going through the latest books, though there, again, the differences were clear. Mary was more interested in serious works of literature to complement her devotion to the Bible, meaning she focused on works with a religious bent, such as *Paradise Lost*. Elizabeth, though she also enjoyed such literature, also liked poetry and philosophy, and even the occasional novel, a genre Mary looked on with disapproval.

After a time, Jane and Mr. Bingley joined them and looked on with laughter in their eyes. "I should have known that I would have time to visit almost every shop in the village before my two sisters would even think of leaving the bookstore."

Elizabeth returned her grin. "Perish the thought! I am convinced we shall not be pried away in anything less than double the time you suggest!"

"For Lizzy, perhaps that is accurate," said Mary. "But I believe I am ready to make my purchases and depart."

With good-natured teasing, her sisters chivvied Elizabeth until she made her selections. She would not do so, however, without returning the favor.

"It is shocking what a number of ogres you all are! Can you not leave me to shop for the written word in peace?"

"If we did that," replied Jane, "I doubt we should see you for the rest of the day, Lizzy."

"I think your sister's devotion to books is charming," said Mr. Collins. "It proves her to be an accomplished woman, one with a great mind that she can read and understand so much."

"You flatter me, Cousin," said Elizabeth. Then she winked at him and added: "And I appreciate it very much. These two will give me an infamous character with no chance to defend myself."

So focused was Elizabeth on their banter, that she was not watching where she was going in the narrow confines of the shop between the various bookshelves. Thus, when she impacted with something, at once soft and unyielding, she might have fallen had she not reached out to steady herself against whatever she had run into. It turned out to be a "whoever" rather than a "whatever."

"Oh my!" said Elizabeth when she discovered she had collided with none other than Georgiana Darcy. The girl appeared as surprised as Elizabeth, though she did not show the revulsion Elizabeth might have expected from one of the Darcy family having such a close encounter with a member of the Bennet clan. Unfortunately, there was one present who was not so circumspect.

"Dearest Georgiana," cooed the dulcet tones of Miss Bingley. The woman stepped into view and grasped Miss Darcy's arm, ostensibly to support her, though her piercing glance at Elizabeth spoke to other motivations. "Perhaps we should depart, for it would not do to allow your brother to see you in such company as this."

"Caroline!" exclaimed Mr. Bingley, while at the same time Elizabeth leveled a quelling look on Miss Bingley.

"It would be best if you said nothing more, Miss Bingley," said Elizabeth, her glare bearing down on the woman. "Perhaps you should remember that neither the Bingleys nor the Darcys are of the Bennets' level of society. It would serve your social aspirations ill if you forgot this and insulted one or several daughters of a baron."

Miss Bingley paled, much to Elizabeth's satisfaction. The Bennet family was not in the habit of throwing their power about or using it as a cudgel against those of a lesser station. In this instance, however, Elizabeth thought it justified in the face of such insolence as Miss Bingley displayed. Though she held Miss Bingley's eyes for some moments, she was satisfied when the other woman looked away, as much in anger as shame, Elizabeth thought.

Then Elizabeth turned back to Miss Darcy, who was watching the scene with pursed lips. "I hope you are unharmed, Miss Darcy?"

"Not at all," replied the girl, turning back to Elizabeth, her manner shy. "It was an accident, nothing more."

"Yes, it was," replied Elizabeth. She grinned at the girl and added: "But battles have been fought for less than this, do you not agree?"

Miss Darcy caught the facetious tone in Elizabeth's voice and laughed aloud. "Yes, I believe you are correct. I suspect there is no need for us to go to war, for there is no insult."

When Miss Bingley made to speak, Elizabeth glared her down again, and she subsided with a pouting huff of annoyance. It appeared Miss Darcy was no fonder of the woman than Elizabeth was, for a faint hint of satisfaction hovered about the corners of her mouth. Then Elizabeth remembered the proprieties of the situation.

"Mr. Bingley," said she, calling to the gentleman glaring at his sister. "It comes to mind that we are not acquainted with this young lady. Might I ask you to perform the office?"

"An excellent notion," said he.

Once again Miss Bingley seemed like she wished to protest, but his glare silenced her. Mr. Bingley provided the necessary presentation, and the ladies all curtseyed to each other, while Mr. Collins bowed. When completed, Elizabeth fixed a wide smile on the girl and said:

"I hope you do not find us presumptuous, Miss Darcy. But I find we have remained unacquainted too long, regardless of whatever silly matter lies between our families."

"Yes, I cannot but agree, Miss Elizabeth," replied the girl. Then she turned to Mr. Bingley. "I hope you are well, sir? Your sister has spoken of you, but I have not had the privilege of your company for some time."

"I am very well, Miss Darcy," said Mr. Bingley. "As you can see, I have been busy of late. I hope your brothers and your father are well?"

"They are," replied Miss Darcy. "My Cousin Anthony is also to join us soon."

"Fitzwilliam!" exclaimed Mr. Bingley. "That is excellent, Miss Darcy, for he is a good man. And how has he been?"

"It is my understanding he is to resign his commission," said Elizabeth. "Or so Lady Charlotte informed me at church on Sunday."

"Yes, that is correct," said Miss Darcy. She seemed a little curious, and then said: "You are friendly with Lady Charlotte?"

"She is one of our closest friends," said Jane. "My father and her father have been friends and allies for many years."

Miss Darcy nodded, deep in thought. While they said nothing more of substance, their conversation continued for several more moments, consisting of pleasantries. None of those present were bold enough to state a wish for future friendship or society, unsurprising, given the situation. But Elizabeth thought she might like to have this shy young girl for a friend, though she knew how unlikely it was.

Then the shop's door swung open and in walked the imposing figure of Mr. Darcy. With one look he took in the situation. It was clear he was not amused.

Chapter IX

*L*ambton was a picturesque town if one cared for that sort of thing. The old Alexander Darcy might not have cared in the slightest—the present man had begun to appreciate the little pleasures in life.

It *was* good to be back in Derbyshire, at Pemberley, he reflected, though only a few short days ago he had lamented his father's summons. While Alexander still considered the notion of watching his own estate a bother, stability had begun to have some appeal. This did not mean Alexander was immune to fun.

"You should go on ahead," said Alexander one morning as he rode with his brother and sister toward the town. "The stitching in my left stirrup is loose—I shall stop at the tanner and have it repaired."

William regarded him momentarily before giving his agreement. "I must stop at the mercantile for a time."

"And I should like to visit the bookstore," said Georgiana. "As I know you are a devotee of the written word, shall you not meet me there after you finish?"

As Alexander might have predicted, William was quick to give his assent. When they turned as one to regard him, Alexander laughed and shook his head. "If you wish it, I shall join you at the bookstore.

Though I am not as devoted as you both, I shall remind you I *can* read."

Both siblings gave him a smile, and Alexander reined his horse away, making for the Tanner's shop on the outskirts of town. The tanner was a tall man in a rough smock, his shop smelling of old leather and other, less pleasant scents. He bowed low when Alexander informed him of the problem and promised to fix it at once. Then he went about his business as Alexander waited, looking about with interest.

"Darcy!" hailed a voice, and Alexander turned, noting the approach of John Smallwood, a friend of longstanding.

"Smallwood!" exclaimed Alexander, pumping his friend's hand with pleasure. "How are you, man?"

"Excellent," replied his friend. "The rumors of your return made their way through the neighborhood some days ago. I see they were not exaggerated."

Alexander grinned and said: "My father required my presence. Otherwise, I might have continued relieving Jameson of his wealth in London."

Smallwood laughed along with him. "Jameson never knows when to quit. One might think he would have realized his lack of skill by now."

"He will never learn," replied Alexander. "And as long as he does not, I shall cheerfully continue to play against him."

In the manner of old friends reunited, the two chatted for some time, imparting details of their doings of late. Smallwood was a man of Alexander's age, who had been a friend as long as he could remember. Their exploits as young boys had been legendary, and Alexander still remembered some of the punishments he had received from his father for some of their more memorable antics.

"Mr. Darcy," interrupted a voice after they had conversed for some moments. "I heard you returned to Derbyshire, but as I did not receive a visit, I thought perhaps the rumors were false."

Turning, Alexander noted a young woman watching him. Her name was Miss Violet Gainsborough, and she was one of the flirtiest young ladies in the neighborhood. Before Alexander had left for London, she had been the focus of his attention; he had considered visiting her when he returned home but thought it would have been a blatant show of favor, one he did not wish to make.

"Miss Gainsborough," replied Alexander with a bow. He flashed her a brilliant smile, for just because he did not wish to marry the girl, there was no reason not to enjoy her company. "I might have come as soon as I arrived in the neighborhood, but six months out of your company is a long time to go without the sun. It is impossible to suppose you are still unattached, for what man could resist you?"

The girl was not embarrassed at all by his flattery; instead, she gazed at him, as bold as brass. "How could I have allowed any other man to charm me, given how much I longed for your return?"

"How could you, indeed?" said Alexander softly. She was a comely girl, one any man would feel lucky to have at his side. It was unfortunate that Alexander had often thought her purpose in flirting with him was to become closer to his older brother. It was no secret that William had never looked twice at her—nor at any other woman, for that matter.

"I shall wait at my father's estate for your coming," said Miss Gainsborough as she turned away. "The thought of resuming our acquaintance pleases me."

As she sauntered away from him, her hips swaying, his friend gave a low whistle. "Do you mean to pursue her?" asked Smallwood.

"Of course not," replied Alexander, fixing his friend with a sidelong look. "With Miss Gainsborough for a wife, one would never be certain her eye would not wander."

Smallwood laughed at his sally. "For that matter, I wonder if the woman *you* marry can be certain *your* eyes will remain fixed on her."

"Nothing could be further from the truth," said Alexander, affecting an injured air.

"Perhaps not, though you give the impression of it, my friend. It was good to see you again, but for now, I must depart."

Wishing his friend well, Alexander farewelled him and returned to the tanner to discover the man had completed his work. Alexander paid him, plus a little extra for his trouble, and turned to depart, deciding to lead his horse into the town by the reins instead of riding in the narrow confines of its roads. And as he walked, he whistled a jaunty tune, once again filled with the contentment of being back in Derbyshire.

As he had considered before, Lambton was a pretty town, one appealing because of its charming, though narrow streets, and the friendliness of its inhabitants. Some might consider the location to have been chosen ill, for it was nestled among the rolling hills of Derbyshire with nary a straight or wide road to its name. That did not bother its inhabitants, for there were few who lived there who did not look back on it fondly if they left.

On the way to the bookstore, Alexander stopped at the milliner's, for his hat was becoming old and in need of replacement. When he departed the store, he stopped for a moment, looking both directions, before continuing on toward the bookstore, which was just down the street. That was when he saw them.

Walking together, giggling behind raised hands as was the wont of young ladies their age were two of the Bennet sisters—including the one who had looked at him so boldly that day on the hill. They were, Alexander could appreciate, comely young girls—but so were all the Bennet sisters. One was fair of face and hair, slender of form and possessed beautiful green eyes and a pert mouth begging to be kissed, while the other was a little taller of stature, dark locks peeking out from under her bonnet, framing her face, with eyes similar to her sister's, though perhaps even prettier.

The two girls stopped short when they saw him, seeming to know at once who he was. Alexander, not thinking much of it—or the infamous feud between Bennet and Darcy—bowed low to greet them. He could never have predicted the response he was to receive.

"Good morning, ladies. How do you do this fine day?"

The two girls looked at him with astonishment for a moment, then they turned to each other and laughed. The shorter girl would not meet his eyes again, but the taller fixed him with a challenging stare, the likes of which he would not have expected to see from a woman twice her age, though much like she had done that day at the hill.

"Mr. Darcy, I presume? I wonder at your presence, though I suppose any audacity from a Darcys should be unsurprising."

"If you recall," said Alexander, amused and confused at the same time, "I merely wished you a good morning. How could I do otherwise when such loveliness is before me?"

"You consider yourself a charmer, I think," replied the girl. "I wonder if you have it in you to please a young woman worthy of being pleased."

"And I presume you consider yourself such a woman?" asked Alexander, more diverted than perhaps he should have been.

The girl strolled toward him, her manner sultry and provocative, and when she reached him, she tapped him on the arm and said: "You would like to know what kind of woman I am. But I do not associate with known rakes and libertines."

"None of which describe me," Alexander found himself saying. "The reality is less scandalous than the rumors."

A throaty laugh was the girl's response. "How utterly expected. I am not surprised you would attempt to ply an innocent maiden such as myself with such tales."

"Lydia," said the other girl, an urgent note in her voice, "perhaps we should leave."

It may have been best for this tête-à-tête to end as the girl said, but the truth was Alexander was enjoying her flirting and unwilling to go away. A part of him wondered how old she was, for she did not appear to be more than seventeen or eighteen. She acted like a woman of five and twenty or more.

The girl—Lydia—considered what her sister said, and then addressed Alexander: "It seems to me this one is much more bark than bite, Kitty. Besides, I told you how much I enjoy mocking them."

"Oh, so this is mocking, is it?" asked Alexander, eyebrows rising in further astonishment.

"It may be—or at least a form of it. It seems to me you are deserving of it."

Why Alexander was deserving of being mocked he was not to discover, for the sound of a loud voice interrupted their confrontation. The two girls turned, Alexander following their eyes, only to be shocked at the sight of the man he least wished to see walking toward them.

"What is the meaning of this?" demanded he, looking alternately at his nieces, then back at Alexander himself. Mr. David Gardiner, for that was who he was, appeared less incensed than Alexander might have expected. That did not make him any less wary of the gentleman.

"Nothing more than exchanging morning greetings, Uncle," said Miss Lydia with a shrug. "Mr. Darcy greeted us, and we responded in kind."

Mr. Gardiner's eyes once again found him, falling on him with the force of a hammer. "He did? It was my impression that Bennets and Darcys did not acknowledge each other."

Miss Lydia huffed as her sister looked frightened. "Do not be silly, Uncle. There is no reason to care that he is a Darcy, and no reason to be uncivil. If someone greets me, I shall respond."

"I am do not think this one is trustworthy, Lydia. You should return to Longbourn. I suppose I shall follow you, for I must have words with your father."

"If you are referring to what happened between us last autumn," said Alexander, "then I apologize without reservation. It was unintentional."

"Do you not think I know that?" said Mr. Gardiner. "That is in the past, and I have no intention of belaboring the point. Of more immediate concern is your reputation regarding young ladies—these two are my nieces, as you must know, and are far bolder than they have any right to be. They are too young to converse with grown men many years their elder in the streets of Lambton.

"Now, since it seems you were the one to initiate a conversation with them, I put the question to you: what do you mean by flirting in the streets with my young nieces?"

"You are asking the wrong person," said Alexander, fixing the man with far more asperity than he had intended. "I may have greeted them, but it was your niece who responded with far more boldness than I might have expected in a woman of questionable morals!"

As soon as the words spilled from his lips, Alexander knew it had been a mistake to utter them. Mr. Gardiner's fists clenched and unclenched, and he appeared ready to attack Alexander for the insult to his family. It was then the benefits of flight occurred to him. He had never been one to back down, but at present, a quick departure may be for the best.

The tension in the bookseller was almost thick enough to walk on, a fact that was not lost on the proprietor. The poor man looked about, knowing of the enmity between Bennet and Darcy, as did everyone within fifty miles of Lambton. Darcy endeavored to smile, to reassure him that no unpleasantness would occur in his shop, but he was uncertain it was anything other than an abject failure.

"Have you finished your shopping, Georgiana?" asked Mr. Darcy of his sister. "If so, perhaps you should make your purchases and depart."

"As I attempted to inform her, Mr. Darcy," said Miss Bingley, her simpering leer as grating as it had ever been. "It would be best for her to avoid such company as this, for you would not wish her to be hurt."

Darcy noted the anger blooming in Miss Elizabeth's eyes and heard Bingley's sharp reprimand; he was not impressed himself. Whatever he or anyone in his family thought of the Bennets, they *were* of the nobility. One did not insult such people lightly.

"It would be best, Miss Bingley," said Darcy, his harsh tone wiping the smile from her face, "if you refrained from such comments. The Darcy family is not friendly with our neighbors, but we have nothing but respect for their position in society."

Miss Bingley looked away in embarrassment, much to Darcy's satisfaction. In that, he was joined by Miss Elizabeth, whose glare at Miss Bingley suggested she had already set the woman down once; it was clear Miss Bingley had learned nothing from the experience. For a moment, Darcy felt a hint of kinship with the young lady, which was both welcome and unsettling. Darcy ignored it and returned his attention to his sister.

"Come, Georgiana, let us purchase your books." He stepped up to her and past Miss Elizabeth, and stood beside her, and as she set her books down for the proprietor to examine, he could not help but add: "Are you well?"

A huff drew his attention back to Miss Elizabeth. "Do you suppose we would be unkind to your sister, Mr. Darcy? What kind of ruffians do you take us for? Or were your words about respecting our position nothing more than words?"

"Miss Elizabeth was very kind to me, Brother," added Georgiana. "*All* the Bennet sisters were excellent."

Though Darcy attempted to discover the words with which he could respond, Miss Elizabeth was quick to state her opinion.

"Whatever you may think of us, Mr. Darcy, we Bennets are a civilized family. We are not barbarians; we will not render unkindness to a young woman because she belongs to a family with whom we disagree. It was lovely to make your sister's acquaintance, and should the occasion permit it, I would like to continue our acquaintance and know more of her."

The woman stepped to his sister and grasped her hands. "You are a wonderful young woman, Miss Darcy. I hope you will not hold my surname against me, for I assure you, I do not think ill of you for yours."

Georgiana responded with a warm smile, as much a surprise to Darcy as anything else that had happened in this shop, for she had always been a shy creature. "Not at all, Miss Elizabeth. Though the relations between our families are strained as ever, I can state with no hesitation that I have seen nothing of untrustworthiness from you or your sisters."

"Thank you, Miss Darcy. Now, if you do not mind, I believe I shall put my books on the counter beside you and wait for my turn to pay for my purchases."

After his sister agreed with a happy smile, Miss Elizabeth did exactly that. Darcy did not know what to say. There *was* nothing to say. Everything Miss Elizabeth had said was the truth, and Darcy did not wish to dispute it. It was something he would need to consider further.

As the proprietor, now looking relieved, tallied their purchases, Bingley stepped close to Darcy. It had been some time since Darcy had the pleasure of his friend's company, and he wondered how he had not missed it.

"I hope there is enough of our friendship left," said Bingley, "for you to take my words in the manner in which I intend them. As I was your close friend for years and am now all but engaged to Miss Bennet, let me tell you without equivocation that there is no reason for this continued mistrust for your families."

"Perhaps there is not, Bingley," replied Darcy. "But it exists nonetheless."

"Then it will fall to you — to all involved — to overcome it. There is something of pride in *both* families, Darcy, and as I know it is a common complaint of each about the other, you should know the Bennets are not any more steeped in it than the Darcys. And as far as I have seen there is nothing untrustworthy about either family, for I have seen the good in you both. I hope you will think on this."

Darcy nodded and Bingley stepped away, leaving Darcy with the realization there was more on which to think than he had expected. As Georgiana had paid for her purchases — by now, the Bennets had finished was well — he thought it best to depart. Thus, offering an arm to his sister as an escort — Darcy ignored Miss Bingley, much to the woman's displeasure — he led her from the shop. Only to find another scene of even greater disquiet.

"As your nieces have noted, I greeted them. It was your niece who responded with far more boldness than I might have expected in a woman of questionable morals!"

The words, ringing among the close quarters of the street could not be misheard by anyone nearby, least of all the man who had been their target. Mr. David Gardiner stood facing Alexander, and from the look of him, Darcy thought he was on the verge of calling Alexander out or attacking him at once. Alexander himself seemed to understand the mistake he had made. Even the two girls with Mr. Gardiner appeared surprised. That did not stop one of them from appearing amused if the slight smile she wore was any sign.

Without conscious agreement, the three men from the bookstore — Darcy, Bingley, and some other man, a Bennet relation — stepped forward and interposed themselves between the two combatants.

"That is enough, I should say," said Darcy, glaring at his brother, while the other two men performed a similar office calming Mr. Gardiner. "That comment was beyond the pale, Alexander. Apologize."

"Of course," said Alexander without attempting to defend himself.

"I offer my unreserved apologies, Miss Lydia, and to you, Mr. Gardiner. It appears my sense deserted me when I said such vile words.."

It seemed to Darcy that Alexander was being serious for a change, for none of his usual glibness was in evidence. Mr. Gardiner seemed to understand this too, for though he still glared at Alexander, he said nothing. That left Miss Lydia to respond.

"Apology accepted. Mr. Darcy. I should not have spoken with such boldness, and for that, I offer my own sincere regrets."

"Not at all," replied Alexander, offering her a low bow. "The greater fault was mine, and I own to it without reservation."

"It seems to me it behooves us all to take great care," said one of the other Bennet sisters, though Darcy did not know her name. "If our families cannot see the good in the other, we had best refrain from statements which are inflammatory or easily misconstrued."

"Thank you, Mary," said Mr. Gardiner. "We should all take heed of your wise words."

"Then we shall depart, Mr. Gardiner," said Darcy, nodding to the other man.

Mr. Gardiner returned his tight nod and gathered his family, including Bingley, and began to herd them down the street. Darcy did the same with his brother and sister, though he could not help but cast a glance back in Miss Elizabeth's direction. The woman had turned to follow her uncle, but her words in the bookshop were ever before him. One thing Fitzwilliam Darcy was coming to understand—Miss Elizabeth Bennet was a rare woman, the likes of whom he had never met.

"Girls," said Mr. Gardiner as they walked away, "I would have you keep your distance from the younger Mr. Darcy. There is something too cavalier about the man, which renders him an unsuitable acquaintance for young ladies of your station."

"There is nothing the matter with Mr. Darcy," said Lydia, her mind not on her uncle's lecture. "The only fault I can attribute to him is a propensity to speak when he should remain silent."

"Lydia," said her uncle, his tone brooking no disagreement.

"Oh, do not concern yourself for me," replied Lydia, turning more of her attention to her uncle. "I have no desire to speak again to Mr. Darcy."

"Then you will oblige me."

With a huff, Lydia said: "I have said I would, have I not?"

Though her uncle's gaze rested on her, he said nothing further. The Bennet sisters were soon on the way back to Longbourn, following the road which led to the estate. Her uncle, after calling for his carriage to journey to the estate and wait for him there, escorted them, as if they were small children in need of a minder. Lydia Bennet was a young woman, only sixteen, but she considered herself mature, and not in need of coddling. She had always loved her uncles, but there were times it seemed they smothered their nieces in thick, cotton blankets.

"Lydia!" hissed Kitty as they were walking. "What did you think you were doing, baiting Mr. Darcy in that fashion?"

"Nothing but a bit of fun, Kitty," replied Lydia. When her sister looked at her with disbelief, Lydia exclaimed: "It was nothing."

"It seemed to me as if you were attempting to flirt with him," muttered Kitty.

"And if I was?" asked Lydia, daring her sister to protest. "What is it to anyone if I have a little fun with that gentleman?"

"You almost provoked a brawl!" hissed Kitty.

"Uncle and Mr. Darcy would not have come to blows," said Lydia.

"You know how protective Uncle is of us," reminded Kitty.

"Well, I did not know he was there." It was nothing more than the truth, though it did not appease her sister. "Very well, then! Though I have already assured my uncle, I shall do the same with you—I shall not speak to Mr. Darcy again. There, are you happy?"

It was clear that Kitty still did not believe her. But she nodded, her gesture seeming to promise she would ensure Lydia kept her word. Lydia did not think it was an issue, to be honest. It had been nothing more than a little harmless flirting. Who cared if the Darcys did not like the Bennets? Should Lydia wish to tease the man, she was determined to do it where her sisters—or overprotective uncles— could not witness.

CHAPTER X

Returning to Pemberley in the company of his siblings was nothing like the lighthearted journey to the town had been. The shock of the sudden confrontation with the Bennet family had rendered Darcy silent, requiring most of their ride back to the estate to consider it. Then contemplation gave way to anger, and Darcy seethed the rest of the way about his brother's stupidity. The events in the bookshop had been benign compared to that between Alexander and Mr. Gardiner.

They were riding down the long drive toward the house, Darcy still wrapped in his thoughts, when his brother's casual indifference to the situation made itself known. "Well, that was almost a spot of trouble, was it not?"

Head whirling to the side to gaze at his brother in astonishment, Darcy fixed him with a fierce glare. "Almost a spot of trouble? A spot of trouble you provoked with your imprudent actions and unthinking words."

"The girl is one of the most brazen chits I have ever met!" exclaimed Alexander, as if that was a valid defense.

"I care not if she was the very Queen of the Night herself!" rejoined Darcy. "It may have escaped your notice, but she is the daughter of a baron and a member of a family with whom the Darcys do not share good relations. In the past, if you look back thirty or forty years, this was a more active feud. There were times when arguments would turn into open fights, and on one occasion two servants engaged in a fight which almost ended in tragedy. I have no desire to return to those days!"

Unable to stomach his brother's further protests, Darcy kicked his horse forward, leaving his siblings behind. This business of calling Alexander back to Pemberley was a mistake—if he did not provoke a man connected to the Bennets to call him out it would be a miracle.

Throwing his reins to a waiting groom, Darcy stalked into the house to make his sentiments known to his father. It was fortunate the man in question was at that very moment walking through the entrance hall.

"This is a mistake, Father," growled Darcy when he caught sight of his sire.

"What is a mistake?" asked his father, mystified as to Darcy's meaning.

"Alexander's presence in Derbyshire," grated Darcy. "If he does not provoke a renewal of active hostility with the Bennets I shall be very surprised. If you do not wish to send him to London again, it would be best if he made his way to Thorndell to manage his own affairs. Anywhere but here would be preferable."

"Has something happened?" asked Mr. Darcy, his countenance darkening.

"What has your eldest son in a tizzy is the incident today in Lambton," said Alexander as he stepped into the hall, Georgiana trailing him in wide-eyed astonishment. "I spoke without thinking, Father. The fault is mine."

Though Alexander's words surprised Darcy, for he might have thought his brother would attempt to minimize what had happened, his father scowled and beckoned them all to follow him. They did so, not taking the time to change after their ride, and after they had entered the sitting-room, Mr. Darcy calling for tea, he turned to his progeny, his arched eyebrow demanding an explanation.

"The Bennet sisters were all in town today," said Darcy, "along with Bingley and some cousin I do not know. The true problem was Alexander's behavior with the youngest Bennet sisters and their uncle's appearance."

There was no need to specify *which* uncle Darcy referenced, for his father understood his meaning at once and scowled in response.

Again, however, Alexander spoke up and accepted responsibility.

"Do not blame Mr. Gardiner, Father, for it was my unthinking words which created the problem."

"It would be best if you inform me what happened," said Mr. Darcy.

The brother shared the task of relating the account of the events in Lambton, Georgiana remaining silent for the most part. Darcy informed his father of their parting when they arrived in town, glossing over everything that had occurred before coming upon the scene in Lambton's streets. When he had finished his account and spoke of the confrontation between Alexander and Mr. Gardiner, Alexander made his communication, and to Darcy's surprise, it was candid. The explanations offered, Mr. Darcy sat back to consider the matter and the potential consequences of what had happened.

Darcy, while his father was thinking, shot his brother a sidelong look. "I am surprised your account was so forthright, Brother."

"I *am* able to take responsibility for my own actions, William."

Though the reply was not in any way facile, it still provoked Darcy's ire. "That is interesting, Alexander, for, by my account, you have rarely accepted the blame for what you have done."

"That is enough," interrupted their father, looking between them, his tone brooking no disagreement. "There is no call to rehash the past—I am much more interested in dealing with the here and now."

Darcy nodded, as did his brother, though Alexander's was an echo of his old indifference. Having their agreement, the elder Darcy directed a chiding look at his son.

"That was very poorly done, Alexander. Not only should you not have spoken to the Bennet sisters at all, but to say what you did about the girl, and to the uncle who is close to the family, no less! It would be best if you stayed away from the Bennets altogether."

"That is a fact," said Darcy, vinegar and salt in equal measures in his tone. "Nothing good can come from any continued attention paid to the youngest Bennets and you should not be drawing attention to yourself—not after what happened last year. Given how the youngest girls have acted, I have little faith in the good behavior of any of them—they seem quite an improper family to me."

"It is a fine thing when you tarnish an entire family based on the actions of one or two," said Alexander.

"The elder sisters were lovely," said Georgiana, though in her usual diffident manner.

Mr. Darcy's eyes found his daughter. "Did something happen

before William entered the bookshop? As I recall, you have said little during this account."

"Miss Elizabeth bumped into me," replied Georgiana. "Then she apologized to me at once, and induced Mr. Bingley to introduce us all to one another." Georgiana paused and an unmistakable expression of distaste came over her. "Miss Bingley found me soon after I parted from William and Alexander, and after meeting the Bennets, she tried to usher me out, with some unkind words directed at the Miss Bennets."

While Darcy exchanged looks with his sister and father, Alexander burst out laughing. "That woman is utterly senseless! Can I assume one of the Miss Bennets put her in her place?"

"Miss Elizabeth," confirmed Georgiana. "She was not amused and let Miss Bingley know in a way that could not be misunderstood. They were very kind to me, insisting our families' animosity should not induce us to incivility. Should I ever have the opportunity, I should like to come to know her better."

"The rancor should be lessened between us," said their father. "But we must dismiss this notion of friendship without a second thought, however, for Darcys do not associate with Bennets."

"It seems to me, Father," said Alexander, "we must forget old prejudices if this ill will between our families is ever to recede."

"That may be true," replied Mr. Darcy, "but there is nothing we can do at present, particularly given the situation with Mr. Gardiner."

"You need not speak on the matter further," said Alexander, interrupting his father's next words. "I know William believes it would be best if I should go to Thorndell, but I am enjoying my time here with you far too much. Aunt Catherine and Cousin Anne are to come, as is Fitzwilliam. You need have no concern for me, for I shall stay away from all Bennets and endeavor to avoid Mr. Gardiner."

Though Darcy was uncertain this was for the best, his father eyed his second son for a moment before giving his assent. "Very well. To be honest, I was loath to give up your company so soon after getting it. If you do as you say, I believe that will be enough."

"It shall be, Father," replied Alexander.

The matter was thus settled, and the three siblings excused themselves to go to their rooms and change into more suitable clothing. Darcy's mind was not on the conversation which had just taken place, for he knew he could not control his brother's actions, nor could he insist his father send him away again. Instead, he considered Georgiana's testimony of the Miss Bennets, comparing it with what he knew of them. And, in particular, he thought of Miss Elizabeth, could imagine the fire in her eyes as she faced down Miss Bingley. What a sight to see that must have been!

The recitation of the day's events to her parents at Longbourn went about how Elizabeth might have predicted it. With Mr. Collins and Uncle Gardiner with them, there was never any question of informing their father, not that any of them would have kept it from him, regardless. Lord Arundel listened to their account in silence, and when her uncle had finished saying his piece, their father turned to Lydia.

"What passed between you, Lydia? Was the younger Darcy improper or in any way threatening?"

"No, Papa," said Lydia, Kitty nodding by her side. "If anything, I believe I might have provoked him, for I teased him."

Lord Arundel's countenance darkened. "You teased him?"

"I did," replied Lydia. Elizabeth could not be more surprised, for her sister did not often confess to misbehavior. "Perhaps I was imprudent, but the man deserved it, with his impertinent greeting."

"It seems to me," said Uncle Gardiner, "it would be best to avoid speaking to members of the Darcy family."

"You are correct, Uncle. I was not thinking when we met Mr. Darcy. It shall not happen again."

As Lord Arundel knew his youngest daughter was headstrong, he watched her for a moment, his gaze searching, before he nodded, albeit slowly. "Very well, as long as you have learned your lesson." Then her father's eyes found Elizabeth herself. "I suppose there was little you could do in the bookshop. It is not as if you could foresee bumping into the girl."

"No, I could not," replied Elizabeth. "And Miss Darcy is not a girl who would seek to cause trouble, regardless. It was clear within two minutes of meeting her that she is shy."

"Be that as it may, I believe it is best to practice simple avoidance."

"Of course, Papa," replied Elizabeth.

"It has come to my mind," interjected Mr. Collins, "that this business between you and the Darcy family is a matter which should not persist. Mr. Darcy, when he entered the shop, struck me as a most gentlemanly man, and given my association with his aunt, Lady Catherine de Bourgh, I can say her ladyship is not a woman who would endure a ruffian in the intimacy of her family.

"Furthermore," said Mr. Collins, his manner now sounding pompous, "This contention must be of the devil. I would urge you, in the strongest manner possible, to take steps to effect a reconciliation between your houses, for who knows what evil this animosity will provoke."

"Yes, I had forgotten of your connection to the Darcys' relation," said Lord Arundel. "You were her parson before inheriting Brownlee, were you not?"

Mr. Collins confirmed her father's memory, prompting Lord Arundel to continue to speak. "I have met Lady Catherine myself. Is she still the same dictatorial woman she was when she was young?"

Mr. Collins paused, considering how he might best answer. Elizabeth had heard him speak in warm tones concerning his previous patroness, though she knew he was observant enough to know when others, even those he respected, did not display perfect behavior. His diplomatic words proved Elizabeth's supposition.

"Lady Catherine *is* rather dictatorial," allowed Mr. Collins. "Though I was only her parson for a short time, she displayed a distressing tendency to meddle in the parsonage's business, and far too much inclination to direct when she should encourage. But she is a good woman for all that, for she cares for others. It is only that she believes she knows best in any situation, whether or not she knows anything of the subject."

"Yes, that is the Lady Catherine I have met," was Lord Arundel's sardonic reply. "It may be as you say, Cousin—perhaps it would be best to end the dispute between us. That may only be accomplished, however, if the Darcys wish it, and at present, I cannot say if they do. For now, the best strategy is avoidance." Lord Arundel's eyes found his youngest daughter. "I hope I have made myself clear?"

"You have," said Lydia, speaking for them all.

And thus, they dropped the subject by mutual consent. During the next few days, Elizabeth found her thoughts returning to the Darcy family with great frequency. These were days where there was little occurring in the neighborhood, which meant the Bennets stayed peacefully at home, though Elizabeth engaged in her favorite pastimes of riding and walking. Though she saw none of the Darcys, she looked about as if expecting to see them, wondering what would happen if she should meet them again. Miss Darcy, she thought, would be reticent, yet friendly, though she could not say how the brothers might act. Elizabeth had no notion of disobeying her father, so it did not signify that she did not encounter them. And so matters continued, until one day when an event occurred which proved to be of great import to Elizabeth's future.

On that occasion, Elizabeth rode out on Midnight, taking in the sights and sounds of the waning winter, noting the onset of spring with gratitude, for she had never liked the colder weather. Whether fate or some unconscious impulse led her she could not understand, but after a time, she found herself on the northern border of Longbourn, leading Midnight up the gentle slope of the hill. When she arrived there, she looked down the valley, though she could not say if she hoped to see anyone. When there was no one in evidence, she sat down under the oak and pulled out her book. Soon she was engrossed in its pages, Midnight grazing nearby on a few hardy shoots which had already poked through the hardened soil.

A few minutes later, Elizabeth looked up to see a rider approaching from the far side of the fence. Given his mount and stature, Elizabeth knew his identity long before he was close enough to make out his features. Rising, Elizabeth thought to go to Midnight and depart.

"Good day, Miss Elizabeth," said Mr. Darcy as he pulled his horse near to the fence. He looked at her for a moment, his eyebrows narrowed in curiosity. "It seems to me you enjoy reading, for this is the second time I have seen you with a book when out of doors. Most people prefer to do their reading when they are inside, and at this time of year, before a roaring fire."

Elizabeth's instinct was to give the gentleman a polite reply to his greeting and excuse herself as her father had instructed. Why she did not, Elizabeth could never determine. Could it have been that fate led them to this spot, led her to the place where Mr. Darcy might come across her? The thought crossed her mind that a meeting at this far-flung location was an unlikely event. She did not know, but something prompted her response, allowing no thought of resisting.

"Before a crackling fire is a place I love to read best, Mr. Darcy. As I am also a lover of nature, however, I occasionally enjoy combining reading and the outdoors."

Mr. Darcy nodded, saying: "Then we are alike in our love of nature, Miss Elizabeth, though I rarely take a book with me when I ride. It occurs to me to wonder if we read the same material."

Amusement welled up within Elizabeth's breast, though she supposed she might as soon have felt insulted by his words. "Do you suppose I read Fanny Burney at all hours of the day and night?"

Mr. Darcy appeared to accept the challenge, for he said: "Not when I have already seen you with a collection of Blake in your hand. What are you reading today?"

"A collection of Cowper, actually," said Elizabeth, holding up the small book she held so he could see the spine. "I will own that I do not always read poetry, for I find I must be in the correct mood to enjoy it. Today is such a beautiful day that I could not resist returning to an old friend."

It seemed Mr. Darcy was impressed. "Then I must presume you have read Donne, Byron, Coleridge, and Chaucer? I already know you are a devotee of Blake."

"And many more," replied Elizabeth. "My father felt that his daughters should be educated in classical and modern literature, so he ensured we were all exposed to it to a certain extent, though some have more affinity than others. But these are not all, for I can speak and read French and Italian, and have some familiarity with Voltaire, Rousseau, and others." Elizabeth paused and laughed. "Jane is also proficient in German, but for myself, I have always found it incomprehensible."

"I am impressed, Miss Elizabeth," said Mr. Darcy, his countenance reflecting his statement. "The accomplishments of the Bennet sisters were unknown to me."

"My father would have it no other way," said Elizabeth. "Papa is a learned man and wished his progeny to be knowledgeable themselves, for he is of the opinion that no enlightened thought can be obtained without education. Mary and I were the most eager of his children, though we have all been trained to think critically."

"Then do you have some favorites? I am interested to learn if your education is equal to that which I received at Cambridge."

While Elizabeth might have suspected the man of sarcasm, the manner in which he spoke, earnest and even a little eager, spoke to his sincerity. What followed was brief—perhaps only thirty minutes of conversation altogether, but in that time they canvassed their likes and dislikes, spoke of their impressions of various works, and contrasted where their opinions differed.

In that short time, Elizabeth discovered Mr. Darcy was partial to Shakespeare's tragedies, whereas she preferred the comedies; learned that Mr. Darcy preferred Donne to Cowper; and discovered the gentleman was widely read on a variety of subjects but preferred philosophy to poetry. Elizabeth found herself responding, informing him of her preferences, speaking of some of the works she had read, and even received some advice of books he thought she might like. By the time she realized that a half-hour had passed, she could only wonder how it had come and gone without her noticing.

"I apologize, Mr. Darcy," said Elizabeth at length, "but I believe I have been here long enough. If I stay much longer, my father will wonder where I am."

"That is understandable, Miss Elizabeth," said Mr. Darcy, seeming to realize for the first time how long they had been together. "I thank you for speaking to me, for it has been a most enlightening conversation."

"It has," was Elizabeth's soft reply.

Then she turned and, without another word, approached Midnight and lifted herself into the saddle. When she turned back to Mr. Darcy, he was watching her, his expression unreadable. For a moment, Elizabeth was almost loath to leave him, though she knew she must.

"Farewell, Mr. Darcy," said she, raising a hand in parting.

"Until next time," replied the gentleman, mirroring her action in response.

As she rode away, Elizabeth wondered if there would be a next time. Though she knew she was breaking her promise to her father, she also realized she wanted to see the gentleman again. She wanted it very much.

Another meeting between members of the Bennet and Darcy clans took place, though unlike the other, the second meeting did not occur away from prying eyes on the edges of two great estates. It was also not a meeting which included anyone bearing the Bennet surname, though Alexander Darcy might have wished to meet anyone other than the man who spied him on the street in Lambton. By the time he saw the gentleman, it was too late to turn and leave.

"Mr. Darcy," said Mr. David Gardiner, stepping up to where Alexander stood, preparing to mount his horse. "I wish to have words with you for a moment."

"It would be best if we did not," said Alexander, wishing to avoid a confrontation. "Let us go our separate ways, Mr. Gardiner, for I have no interest in an argument."

"There is no need for us to argue," replied Mr. Gardiner. "I only wish to impart a message, after which we may part as amicably as possible."

Alexander eyed the other man for a moment, and noting he did not seem belligerent, and agreed to listen to him. In fact, it seemed to him he could not avoid it without provoking the argument he did not wish to have.

"The reason I wish to speak with you is simple," said Mr. Gardiner. "Your reputation precedes you, sir. Tales of your exploits are well known in town, and it is for this reason, more than any difficulty between our two families, which prompts me to insist you stay away from my nieces."

"Oh?" asked Alexander, feeling a little annoyed. "Have you appointed yourself their protector then? I might have thought Lord Arundel, being a baron, would fight his own battles."

"Lord Arundel is capable of defending his family, sir; you would not be wise to make any insinuations. Be that as it may, I am closely connected to the Bennet family, and have an interest in protecting my nieces. I do not usurp my brother's position; I reinforce it."

"Then you need not fear, Mr. Gardiner," said Alexander. "My reputation is exaggerated, though I will own I have been a little wild in my youth. Despite this, I have come to the same conclusion myself—I have no desire to provoke unpleasantness between our families and every desire to keep my distance. Your nieces are safe from me."

The way Mr. Gardiner watched him, Alexander thought the man searching him to see if he was telling the truth. After a moment of this, Alexander sighed.

"I know not what I must do to prove myself to you."

"I shall take your word as a gentleman," said Mr. Gardiner. "If you offer it, I shall accept it."

"Then I do," replied Alexander.

"Good," said Mr. Gardiner. "Then I bid you a good day."

Mr. Gardiner tipped his hat and walked away, leaving Alexander watching him as he went. After a moment Mr. Gardiner was out of sight, and Alexander mounted his horse to return to Pemberley.

Alexander decided his father and siblings did not need to know of the meeting with Mr. Gardiner. The man had issued his demands and Alexander had responded the way his father had required him only days before. Since there had been no unpleasantness, it did not bear further consideration.

As it had many times in the past few days, the memory of Lydia Bennet returned to him as he allowed his mount its head to return to Pemberley. The girl was interesting, and Alexander had not felt that way about a woman for some time. Her manner had been so unlike anything he had seen before, he wondered what kind of girl she was. In some ways, she reminded him of Miss Gainsborough, though that woman was more calculating than Miss Lydia. Miss Lydia was more of a flirt.

Alexander did not know what to make of her, but he supposed it did not matter. The Bennets and their connections were to be shunned, and he would gain no more insight into Miss Lydia. It was a shame, for he found himself thinking about her more often than he should.

CHAPTER XI

*D*arcy could not be sure why he had approached Miss Elizabeth. It was best, as his father said, if the Darcy family avoided all contact with their Bennet neighbors, for as Darcy had said himself, continued clashes could provoke a return to a more active conflict. None of them wished for that, the Bennets as much as the Darcys.

But something had spurred Darcy on, some unconscious well of fascination for the second-eldest Bennet daughter. What was it? Darcy could not be certain, though he often thought on the matter. She was, as he had already thought many times, unlike any other woman he had ever met. The matter of the Bennet sisters' education he could only applaud, for Darcy had never been of the opinion that women should concentrate on "proper" activities. The world was a large place, and there were many situations in which a person could find themselves; it was best she possess knowledge of the world around her, so she was prepared to live in it.

When Darcy had approached the hill and seen Miss Elizabeth sitting under the gnarled old oak tree, her attention focused on the pages before her, he had almost turned his horse around and returned from whence he came. That would have been the prudent course. The sight of her immersed in her study, however, had called to him, and as he had approached, the appeal of the woman's person was nigh overpowering. When she had looked up and seen him—and it had not missed Darcy's attention that she had made to leave at once—he had been lost, any thought of departing gone in favor of the need to speak to her, to be the focus of her attention. Their conversation had left him even more impressed.

Though his introspection was a constant companion those days, Darcy soon realized he was not the only member of his family so afflicted. It was more easily seen in Alexander, who was a more open sort of man than Darcy ever had been. But when he asked, Alexander was quick to brush off any attempt to discover what was on his mind.

"There is nothing the matter with me, William. There are many thoughts on my mind, not the least of which is this situation with the Bennets. I have also been thinking about my estate."

That last admission surprised Darcy. "Thorndell?"

"That is its name, is it not?" asked Alexander, amusement dripping from his voice. "I have not given it the attention I should have—of this, I am well aware. As I am now five and twenty and Father has declared his desire to pass much of Pemberley's management to you, it should not be surprising I should begin to think of Thorndell."

"Thorndell is a picturesque estate," said Georgiana, who was with them in the sitting-room. "William took me there just after you left for London. I believe with a woman's touch it would become a wonderful home."

Alexander laughed. "Are you now attempting to inform me it is time I married, Sister?"

"I would never presume to do so," said Georgiana, though her twinkling eyes belied her denial. "Before too many years have passed, you will need to consider such things."

With a shaken head, Alexander said: "You are correct, Georgiana, but I believe I am not ready to be shackled to a woman just yet. Many men of our set do not marry until they are thirty. William here is seven and twenty and still has no interest in marrying."

This talk of marriage and Darcy's age caused the image of Miss Elizabeth Bennet to flash before his eyes. Darcy shook the image away, knowing it was silly to think such things of a woman whose family was an enemy of his.

"It is not that I have no interest in marrying," replied Darcy. "It is only that I have never found a woman I wish to come to know better." Even as he said it, something in Darcy's mind whispered there *was* such a woman. But she was unsuitable in every way.

"Then perhaps you should surrender and marry Anne," replied Alexander to Georgiana's amusement. "If you did so, at least you would make Aunt Catherine happy."

"At the expense of my own happiness," grumbled Darcy.

"This is a fine representation of Cousin Anne!" protested Georgiana. "She is a lovely young woman, and one I believe you find interesting."

"That is true," replied Darcy. "But I also remember Anne as a child, for she is a little younger than Alexander, if you recall. Though I love Anne as a Cousin, engaging in piracy, sword fights, and other such play diminished my interest in her as a woman."

"And you know Anne has no more desire to marry William than he has to marry her," added Alexander. "I understand his reasons, for I do not think I could marry her either."

"As long as you are not dismissing her because she is not suitable," said Georgiana, trying—and failing—to glare at her brothers when they were both aware of her continued mirth. Then she addressed Darcy again. "If you or Anne were to marry, Aunt Catherine would cease promoting the match with such fervor."

Alexander snorted his disdain. "Anne marrying is unlikely, not when Aunt Catherine is so set on her marrying our brother."

"Then William must marry. Not only would he find his happiness, but he would free Anne to find hers."

"I believe she has you there, Brother," said Alexander, fixing Darcy with a sidelong look. "The sooner you find a wife, the better Anne's position will be. Perhaps we can find a man of the neighborhood to pay court to her when she comes."

"They would face the same logistical problems as I," replied Darcy. "Rosings is a large estate and would be difficult to manage from such a great distance as this. It is not Appleton or Blackfish Bay."

Alexander nodded his understanding, for Darcy had just named two of the more profitable Darcy satellite estates. Rosings was an estate of seven to eight thousand a year, though it was not as diverse as Pemberley because of its location in the garden of England. By contrast, Blackfish Bay on the coast in Lincolnshire generated about two thousand a year, while Appleton Court was smaller, only generating three quarters that much. To manage Rosings, Darcy knew he must spend at least two or three months a year there, and while he could do it by leaving early for the season or returning late, Kent was not Derbyshire—he much preferred the latter.

"Perhaps it would be difficult to manage," said Alexander, "but it would be a good estate to pass on to a second son."

"That is true," replied Darcy. "But the fact remains that I am not interested in Anne as a potential wife. I prefer to find someone with whom I can build a relationship of mutual affection, and I know Anne would like the same.

"In truth, it has always surprised me that *you* were not put forth as a match for Anne." Alexander returned his look, a question contained within. "You are the younger son," explained Darcy. "Though Thorndell is a good estate, it is not Pemberley and all its associated interests. Gaining Rosings would not make your future wealth the equal of mine, but it would do much to raise your consequence."

"Have I ever given the impression of envy?" asked Alexander. When Darcy denied it, he shook his head and continued, saying: "Given the manner in which I have lived my life, the thought of managing Thorndell alone is daunting, to say nothing of adding Rosings."

"That may be so, but it would have made more sense from the perspective of fortune. I never needed Rosings, but it would enhance your position beyond measure."

"Come, William," said Alexander, "I know you understand Aunt Catherine better than this. The reason she wished to marry Anne to you is *precisely* that you are wealthier than I. Lady Catherine's interest is in creating a family dynasty, if you will. I believe she may even have designs on a title."

"In that, you would be correct." Detecting his siblings' looks askance, Darcy elaborated: "Aunt Catherine has said nothing direct to me, but she has insinuated it more than once."

"That is my aunt," said Alexander, laughing while shaking his head.

It was at that moment the door opened and Mrs. Reynolds showed a visitor into the room. Darcy and his brother rose, accompanied by their sister, and got his first look at the woman who had entered the room. It was one of the most fortune-seeking females in the neighborhood, a woman who equaled Miss Bingley in her attempts to attach herself to the Darcy family. Oh, her attempts had never been overt—with one exception—for Darcy was well able to fend her off. Even so, Darcy knew how dangerous this viper could be.

"Miss Gainsborough!" said Alexander. The tone of his voice prompted Darcy to glance at his brother, and he noted Alexander's countenance was as closed as he had ever seen.

"Mr. Darcy," said the young woman smoothly. She then greeted Darcy himself in a more perfunctory manner before turning her attention to Georgiana. "Dear Miss Darcy, how are you this morning? It has been an age since I last saw you!"

Darcy could not have been more surprised, for he did not think Georgiana was acquainted with the other woman. Georgiana's countenance mirrored her brothers' surprise as she stammered for an answer.

"Miss Gainsborough. How wonderful it is to see you."

"The pleasure is all mine. I had hoped you would visit me, but since you did not come, I thought I would take the first step."

It did not miss Darcy's notice that while she spoke to Georgiana, her eyes never left Alexander, and he wondered what the woman could mean. A thought niggled its way through Darcy's mind, and he remembered a party at one of the neighboring estates, a brief glimpse he had gotten of Alexander sitting close to this woman, laughing with her. He also remembered when her eyes had found Darcy's during that interlude. Was Alexander aware the woman was attempting to come closer to Darcy through him?

As she was already here, there was nothing to do but sit with her. Georgiana ordered tea and they sat chatting for some time—Darcy said little, and though it surprised him, Alexander said little more. The visit passed as many other morning visits, the conversation consisting of the small talk Darcy found to be so dull. After they drank their tea, however, there was a slight change in the dynamic, as Miss Gainsborough turned her attention to Darcy and his brother.

"I am pleased to see you back in Lambton, Mr. Darcy. There was some talk Mr. Gardiner that he would call you out for the incident last summer."

"It was nothing more than an accident," replied Alexander. "Mr. Gardiner understands this. We have settled our differences."

"That you have done so speaks well of you," simpered Miss Gainsborough. "Then you will not be departing Derbyshire for some time?"

"I believe I am quite settled here for the present."

It was when she fixed him with a beaming smile that Darcy had enough of the game. "Excuse me, Miss Gainsborough, but I was not aware you were acquainted with my sister."

The look with which Miss Gainsborough regarded him was all insincerity hidden in shock. "We met in Lambton, did we not Miss Darcy?" The smile with which she regarded Georgiana did not make

Darcy feel confident at all. "I liked your sister at once, for there is something pure and innocent about her which calls to anyone who listens."

"So you were not formally introduced," said Darcy, deciding bluntness was the best way to deal with her. When she appeared surprised anew he clarified: "The usual protocol is for someone known to you both to introduce you. Where a family moves into a neighborhood, gentlemen of the neighborhood visit the newcomer and introduce themselves, then the families become acquainted through their auspices. My sister is not yet out, and has not, to the best of my knowledge, been introduced to you in such a setting."

"In the instance in question, we took the onus on ourselves, Mr. Darcy," said Miss Gainsborough. "There was no one else to perform the office."

"From that, I infer you have not made Georgiana's formal acquaintance." Darcy shook his head. "I am sure you mean well, Miss Gainsborough," Darcy knew *that* was furthest from the truth, "but you will find the Darcy family prefers to follow the forms."

"With that, I think the time for your visit has elapsed," said Alexander. "Please come with me, Miss Gainsborough, for I shall escort you to your carriage."

It seemed to Darcy the woman was more than a little shocked at her summary dismissal. She said her farewells to Georgiana in an affectionate manner, though she did nothing more than curtsey to Darcy. Then she exited the sitting-room when his brother bowed and motioned her toward the door.

Curious to see what Alexander planned, Darcy stepped from the room and followed them the short distance to the entrance hall. When they arrived there, he saw his brother lean down and say something to her, and from her pursed lips, it was clear she did not appreciate it, whatever it was. Having seen enough, Darcy returned to the sitting-room and stepped in, regarding his sister with a raised eyebrow, receiving a huff in reply.

"We exchanged a few words," said Georgiana. "And the incident to which she refers occurred over two months ago!"

Darcy shook his head. "It is as I suspected. Whether her target was Alexander or me I know not, but it seems she seized on the excuse of your brief meeting to visit."

"Oh, her ultimate target was you, of course," said Alexander as he stepped into the room. "It is possible she might turn her attention to me if she knew you were unattainable, but she has always had her eye on the greater prize."

Nodding, Darcy shook his head. "I am pleased you have seen that for yourself. Miss Gainsborough is the most conniving woman I have ever seen. Three months ago, she attempted to engineer a compromise with me. I gave her to understand I would not marry her even if she succeeded."

Alexander laughed. "Then either she did not believe you, or she has turned her attention to me."

"The latter, if I am any judge, though there may still be some hint of the former." Darcy paused and peered at his brother, asking: "What did you tell her when she was leaving?"

"I reminded her not to return until she has *properly* made our sister's acquaintance. Since I have no notion of that happening soon, I hope we will be free of her for some time."

"Excellent," said Darcy.

The siblings separated then to their various activities, Georgiana to the music room, while Alexander took himself to another part of the house. Darcy made his way to the billiard-room. As he played, he considered Miss Gainsborough, amused by the woman's audacity. Though she was a pretty girl, not without charms, her devious nature repelled him; he would never marry such a woman. She was not at all like Miss Elizabeth Bennet—there was a woman who would never exert herself to such stratagems employed by the likes of Miss Gainsborough. And she was much prettier too.

Rain was not fun—or so the youngest Bennet told his sisters on several occasions.

"I wish it was not raining today," whined Thomas, much to his sisters' amusement.

"Do you not take your lessons at this time of day?" asked Mary, her pointed question delivered without taking her eyes from her book."

"Yes," replied Thomas, a hint of smugness in his tone as he added: "But Master Davies was ill this morning and allowed me to have the day to myself."

"Much to our chagrin," said Lady Margaret, fixing her youngest with a hard glare. "Though Master Davies may not be present to give you formal lessons, it does not follow you should be engaged in idleness and pestering your sisters, young man."

"But Mother," whined Thomas in a manner used by young children since the dawn of time.

"Perhaps we should find something to occupy our brother," said

Elizabeth. "I believe I would also benefit from an activity other than embroidery."

"You never wish to embroider, Lizzy," said Jane as Thomas darted forward with a whoop and hugged his sister with boundless enthusiasm.

"Yes, you are correct," replied Elizabeth, embracing her brother while ensuring he avoided her needle. "But at present, I believe we could all do with a little fun activity. Shall we not join Thomas in his games for a time?"

Kitty and Lydia readily agreed, and while Jane and Mary were more reserved, they also affirmed their willingness. Mr. Bingley, who was visiting Jane, proclaimed it an excellent notion, even calling out several suggestions for games they play, and Mr. Collins informed them he had no objection to taking part. Their mother, unsurprising to anyone present, declined their invitation, leaving the room instead, saying she needed to speak with Mrs. Hill, their housekeeper. The most surprising agreement came from their uncle, who entered the room soon after Lady Margaret left it.

"That sounds like an excellent idea," said he, rubbing his hands together. "Tell me, Tommy; what shall we play?"

Thomas thought for a moment, then raised his eyes to his uncle, saying: "Shall we not play sardines?" Then, with more enthusiasm added: "Yes, let us play sardines, for it shall be ever so much fun! I shall hide first!"

Though the rest of the adults looked at each other with some amusement, Thomas, eager to get on with the game, ran from the room, his voice floating back to them: "Count to fifty, then you may find me!"

"I think this may not be a good idea," said Mary, her gaze falling on Mr. Bingley and Jane.

Though Jane blushed, the response came from Uncle Gardiner. "I believe we may dispense with the proprieties when playing a children's game." The gentleman paused and looked at the two couples—he included Mary and Mr. Collins in his scrutiny. "Should one of you hide and one of the gentlemen is the first to find you, I must insist on your good behavior."

While Jane and Mary's countenances bloomed in embarrassment, Elizabeth, Kitty, and Lydia were not reticent about voicing their amusement. Mr. Collins was quick to assure Mr. Gardiner, in a most serious fashion, he would never dream of taking advantage of Mary, who glared at her uncle, informing him she did not find his jesting at all amusing. It fell to Elizabeth to rescue them.

"Is it not now time to search for Thomas?"

They agreed and split up, each going to a separate part of the house to search for the youngest member of the family, though Elizabeth noted that Mr. Bingley and Jane exited in the same direction. Elizabeth, having played this game with her brother before, had some idea as to his favorite places to hide, and took herself above stairs to the family apartments. The first two places she checked revealed nothing, but the third — in his mother's dressing room — yielded the young boy.

"Oh bother!" exclaimed Thomas when he saw her. "Why do you always find me so quickly, Lizzy?"

"Because you do not vary your favorite locations, dear brother," replied Elizabeth, settling in with her brother behind a row of their mother's dresses. "You must find new places to hide, for I believe I know all you use at present."

Thomas grumbled but did not respond. Looking about, Elizabeth laughed a little and embraced him again, saying: "I hope Mama does not discover us in here, for I am certain she will not be pleased."

"But we are playing a game!" protested Thomas.

"Do you believe Mama will make any distinction?" asked Elizabeth. Thomas frowned, and when he did not respond, Elizabeth said: "Do not concern yourself, Thomas, for Mama may be unhappy, but the rest of us shall blunt her anger. Now, we should be quiet, for we shall be found if we do not."

The others found them after a time, first Kitty, and then soon after Lydia. Jane then found them with Mr. Bingley in tow — given the wide eyes the gentleman sported, Elizabeth thought he never would have ventured into the mistress's chambers regardless of the game had Jane not coaxed him in. Then Mr. Gardiner discovered them. After the gentleman's arrival, they waited for some time until Mary came in and looked down on them with some disapproval.

"Mr. Collins will not enter this room," said she, much to the younger girls' amusement. "I am surprised Mr. Bingley and my uncle would."

With a laugh, Elizabeth rose, followed by the rest of those hunkered down behind the clothing, and said: "Perhaps we should confine our game to the lower floor so all may participate."

"That would be best," said Mary, the asperity not gone from her voice.

When they all trooped outside Lady Margaret's bedchambers, they found Mr. Collins waiting awkwardly, though there was no sign of

Lady Margaret, for which they were all grateful. The new rules established, Mr. Collins—as the only one who had not found them—was sent off to hide, and he took himself downstairs, though it was clear he was embarrassed and unsure.

By the time they declared the game finished, Elizabeth thought they had all had a grand time. Mr. Collins's hiding had been something of a failure, for he had chosen a spot behind a sofa in the sitting-room, a place which was quickly found and could not accommodate more than a few of them. But Thomas's cries of joy every time they all came together again warmed their hearts and brought them closer together. Then Elizabeth ordered hot chocolate for them all, a treat only served on special occasions because of its scarcity and expense.

After the hot chocolate arrived and they were all nursing cups of the sweet, steaming liquid, they sat in the sitting-room chatting about their fun that afternoon. Thomas, Elizabeth noted, was concentrating on his treat, though she noticed his boundless energy was tempered, no doubt by the exertions of the day. Uncle Gardiner, who sat beside her, noted her look and chuckled as he sipped his drink.

"A good boy, your brother. Some day he will be a fine master of this estate."

"He will be," replied Elizabeth. "His birth was such a joyous occasion—my mother had despaired of ever bearing an heir for her husband."

"We were all happy for her, though your father spoke many times of his contentment with having only five beautiful daughters."

Elizabeth smiled at her uncle and turned her attention again to her cup. Uncle Gardiner was silent for a moment before speaking again.

"I see that Mr. Collins's admiration of your younger sister has become more noticeable."

Turning her smile on the couple, Elizabeth glanced at her sister, noting Mary in close conversation with their cousin. "Yes, I believe it has. Mr. Collins seems to lack a certain confidence when it comes to my sister, but I believe they are making progress."

"It is the same for any man his age," replied her uncle. "Though we all project confidence, there is still a hint of the little boy left in us, no matter what age we attain. There is always some fear that the woman we admire will reject us—it takes time for a man to gather his courage together."

"Is that so?" asked Elizabeth with a laugh. "I will own I have seen nothing of it in Mr. Bingley."

"Maybe not. But Jane has been far more open in her returning admiration than Mary. Your younger sister is not a woman who responds with anything other than the subtlest hints."

"I suppose you must be correct."

Uncle Gardiner nodded and sipped his chocolate. "He will make her a good husband when he gets up his courage to propose. Mr. Collins is a bit of a simple man, but he is a good man, one who will move heaven and earth to protect her."

"That he will," said Elizabeth. "Mr. Collins is exactly what Mary needs."

They fell silent after that, but Elizabeth's thoughts were not also quiet. As they all concentrated on the sweet liquid in their cups, she considered her sisters, noting the contrast in their courtships, their different relationships with their suitors. Both would find their happiness, she knew, and she could only hope she could find a man as devoted to her as Mr. Bingley and Mr. Collins were to her sisters.

The image of a tall man, dark and handsome, with an air of mysterious brooding flashed through Elizabeth's mind, but she pushed it away. Such thoughts were nonsensical. Elizabeth did not need to hurry to search for her future spouse, for there was plenty of time to find him. Though she was certain she would soon inherit the title "Miss Bennet," and her younger sister would follow their elder into matrimony, Elizabeth could feel nothing but the contentment of her situation.

CHAPTER XII

Miss Violet Gainsborough was not the only woman on the prowl trying to capture one of the Pemberley men. This was amply displayed the day after the rain ceased when the more common visitor imposed herself on Georgiana's peace.

"Dear Georgiana!" exclaimed Miss Bingley as was her wont when Mrs. Reynolds showed her into the room. Georgiana did not miss the housekeeper's disapproving glance at the woman, but as a good servant with extensive experience, she did not allow the guest to notice her censure. Georgiana smiled at her housekeeper, giving her permission to leave the room.

"How unfortunate was yesterday's weather," said the woman as she sat nearby, "for it prevented me from visiting you." The woman paused and sniffed. "Charles spent the entire day at Longbourn, leaving me alone at Netherfield."

'Was your mother not there?" asked Georgiana in a show of innocence, avoiding the subject of the Bennets. "I had thought she had returned from Norfolk."

"Yes, my mother was there, and I adore her so. But I longed to see you too. How have you been?"

"Very well, Miss Bingley."

"And are your brothers about? I should like to pay my respects to them during my visit."

"Oh, Alexander is about," replied Georgiana, "but William had some business in Lambton this morning and informed us he would not return for some hours."

As Georgiana might have predicted, Miss Bingley was put out by this news, though she attempted to brush it aside. "Then I suppose we must content ourselves with each other's company. Shall we remove to the music room? Your playing is so divine, I should like to hear you again."

They did not move to the music room, for Georgiana had no desire to endure Miss Bingley's false praise that morning, for a morning in the music room would increase the level of flattery to near sickening levels. Instead, they remained in the sitting-room conversing; rather, Miss Bingley talked, and Georgiana listened more than anything else.

Though Georgiana would not call the woman completely shallow and conniving, she well knew that Miss Bingley's exclamations of friendship were aimed at obtaining William's good opinion. Georgiana thought Miss Bingley esteemed her on some level, but she could not imagine Miss Bingley visiting her if she did not have a handsome and eligible elder brother. When considering Georgiana's more tender age compared with Miss Bingley's status as a woman full-grown, she supposed the woman would prefer to be among others her own age. But the desire to obtain the position of Pemberley's future mistress was always at the forefront of Mis Bingley's thought, rendering the desire for friends her own age secondary.

They stayed in this attitude for some time, and as she ever did, Miss Bingley stayed past the time of normal visiting hours. Georgiana was reflecting on the benefits of reminding Miss Bingley of the time—she had long stopped paying much attention to the woman's prattle—when Alexander found them.

"You have my apologies, Sister, for I did not know you had a visitor."

Though Miss Bingley had looked up with hope and expectation when he entered, the opening of the door had not yielded the correct brother, and she looked away a little crestfallen. That did not stop Alexander, who knew very well Miss Bingley's purpose for being there.

"Good day, Miss Bingley," said he and, stepping forward, he caught up her hand and bestowed a lingering kiss on its back. "It has been much too long, for I believe we have not met since the last assembly before I departed for London. I have missed having the pleasure of your company."

Georgiana stifled a giggle at her brother's overt flattery, though she attempted to send a glare in his direction. That Alexander ignored it was no surprise to Georgiana and she was far too amused to offer any protest.

"Well . . . That is to say, I am surprised by your perfect recollection, sir," said Miss Bingley, her words becoming firmer though she stammered at first.

"Who could forget it?" asked Alexander. "It was a wonderful night, in particular, the dance we shared. Do you not agree?"

While Miss Bingley eyed him, Alexander returned her look with one of his own which Georgiana could only call smitten. Miss Bingley did not seem impressed by his display, for she turned to Georgiana, intent upon ignoring him.

"Have I told you of the party I attended at the Danforth estate last week? It was a most wonderful event, for Miss Danforth's performance on the pianoforte is exquisite—almost the equal of your own."

"Do tell," said Alexander before Georgiana could form a response. "Perhaps she is excellent when sitting at the instrument, but I cannot call Miss Danforth anything other than dull otherwise. I should much rather speak of you, Miss Bingley."

The woman blushed crimson, but she attempted to continue speaking of her recent experience. As she spoke, Alexander continued to interrupt, essaying little compliments designed to flirt with Miss Bingley, who was having no part of it. The longer she talked, however, the more frustrated Miss Bingley became, and a time or two she snapped back at Alexander's obvious flirting, not that it deterred him.

After a time of this, the woman left the topic of the party and exclaimed: "What a fine thing it is to be at Pemberley today! You are blessed, Georgiana, for it is the dearest place in the world!"

"If you saw Thorndell, your opinion might be different," said Alexander, his most blatant attempt to distract her yet. "Thorndell is my estate, you understand, and though Pemberley is larger, in sheer terms of beauty I do not think Thorndell can be exceeded. Perhaps one day you may see it, Miss Bingley, for I should like to show it to you."

Miss Bingley's mouth fell open at Alexander's obvious insinuation, but it was not long before she turned away, a brittle smile fixed on Georgiana. "It seems I have stayed past the time of our visit, Georgiana. You have my apologies and my regrets, but I believe I should now depart."

Then rising, and giving a brief curtsey, she fled the room, the sound of Alexander's voice following her out into the hall.

"But Miss Bingley, I wish to tell you more about Thorndell!"

The sound of the woman's footsteps quickened, and she was soon beyond the range of their hearing. Alexander turned an amused grin at Georgiana, who was fighting to maintain a frown of asperity.

"There, Georgiana, I have rid you of your unwanted visitor. Shall you not thank me for my magnanimous assistance?"

Georgiana could not help the laughter which burst forth, though she attempted to cover it up with a scowl. "That was poorly one, Alexander. Why, when William marries, the woman might remember your actions and decide *you* are the Darcy brother she wishes to capture."

A snort was her brother's response. "I believe you will find I can fend off Miss Bingley. There is no more chance of her marrying me than she has of capturing William."

"Then why did you run her off?" demanded Georgiana.

"Were you enjoying her company?" asked Alexander with a raised eyebrow.

"No, but that is beside the point."

"I that case, dear Sister," said Alexander, sending her a wink, "the next time she comes, I shall leave you to it. My purpose was nothing more than to spare you her company for the rest of the day, for she seemed quite settled here. If my interference was officious, I apologize."

With a final grin, Alexander turned and let himself out of the room, Georgiana watching him with equal parts asperity and mirth. She supposed she should be grateful for his interference, and the thought of Miss Bingley's haste to leave did provoke her to laughter again. Alexander was audacious—he had best take care, for who knew what response he might provoke?

Darcy was uncertain what he was doing, but all his arguments were ineffective, vain thoughts rumbling in the back of his mind, neither heeded nor wanted. While his actions seemed foolhardy, he had not yet learned to condemn them, and if this torment, so sweet and aching, was wrong, then perhaps all his previous conceptions were also incorrect. All he knew was that he left that morning to go to Lambton, saw Miss Elizabeth in the town, and in an instant of decision, arranged so he would meet her as they were leaving, yet far enough away that their discourse would not be noticed.

"Miss Elizabeth," said he, inclining his head as he sat on his steed. "I see you have come to Lambton again today."

"I have, Mr. Darcy," said she. "In fact, I often come here."

For a time, their paths to return to their homes would be the same, he motioned on, somewhat surprised when she assented. As they turned their horses as one onto the road, Miss Elizabeth looked back at him.

"My uncle is the parson at Lambton church, as you must know — I often visit him or stop to speak with Mrs. Gardiner. Lambton is also a place to find some amusement, though it is not as exciting as if a regiment of officers were quartered there."

"You appreciate a man in a red coat?"

Miss Elizabeth laughed. "It seems to me any young maiden would feel the call of such adventurous fellows, but I am no more enamored of a man in scarlet than the next woman. If they had interesting tales to tell of exotic locations and other cultures, I would be intrigued."

"Then you will not find that among a company of militia, Miss Elizabeth. My cousin, Colonel Fitzwilliam, has many tales to tell, and as he is in the regulars, *some* of them may even be true."

The woman's laughter was a tinkling bell, its chimes finding an echo in the beating of Darcy's heart. "I suppose you are attempting to inform me that militia officers, by contrast, lead rather dull lives."

"So my cousin would inform you if he was here."

"When I spoke to Lady Charlotte Lucas, she informed me he was expected before long?"

"Within a few days," replied Darcy.

"It must be a great relief to know he is leaving active service for the life of a gentleman."

"We all are thankful. My aunt, in particular, cannot be more grateful her younger son has sold his commission, and even happier that he shall marry the daughter of an earl." Darcy paused, wondering if what he meant to say next would make him sound proud. Then again, she was the daughter of a baron — she must have heard much worse. "The Chesterfield earldom is peculiar in that the title may be passed down through the female line. Though Fitzwilliam will never be an earl himself and must take the earl's family name as his own, he will be the father of the next Earl of Chesterfield."

"Yes, I had heard something of that nature," replied Miss Elizabeth, her manner indicating she had seen nothing into his comment he had not intended. "As it is a love match — or so I have heard — it is very fortunate for Colonel Fitzwilliam, as it also provides for his future."

"It does," agreed Darcy.

For several moments they rode on in silence, Darcy wishing to say more to this woman, but feeling bereft of his senses, unable to think of anything interesting to say to her. Miss Elizabeth, it seemed to him, did not suffer from an inability to converse—everything he knew of her suggested that was out of the question. The silence was comfortable, however, which was a good sign, if one cared to interpret it in such a way. While he did not know why Darcy wished it to be so.

"I am curious," said Darcy at length. When Miss Elizabeth regarded him askance, he continued: "When we all met in the bookshop there was a tall gentleman with you. Though I assume he is a relation, I do not believe I have seen him before."

"Mr. Collins," said Miss Elizabeth, her face graced with a slight smile. "He is my father's cousin, though none of us can quite remember to what degree. When he was a boy, my father was close to Mr. Collins's father and has remained so with his son. The elder Mr. Collins was a parson and his son followed in his stead. But a year ago he inherited an estate in Nottinghamshire. Since that inheritance, he has been there, learning the craft of being a gentleman. This is the first time he has been with us in some years."

"That explains it then," said Darcy. "It is my perception your family does not have many Bennet relations."

"That is true," replied Miss Elizabeth. "Mr. Collins is the only one with whom we are at all close—most of our relations are from my mother's family. Of possible interest to you is Mr. Collins claims a connection close to your family."

"Indeed?" asked Darcy, uncertain what to make of this revelation. "How so, Miss Elizabeth?"

"After Mr. Collins attained his ordination, he came to the notice of one Lady Catherine de Bourgh, who I believe is your aunt. Lady Catherine installed him as the rector of Hunsford, where I believe he stayed for less than a year before he inherited his estate."

Darcy could not help the slight grimace of distaste, and it seemed Miss Elizabeth had seen it. Though he could have seen her becoming angered by it, she seemed to interpret it correctly, for she grinned at him and waited for his explanation.

"Being chosen as Lady Catherine's parson is not a ringing endorsement of his character, Miss Elizabeth," said Darcy, hoping to explain with swiftness. "My aunt surrounds herself with sycophants and toadies, people who would never dare contradict her. It is not my purpose to insult Mr. Collins, but if you had known her last parson, you would understand."

By this time Miss Elizabeth was laughing, a matter of some relief to Darcy. "In this, I cannot but believe your assertions, Mr. Darcy, for Mr. Collins's accounts of his time as the parson of Hunsford match your account in every particular. It seems it pleased Lady Catherine to be rid of my cousin, for he did not display the 'proper level of respect' in her words."

They laughed together, Darcy's mirth full of appreciation that he had not offended her. Then Darcy added: "You must inform your cousin that Lady Catherine is to visit us and is to arrive within a few days of Fitzwilliam's coming."

"Then I shall be sure to inform him!" exclaimed Miss Elizabeth, still laughing. "Though I do not know if the lady will appreciate the opportunity to become reacquainted with her former parson, Mr. Collins speaks in warm terms of Lady Catherine."

Darcy nodded. By this time, they had arrived at the turnoff which led to Pemberley, and Darcy, though he would have preferred to continue riding with her, knew it was best if he returned to his home. It was a wonder they had come upon no one as they had ridden down the road, for it was not an untraveled path. Fate, it seemed, had been tempted enough that day.

"Thank you, Miss Elizabeth, for this interesting conversation. Since you have traveled this road many times, I shall assume I am not required to escort you to the road to Longbourn."

"Should I still think of you as ungentlemanly," said she, her laughter contradicting her words, "I could use this as a reason to think ill of you, for is it not polite to offer an escort to a helpless female!"

"Perhaps it is," said Darcy with a grin. "But I neither consider you helpless nor do I think any good could come from being discovered together."

"You are correct, of course," said Miss Elizabeth, her manner become more serious again. "My father has asked there be no contact between any of us and any of your family. In light of that fact, I shall wish you a good day, Mr. Darcy."

"Good day, Miss Elizabeth," said Darcy, nodding as she heeled her horse away.

In a day full of foolhardy actions, sitting on his horse, watching her until she disappeared in the distance may have been the most imprudent. Several emotions had ignited within Darcy's breast, stoking the admiration he already felt for her into a burning flame. Not only was the woman intelligent, her personality magnetic, but life shining in her eyes, the joy of life she illuminated for all to see like the sweetest ambrosia. Darcy could imagine becoming drunk with nothing more than her presence. He could imagine it very well.

The first meeting with Mr. Darcy was exactly that—the first. Elizabeth could not quite understand how it had come about, but something compelled her out of doors many times in the subsequent days, and on most of those she met with Mr. Darcy. It may have been the man had an uncanny sense of where she could be found, or maybe he had bribed one of Longbourn's servants to report her movements to him. Regardless, whether she walked to the boundary between estates, rode to Lambton, visited her favorite meadow, or meandered some long-forgotten trails about the neighborhood, Mr. Darcy was there, eager to meet and speak with her.

Elizabeth supposed she should feel guilty for disobeying her father's instructions. Obedience had never been one of Elizabeth's strengths, but she had always respected her father's authority. But she could not find it in herself to flee Mr. Darcy when perhaps she should. There was something about the gentleman that called to her, pleaded her to accept his overtures. She did not set out, intending to find the gentleman. Elizabeth did not think he was consciously searching for her either.

Over the course of those few meetings, however, Elizabeth came to realize that all her family's prejudice against the Darcy family was incorrect, at least regarding Mr. Fitzwilliam Darcy. It was nothing more than silliness, for Elizabeth came to know the man, their discussions illuminating his character to her, teaching her that this was a good man, one who was serious in the performance of his duties, but tender and true in the application of his affections. Soon, Elizabeth began to feel as if his affections might include her.

"Can you tell me about your family?" asked he one significant day when they had been speaking together for some time. Then he looked away in embarrassment and added: "The distance between our families is such that I have little knowledge of them, other than what I have observed. I would like . . . It would please me to learn more."

Flattered by his interest which she knew was no disguise, Elizabeth began to speak of the members of her family, from the baron with his quixotic sense of humor and learned ways, to her mother's focus on her family and upholding their position in society. When she reached her sisters, Elizabeth's smile grew warm as she considered Jane and the relationship they had always shared.

"Jane is an angel," said Elizabeth. "There is no other way to describe her."

Mr. Darcy laughed. "That is what Bingley says about your sister, Miss Elizabeth, so I find it amusing. Then again, I have often heard Bingley refer to any woman he admires as an angel."

"In Jane's case, he is correct. I have never met another with such intrinsic goodness as Jane." Elizabeth smiled and added: "If it were any other man, I might, perhaps, concern myself for Mr. Bingley's wandering heart, for I have also heard tales of his exploits. But having witnessed him with Jane, I believe his heart has found a place where it may rest for the remainder of his life, for he is entirely devoted to her."

"I did not mean to suggest he was fickle," replied Darcy. "It was clear within moments of learning of his intentions he had found the woman he meant to make his. I hope you did not think I was belittling their connection."

It had often been this way between them. Little comments with no ill intent were explained to ensure there was no confusion, for neither wished to offend the other. It was unsurprising that they would wish to avoid misinterpretation. On the other hand, Elizabeth could not decipher why it was so important they understand each other perfectly.

"No, Mr. Darcy—nothing was further from my mind. I am content knowing that Jane shall find her happiness and that Mary, also, is close to obtaining hers. Mr. Collins, my father's cousin, is expected to offer for Mary; I believe she means to accept him. Mary is like I am in her studious nature, but much more so. She is also more serious, which, I believe, will suit Mr. Collins very well.

"As for my two youngest sisters, Kitty and Lydia are more adventurous than the rest of us, but though they can become somewhat boisterous, they are, at heart, good girls. Kitty, though she is the elder, is the follower, while Lydia is the leader. Kitty enjoys music and plays the pianoforte very well, while Lydia is more inclined to the arts. Should you see some of her paintings, you would declare her talented."

Mr. Darcy paused for a moment, seeming to consider his words with care. "Your young sisters are bold."

"That is an understatement," replied Elizabeth with a laugh. "Both are often more fearless than I believe wise, particularly on Lydia's part. She pushes the boundaries of good behavior, but she is not improper. Both my sisters are still immature and require a little more growth, but I am certain they will obtain it as they grow."

"And what of Miss Elizabeth Bennet?" asked Darcy.

Elizabeth favored him with a smile which he returned without hesitation. "There is much of me I believe you already know, Mr. Darcy. I love music, but I don't practice as much as I should; I love books and reading; I am fond of nature, and love nothing better than a walk out of doors or a ride on my beloved mare; and I am fond of society.

"Now, that is enough of my family—can you tell me of yours?"

With a nod, Mr. Darcy began to explain something of his own family. His mother, Elizabeth knew, had passed away some years ago, and had left a great wound in his family which persisted to this day. Mr. Darcy the elder had been devoted to his wife and had taken her death hard, and though his sons had urged him to look for another companion, he had declared his intention to stay true to his lost love. The very notion appealed to the romantic in Elizabeth, filling her heart with admiration for this absent gentleman. Mr. Darcy informed her of his mother's family, and spoke of them with the warmest regards, asserting they were the humblest titled family he had ever know.

"As for my sister and brother," said Mr. Darcy, "Georgiana, as I am certain you have noticed, is shy, though she is sweet when you come to know her. The pianoforte is the most important thing in her life, though she is accomplished at other activities as well."

"Yes, Mr. Darcy—I can see that very well."

Mr. Darcy grinned. "Your reaction to meeting her was telling, Miss Elizabeth. Should the situation between our families change, it would benefit her to come to know you better. As for my brother, at times we have not got on at all. Alexander is everything I am not, for he is easy in society and possesses a way with the ladies that I have never had."

"You make him sound like quite the rake!"

Shaking his head, Mr. Darcy denied it, saying: "While I have always thought Alexander was less disciplined than he should be, he has never been a rake. Many of the tales told of him are exaggerated. Sometimes he has gambled and I would prefer a more proper attitude with the ladies, but he has always been scrupulously honest, even if he is not eager to accept responsibility for his actions. And if he loses somewhat at the gaming tables, he has never allowed himself to gamble away a fortune. Alexander has changed since he has come back to Pemberley, has acquired a hint of maturity I despaired of him ever gaining."

Elizabeth nodded, not responding. Though she had never thought the worst of the youngest Mr. Darcy—she did not know him, after all—

his meeting with Lydia had made her wonder. It was, perhaps, a surprise, but Elizabeth found herself trusting Mr. Darcy's account of his brother.

"What of your uncle?" asked Mr. Darcy, returning Elizabeth's attention. "You have not mentioned him."

"I have two close uncles, Mr. Darcy," said Elizabeth. "The younger, Mr. Edward Gardiner is the parson of Lambton. It has come to my attention you speak to his wife on occasion."

"Mrs. Gardiner is an excellent lady," replied Mr. Darcy.

"That she is," said Elizabeth. "As for David Gardiner, my other uncle, he is a good man. It is only that he is protective of us, and for that, I believe you can blame my father, who is not by any stretch of the imagination a taskmaster."

Mr. Darcy glanced at her and said: "The situation between your uncle and my brother is largely resolved."

There was a hint of a question in his tone, and Elizabeth nodded her agreement. "My uncle claims he has no quarrel with your brother. The current issue is he knows your brother's reputation and is uneasy because of his recent meeting with my sister."

"I do not believe Alexander meant any harm."

Elizabeth sighed. "Nor do I, Mr. Darcy. But since this resentment between our families continues to fester, I believe it would be best to keep us apart, and, in particular, keep Alexander and Lydia from meeting."

"With that, I cannot but agree, Miss Elizabeth."

Their last few words reminded both that their current meetings violated their fathers' decrees. Though Elizabeth did not see any harm in Mr. Darcy and had begun to esteem him, she knew she should not be meeting him in such a fashion. Thus, it was a short time later that they parted, each going their separate ways, likely with the same resolution of ending their meetings. For Elizabeth, the thought of giving up Mr. Darcy's society, even the secret encounters in which they had engaged, filled her with regret. But her father had commanded it, and Elizabeth knew she must obey at last.

CHAPTER XIII

*W*ithin a few days of Darcy's last meeting with Miss Elizabeth, another arrived at Pemberley to swell their family party.

Darcy had not intended it to be their last meeting, for the desire to meet her still burned in his breast, a fierce, bright flame he could never imagine extinguishing. Their conversation during that meeting had reminded him, however, that his father—and hers—had commanded that there be no contact between the two families. Darcy had always been a dutiful and obedient son and could not remember a time when he had defied his father's decrees. That was enough to keep him from seeking to meet Miss Elizabeth again.

It was fortunate, therefore, that his cousin arrived to provide a distraction. Fitzwilliam was, in some respects, like Alexander, though he had never been one to gamble. He was, perhaps, a little freer with his attentions toward the ladies than Darcy, but he was not cavalier. Moreover, he was an excellent man, one who had shown his mettle repeatedly in his service of the crown and his devotion to his family. Darcy had always been closer to his cousin than even his younger brother—Fitzwilliam was Darcy's truest friend, even more so than Bingley had been.

"I offer my thanks to you, Uncle," said Fitzwilliam after he had arrived and made himself presentable. "Your offer to host me at present is very much appreciated."

"We would not wish you to pine for your betrothed at Snowlock," said a laughing Alexander. "Perish the very thought!"

Fitzwilliam grinned at the younger Darcy. The two had always been close, though the age difference meant they were not as friendly as Darcy had always been with his cousin. But they were much alike in temperament, their sense of humor similar, their views of life, love, and what constituted happiness aligned.

"Perhaps someday *you* will discover the torture of being separated from your beloved, Alexander," said Fitzwilliam. "Until then you may laugh at me as much as you like. When that day comes, however, *I* shall laugh the loudest."

"There is no doubt in my mind you shall," replied Alexander.

The banter between the two more verbose members of the party was always amusing, and that day was no different. Throughout the afternoon they teased each other, their subjects ranging from the state of their love lives to outrageous stories of their exploits—which Fitzwilliam won without question, in Darcy's mind—to even some commentary about who the better horseman was. In this fashion they were all entertained until the supper hour arrived.

When they sat down to dinner that evening, the conversation continued to flow with ease. As Fitzwilliam had been heretofore a member of the army for close to a decade, the members of the Darcy family were quick to congratulate him on his change to civilian status.

"It has been a way of life for me since I left university," said Fitzwilliam in a candid moment during dinner. "In some ways, I miss it." The man paused and grinned. "Oh, I do not miss the chill of sleeping in a tent, being sent on errands on whatever whim by a commanding officer, and I shall certainly not miss being the target of French bayonets. But it *is* an adjustment, and one which shall take some time to make, I should think."

"I have always heard," said Alexander, "that there is nothing more exhilarating than being the target of another's guns, as long as their skills are poor."

Though Mr. Darcy reprimanded his son for such an unsuitable remark at the dinner table, Fitzwilliam grinned. "There is some truth to that. The problem is that sooner or later someone in the French army will teach their recruits how to shoot straight. Eventually, everyone's luck runs out. Though I was pleased to do my duty and serve the crown, I am not sad to leave the horrors of war behind. You were fortunate, Cousin, that you had an estate ready for you and did not need to seek a profession."

"Well do I know it," replied Alexander, nary a hint of nonchalance in his tone. "If I had, I doubt I would have chosen the army, regardless. I believe I would make a better parson than a soldier."

"And as you would not make a good parson," said Mr. Darcy, "the notion of what a poor soldier you would be causes one to shudder."

The mirth released at Mr. Darcy's sally encompassed them all, Alexander laughing the loudest. "That is the truth!"

"It is also beneficial for you," said Darcy, "that Lord Chesterfield is a vigorous man who will not require you to take over the estate business at once."

"No," replied Fitzwilliam. "Nor will I bother with all the political maneuvering in the House of Lords, for I shall not be an earl—I am more than happy to leave that to my future son. The estate business I assume he will transfer to me after the wedding. Until then, I mean to enjoy my freedom."

The family voiced their approval, after which Fitzwilliam turned to Alexander and fixed him with an appraising look. "I will own my surprise at hearing that you were returning to Pemberley. Has the situation improved? I cannot imagine the incessant and silly quarrel with the Bennet family has abated to any great degree."

Since Alexander did not seem interested in responding, it fell to Darcy and his father to relate the reasons for Alexander's return. Fitzwilliam listened, curiosity alive in his countenance, and he nodded when the explanation was complete.

"That is reasonable," said he. A grin came over his countenance and he said: "I have heard my father has begun to turn estate matters at Snowlock and the other properties over to James, though his time of freedom lasted longer than yours."

"But James has been managing the estates attached to the viscountcy for several years," reminded Mr. Darcy.

"That is true," replied Fitzwilliam. "But those estates are not as large."

"I think, in James's case," said Darcy, "the bigger issue will be learning to deal with the politicking which goes with the earldom."

"I would agree," said Fitzwilliam with a nod. "As a viscount, he is not immune to it, but he has not had the burden of the family's political agenda. Someday he will be a leader of our faction in parliament."

Fitzwilliam then turned back to Alexander. "And what of Mr. Gardiner? Has he not stormed Pemberley's walls, baying for your blood?"

"Mr. Gardiner is more level-headed than that," said Mr. Darcy. "If it were a Bennet, that may very well have happened."

Darcy wished to speak up, to inform his father he was wrong, but the words would not come. He had little desire for his relations to learn of his meetings with Miss Elizabeth, and it would be difficult to explain the reasons for his thoughts should he speak. Even so, Darcy could not but think his father was wrong. The baron was, by all accounts and what Darcy had observed of him on occasion, a mild, scholarly sort of man, and though he had only seen Mr. Collins once, he could not imagine the former parson behaving in the manner his father suggested.

Though Darcy hesitated to voice his concern, Fitzwilliam was not thus afflicted. "If you wish my opinion, I think the matter is a silly one. I cannot say I know the baron to any great degree, but I have spoken with him on occasion. My father says he is perfectly unassuming."

The frown this opinion produced from the elder Darcy did not miss Fitzwilliam's attention, but he did not make a response. The Darcy family knew their close relations, though they rarely associated with the Bennets, would not shun them because the Darcys wished it. Fitzwilliam's family thought the dispute was sheer nonsense.

"Of more importance," said Mr. Darcy, changing the subject and giving the impression the Bennet family was a distasteful subject, "is the forthcoming visit of our de Bourgh relations."

"Ah, yes," said Fitzwilliam, grinning at them all. "It is fortunate that I am to be graced with the presence of my demanding aunt while I am staying with you all. I am certain I shall be subjected to an inquisition the moment she walks through the door, the subject of which will be the fact that England has yet to defeat the French Tyrant. No doubt, the fault will be mine!"

They all laughed, knowing that while the prediction may be silliness, Lady Catherine was capable of making them all miserable within moments of entering. Alexander, however, set them all straight on that point.

"If you think that, I must believe you insensible, Cousin. You know the first words out of her mouth will concern William and Anne's forthcoming marriage."

The understated laughter became open hilarity, for they were all aware of the truth of Alexander's words. Mr. Darcy, however, was less amused than the others, for while he chuckled, his countenance soon turned dark.

"Should Catherine attempt to do so, I shall inform her she will not be welcome to stay with us. I have no desire to listen to weeks of her insisting on the match that no one other that she desires."

"Thank you, Father," said Darcy. "I would appreciate Lady Catherine receiving a set down on the matter, for I have no desire to listen to it myself."

"Come now, Darcy," jested Fitzwilliam, "a spring wedding would be just the thing. Of course, as it is more Lady Catherine's wish than anyone else, perhaps *she* may take the bride's position for herself, for she would not wish for her daughter to take all the attention!"

Laughter erupted again, and this time Mr. Darcy did not stint in allowing his mirth free reign. The amusing picture of his aunt, a similar age of his father, taking her daughter's place, or leading them both into the church by the ears was much more amusing than it should have been. In this manner they spent the rest of the evening, their conversation so engaging that Darcy forgot about Miss Elizabeth. Perhaps he only thought of her once every other minute, instead of every minute of the evening, but it was a start.

"What do you think of this matter of the Bennets and the Darcys?"

Lady Charlotte Lucas, the young woman with whom Fitzwilliam was walking, gave him a curious glance. "Has that old matter reared its ugly head yet again?"

"Nothing in particular of which I am aware," replied Fitzwilliam. "The subject came up at the dinner table after I arrived last night, and I had wondered if something *had* happened to raise tempers yet again."

Lady Charlotte grew silent and reflective, which was agreeable to Fitzwilliam, for though he loved to speak with her, to hear her voice and enjoy her opinions, it was no hardship to observe her. She was a lovely woman, tall and graceful, her form slender and possessing all the right curves, her countenance handsome. Her head was crowned with a mass of glorious golden curls tied back in a simple knot, for she was no pretentious woman concerned about appearances. Darcy had always displayed a preference for women with darker coloring, mahogany hair and dark brown eyes, but Fitzwilliam men preferred their women to look like the Norse goddesses of old: blue of eye and blonde of hair.

And this woman was soon to be his. Fitzwilliam could hardly believe the good fortune his life had taken. At one time, he had loved this woman from afar—had adored her from their first meeting—

worshipped her, convinced she would never see him as anything other than a poor soldier. A visit to Pemberley the previous year had changed all that, had given him some hope that she might return his feelings. It was then, during a visit at Christmastide, that he had taken his chance, had proposed, and to his everlasting joy, she had accepted him.

"There is nothing of which I am aware," replied Lady Charlotte at last. "I have heard there was a confrontation in Lambton between Mr. Gardiner and your younger cousin, but the details are unknown to society, and neither family will speak of it."

"Do you think they will come to blows again?"

"Elizabeth does not think so." At Fitzwilliam's interested glance, Lady Charlotte was induced to be explicit. "As you are aware, Miss Elizabeth Bennet is among my closest friends, and I consider her sister Jane a good friend too. I have had occasion to speak with the eldest Bennet sisters on the subject, and they have both assured me their uncle holds no grudges in the matter. It was an accident—he is well healed, and little inclined to pursue vengeance."

Fitzwilliam laughed. "I wonder what my relations will say to know my future wife is an intimate of their evil enemies, the Bennets."

"It is of little significance to me what your relations think," said Lady Charlotte, her gaze challenging, daring him to disagree. "And they should already know, for I have never hidden it."

"Of course, it is not," said Fitzwilliam. "I neither wish to compel you to throw them off or disapprove of those whom you call friends, my love."

"Then what is your purpose for raising the subject?"

"I am not certain," confessed Fitzwilliam. "There was something . . . . Well, I do not know. Something off about Darcy's behavior last night."

Now he had his betrothed's full attention. "In what way?"

With a shrug, Fitzwilliam said: "Perhaps it was not off. It is simply that Darcy, though he does not say much on the subject, has always followed his father in condemning the Bennets. Yesterday, however, he seemed almost . . . restrained. It was as if he did not wish to say anything negative about the Bennets, though he has never been so discreet in the past."

"Is it because he has realized continued enmity is futile?"

"I don't know. It may be." Fitzwilliam paused and considered the matter. "It may be nothing, for my cousin can be taciturn at the best of times. But I know Darcy well—as well as any other man, I will wager.

There is nothing, in particular, I can point to and say his behavior is strange, but the notion there is something happening of which I am not aware will not leave me."

"Is this where you inform me you intend to follow your cousin to determine what he is doing?" teased Lady Charlotte.

Fitzwilliam guffawed and captured her hand in his, bringing it to his lips. "That is a brilliant idea, my sweet."

Had he been so inclined, Fitzwilliam might have predicted her reaction in advance. "I hardly think that is proper, Anthony."

"No, I suppose it would not be," replied Anthony. "It is not as if I suspect him of fraternizing with one of the Bennet sisters, so there is little reason to do so anyway."

"Now that is a solution which would heal the breach between the families," said Lady Charlotte with a sigh. "Marriage has healed many a feud in the past."

"I doubt they would ever be in a position to marry their scions to each other," muttered Fitzwilliam. "While I cannot speak of the Bennets' feelings on the matter, my relations would rather abandon Pemberley itself than have anything to do with the Bennets."

"And when they attend the same events," added Lady Charlotte, "it seems as if there are two armed camps, for they will not approach each other."

The comment set off the genesis of an idea in Fitzwilliam's mind, and he considered it for a moment. Armed camps were something with which he was familiar, and there were ways to bridge them. Should the Bennet and Darcy families come together in a situation where they must have *some* contact, would that not force them to be civil with each other? Then, could that not be used to affect a thawing of their relations?

"Do the Bennets and Darcys often attend events together?"

"There are certain intricacies of the neighborhood's society," said Lady Charlotte. "Each family has those with whom they prefer to interact, and most events are planned with one or the other clique invited. At assemblies, they come together, of course, but as those in Lambton's public halls tend to be large, they avoid interacting."

"Then what if we put them in a situation more intimate, where they will have no choice but to interact?" At Lady Charlotte's uncomprehending look, Fitzwilliam elaborated. "Do you not plan a ball every year at Lucas Manor? Your father's house is large, but the ballroom is not as large as the assembly rooms. Who do you usually invite?"

"We snub neither family by inviting the other," said Lady Charlotte, her frown suggesting she understood what he was saying. "Having said that, I cannot remember the last time the Bennets and Darcys attended together. Last year the Bennets made for London early, and were absent."

"This year both are still in Derbyshire," said Fitzwilliam with a grin. "Unless one of them decamps in haste—and I know it will not be the Darcys, as our de Bourgh relations are to join us at Pemberley—they cannot avoid each other unless they wish to offend your father."

Lady Charlotte laughed. "Are you not concerned about the breakout of war in England?"

"The Bennets, by all account, have nothing but daughters in their ranks, except for the youngest, who is still too young to attend. I can control my cousins."

"It is an audacious notion, and it might fail in a spectacular fashion."

"It also may be a means of *beginning* to shape a rapprochement between them."

Though she thought about it for a moment, Lady Charlotte smiled at length and shrugged. "Yes, I suppose it may be possible."

"Then it is decided," said Fitzwilliam with a grin.

Kitty Bennet was not the most noticeable of the Bennet sisters. Then again, Kitty had never attempted to be noticeable. Aware of her strengths, Kitty had always contented herself with allowing others to garner attention, for she was not comfortable with it—in this, she was like her elder sister, Mary.

It was this, in part, that made her closeness with Lydia work so well. Lydia, far from avoiding attention, reveled in it, often going out of her way to ensure she received it. Lydia was the acknowledged leader of the pair and Kitty the follower, for she knew she had no talent for leading.

There were times, however, when Kitty wished her younger sister was not so brash. Not that Lydia was improper. Lydia knew how to behave, knew what was expected of her as a young woman and daughter of a baron. It was only that Lydia seemed to delight in pushing those boundaries, in testing how far she could bend the rules of polite society. Kitty could not understand it, for though the greater force of Lydia's personality often swept her along in her sister's wake, Kitty would never have gone so far herself.

This business with the Darcys was, in Kitty's opinion, a matter which they should not test, for there was too much opportunity for misunderstanding, and with it, a greater possibility for trouble. And yet, Lydia, with her usual boldness, could not help but push. A good example happened that morning in Lambton.

The Bennet sisters often went thither, especially the younger ones. They would congregate with their friends there, patronize the shops for news, amusement, and purchase whatever caught their fancy and often visited their Aunt Madeline at the parsonage. On that morning Kitty was not certain what had led them there, but when they met one of the Darcy family, they did not depart at once as their father had instructed.

It happened as they were outside the milliners, looking inside the window at a bonnet Lydia had pointed out. They debated the merits of the hat for some moments, Lydia thinking it was fine, while Kitty did not like it at all. Then Lydia seemed to go still for a moment, though Kitty could see nothing extraordinary to affect her so, and then she turned.

"Well, well, if it is not Mr. Alexander Darcy, gracing the streets of Lambton again with his presence."

Turning, Kitty saw that it *was* Mr. Darcy, passing the street on the other side. That he had seen them was clear in the glances he shot at them, but it seemed the recent confrontations had taught him caution, for he endeavored to pass them without acknowledging Lydia's words.

"You see, Kitty?" said Lydia loudly. "That is the problem. There is no room for civility. Until we can be civil with one another, we shall remain at odds."

"That is a sentiment with which I happen to agree."

The sisters turned to look at the gentleman, noting he had stopped and was now regarding them. Though uncomfortable, Kitty noticed Lydia meeting his gaze, as bold as ever.

"Then you confess the Darcy family is in the wrong?" asked Lydia, arching an eyebrow at Mr. Darcy.

"I believe I said no such thing," refuted the gentleman, though his pleasant expression never wavered. "It seems to me, Miss Lydia, that no one is at fault in the dispute. Or perhaps it is more correct to say we are *all* at fault."

In spite of herself, Kitty was interested in why he would say such a thing, and Lydia was no less intrigued. "On what do you base that opinion?"

"Why, on the length of the dispute. There is no one alive who remembers how it began; thus, I would suggest it is that person or persons who are responsible, not anyone of us who must live with the consequences. To the best of my knowledge, none of us have offended anyone from the opposite side."

"Did you not injure my uncle?" asked Lydia. While Kitty might have thought her sister would pose such a question with an air of accusation, Lydia's tone was light, almost unconcerned.

It seemed Mr. Darcy saw it too, for his response was not as defensive as it might have been. "Perhaps you do not know, Miss Lydia, but we both shared a certain level of blame for that incident. Mr. Gardiner himself has told me he bears me no ill will."

At that moment, a young woman of the neighborhood, someone Kitty had seen but never met, passed them on the street, her head turned in interest toward them. Reminded of her father's decree, Kitty thought it was best they departed, prompting her to tug on Lydia's sleeve.

"Lydia, remember what Papa said."

Though Lydia appeared about to dispute Kitty's assertion, Mr. Darcy spoke up: "Yes, I believe that would be for the best." The gentleman smiled at Kitty, adding: "If your father is anything like mine, he has warned you away from all Darcys."

"Why, does your father warn you from all Darcys?" asked Lydia.

Mr. Darcy roared with laughter. "Oh, you are a saucy one, Miss Lydia. I can see a man must be sharp to keep up with you."

On what looked like the impulse of the moment, Mr. Darcy crossed to them and caught up Lydia's hand, bowing and kissing it. Then he did the same with Kitty, winking outrageously.

"I should not like to make trouble for such interesting ladies as yourselves, so I shall take myself from your presence. Until next time."

With one further bow, the gentleman turned and walked away, his stride brisk, the sound of a whistled tune floating back to them. In a moment he left their sight, leaving the two bemused girls to turn and make their way home. Kitty's bemusement lasted only a moment, for she soon turned to her sister and scolded her.

"Lydia! You know we are not to speak to the Darcys. Why do you persist in doing so?"

"As I informed you before, I like to tease Mr. Darcy," was Lydia's blithe reply.

When Kitty continued to glare, Lydia threw her hands up. "Very well! I shall not speak to them anymore."

"You said that before," reminded Kitty.

"I did," was Lydia's careless reply. "This time I shall keep my word, though I do not know why we should avoid such a charming man as Mr. Darcy."

Then Lydia fell silent and stalked on ahead, leaving Kitty to hurry to catch up. The way Lydia had phrased her final comment was enough to make Kitty suspicious, for she thought Lydia had no intention of keeping her promise.

CHAPTER XIV

$\mathcal{C}$onsidering the expected arrival of Lady Catherine and her daughter that day, Darcy decided a morning ride would be just the thing to prepare himself to endure his aunt. Thus, he had his mount ready and was in the saddle early, eager to escape for a time.

As the fields and hills of Pemberley flew past the speeding mount, Darcy considered what Lady Catherine's arrival meant for the family. Though she was family, the woman was difficult to bear, being both dictatorial and insistent on her favorite wish being gratified. Had Darcy been at all of a mind to grant her wish, she still would not have seen its successful completion, for Anne was as little inclined to marry Darcy as the reverse.

Lady Catherine, however, could not see this. While she did not speak of the matter to the exclusion of all other subjects, her conversation was directed thither more often than Darcy might wish, a circumstance which made her society intolerable. It was Darcy's great relief that his father still lived and had never been inclined to bow to Lady Catherine's demands, for Darcy could not imagine what she would be like if his father, instead of his mother, had passed on!

Darcy enjoyed riding and indulged often, for he found himself soothed by the pounding of the horse's hooves on the turf, the feel of the wind rushing through his hair. The air that morning was a little brisk, made colder with the quick movement of man and beast, and soon Darcy felt his cheeks becoming cold and his ears lose feeling. But he pressed on, enjoying the ride otherwise.

Though Darcy traveled with no specific destination in mind, he rode the boundaries of Pemberley, looking down on the valley below through the trees, wondering at the beauty of his family estate. At one point he came close to the border with the road that led to Lambton, but being in no mood to encounter anyone, he skirted the village and continued on.

Then he steered his mount into the little meadow in the triangle near the borders of Longbourn and Netherfield. Miss Elizabeth Bennet was not there.

With a sigh, Darcy turned his horse away and pointed him back toward Pemberley in the distance, trying to understand why he was so disappointed he was not to see her that day. Had he not determined it was best to avoid the woman, to submit to his father's edict and not tempt fate? Darcy did not know what to think of the sudden longing which welled up within him to see Miss Elizabeth again. Was he beginning to fall in love with the temptress?

Darcy could not be certain. Thoughts of the woman warmed him and he often considered her when least expected, marveling over her perfections, or recalling some bit of conversation they had exchanged. Never having considered himself a romantic man, Darcy could not quite determine how he felt about being lost to a woman's power. What he did know was that it would be exquisite torture to lose his heart to the young woman, for he did not know how his love could ever be expressed, let alone returned. It was just as well he had not come across her, for no good could come of continuing to meet her. At least, that was what Darcy told himself.

At length, his mount hanging its head in weariness, Darcy walked into the yard at Pemberley, making his way toward the stables, feeling as worn out as his trusty horse. His exhaustion was as much because of the thoughts swirling about in his head as it was the exertions of the morning. There he met Fitzwilliam, who had just come out of the house.

"Ho, Darcy!" called he in greeting. "I see you have returned. Was there estate business to attend to this morning?"

"Nothing of note," replied Darcy.

He dismounted and led the weary animal into the building, noting as it began to pick up at the smell of oats and hay which permeated the stables. No doubt the stallion would appreciate a hint of water to go along with the expected sustenance.

"It seems you have ridden your mount hard," observed Fitzwilliam. "Are you attempting to escape from something, or did your horse slip your control?"

"Do you not enjoy an occasional gallop yourself?" asked Darcy.

Fitzwilliam regarded him for a moment before saying: "Yes, I do. But it seems to me you have been a little . . . I am not sure, to be honest, but a little off of late. Has something been affecting you?"

"Nothing in particular," said Darcy, though the sight of a beautiful young woman with laughing eyes rose in his mind. To cover this, Darcy continued about his tasks, rubbing his mount down with wool. "You need not have any concern for me, Fitzwilliam. I am well."

"I have noted my brother riding often since my return to Pemberley," came the voice of Alexander. Darcy looked up to see his brother standing by the stall's entrance, leaning against the jam, looking at them with amusement.

"It is nothing more than my usual habit," replied Darcy, hoping to keep a defensive note from his voice. "When have you ever known me to remain sedentary in the house when I may be out of doors?"

"That is true," said Alexander, his manner showing he had not much interest in the subject.

Completing his tasks, Darcy turned and exited the stall, pulling his brother and cousin along with him. What they were doing there, or whether they had been waiting for him he could not say, but Darcy ignored it for the moment. If he did not comment further, perhaps they would forget the matter altogether.

"You know," said Fitzwilliam as they walked, "I have not seen Bingley about since I came. That is odd, for he is always nearby."

"When you put it that way," said Alexander with a snicker, "you make him sound like a puppy."

Fitzwilliam snorted. "That is not a bad description, but I mean no such thing. Darcy has always been close to him, so it surprises me I have not seen him since I arrived."

"That would be because Bingley has committed great treachery!" said Alexander, a hint of the dramatic in his tone. Darcy scowled at his brother, but Alexander paid no notice, not that he had expected he would.

"Betrayal?" asked Fitzwilliam, apparently catching Alexander's tone and grinning in response to the joke. "In what way has Darcy's most loyal follower betrayed him?"

Taking the steps to the manor two at a time, Darcy attempted to leave his tormentors behind. It was all in vain, however, as they simply followed him, and from thence to the grand staircase and up to his room where it was his intention to change.

"It seems our Bingley has grown a backbone and defied William by paying attention to Miss Jane Bennet."

Fitzwilliam whistled low and said: "That is serious, indeed. Good for Bingley! I never would have thought he had it in him!"

"I only hope he does not regret his experience," grunted Darcy as he ducked into his room, hoping his companions would not follow him. It was a vain hope, for they were hard on his heels.

"Regret?" echoed Fitzwilliam. "Though I will own to not knowing the Bennet family well, I seem to recall Miss Jane Bennet is a lovely young lady and kind to everyone she meets. You do not suppose she would stoop to hurting Bingley, do you?"

"William believes she has drawn him in," supplied Alexander.

"That is a bag of moonshine! What motive could the daughter of a baron have for drawing in a man of Bingley's social background? The Bingleys are new money, however you look at it, and a decided step down for Miss Bennet. Unless there is some issue with insolvency."

"None of which I am aware," replied Alexander.

"Nor would I have expected any such difficulty," said Fitzwilliam. "Lord Arundel is a scholarly man, one not given to gaming or the like, and his son is but ten years of age. While it is possible some investment might have failed, leaving financial difficulties, the Bennets still possess Longbourn, which appears to be a profitable estate. Thus, the only reason Miss Bennet would encourage Bingley is for pure inclination."

The way Fitzwilliam regarded him Darcy knew it demanded a response. As Snell, his valet, pulled Darcy's jacket from his shoulders and untied his cravat, Darcy gave his cousin a grudging nod.

"Yes, that is the truth, Fitzwilliam. The baron is experiencing no difficulties of which I am aware, and Bingley is besotted with Miss Bennet."

"Then you can have nothing to say on the matter."

"I *have* nothing to say on the matter," Darcy replied, his response shorter than he had intended. "But it does not follow that I must approve." Darcy's own interest in Miss Bennet's younger sister gave the lie to this assertion, though he attempted to tamp down on his thoughts.

"No, I suppose it does not," replied Fitzwilliam. "But I would remind you of this, Darcy: Bingley has been a good friend of yours for many years now. It would be foolish of you to throw away that friendship because of this silly dispute with the Bennet family."

Fitzwilliam turned and departed, and after a moment, upon giving him a significant look, Alexander did likewise. Darcy knew they were correct, for even if he did not possess these confusing feelings for Miss Elizabeth, what was it to him who Bingley courted and married? This dispute with the Bennets was coloring everything the Darcy family said or did, and the opinion it should cease was growing in Darcy's heart every day.

When Darcy descended the stairs, his thoughts still consumed by the situation with Bingley, he discovered a most unwelcome visitor, one who could often be found at Pemberley of late.

"Good morning, Mr. Darcy. How wonderful it is to see you this morning."

Miss Bingley, who had spoken, looked on him with shining eyes full of yearning, and for a moment Darcy wondered if this was what a side of beef felt like when watched by a pack of hungry dogs. Georgiana, who had been sitting with Miss Bingley, rolled her eyes, while Alexander and Fitzwilliam grinned at him.

"Yes, Darcy," said Fitzwilliam with a wide smirk. "Miss Bingley is visiting this morning. Is it not wonderful to see her here today?"

The beaming smile with which Miss Bingley regarded him suggested she had not caught the hint of irony or the note of mocking in Fitzwilliam's tone. Then again, the woman was adept at seeing and hearing that which she wished to see and hear, so it was not at all surprising. Knowing it would be a long visit, Darcy greeted Miss Bingley and situated himself as far away from her as he could and remain polite.

It was no more than five minutes later when the sound of voices interrupted their visit. Then the elder Darcy led Lady Catherine and Anne into the room, prompting those within to stand. Darcy had not counted on the early arrival of his family, but the thought struck him that exchanging Miss Bingley's company for Lady Catherine's was akin to escaping Scylla, only to run afoul of Charybdis.

"Lady Catherine," said Darcy, serving as spokesman for them all. "It is a surprise to see you; we were not expecting you until late this afternoon."

"Fitzwilliam," said Lady Catherine—she was the only member of the family who never called him by the diminutive of his name, instead preferring to use his full name. "Anne and I made good time yesterday and stopped in Derby. From thence it was a short ride to Pemberley."

"It is a short journey, indeed, from Derby. Welcome to Pemberley."

The family members long sundered exchanged greetings—the Darcys had not been in the de Bourghs' company since the previous Easter. While this was going on, Miss Bingley was watching the scene, eager to make the newcomers' acquaintance.

"I see you have a visitor this morning," said Lady Catherine, eying Miss Bingley. The woman puffed herself in pride at being noticed, and even more so when Lady Catherine requested an introduction, to which Georgiana did the honors.

"Bingley, Bingley," said Lady Catherine in thought. "Is that not the name of that friend of yours from university?"

"The same," said Darcy. "Miss Bingley is my friend's younger sister."

Though Miss Bingley beamed at the attention Lady Catherine was showing her, Darcy knew it would not last, for Lady Catherine had definite ideas about the right sort of people. This became clear as soon as the lady opened her mouth.

"Then it must be a privilege to receive the Darcys' attention, for those of your background can not expect such favor. You should return to your home, for now is a time for family."

"Catherine," said Mr. Darcy in a warning tone, "please do not order about my daughter's visitor as if Pemberley was your home."

"It is no trouble, Mr. Darcy," said Miss Bingley, showing remarkable composure Darcy would not have expected from her. "Of course, you wish to congregate as a family. I shall return to Netherfield and visit Georgiana again another day."

The woman made her good-byes, with affection to Georgiana, reserved to Lady Catherine and Anne, and friendliness with the rest of the family, and departed. It was clear Mr. Darcy was not happy with his sister by marriage, but she spoke before he could open his mouth.

"It does no good to encourage closeness with the lower classes, Georgiana," said Lady Catherine, fixing her niece with a gimlet eye. "Remember your lineage."

"That is enough, Catherine," said Mr. Darcy. "My daughter may count whomever she chooses as a friend, for it is none of your concern."

It was clear Lady Catherine would like to dispute the matter, but she receded, albeit with little grace. "Yes, well, Anne and I cannot be happier to be here. Perhaps this will finally be the year we shall have a happy announcement."

As one the company groaned, though Mr. Darcy was not at all amused. "Let us be clear on one subject, Catherine. There is to be no mention of your desire for William and Anne to marry, for I will not have it. If they were inclined to each other I should support them — as they are not, I will not have you browbeating them into obliging you."

"Thank heavens!" exclaimed Anne before her mother could muster a response. They all turned to her with surprise, but Anne laughed and reached out to touch Darcy's arm. "I hope I have not offended you, Cousin, for it was not my intention. We are not suited, for you are far too solemn for me."

"There is no offense," said Darcy before Lady Catherine could interject. "My feelings are identical to yours."

"Then that is the end of the matter," said Mr. Darcy. "With this behind us, I hope we enjoy an excellent visit together."

Lady Catherine, they all knew, was not willing to confess defeat just yet, but for the moment she seemed to have been silenced. How long that would last Darcy could not say. Darcy elected to ignore her and enjoy the reprieve.

It was a common occurrence for the Bennet sisters to go into Lambton to assist their aunt in her various charities. Mrs. Gardiner was active in the community, not only as the parson's wife but also in society, with those of the town who were lacking in necessities. There were several groups active in the neighborhood, and they provided many provisions, such as food and clothing to those in need. Lady Margaret had always thought it beneficial for her girls to become involved themselves, informing them when they protested that it helped build character to assist those less fortunate and see how they lived their lives.

On a particular day, the Bennet sisters made their way to Lambton to join their aunt in sewing clothes for some of the tenant children in need in the neighborhood. While Elizabeth had never enjoyed sewing, as her stitches were not so neat and even as Jane's, she enjoyed visiting with her. It was during this bit of visiting that Elizabeth let slip an important piece of information, thereafter relieved her sisters were too busy in their own conversations to overhear.

"I have not seen you as much of late in Lambton," observed Mrs. Gardiner. "Have the attractions of this fair town paled?"

"No, Aunt," said Elizabeth.

"Then I am delighted to hear it, for you know my opinion of Lambton. Though I have lived nowhere else, I think it the dearest place in the world."

It was an oft-stated view, and Elizabeth had heard it many times, not that she disagreed. "No, Lambton has not lost its charms. But I cannot always be coming and going to and from Lambton."

Mrs. Gardiner regarded her with interest. "Have other matters occupied your time?"

With that prompting, Elizabeth turned her attention to the various events of late, Mr. Bingley's continued efforts in wooing Jane, mixed with some of her doings at home. Elizabeth even spoke of their game of sardines, which provoked Mrs. Gardiner to laughter as she imagined her serious brother-in-law engaging in a child's game. They also spoke of the confrontation between Mr. Gardiner and the younger Mr. Darcy, a conversation that led to Elizabeth's error.

"I am glad nothing came of it," said Mrs. Gardiner, referring to the separation of the combatants that day outside the bookshop. "Though I would see the breach between the families healed, there can be no good for David to confront Mr. Darcy in the middle of the street."

"That is true," said Elizabeth. She paused, concentrating on a bit of tricky stitching, her guard down when she observed: "I wish my family would come to see, as I have, the Darcy family is not all bad."

Mrs. Gardiner's level look did not capture Elizabeth's attention at once, so for a moment, she did not realize she had made an error. "How have you 'come to know' the Darcy family, Lizzy?"

The belated comprehension of her mistake led Elizabeth to dissemble. "It is only that I now understand we should not be arguing in this way. Georgiana Darcy, whom we met in the bookshop, is a shy and unassuming girl, and the rest of the family do not seem to be as reprehensible as we Bennets have always thought."

Mrs. Gardiner's look did not abate. "As you know, I have spoken with Miss Darcy several times, as I have with her brother. I cannot but agree with you. However, your statement speaks to some further knowledge than a short meeting in a shop."

Though Elizabeth twisted and turned in a metaphoric sense and tried to avoid Mrs. Gardiner's inquiry, it soon became clear there was no way to evade her questions. Before she spoke, Elizabeth glanced about at her sisters, noting that Kitty and Lydia were chattering amongst themselves, while Jane and Mary were also speaking softly. As the younger sisters were closer to them than the elder, Elizabeth felt confident they would not overhear.

"I . . ." Elizabeth hesitated, uncertain how to explain before deciding there was nothing she could do except say it. "I have met Mr.

Darcy several times during my walks and rides."

"Met Mr. Darcy?" echoed Mrs. Gardiner. "I was not even aware you *know* Mr. Darcy, Lizzy." Mrs. Gardiner's eyes narrowed and she said: "Of which Mr. Darcy are we speaking? Not the younger man."

"No," replied Elizabeth, feeling her cheeks heating with embarrassment. "It was Mr. Fitzwilliam Darcy."

"Please tell me all, Lizzy," said Mrs. Gardiner, though it was more of a demand than a request.

Hesitant though she was, Elizabeth related her initial meeting with Mr. Darcy at Oakham Mount and riding back to the road to Longbourn with him during their next encounter. Then she covered their subsequent meetings, whether while walking the boundaries of Longbourn, the meetings in the meadow, and even a brief conversation in Lambton. As she spoke, Elizabeth's aunt listened with growing astonishment, and when she had finished relating her tale, Mrs. Gardiner was not slow to voice her opinion.

"Lizzy, have you considered the consequences of your actions?" When Elizabeth looked away, Mrs. Gardiner said: "Your father, at the very least, will not be pleased. I might have expected this disobedience from Lydia, but never from you."

"Lydia is headstrong," said Elizabeth, feeling the need to defend her sister, "but she is a good girl."

"It appears obstinacy is not only a part of your sister's character," said Mrs. Gardiner, her pointed look making Elizabeth feel uncomfortable.

"I know of my father's displeasure should this become known," said Elizabeth. "However, I shall also point out I have realized through our meetings I have misjudged Mr. Darcy. The gentleman is not a devil as my family had always taken all Darcys to be."

Mrs. Gardiner's mien softened. "Yes, that is a definite benefit of such meetings. If only your family could see the Darcys as they truly are, perhaps this disagreement could be put to rest."

"It is not only the Bennets," said Elizabeth. "I have it on good authority that the Darcy family feels the same way about *us* as we do about *them*."

Mr. Gardiner nodded but did not speak, after which Elizabeth added: "You need not worry, Aunt, for I have not met Mr. Darcy for some days now. It is my conjecture that he has realized, as much as I, that there is little reason to continue to dispute between us, but he also understands he cannot disobey *his* father as I cannot disobey *mine*."

Once again Mrs. Gardiner regarded Elizabeth closely, though she did not speak for the moment. Though Elizabeth wondered what her aunt might say, she would not have expected it when it came.

"Elizabeth, have you considered the possibility that this hostility between your families might be resolved by your connection to Mr. Darcy?"

For a moment Elizabeth could not understand her aunt's meaning. Then the inference became clear and she gasped. It was fortunate her sisters were still engaged in their own conversations, for Elizabeth thought she might have been asked to explain herself.

"Can you mean what I think you mean?" asked Elizabeth, though her words were little more than a squeak. It seemed that outburst did garner her sisters' attention. Mrs. Gardiner smiled, however, and made some jest—Elizabeth did not even hear it—prompting her sisters to return to their own conversations.

"I am not in love with Mr. Darcy," hissed Elizabeth, fixing her aunt with a glare.

"There must be something there, Lizzy," said Mrs. Gardiner. "Otherwise, I do not believe you would put your father's instructions aside with such ease."

The observation brought Elizabeth up short, bereft of any response. Mrs. Gardiner smiled and clasped Elizabeth's hand. "I would ask you to take great care, Elizabeth. It is not my contention that you *are* in love with the gentleman, but I would abjure you to ask yourself *why* you have chosen to put aside your father's commands. Further, if you meet with Mr. Darcy again, try to discover the gentleman's feelings. I do not ask you to throw yourself into his arms; I ask you to understand what you are about, what the gentleman is about."

Soon after, the Bennet sisters departed. They took some time to peruse the shops in Lambton, separating to visit those locations of interest to each sister. Elizabeth had no thoughts for her sisters and had little attention for any of her activities. Most of her remaining time in Lambton she wandered deep in thought. But there was little resolution she could find in her reminiscences. Confusion reigned, and Elizabeth did not know how to resolve it.

CHAPTER XV

*L*ife with Lady Catherine at Pemberley was a constant state of vexation, for the woman was not shy about stating her opinion whenever the opportunity presented itself. Though Darcy had always held his aunt in a certain exasperated affection, her continual direction, advice, and comments about how *wonderful* it would be if he were to do his duty and propose to Anne could not help but grate on his nerves. His father, though it was clear she also annoyed him left well enough alone, as she was not trumpeting the engagement to all and sundry. This left Darcy with little option other than to escape from the house as much as he was able.

On a day not long after his aunt's arrival, Darcy rode out in the company of his cousin and brother, and the three riders, after following the paths of the estate for a time, decided to make for Lambton. The sounds of the horses' hooves against the roads, accompanied by the swaying gait of his mount soothed Darcy, helping him forget the stresses of his aunt's presence. Then a strain of another sort presented itself.

"Bingley!" exclaimed his cousin as they approached the town. Darcy, who had been lost in thought, had not noticed his friend, and he looked up, noting Bingley's presence and his smile of pleasure for

Fitzwilliam. The two men came together and shook hands, both at their irrepressible best.

"Fitzwilliam. I heard you were to return to Pemberley, though not that you had arrived."

"It is even worse, Bingley," said Fitzwilliam in a low voice, as if imparting a secret. "Pemberley, you see has been taken by invaders from Kent, pitiless mercenaries intent upon carrying my cousin away captive for their nefarious schemes!"

Bingley laughed, though the look he shot at Darcy betrayed a hint of nervousness.

"Come now, Fitzwilliam," said Alexander, guiding his horse forward to make his own greetings. "You know only *one* invader is determined on such despicable actions. Anne has the sense to wish nothing to do with William for a husband!"

The three men laughed while Darcy looked on, uncertain what he should do. Little desire though he had to end his friendship with Bingley, they also had not spoken since Bingley had announced his intentions for the eldest Bennet, outside of his few words in the bookshop. How he should act, Darcy could not decipher.

"It is my understanding you have braved the viper's den to pay court to the eldest daughter of Baron Arundel."

Bingley shot Darcy a look at Fitzwilliam's statement, and Darcy attempted to smile, hoping his friend understood Darcy had said nothing derogatory of the young woman. It was fortunate Fitzwilliam interpreted the look correctly.

"Oh, do not look so at Darcy. Though I heard of it soon after my arrival, Darcy had little to say on the matter and did not attempt to poison me against Miss Bennet. From what I remember, she is a beautiful young woman, the type I would expect you to pursue, given what I know of your preferences."

"She is," said Bingley with a soft smile. "There is no woman of my acquaintance who is better than she. I am a lucky man."

"Or she is a lucky woman," said Fitzwilliam.

"Perhaps," replies Bingley. Then he fixed Fitzwilliam with a look and said: "It is a surprise you would speak to me, considering the situation. I might have thought you would shun me."

"Might I assume you are speaking of this silly dispute between the Darcys and the Bennets?"

When Bingley nodded, Fitzwilliam's snort informed them all of his opinion on the matter. "As I said, I think it is akin to a spat between children. Regardless, the matter is a *Darcy* concern, not one to plague anyone bearing the name Fitzwilliam. I have met various Bennets at different times, and I have no disliking for any of them."

"Furthermore," added Fitzwilliam, shooting a look at Darcy before his eyes found Bingley again, "the Darcys are my relations, and I support and respect them. But I choose my own friends, and if they have any problem with that, it is *their* problem. I will not shun you for your feelings for a worthy young woman, of that I can assure you."

"Thank you, Fitzwilliam," said Bingley, his voice laden with feeling.

"For my part," said Darcy, speaking on instinct and without thinking, "I do not wish to lose your friendship because of such trivial concerns, Bingley." Pausing, Darcy struggled to say something more when his friend's eyes found him. When he felt the weight of all their eyes upon him, he shrugged and said: "It has taken me too long to realize this, I know, but losing your friendship is something I would regret the rest of my life."

"Then you will withstand my Bennet bride?" asked Bingley.

Darcy laughed, feeling free for the first time in weeks. "As my cousin said, she seems like an excellent young woman. I shall try not to hold a grudge against her should she marry such an unworthy sod as you."

With a wide grin, Bingley urged his horse forward, clasping Darcy's forearm, Darcy returning the gesture. "I thank you, my friend. Though I knew I was risking the loss of your friendship, I am glad that has not happened. I have had no firmer friend than you."

"The feeling is mutual," replied Darcy. "Please do not hold my tardy acceptance of your ability to make your own choices against me."

"Of course not," replied Bingley with a grin. "Do not think you are free of being reminded of it, though. I shall ensure to do so at every opportunity."

"With such a cousin as Fitzwilliam, I am accustomed to such teasing."

"As you should be," replied Fitzwilliam with a grin. Then he turned back to Bingley. "Where are you bound, Bingley? Shall we ride on to Lambton together?"

"I have just completed some business there," said Bingley. "At present, I am for Longbourn. I hope you will forgive me if I find Miss Bennet's company preferable to yours."

"Methinks someone is entangled in a woman's web," said Alexander.

"And content to be so," replied Bingley with a grin. "But if you are willing, perhaps we could ride together tomorrow."

They discussed and agreed upon their plans for the morrow, and soon Bingley farewelled them and went on his way. For the past weeks, Darcy had been agonizing over his friendship with Bingley, wishing there was some way to restore it. Now that it was repaired, he was floating on a sea of relief. The words he had spoken were not idle praise—Bingley was as good a friend as Darcy ever had, and to keep his friendship was all Darcy had ever wished.

"I see you have come to your senses," said Fitzwilliam as they rode on toward the town.

"As you said," replied Darcy, "the business in question was no reason to lose a friendship."

"Perhaps there is hope for us yet," said Alexander. "The question is, will Father allow a Bennet at our table after Bingley marries, even after she resigns her maiden name in favor of his?"

It was a question to which Darcy did not know the answer. As fond of Bingley as the elder Darcy was, it was possible he might see reason and allow it, since the lady was quiet and unassuming. It was a discussion for another time, however, for they soon entered the town. And there, Darcy saw her.

Miss Elizabeth Bennet. Darcy drank in the sight of her, fighting her allure which urged him to take her in his arms, to kiss her with abandon, as a man kisses his lover. It was with the utmost self-control that Darcy refrained, instead turning his attention to finding some way to inform her he wished to see her again. The three riders progressed down the street toward where Miss Elizabeth stood with her mount speaking with someone of the town. Then, as they were passing, Miss Elizabeth climbed into the saddle, which provided Darcy an opportunity, behind his cousin and brother as he was.

"Meet me at the meadow," said Darcy in a low voice without stopping.

Though the young woman appeared startled, Darcy dared not wait for a response. Keeping pace, he continued on behind his companions, listening to their banter and laughter. They separated soon after that, Darcy informing them he meant to visit the bookshop, but after only a perfunctory glance about the shop, he was soon out the door and on his mount again, making his way out of town.

The ride to the meadow seemed interminable, such was his desperation to see the young woman again. As he rode, thoughts of arriving only to find an empty field with no Miss Bennet in attendance plagued him. Darcy was certain she had heard his request. Had she decided to humor him? Though he could not know, he thought it likely she had chosen to follow her father's command after their last meeting, much as Darcy had himself.

When Darcy urged his mouth through the trees toward the bit of clear space, for a moment he thought she was not there. Then, through the trees, he caught a hint of the lavender color of her dress. And soon he emerged, the woman sitting on a rock with a book, much like the first time Darcy had seen her there. She had come.

"Miss Bennet."

The tall figure of Mr. Darcy emerging from the trees set Elizabeth's heart to racing, and she put her book down and rose as he approached. Not having noticed him in Lambton, hearing the whispered request to meet him had surprised her. For a moment, Elizabeth had thought to refuse in deference to her father's wishes. Then the memory of her last meeting with him and the silent longing of her heart overwhelmed any rational objection, and she had made her way there, alive with impatience for his coming.

Once in place, she had taken her book out of her saddlebag to read while she waited for him, but there was no room for concentration in her heart that day. The anticipation for Mr. Darcy's arrival rendered her unable to give her attention to the words, and more than once she had risen from her place on the rock to pace, attempting to expend the nervous tension racing through her. It was fortunate, she thought, that she had situated herself again on the rock before he made his appearance, for she did not know how she would explain her behavior if he saw her.

"Mr. Darcy," said she in response to his greeting, though not without a shudder at the way he caressed her name as he spoke.

The gentleman vaulted down from his saddle and approached her, stopping before her and taking one hand between his. "I hope you will not find me too forward, Miss Elizabeth, but I longed to see you again. These past days of our separation have been torturous."

A fire began burning deep within Elizabeth's soul, and so moved was she that she could only whisper in response: "I have felt it too, sir."

The wide smile with which the gentleman regarded her spoke of promise, a promise of love and devotion, of everything for which she could ever have wished. Of a life of fidelity and trust. Elizabeth had never been jealous of her sisters Jane and Mary, who seemed to find their happiness with little effort. At that moment, however, Elizabeth was certain that what she had found rivaled theirs in a way that suited her in every way. The obstacles in their path, though she knew they would rear their ugly heads, fell away as if they were nothing, allowing Elizabeth to immerse herself in the moment.

"I have longed to see you, Miss Elizabeth," said Mr. Darcy.

Elizabeth laughed. "It seems to me you are repeating yourself, sir."

The smile he gave her seemed to confirm every hint of Elizabeth's feelings for this tall, enigmatic man. The feelings which had been building within her burst forth in her own beaming smile for him and the gentleman raised her hand to his lips, gracing it with a featherlight kiss, lingering, yet imparting every hint of his regard.

"Then I think we should not allow so much time to pass between meetings again."

A hint of the admonition administered by her father made Elizabeth pause, for her happiness receded a moment. Mr. Darcy must have seen it flee, for he became serious in an instant.

"Can I suppose your father has forbidden such meetings, as mine has?" asked Elizabeth, searching the gentleman for the truth.

"Yes, he has," said Mr. Darcy. "Can we sit while we discuss this matter?"

Nodding her acquiescence, Elizabeth allowed him to lead her to the nearby rock, where Mr. Darcy saw to her comfort before situating himself at her side. Never once in this maneuvering did he release his grip on her hand. Though worry over her father's decrees had cast a pall over her earlier feelings of bliss, Elizabeth could no more remove her hand from his than she could walk to the moon.

"The first thing I would have you know," began Mr. Darcy, "is that I would not cast my father's instructions aside without reason. Nothing less than the most extraordinary circumstances has provoked me to do so."

"And you consider *these* extraordinary circumstances?" asked Elizabeth, uncertain as to his meaning.

"I consider *you* extraordinary, Miss Elizabeth," replied he.

Elizabeth felt her cheeks heat, as much because of his open admiration as his words. Though she could not speak for a moment, Mr. Darcy did not fill the void, and soon she felt the ability to return to her.

"I feel the same way."

That small declaration prompted a brilliant smile to infuse his countenance, and he raised her hand to his mouth again, this time his kiss more forceful, more sensual. Every hair on the back of her hand stood up in response to his ministrations, leaving Elizabeth to wonder what the sensation would be like if he kissed her!

"Then we are agreed," said he.

"We are," replied Elizabeth. "To act as the voice of reason, however, I doubt our fathers would consider our feelings adequate grounds to ignore their instructions. Especially when you consider we were not supposed to have met enough to *form* our feelings."

"To that, I can offer no rebuttal. Though some might consider it mere sophistry, I shall argue a higher calling."

"In what way?' asked Elizabeth, amused by his grandiose statement.

"If you consider that we two may be the means by which our families' enmity may end."

Elizabeth's breath caught in her throat and she gazed at Mr. Darcy with amazement. "That is premature, sir!"

Perhaps it is," replied Mr. Darcy. "Do not mistake me, Miss Elizabeth—I do not offer a proposal at present. However, it has often been said I am a man who knows what I want. Though we have not known each other long, I can state with no hint of doubt that you are everything I could ever want in a woman.

"It is not my intention to press you, though it may seem that way." Mr. Darcy paused, his gaze seeming to pass right through to her heart. "Even if matters between us do not end as I have come to wish, we have each learned that those of the other side of the dispute are not evil, have we not?"

"We have," replied Elizabeth. "Then through our friendship, when we acknowledge it, we may heal the breach between us."

"I hope you will not think less of me if I hope *friendship* is not all there ever is between us, Miss Elizabeth. In essentials, however, you are correct. All it takes is a single step—any journey has such a small beginning."

"We shall have to take great care," replied Elizabeth softly. "Not only in how to make our families know of our connection, regardless of what it is, but also that we do not make matters worse."

"There is little chance of that, I should think," replied Mr. Darcy. "It is my hope, Miss Elizabeth, that you will accept that risk. I wish for nothing more."

Though she thought on the matter for a moment, Elizabeth knew the answer to his unstated question. The thought of enduring his absence again, of ending these meetings, of turning away from him and never experiencing his friendship again caused her to weep inside. To never explore what lay between them and discover if it could be something more left her feeling as if she were wasting her life. No, there was no fighting against this. It was in every way unfathomable.

"There is nothing to risk, Mr. Darcy," replied Elizabeth. "The greater risk is to separate now, never knowing what might have been."

"Then we see matters alike."

With such questions resolved between them, they stayed that way for some time—much longer than perhaps they should have. What passed between them was a mingling of shared confidences, little endearments, a discussion of how they should handle the future, interspersed with brief silences in which they enjoyed each other's company. More than anything else, they allowed themselves to feel— the regard each possessed for the other, the newness of admiration and trust. The first steps on the path to love without equal.

"You will never guess what I have just discovered!"

Lady Charlotte's eyes widened at Fitzwilliam's sudden declaration upon entering the room. It seemed, however, the lady understood the essence of his excitement and amusement and was infected by it, for she invited him to sit nearby and fixed him with a questioning gaze. Fitzwilliam, eager to relay his news, lost no time in speaking.

"Darcy and Miss Elizabeth Bennet have been meeting in secret!"

Amusement gave way to shock, leaving Lady Charlotte gaping at him. "Meeting in secret?"

"Well, perhaps I should say they met in secret today," said Fitzwilliam, fixing his fiancée with a grin. "Given how cozy they seemed with each other, however, I suspect today was not the first time."

"You must tell me what you have discovered, Anthony."

"Darcy has been acting odd of late," replied Fitzwilliam. "In fact, I date it back to the time of my arrival. He is very closed, as you know— reticent and even taciturn. Whereas he has often been said to be intense, focused on his ambitions, of late he has, at times, been almost inattentive, introspective. While he is not a stranger to introspection, it has seemed to me this time that his reminiscences are softer, somehow pleasanter than what I have often seen in him.

"This morning, he, Alexander, and I rode into Lambton. We passed Miss Elizabeth speaking to someone on the street; I happened to look back at the exact moment he leaned over and said something to her as he passed by. Then he gave us some silly excuse of wishing to go into the bookshop and we parted."

"It seems he did not do so," observed Lady Charlotte.

"Oh, he did," replied Fitzwilliam with a grin. "But his stay there was no more than thirty seconds. When he came out, he went straight for his horse and hurried out of town. If he had not been so inattentive, he might have spotted me following him."

"He met with Elizabeth?" asked Lady Charlotte.

"There is a small meadow hidden within the trees just off the road joining the two estates to Lambton. It is nestled up against both estates, a small, rocky little plot I found rather picturesque. When Darcy entered, I tied my horse to a tree and followed on foot, and when I neared the edge of the trees, I found Darcy sitting beside Miss Elizabeth on a stone, her hand ensconced within his!"

Lady Charlotte's eyes widened, and she shook her head. "I might never have expected Elizabeth to behave in such a manner. During the last assembly, I overheard an exchange between them which betrayed no lack of asperity."

"Then they have moved beyond those feelings," replied Fitzwilliam. "Should I hazard a guess, I would say that they are close to being in love with each other."

A sigh escaped Lady Charlotte's lips, though she smiled at him. "That is so romantic, Anthony. I know you are seeing the humor in the situation, but my thoughts are different. Two people whose families are enemies have seen beyond it, have given themselves over to the other, have put their trust and their devotion in the other. I cannot help but wonder if they will regret it someday."

"Star-crossed lovers?" asked Fitzwilliam, waggling his eyebrows. "Lovers fated to meet and love for a brief time before their families' implacable resentment causes them to tear apart in tragedy?"

Lady Charlotte swatted at him. "I do not think they will end entwined in a lovers' death embrace like the Montague and Capulet of tragic lore."

"We shall have to see they do not."

"I do not think we should interfere, Anthony," said Lady Charlotte, hesitation clear in her manner. "It has the great potential to rebound upon us, make the situation even worse."

"It is not my contention we should announce their betrothal at your ball," said Fitzwilliam. "However, I am more convinced than ever the ball allows us the opportunity to have the Bennets and Darcys in one room together, to affect a détente between them. If relations between their families warm, that should give them the opportunity to realize whatever future they desire."

It was a compelling argument, Fitzwilliam thought, and he could see Charlotte begin to be swayed by it. She gave a slow nod, her gaze inward, considering the possibilities.

"There is little harm in having them both together here," said she. "There have been enough times when both families have been in attendance at various functions."

Fitzwilliam nodded, adding: "I am Darcy's cousin, and I am known to the baron also. If we can induce them to see the other in a different light, it will go a long way toward thawing relations between them."

"Both the Bennets and Darcys are to attend our ball this year?"

Fitzwilliam and Lady Charlotte looked up as one to see her father regarding them, some concern etched upon his brow. It was clear to Fitzwilliam he had heard nothing of Darcy and Miss Elizabeth, or he was certain the earl would have spoken of the matter. Eager to avoid speaking of the subject, Fitzwilliam essayed to speak first.

"It is time for this silly dispute to end, my lord. My relations have attended other functions with the Bennets in the past."

"Yes, they have," replied Lord Chesterfield. "This concerted effort to bring them all to my home at once is different. I wonder if it is wise."

"No reconciliation can ever be achieved if they refuse to meet," said Fitzwilliam. "We do not mean to push, nor do we mean to insist. They must attempt to reconcile, or it shall all come to naught. But I think the opportunity is there, particularly with Bingley's pursuit of Miss Bennet and his connection with the Darcy family. I, myself, witnessed Darcy and Bingley's reconciliation and Darcy's pledge to accept Bingley's future Bennet wife—there must be some congress between them, and Mr. Darcy may be induced to accept the future Mrs. Bingley into his home. To me, this is a good place to begin that process."

"You agree with this, Charlotte?"

"The Lucases have long known the Bennets and the Darcys are good people, though they persist in this silly disagreement. If we can bring greater peace in the neighborhood, I believe we should do everything we can to forward that ideal, Papa."

Lord Chesterfield smiled and approached his only daughter, kissing the top of her head. "It is a worthy objective, my dear. But let us take care, shall we? The possibility exists that the situation may be made worse."

"Of course."

With a smile and a nod, the earl excused himself. When he was gone, Lady Charlotte turned to Fitzwilliam and fixed him with an arch look.

"I noted you did not speak of Mr. Darcy and Miss Elizabeth."

"It seems best to keep that to ourselves," rejoined Fitzwilliam.

"I agree," replied she. "Then we have some planning we must do."

With a grin, Fitzwilliam set to it with a will. As they spoke of the possibilities, he wondered if Darcy might ask Miss Elizabeth to dance in front of everyone. It may be a shock to them all, but sometimes shocks serve a purpose, for they jerk one out of one's complacency. Yes, Fitzwilliam thought a bolt from above might be just the thing to end this interminable warfare once and for all. And it just might guarantee his cousin's happiness at the same time.

CHAPTER XVI

*A*nne de Bourgh was an observant young woman. Having lived her entire life with a mother bombastic and overbearing, one who did not care to hear another's opinion, Anne had learned to keep her own counsel, to listen and watch rather than comment. It had saved her many a reprimand and allowed her to form her own opinions, rather than have her mother dictate to her what she thought Anne's opinions should be.

Thus, the behavior of her cousin startled her. Oh, not that Anthony was not usually irreverent and jovial, or that he did not tease her other cousin—those were well-established habits those in the family had seen for many years. Anne did not think she had ever seen him taunt William to this extent, and when he continued, it drew Anne's greater interest.

"Well, Darcy," said Fitzwilliam one afternoon while they were all together in Pemberley's sitting-room, "I wonder if I should be offended you left us in Lambton this morning."

"I do not know why you cared," said Alexander. "You were so eager to depart to see your lady, I did not know you had noted my brother's absence."

"Of course, I noticed it!" exclaimed Anthony. "Just because I wished to see my betrothed does not mean I am unaware of what is occurring around me. Considering how much Darcy has been riding of late, I should wonder if he has a paramour hidden in the woods somewhere."

"Do not make such jests, Fitzwilliam!" snapped Lady Catherine. "Why should Darcy search for a lady in the woods when Anne is here and willing to provide companionship?"

It was no surprise to anyone when the elder Darcy cleared his throat, a pointed reminder, though he did not look up from the book in his hands. Anne's mother understood the rebuke at once, though she accepted it with as little grace as she ever did. Alexander turned to Anne and grinned, which she returned, but she was more interested in Darcy's response—which was to glare at his cousin—and Anthony's challenging look.

"Why you would suspect me of such things I cannot understand," replied Darcy to Lady Catherine's nod of satisfaction.

Unlike her mother, Anne noted that Darcy did not deny he had seen another woman on his ride that morning. The thought of staid Darcy doing something so improper as meeting a young woman in the woods was so unlikely as to seem absurd, but the continued discussion between them piqued Anne's interest and stoked her suspicions.

"I did not say you were," replied Anthony, his manner at once flippant and probing. "I suggested that had you been a little more adventurous, I might have thought you interested in a young lady of surprising identity."

At this, Mr. Darcy put down his book and eyed Anthony. "Do you have some knowledge the rest of us do not?"

"We all know William very well, Uncle," replied Anthony. "There can be no suspicion he is behaving in any way improper. *If* he is interested in a young lady, I should think you would applaud him, for it seems to me it is high time he thinks of marriage and producing the next heir of Pemberley."

"I think—" began Lady Catherine, only for Mr. Darcy to cut her off.

"We are all very aware of what you think, Catherine, and I would remind you I do not agree." Lady Catherine huffed but did not press the point. Mr. Darcy turned to regard his son. "Anthony *is* correct, William. As you are now seven and twenty, it is time you began to think about taking a wife."

"I understand my responsibilities, Father," said Darcy. "There is no need to lecture me on this matter."

Though Mr. Darcy gazed at his son a few moments, interspersed with glances at Fitzwilliam, it seemed he decided it was nothing more than the banter between close cousins and returned to his book. What he did not see, but Anne noticed, was William's glare at Anthony, who responded with his own brand of insouciance.

No one said anything further, which served to keep the peace, but Anne remained watchful, and the pattern continued. Anthony continued to make little digs at his cousin, though outside his uncle or aunt's hearing, and while Darcy appeared annoyed at first, soon he seemed to decide it was nothing more than Anthony's continued teasing and began to respond in kind. Anne did not miss the fact that Darcy continued to ride out on a near-daily basis, sometimes staying out for hours at a time.

It was clear questioning Darcy on the matter was akin to speaking to Pemberley's cornerstone and expecting an answer. Likewise, approaching Anthony would see her inquiry treated as nothing more than a joke, and Alexander was little better, even if he *knew* anything of the matter. She could not approach her uncle or mother for obvious reasons, so Anne determined to see if the one other member of the party knew anything, little likely though that seemed.

The opportunity presented itself a few days later. Miss Bingley was still a frequent visitor, despite Lady Catherine's words the day of their arrival, and while Anne knew Georgiana tolerated the woman and knew she visited to be in William's company, Anne also saw in her a genuine affection for Georgiana. If she came to see William, her ploy was an abject failure, so much was he absent those days. Lady Catherine was almost always present, her manner one of watchful vigilance; it was fortunate she did not say much, for Anne knew anything she deigned to say to Miss Bingley would be an embarrassment. On the day in question, Miss Bingley departed after her visit and Lady Catherine retired to her rooms, and as the gentlemen were all elsewhere, Anne was alone with Georgiana.

"I am sorry if my words are offensive," said Georgiana with a sigh of relief, "but hosting Miss Bingley when your mother is present is more than a little trying."

Anne fixed her young cousin with a grin. "Is my mother that fearsome?"

"Not at Pemberley," replied Georgiana. "But I know she is waiting for any pretext to condemn us and see Miss Bingley dismissed from the house. And Miss Bingley, though I believe she is a good sort of person, wishes to see my brother more than she visits me. It is all so vexing!"

"I can see that it is," replied Anne. "Perhaps if your brother were to marry, these visits from Miss Bingley would cease. Or at the very least you would have someone here to assist without having to deal with the woman yourself."

"Oh, do not misunderstand me," said Georgiana. "I like Miss Bingley well enough. But I can see the ulterior motives in her actions. Is it too much to ask that those who visit me do so from a desire to speak to *me* rather than impress my brother?"

"No, Georgiana," replied Anne. "it is not too much to ask at all." Anne paused, considering how to best phrase her question, before saying: "I suppose there is nothing to Anthony's teasing of late? Do you know if your brother is interested in a woman?"

"I do not," replied Georgiana, dashing Anne's hope of obtaining answers to her questions. "But I should like it very much if he would marry, for I have always wished to have a sister. Brothers are excellent for providing protection and carrying one on their shoulders, but I have long outgrown such frivolities and wish for a woman to whom I can talk."

"Yes, I can imagine that. But you must own that your position is so much better than my own; why, I have no siblings upon whom I may rely!"

Georgiana laughed. "I suppose I must be grateful for those blessings I have received."

Though it was clear Georgiana knew little of her eldest brother's activities, Anne was convinced there was something to Anthony's teasing. The question was, how to discover the truth. No answers presented themselves, but an invitation to a ball arrived a few days later and provided a distraction.

"The yearly ball at Lord Chesterfield's estate," said Mr. Darcy when he inspected the invitation. "I had wondered if they planned to hold it this year."

"Why should they not, Uncle?" asked Fitzwilliam. "Lady Charlotte has been hard at work of late preparing for it, and I have given her some little assistance."

"Oh, is it to be your engagement ball?" asked Georgiana, nearly jumping in her seat with excitement.

"Nothing so lavish," replied Anthony, grinning at his cousin. "However, I believe it will be an event of some interest this year, not least of which is that it is the first ball since our engagement."

"It is always the social event of the neighborhood," said Uncle Darcy. "It also signals an exodus of the neighborhood families for

London and the season, for most do not depart without first attending the earl."

"Are we to go to London this year, Uncle?" asked Anne. "It was my understanding we were to be here most of the spring."

"If you were to canvass my opinion," said Alexander, "I should prefer to stay in Derbyshire this year."

"*You* wish to stay in Derbyshire?" asked William with clear disbelief.

"You forget, Brother," replied Alexander, "I have just returned from spending six months in London. At present, I am content at Pemberley and have little desire to go to town."

That was out of character for Alexander who had always clamored to go to London as soon as possible. Though most of the family regarded him with curiosity, he showed no signs of being aware of it. Uncle Darcy rescued him by shrugging and turning back to the subject at hand.

"I suppose the Darcy family must make an appearance in town, but at present, I will confess I am comfortable at Pemberley. Perhaps we shall go later in the season."

"But we shall attend the ball," said Anne.

"One does not reject an invitation from the highest-ranked family in the neighborhood," said Anthony, though Anne could hear from his tone he was using a hint of facetious humor.

"Of course, we shall attend," said Uncle Darcy. "The earl and his family have been friends for many years." The gentleman paused and his mouth twisted in distaste. "I suppose the Bennet family will also be invited."

"Though I have assisted when asked," replied Anthony, his answer a trifle too bland, "the guest list is Lady Charlotte's privilege to create. With such distaste as you betray at the mere notion of attending together with the Bennets, I might suppose the Bennets and Darcys cannot be in the same room with each other or they will come to blows."

"No, we have attended together before, that is true enough. Last year the Bennets were in London early for the season, so we were not required to endure them."

"They are still in Derbyshire this year, Father," replied Darcy. "Though the earl is of a higher rank than Lord Arundel, it would not do to offend him by excluding him from the invitation list."

"Yes, I understand that," replied Mr. Darcy. Then he shrugged. "It is well, I suppose. We have ignored the Bennet family in the past—this time shall be little different."

The exchanged heightened Anne's suspicions. It all made sense—Anthony teasing William about some nameless paramour, his insinuation it was some woman William felt compelled to meet in secret, not to mention Darcy's initial defensive response. Anne did not know the Bennet family at all and had only had the most superficial of contact with the eldest daughters. Could there be something to her suspicions? Could Darcy be interested in one of the Bennet women?

That was a circumstance which could prove divisive, considering what Anne's uncle had just said about the Bennet family. Could Darcy be provoking that dragon, waking him to fire and calamity? Anne did not know. But she resolved to watch Darcy at the ball, to see if he showed an undue level of interest in a young woman, and to discover if the woman was a Bennet. Anne would not interfere—like most of the family who did not carry the surname Darcy, she thought the dispute was tiresome. If Darcy was intent upon paying his addresses to a Bennet, he would need all the support he could muster.

At Longbourn the response to the invitation was similar to that which occurred at Pemberley. The difference was that Elizabeth was not present to witness it—or at least to witness the family's first reactions.

These past days had been wonderful for Elizabeth, for she had walked or ridden out every day—except Sunday—to meet with Mr. Darcy. Any shame Elizabeth might have felt for disobeying her father's orders had all but disappeared. While it was not laudable to disregard her beloved sire's instructions, Mr. Darcy's contention that their families might be brought closer together by their association had found fertile ground, so much that the memory of her father's wishes was fading, drifting away in a sea of contrary emotions.

It was becoming more apparent with every passing day that Mr. Fitzwilliam Darcy, he of the reticent disposition and proud reputation, was a man who felt deeply, but did not always know how to express those feelings. When with Elizabeth, he displayed his emotions in an understated manner, in the way he gave her his full attention when she spoke or showed his respect for her opinions. In a very real way, Elizabeth was coming to understand that Mr. Darcy was the best man she had ever known, a man with whom she could see herself spending the rest of her life.

Would he come to that same conclusion? Would he defy all their families' enmity and propose, knowing it might set tempers to flaring? Elizabeth could not know what the future would bring. The more

Elizabeth spoke to him, the more she yearned for that outcome. The feelings of heady new love were threatening to overtake her, and only the need to remain circumspect kept her in check.

The day the invitation arrived, Elizabeth had returned home, the euphoria of love's first bloom threatening to burst forth and betray her secret. It was this, as much as the desire to play with her brother, which prompted her to suggest they take themselves outside that day.

And they had a grand time doing it. Though there were still no frogs in evidence, Elizabeth assured her brother they would be out in force that summer, allowing them to capture some as he still insisted he wished to do. Instead, they romped about, chasing after each other, inspecting the banks of the river for any sign of tadpoles, and skipping stones.

"I believe I should like to wade in the water, Lizzy," said Thomas, as he looked with eager longing at the flowing river.

"At present, you would find it too cold," replied Elizabeth. "It is full of winter snows flowing out from the peaks, which makes it colder than it would be in the summer." Elizabeth paused and fixed the river with a critical look, saying: "I believe it is also flowing higher than normal."

"Why would it do that?" asked Thomas.

"If there is more snow, then there is more to melt," replied Elizabeth. "A heavy rain lasting for days will also affect it, for that water has to go somewhere."

Thomas looked up at her. "Do you think it will rain again?"

A clap of thunder interrupted them, and they both looked skyward to a tall, dark band of boiling clouds headed their way. To further punctuate the tempest bearing down upon them, fat, cold raindrops began to fall about them, only a few at the beginning, but gaining in volume and size within a short period.

Shrieking with laughter, the two ran for the house looming in the distance, Elizabeth tugging her brother's hand as she raced for safety. By the time they reached shelter, the rain was pouring down in thick, heavy sheets, the two intrepid explorers dripping puddles of water as they slipped in through a back entrance.

Lady Margaret had anticipated them, for she was there waiting, looking on with disapproval, her foot tapping her displeasure. Two maids waited nearby, and neither stinted in fixing Elizabeth with amused grins, even as they stepped forward with towels to dry and warm. Behind them a loud clap of thunder once again pierced the landscape, the accompanying lightning illuminating the darkened sky at irregular intervals, declaring the outside world unfit for man or beast.

"You will become ill if you persist in this recklessness," tutted Lady Margaret as she directed the servants to take them to their rooms for a change of clothes. "Sometimes I wonder at your trying my nerves like this, for I have never seen two such disobedient children!"

"We are well, Mama," said Elizabeth, catching her mother's hand and squeezing. "A little rain will not hurt us as long as we dry ourselves at once."

"Then be off with you," said Lady Margaret, shooing them away. "There will be warm tea and chocolate in the sitting-room when you come down again."

Thomas gave a whoop of joy and dashed toward the stairs, trailing a stream of water behind him. Elizabeth smiled at her brother and followed, though more mindful of her wet state, while her mother grumbled and walked behind. Lucy, Elizabeth's maid, assisted her in drying, repairing the damage to her hair, and dressing in a new gown, and when her appearance was again adequate, Elizabeth collected her brother, also sporting dry clothes and wet locks, neatly combed, and they made their way to where the family had gathered. There she discovered they had received a visitor while she and her brother had been otherwise engaged.

"I see you have been causing mischief again, Master Thomas," said Mr. Bingley, grinning as he stepped forward to greet them.

"No mischief, Mr. Bingley," said Thomas. "Lizzy and I were playing down by the river."

"Ah, a worthy endeavor," said Mr. Bingley. "I remember doing the same when I was a boy. One can find great adventures when there is running water nearby."

"Will you tell me of your adventures?" asked Thomas eagerly.

"Of course, I shall," replied Mr. Bingley. "Let us get you some chocolate and biscuits and I shall share with you the tales of my adventures."

As Mr. Bingley led the enraptured young boy away, Elizabeth's eyes found her sister Jane. Taking a cup of chocolate and a biscuit for herself, Elizabeth sat beside Jane and raised an eyebrow at her while sipping from her cup.

"It is fortunate Mr. Bingley arrived before the storm," said Elizabeth.

"Yes, it is," replied Jane, though she said nothing further. By this time, Thomas was ensconced beside Mr. Bingley listening, eyes wide and riveted to the gentleman.

"Mr. Bingley is very good with Thomas, is he not?" added Elizabeth. "One might even think he will make a good father one day."

Jane laughed and wagged a finger at Elizabeth. "Though I cannot dispute that observation, I do not wish to speak when there is yet nothing to report."

"There is not *at this time*. But it would surprise me if there is not something soon."

With a pinkish cast to her cheeks, Jane changed the subject. "The invitation for the ball at Lucas Manor arrived while you were out with Thomas."

"Has it?" said Elizabeth.

For a moment, an image of dancing with Mr. Darcy appeared in her mind, causing all sorts of delightful sensations in its wake. Then Elizabeth sobered, for it was not likely she would have the opportunity to dance with the gentleman—not with the continued and unresolved issue of their families. But it was a wonderful dream, and Elizabeth thought she might just indulge in some lazy fantasies when she was at liberty to do so in the privacy of her own room.

"As the invitation includes me," said Mr. Collins, nodding to the rest of the family, "I believe I should like to take the opportunity to solicit Mary's hand for the first sets."

Mary, though blushing, agreed, which brought out a beaming smile in her suitor. Mr. Bingley looked up, and not to be outdone, made the same request of Jane, though he carried it one step further.

"And the supper set, if you please."

"Of course, Mr. Bingley," said Jane, this time with nary a hint of embarrassment.

It was at this moment that Elizabeth felt the first feelings of envy for her sisters stirring in her heart. Jane and Mary were excellent young women and deserving of the attentions of their gentlemen. At the same time, Elizabeth wished *she* could also enjoy the same attention without provoking a family crisis for both families. *Someday* . . . Elizabeth promised herself.

"There is one other matter of which I should inform you," said Mr. Bingley. "As you know, I argued with Darcy when I informed him of my intention to court you. I am now happy to say that our friendship has been restored."

"Has it?" asked Lord Arundel.

While his question was light, there was a hint of hardness about his mouth and eyes which no one but those who knew him well would see. Mr. Bingley, it appeared, was not one of those who could read his lordship's moods with any accuracy.

"Yes, it has," replied Mr. Bingley, happiness evident in his response. "At first, when he informed me of his intention to accept Miss Bennet, I was uncertain, but in subsequent meetings, he has convinced me. I would not have yielded regardless, but I feel fortunate to know I have not lost such a good friend as Darcy because of his fool stiff-necked pride."

"I recommend you be doubly certain, Mr. Bingley," said Lady Margaret with a superior sniff. "Those Darcys are shifty, untrustworthy sort of people."

"Believe me, my lady," said Bingley, "I would not be telling you this if I was uncertain."

Lord Arundel regarded Mr. Bingley for some moments before he shrugged. "It is, of course, your prerogative to choose your own friends, and I shall not attempt to direct you. The only concern I have is that Mr. Darcy is cordial at the very least to my daughter, and that cordiality is mirrored in the rest of his family."

"The Darcy family are excellent people, Lord Arundel," said Mr. Bingley, and while she might have thought a man would take a conciliatory tone with a peer, Mr. Bingley's manner was firm. "I have no expectation of any misbehavior by my friend or his family, but should anything occur, Jane will always have my allegiance and support."

"A sensible stance, Mr. Bingley," said Elizabeth. "I, too, would expect nothing untoward from the Darcy family."

Lord Arundel's eyes swung to Elizabeth. "It is interesting to hear you say so, Daughter. Do you have any particular knowledge of that family?"

"Only what is commonly acknowledged," replied Elizabeth. "When we met Miss Darcy in the bookshop I determined at once there was little evil to be found in her, for I found she is naught but a shy girl. Then when Mr. Darcy came in, there was nothing about him I found objectionable. I find this dispute to be silly, at the very least. It should be buried in the past where it belongs."

"Never have truer words been spoken," interrupted Mr. Collins. "That is my recommendation also, Cousin."

Though he heard his cousin and nodded in response, Lord Arundel continued to regard Elizabeth, and she wondered for a moment if she had said more than she ought. After a few moments, her father shrugged.

"What you speak is the truth. I have little reason to argue with the Darcys, but the distrust of generations is difficult to overcome. Perhaps yours shall be the generation that allows the matter to rest. For the present master of Pemberley and I, we are too set in our ways to change."

Having made his point, Lord Arundel turned back to his book. Desultory conversations continued about the room, Mr. Bingley and Thomas with Jane nearby, and Mary with Mr. Collins, but Elizabeth found herself lost in thought. Her father had hit on the truth of the matter, that it was up to Elizabeth and Mr. Darcy, along with Mr. Bingley with his connection to the Darcy family, and Jane, who would be his wife, to bridge the distance. Suddenly it did not seem like such a daunting task.

CHAPTER XVII

*T*he deluge which had doused Elizabeth and Thomas proved to be the opening chapter in several days of rain. It was not a constant torrent, but an intermittent mixture of drizzle, heavier rainfall, with periods of gray clouds and the occasional break where the sun showed a tired and wan face to the world. As such, Elizabeth could find no time to go out to meet Mr. Darcy, for not only would she be miserable on her poor horse, but her mother would abuse her for putting her health at risk in such a manner.

Thus, when the day came that the sun was once again out in all its glory, Elizabeth could not resist the temptation to saddle Midnight and ride out. This, however, did not escape her mother's attention.

"I believe I should rather you wait an extra day, Lizzy," said she when she came across Elizabeth dressed in a riding habit walking toward the entrance. "It is still cold outdoors."

"Perhaps it is," replied Elizabeth, kissing her mother's cheek. "But I have been trapped inside for some days and long for the wind upon my face. I shall take care not to stray too far or stay out too long."

Though her mother regarded her for several minutes and Elizabeth thought she was considering whether to forbid her, she relented. "You will do what you please, I suppose, for you have always been the most headstrong of my girls."

Elizabeth laughed and said: "Yes, I will own I am headstrong. The title of the *most* headstrong, however, more properly belongs to your youngest, in my opinion."

"You are both peas in a pod in that respect," said Lady Margaret. Then she made a shooing motion with her hand, saying: "Off with you, then. Should you not return in two hours, I shall dispatch a search party to discover you."

With a laugh, Elizabeth was quick to follow her mother's command. The stable, warm with the bodies of the Bennet collection of equines, carried the scent of horse Elizabeth had always loved, and she slipped inside, eager to be on her way. Midnight waited for her, the grooms having already prepared her for their ride, and after a few words of thanks, and a greeting for Midnight—completed with a wizened old apple—she swung herself into the saddle and was off.

The fields of the estate were particularly lovely that morning, shining with the dampness of the past few days. Soon, Elizabeth knew, the farmers of the estate would dot the land, busily planting seeds harvested the previous year to provide their summer crops. Then the land would come alive with the bounty of the season. To all these things, though Elizabeth often watched and marveled, she was indifferent that morning, for she was eager to see the one person she had missed these past few days. In a few short minutes, Elizabeth discovered his turn of mind had been the same as hers.

"Miss Elizabeth," said Mr. Darcy from where he sat on their rock, a dry patch already warming in the morning sun. "I hoped you would come this way this morning."

"As I hoped to see you," said Elizabeth, allowing him to help her out of the saddle.

From Elizabeth's saddlebag, she produced an old blanket which she spread upon the rock, then took her seat by the gentleman's side, close enough to feel the heat from his body. They sat in this attitude for some time, speaking of diverse matters, both enjoying the sound of the other's voice. It had often been thus, for they had learned that conversation between them was effortless as if they had known each other all their lives. Then the conversation took a turn which Elizabeth thought it must, to the significant event which loomed on the horizon.

"We have also received an invitation to the ball," said Elizabeth when Mr. Darcy made a similar comment.

Mr. Darcy fixed her with a wry grin. "Do you think our families shall behave well enough to allow us to enjoy the evening?"

Shaking her head, Elizabeth said: "It is not as if we have not attended the same events before. The last assembly, for example."

"That is true." Mr. Darcy paused and then turned to face her, his manner serious. "Though we have spoken of this before, I believe the coming ball is an opportunity to see each other in a different light from the one we have often cherished."

"Cherished is an interesting word," replied Elizabeth.

Mr. Darcy chuckled and said: "Perhaps it is. But can you deny it? The dispute between our families has become an old and valued friend over the years. It is easier to hold to the enmity of the past, for it takes much more effort to resolve it."

"I agree," replied Elizabeth. "It has often been my observation that members of my family will often make comments with no true knowledge and with no proof. Mr. Collins has attempted to induce us to see this, but until recent events persuaded me to examine our behavior, I believe I was as caught up in it as any of my family."

"Surely you did not make such comments."

Elizabeth fixed the gentleman with a wry smile. "Do you not recall our exchange the night of the assembly? Yes, I allowed myself to make comments of that sort on occasion, but I saw no purpose in them. But I will not claim to be blameless in this matter. To be honest, I do not think any of us can claim innocence."

"Then our families are not prepared to bridge the gap between us."

"At present, I think some distance may still be for the best," replied Elizabeth. "Can you imagine your father and mine speaking without acrimony between them? There is little to gain from pressing the issue before they are prepared to accept it."

For a moment, Elizabeth fell silent, and Mr. Darcy, sensing she had something further to say, watched her, waiting for her to speak. "A thought has come to my mind, something my father said a few days ago." When Mr. Darcy cocked his head to the side, Elizabeth continued, saying: "He suggested it would be *our* generation who would heal the breach between our families, claiming that he and your father were too set in their ways to attempt a settlement. Though I might wish it otherwise, I believe he is correct."

"We have spoken of this before, have we not?" asked Mr. Darcy.

"Yes, though obliquely," asserted Elizabeth. "I realized it was true in a way I had not before. In this instance, my father is correct—for the breach between our two families to heal, we must show them the way."

The way Mr. Darcy gazed at her, Elizabeth wondered if he would propose on the spot. Perhaps it might have been better if he had, for the next words he spoke did not sit well with her.

"Then you must be correct." Mr. Darcy laughed and added: "For I cannot ever see your uncle, for one, letting his resentment toward my brother dissipate unless there was no other choice."

"Uncle Gardiner has told me himself he holds no grudges," protested Elizabeth. "I know you do not know my uncle, Mr. Darcy, but he is a good man, only he is one who takes a prodigious amount of care of us all."

"I am certain he does." Elizabeth wondered if the patronizing tone she heard in his voice was more than her own imagination. "It is also clear he has little love for my brother."

This was true, though the way Mr. Darcy said it, Elizabeth felt the sting of his words. They were unfair to her uncle, she thought, for he was one of the finest men she knew.

"How I wish we could associate without disguise!" exclaimed Mr. Darcy, drawing Elizabeth away from her thoughts and her annoyance. When she looked back at him, it was to witness the intensity of his gaze, his eyes upon her, almost devouring her where she sat. "If we could be free in our admiration, I might have the pleasure of dancing with you at Lord Chesterfield's ball!"

"Perhaps enough progress shall be made during the ball that it will be possible to ask me later in the evening."

"Will you save the supper set for me?"

Elizabeth blushed and looked down. "I shall as long as I can, Mr. Darcy. But you must recall that a woman, if asked for a dance, cannot refuse, lest she has no option but to sit out for the rest of the evening. Should someone else ask for those dances, I must accept, or lose all enjoyment."

"One might think you would be eager to dance only with me," said Mr. Darcy, the turn of his countenance informing Elizabeth that he was teasing. "It would be a small sacrifice to refuse to dance with any other, I should think."

"Do *you* intend to refrain from dancing?" asked Elizabeth, her manner pointed.

"It should be a punishment to dance with anyone other than you, so I had best refuse."

Eyes narrowed, Elizabeth glared at him. "I have it on good authority you dislike dancing."

"I assure you, Miss Elizabeth, that I enjoy dancing if it is with you."

"You have never danced with me."

"No," replied Mr. Darcy, his countenance suffused with amusement. "But if the reality is anything like I imagine, it must be pure bliss."

Elizabeth felt the heat spreading over her cheeks and ducked her head. "It is only a dance," was all she could say.

"No, Miss Elizabeth," replied Mr. Darcy. "It is the beginning of a lifetime."

Though almost overcome by emotion, Elizabeth pushed it away and fixed him with a pointed look. "That sounded like the prelude to a proposal, Mr. Darcy."

"It is not yet," replied Mr. Darcy. "But that day is approaching."

"Now, there is something else I wish to discuss." Elizabeth glanced askance at him, and Mr. Darcy obliged her unspoken question, explaining: "It seemed to me that I offended you with my words about your uncle. Is that so?"

Marveling at the way he already appeared capable of reading her moods, Elizabeth nodded.

"Then it behooves us both to take care in which we say," said Mr. Darcy. "I offer my unreserved apologies, Miss Elizabeth, for I did not intend to cast shade on your uncle, for I am certain he is a good man. That I came closer than I would ever wish to offending you concerns me. I never want misunderstandings to arise between us."

"It is understandable, Mr. Darcy," said Elizabeth, though agreeing with him in every particular. "It may as easily have been I who made a thoughtless comment about your brother. He *does* have a certain reputation in the neighborhood."

Mr. Darcy chuckled and nodded. "He does at that. There is something . . . Well, Alexander has changed since he returned. I do not suggest he has thrown off his careless ways in their entirety, but he is more serious than I have ever known him to be."

"And that illustrates the unfairness of such a comment," said Elizabeth. "I do not *know* your brother—I should not presume to judge him."

"That is what I am saying, Miss Elizabeth. The misunderstandings between our families also have the potential to spawn misunderstandings between *us*. We must take care in what we say, and if there is any ambiguity, we must clarify, for I would not wish to be at odds with you due to a silly comment made without adequate consideration."

"I agree," replied Elizabeth.

For a time, they fell silent, each thinking on the situation in which they found themselves. Elizabeth thought of what he had said of her uncle and how easy it might have been for her to respond in kind, to accuse where there was no reason to do so, to take offense where none was intended. If she had, the result of their meeting that day would have been so much different. Elizabeth did not wish to part with him in acrimony.

"Shall I see you again before the ball?" asked Mr. Darcy, pulling Elizabeth from her thoughts only a few moments later.

Elizabeth considered the question and shook her head. "It is for the best we do not meet again. The Bingleys are to come to Longbourn for dinner tomorrow evening, and my mother will require assistance in the preparations. Moreover, I would not wish to tempt fate by meeting too often, for it may provoke someone to curiosity or suspicion."

That Mr. Darcy was disappointed Elizabeth expected — she was not happy herself. But they both understood her point. If her father or her uncle discovered their frequent meetings, there would be trouble, and the ability to see each other again would disappear. It would be best to hold themselves back, for Elizabeth did not wish to contemplate days on end without his company.

"It is unfortunate," said Mr. Darcy, "but I believe you have the right of it. Though we will not be at liberty to speak, I suspect, I shall anticipate seeing you at the ball."

It was then Elizabeth knew that evening would be excruciating. To be at a ball with Mr. Darcy in what should be a happy time, a time for love, bold statements of affection and acknowledgment before the neighborhood, and yet be unable to show her feelings would be difficult. Elizabeth did not know how she would endure it.

But endure it she must. They rose and said their good-byes, Mr. Darcy holding her hands and raising them to his lips in a motion both loving and longing. Then he helped her into the saddle again and bade her farewell, watching rooted to the spot as she rode away. Elizabeth turned to look at him again many times as she departed, pressing her hands to her lips and blowing kisses his way. Mr. Darcy's eyes never left her until she could no longer see him among the trees.

Feeling as bereft as he ever had, Darcy mounted his own horse once he lost sight of Miss Elizabeth and turned back toward Pemberley. In a moment of decision, he opted to eschew the path which would lead him back to the road, and instead made his way through the barrier of trees to the valley in which Pemberley stood, and from thence through the fields back to the estate. And as he rode, Darcy wondered if Miss

Elizabeth was lamenting their inability to proclaim their courtship to the world, to let the light of their love show forth as so many other young couples had before them.

Upon returning to Pemberley, Darcy found himself at sixes and sevens, uncertain what he should do or how he should occupy himself. Every moment spent out of Miss Elizabeth's company now seemed like a lifetime, every instant a punishment. Darcy began to long for the ball, though he had never wished for such an amusement before— even if he could not dance with Miss Elizabeth, at least he could see her, be within the range of her incandescence. What exquisite torture this business of love was!

"Darcy," said Fitzwilliam when his cousin found him in the library later that day. "What is the matter with you, old man? It seems to me you have been moping about since your return this morning."

"There is nothing the matter with me," said Darcy, wondering again if Fitzwilliam knew something of his recent activities.

"Then perhaps you would join me in a game of billiards?" offered his cousin. "It would take both our minds off the upcoming ball."

Though Darcy agreed, he wondered as to his cousin's meaning. "Why should I require distraction from the upcoming ball? For that matter, why should you?"

"Because I," replied Fitzwilliam, his glib tone a little overdone, "shall not see Lady Charlotte until we arrive at Lucas Lodge. As for your distraction, I suspect it is because of your typical disinclination for such activities."

"I am not against attending, I assure you," said Darcy as his cousin racked the balls.

"If you are not," said Alexander, entering the room, "it is the first time I have ever seen it. You have never cared for such amusements before."

"I still do not," replied Darcy, taking a cue from the rack. "But that does not mean I do not wish to go."

"I am glad to hear it," said Fitzwilliam, passing Alexander a cue before taking one himself. "For I wish the Darcy family to acquit themselves well, for Lady Charlotte and her father are to be my family."

"I believe the earl knows of our characters," replied Alexander with a grin. "He well knows I am eager to dance, and Darcy detests it, and he understands our father's disinclination also. I only hope he understands our aunt, for she could try the patience of a saint."

"Oh?" asked Fitzwilliam amused, while Darcy took the first shot.

"Has Lady Catherine again made her opinions known?"

Alexander shrugged. "She is in the middle of some disagreement with Anne, though I did not remain long enough to discover the subject of it."

Fitzwilliam snorted as Darcy lined up his second shot, sinking the ball into the side pocket with a satisfying clack. When his third bounced off the edge of the hole and out again, he relinquished the table to his cousin.

"When is Lady Catherine not disagreeing with someone about something?" asked Darcy. "To the best of my knowledge, Lord Chesterfield is acquainted with our aunt."

"I hope he is. Then he will not hold our connection against us."

Fitzwilliam's snort preceded his own shot, which rolled into the hole at the end of the table. They continued in this fashion for some time after, random comments interspersed with their turns at the table. Though Darcy found himself distracted in the first pair of games which was reflected in the results, the third and fourth he found himself more at ease and did much better. When they quit the room, Darcy found himself more focused, though still missing Miss Elizabeth's company.

"Darcy, I see you have come," said Lady Catherine the moment the cousins stepped into the sitting-room. "You must speak some sense into Anne."

"Oh?" asked Darcy, noting the way Anne looked heavenward at her mother's words. "For what reason would I presume to correct your daughter?"

"Because," said Anne, her exasperation clear in her voice, "my mother does not approve of my seeking the acquaintance of the daughters of a baron, ladies who are above me by every measure of society."

Having some sense of what the dispute consisted, Darcy turned his gaze on his aunt, as Fitzwilliam and Alexander snickered their amusement.

"I said no such thing!" snapped Lady Catherine. "The only thing I suggested was that it was best to avoid *this particular* family, for their relations with *our* family are not at all cordial."

"And my response," said Anne, "was that *I* am not a Darcy, and do not feel bound by this ridiculous dispute."

"The same point I have made myself," interjected Fitzwilliam.

"You forget, Anne," said Lady Catherine, ignoring her nephew, "that I have met the baron."

"Indeed, I have not forgotten," was Anne's wry reply. "For you have informed me of it yourself at least a dozen times in the past half hour."

Lady Catherine silenced her daughter by means of a piercing glare, but the same did not work against the gentlemen, who all thought the matter was vastly amusing. Lady Catherine sniffed and turned her attention back to Anne when her attempt to cow them failed.

"These Bennets are artful people and should receive no respect from us. The baron as a sardonic man made up of quick, biting parts, and equal measures of sarcasm and contemptuous disdain. I do not know why anyone gives them any consequence."

"Because he is a baron, Catherine," said the elder Darcy. "Lord Arundel has standing in society and is, in fact, higher than anyone here can boast."

"And *I* am the daughter of an earl!" cried Lady Catherine.

"Yes, but you are not of the peerage yourself," said Mr. Darcy agreeably. "When you married, you took the social level of your husband, if you recall. Sir Lewis, good man though he was, was a knight, below Lord Arundel in society. That title you hold is, after all, a courtesy."

"Why do you persist in attempting to denigrate me?"

"If you are offended, I apologize, for I intend no denigration—you mistook my meaning. I spoke nothing more than the truth. You all understand *my* feelings for Lord Arundel and his family, so there is no need to repeat them. But I do not make the mistake of thinking because I do not care for him that I may dismiss him without a second thought. A baron is the lowest rank on the scale of the peerage, but even that carries much influence in our society."

It seemed Lady Catherine understood she had lost this skirmish, for she did nothing more than grunt her agreement. Having made his point, Mr. Darcy turned to Anne. "You wish to make the acquaintance of the Bennets?"

"I do," replied Anne. "Everything I have heard about them suggests the eldest are true gems. I am also curious, for I wonder what manner of ogres these people must be to have earned the undying animosity of such a congenial family as yours."

Mr. Darcy laughed, as did several others in the room, though Lady Catherine continued to scowl. Darcy used the opportunity to inject his opinion into the conversation.

"You must also remember that the walls are even now crumbling between us." When his father turned to him askance, Darcy clarified: "Unless you mean to throw off Bingley's friendship, we must accept one of the Bennet sisters into our home. From what I have heard, a proposal is imminent."

"Mr. Bingley shall be so happy," said Georgiana. "When I met Miss Bennet in the bookshop, she struck me as a lovely woman."

Though Mr. Darcy did not reply to Georgiana's assertion, he appeared thoughtful. "I am uncertain how I might have missed it, William, but you speak the truth. As I am as fond of Bingley's society as you are, I suppose there is little we can do but accept her when he brings her here."

"Do not sound as if Bingley is bringing a murderer into your midst, Uncle!" exclaimed Fitzwilliam with a laugh.

"Yes, well, she *is* a Bennet," replied Mr. Darcy.

Everyone in the room caught the undertone of irony in his words and they all laughed, except for Lady Catherine, who huffed and glared at them all in grumpy silence. Though Darcy thought the lady was sillier than usual, he thought he understood her antipathy for the Bennet family. Lady Catherine, on general principle, was against any young lady being at all cordial with Darcy, for the simple fact that she wished him to marry her daughter, and in her mind, if there was no one else who was a potential wife, he would choose Anne. It was an inane way of looking at it, but so very quintessential of his aunt's thinking.

Of more import to Darcy was this short conversation between his family and his father's acceptance of the inevitability of Jane Bennet finding her way into their circle. If his father was willing to accept *Bingley's* future wife, it was possible he might be induced to accept Darcy's choice too. The hope in Darcy's heart rose apace, for he could now imagine a future where he might acknowledge the love in his heart to his family.

Chapter XVIII

The day of the dinner with the Bingley family was witness to a significant and long-awaited event. Even Jane had not expected Mr. Bingley at Longbourn that morning, and when he arrived, full of nervous energy and excitement, Elizabeth suspected she knew what he planned.

The couple walked out to the gardens behind the house, and when they were gone, the sisters' excitement made itself known in their enthusiastic conjectures, for they all thought they knew what was happening. Lydia, as was her wont, was the sister who exclaimed the loudest.

"This is most unfair," said she, "for I had always intended to be the first sister to marry!"

It was an old and worn jest Lydia had been using since she had been old enough to know what marriage was, though Elizabeth had often wondered if it *was* a jest. Lady Margaret hushed her youngest daughter and Lydia, though she still pouted, turned to Kitty and started whispering with her. It was not long before the couple returned, and the matter was confirmed.

"Mr. Bingley has gone to Papa," said Jane the moment she re-entered the sitting-room.

Knowing what it all meant, the sisters gathered around her, laughing congratulations flowing between them. Elizabeth laughed along with the rest, content that Jane's situation was now settled. It was fortunate, she reflected, that her parents possessed the characters they did, for she did not think many of their level would approve of their daughter marrying a man of Mr. Bingley's position in society. Jane would not be denied her happiness, and Elizabeth could not be any more pleased for her sister.

Soon, Lord Arundel came out with a beaming Mr. Bingley and announced the engagement to the family, leading to the congratulations flowing even more freely. Mr. Bingley, standing by Jane, accepted them with his ebullient cheer, and when Mr. Collins came, the gentleman had some choice words for him.

"I might wonder, sir, why you have allowed me to upstage you in this matter," said a laughing Mr. Bingley. "Shall you eventually take a similar step with your own Bennet sister, or is several years of acquaintance not enough for you to come to the point?"

It amused Elizabeth to hear Mr. Bingley's teasing words, though it appeared Mary was not so pleased. The target of Mr. Bingley's provocation, however, was not affected in the slightest.

"Everything in its proper season, Mr. Bingley. In the future, I believe calling you brother shall please me."

As this was the most open statement of intent Mr. Collins had ever made, Mary blushed, though it did not seem she was at all averse to the gentleman's declaration.

The occasion called for a celebration, and while Elizabeth thought there would be much more of that the coming evening, they could not allow Mr. Bingley to depart without acknowledging what had happened. Lady Margaret called to the kitchens for some spiced wine, and they all raised their glasses in hearty congratulations, toasting the couple's future happiness.

It was while she was ensconced in the bosom of her family as they applauded the successful conclusion to Mr. Bingley's courtship of Longbourn's eldest daughter that Elizabeth felt a little envy once again creep into the corners of her heart. And just like the last time she had felt this, it was not for Jane's good fortune, but the freedom she had to express her devotion to the man of her heart. Elizabeth longed for that freedom.

For Mr. Darcy now owned an indisputable portion of her heart. In fact, he owned all of it. Perhaps someday there would come a time when she would be at liberty to show her devotion to all. But that time was not now, and a part of her longed for that happiness Jane now experienced.

It was the knowledge that her beloved sister deserved whatever good thing came her way which allowed Elizabeth to fix her attention on the good in the situation rather than the uncertainty of her own. Mr. Bingley stayed only a short time, for the family was due back that evening. While he was there, Elizabeth allowed herself the freedom to rejoice in her sister's good fortune. There would be time to mull over her own future in the confines of her own room.

Having successfully proposed to his angel, Charles Bingley could not return to Netherfield without informing his friend of his good fortune. Darcy had not always supported Bingley's pursuit of the eldest Bennet daughter, but his eventual acceptance had meant the world to Bingley. The trick was to inform Darcy but to refrain from making a scene of the matter, for though Darcy had accepted Bingley's intention to offer for Miss Bennet, Bingley was still uncertain of the man's father's feelings on the subject. Mr. Robert Darcy was a man Bingley respected as much as he had ever respected any man, including his own father. Bingley would tread carefully where the elder gentleman was concerned.

It was fortunate, then, that Bingley found his friend alone that morning and could communicate his good news in private. When he had done so, Darcy congratulated him and gave him a hearty slap on the back.

"That is excellent news, my friend. Now we have only to discover what Miss Bennet sees in you, for I am not convinced she understands what trials she is taking on."

Even had Darcy meant it as a serious insult, Bingley did not think he had it in him to feel offense that day, for his mood was far too good. "Yes, well, let us not inform her too quickly, shall we? I would not wish to scare her away before the wedding has even taken place."

Darcy laughed and agreed. "Believe me, Bingley, I shall keep my thoughts on the matter to myself."

For perhaps half an hour Bingley stayed at Pemberley speaking of his good fortune, for Bingley was of the opinion he could never speak enough of the perfections of Miss Jane Bennet, soon to be Mrs. Bingley. Darcy, after his initial congratulations, did not say much, but it had often been this way between the friends. Bingley thought his friend's mind was on another subject entirely, for he often stared at nothing, seeing nothing. Again, this was not out of character, and as Darcy answered in all the appropriate places, Bingley did not think much about his friend's reticence.

Upon leaving Pemberley, Bingley returned to Netherfield to prepare for the evening, and while there discovered an impediment to the evening's entertainment. Bingley spent the rest of the morning dealing with some estate business, but when he found his mother at luncheon, she communicated an unforeseen problem to him.

"Caroline sent word through her maid that she will not join us for luncheon," said Mrs. Bingley when he sat with her at the table. "She claims a headache."

Bingley saw through Caroline's actions in an instant. "She does not wish to attend tonight's dinner."

Though his mother did not reply, Bingley was observant enough to discern that her thoughts on the matter were identical to his. For a moment, Bingley contemplated what he should do when he decided he must not allow his sister's designs to stand. Motioning to a nearby footman, Darcy had the housekeeper summoned.

"Please instruct my sister's maid that she is to inform her mistress to present herself here in no more than fifteen minutes."

If the housekeeper was at all surprised by the uncompromising quality of his instruction, she did not show it. The woman went away, leaving him alone with his mother as luncheon was served. Mrs. Bingley was nervous about the situation, as evidenced in her glances and the uncertainty in her eyes.

"I would prefer you did not argue with your sister, Charles. Nothing good can come of it."

"There will be no argument, Mother," replied Bingley, helping himself to some of the dishes placed on the table. "I cannot allow Caroline to offend the Bennet family, and I will inform her of a certain piece of important information she now lacks."

Mrs. Bingley nodded—Bingley had informed her of his engagement as soon as he arrived home, much to her delight—and turned to her meal. As the minutes passed, Bingley watched the clock, waiting for the exact moment when the fifteen minutes he had allotted were passed. If Caroline did not arrive within that time, Bingley would not lose any time in dragging her from her apartments. It was fortunate she entered the room as the last seconds of that fifteen minutes expired.

"Was it necessary to order me from my room, Charles?" asked his sister, sporting a cold compress on her forehead. "As I told Betty to inform you all, I have a headache today."

A lesson Bingley had learned from the Darcy family was never to allow the servants to witness a family disagreement. Knowing this would not reflect well on any of them, he dismissed the attending footmen, ensuring the doors had been closed behind them, before turning his attention to his sister.

"Do not think me witless, Caroline," said Bingley, though in a tone designed to foster conciliation. "I am well aware your aching head has made an appearance the day that we are to go to Longbourn for dinner."

"If you believe I can command my head to ache whenever I please, you grossly overestimate my control."

Bingley shook his head with annoyance. "Caroline, I do not understand you. I do not assert that you are shallow, but we have all known of your desire to rise in society. Will a connection to the noble family of Bennet not be a feather in our cap?"

"I have nothing against the Bennet family," said Caroline; Bingley thought she was telling the truth. "It is my contention, however, that having been long aligned with the Darcy family, you are betraying our friendship with them."

"It is not as much of a betrayal as you think," replied Bingley. "Darcy himself supports me in my pursuit of Miss Bennet, and I doubt he would do that if he opposed my actions."

Caroline looked away, but he could not mistake the thin line of her lips betraying her displeasure. Eager as she was to provoke Darcy's interest and become the future mistress of Pemberley, she still assumed that a Bennet bride for her brother would lower her chances of eliciting a proposal from Darcy. Though he had tried to inform her that Darcy had no interest in her as a prospective bride, Caroline had never listened, and Bingley was not about to belabor that point.

"In this instance, your defiance is detrimental, Caroline, for you lack a certain piece of information which would make your path clear."

When his sister glanced at him, suspicion in her eyes, Bingley nodded and said: "Yes, as you have likely already guessed, I proposed to Miss Bennet this morning; she accepted me. I am now engaged, and all your protests will not change it.

"Upon leaving Longbourn I traveled to Pemberley, and Darcy congratulated me on my engagement, so there is no reason to suppose he will throw off my friendship. If he were to do so, I would regret it, but it would not cause me a moment's hesitation. I am set on my course and have been for some time. No dissent will sway me."

Dismayed, Caroline closed her eyes and shook her head. "I wish you had acted with more restraint, Charles. This will damage us in the eyes of the Darcys, and more particular in Mr. Darcy's eyes, regardless of what his son thinks."

"I expect better of Mr. Darcy than that," replied Bingley. "Regardless, it does not signify. The engagement is real and I will not repent for asking for the hand of the woman I love. As for today's dinner, the Bingley family will *all* be attending. I shall not insult my future family by allowing you to plead a nonexistent headache. Unless you are confined to your bed with obvious illness, you *will* attend with us."

"In this matter," interrupted Mrs. Bingley, "I support Charles. There is nothing you can do but smile and accept the situation. Let us make a good impression, Caroline, for I know you enjoy Miss Bennet's company."

"On the few occasions I have visited with her," said Caroline, though grudgingly, "I have found her to be a sweet woman. The youngest sisters, however, are not their sister's equal in manners, and I find them intolerable."

"Then you are need not speak to them," said Bingley. "But there will be no veiled remarks about anyone in the family. You will attend tonight, Caroline—I insist upon it."

Later, when the driver brought the Bingley carriage to the front door in anticipation of their departure, Caroline was on hand as he had required. There was little enthusiasm in her and Bingley knew she would rather not be there at all, but she had obeyed—that was the important point. Caroline was well enough schooled in how to behave that she would hide her rancor, and the desire to avoid offending a family of high consequence would be foremost in her mind. Thus, Bingley turned his attention away from his unhappy sister and toward what he was certain would be a marvelous night in company with Miss Bennet.

It was obvious to anyone who cared to look that Miss Bingley was not happy to be at Longbourn that night. Elizabeth was not an unobservant woman, having had engaged in the study of more difficult persons in the past than Caroline Bingley. Of more importance to Miss Bingley's visit to Longbourn that evening, was that other members of the family who were not inclined to be as forgiving could see it also.

"Mrs. Bingley," exclaimed Elizabeth's mother when the housekeeper showed the Bingley family into the room. "We are so pleased to have you with us this evening, and words cannot describe our excitement for the engagement of our dearest Jane to your son."

"Thank you, Lady Margaret," said Mrs. Bingley. "I am delighted with the welcome you and your family have shown my family, and in particular to my son. I believe I may say, with no hint of hyperbole, that your affability has been unmatched."

"We have done nothing extraordinary, my dear," replied Lady Margaret, pressing Mrs. Bingley's hands. "Your son is an excellent man. You should be proud of him."

Then Lady Margaret turned to Miss Bingley and welcomed her, saying: "We all welcome you to our home too, Miss Bingley. I believe at one time you and Jane were excellent friends, though it has been some time since we have seen you at Longbourn. Let this be a new beginning of your former friendship, for you are soon to be sisters."

"Thank you, Lady Margaret," said Miss Bingley, giving her hostess a correct curtsey. "My brother is gaining the best of women to be his new wife; I could not be any happier."

Though Miss Bingley's words were all that was correct, her lack of enthusiasm spoke to her true feelings on the subject. Elizabeth would not accuse the woman of thinking herself better than the daughters of a baron, though she remembered Miss Bingley's insolent words from the bookshop. To anyone who knew Miss Bingley's character, however, her wish that her brother had approached *another* lady of high society could not be misunderstood.

"Come, Mrs. Bingley," said Lady Margaret, ignoring Miss Bingley's lack of enthusiasm, "let us speak together for a time, for I have several ideas for the upcoming celebration, and would hear your sentiments."

Flattered at the wife of a peer asking for her opinion, Mrs. Bingley went along with her, and soon they were seated together, debating the benefits of satin versus lace, from what Elizabeth could hear. Mr. Bingley stood with Jane speaking lightly, and unless Elizabeth missed her guess, the gentleman had calculated the inclusion of his sister to ensure she did not embarrass him with her behavior. Miss Bingley did not say much, and after a time, Mr. Bingley seemed to forget all about his sister as he fixed his attention on Jane.

The addition of Mr. Gardiner to their party, along with Mr. Collins, evened the numbers out a little, though the gentlemen were still outnumbered. The rest of the party was separated by sexes, as Lord Arundel stood with his brother-in-law and Mr. Collins, though the latter abandoned them after some time for Mary's company. Kitty and Lydia sat together as was their wont, and once Mr. Collins was close to Mary, Elizabeth contented herself with the society of her youngest sisters. When she drifted away from Mr. Bingley and Jane, Miss Bingley sat alone, and while she spoke on occasion, she spent more time in thought, though Elizabeth could not divine the content of those ruminations.

Dinner continued in a like manner, though in the dining room Miss Bingley's isolation was even more apparent. As Mr. Bingley sat in the position of honor at Lady Margaret's right, and Mrs. Bingley occupied a similar location beside Lord Arundel, Miss Bingley seemed to feel the lowness of her position in the middle of the table near Elizabeth's younger sisters. It did not make her unruly, but her lack of interest in speaking to anyone became obvious to them all. As dinner progressed, this situation became more pronounced, until Uncle Gardiner appeared determined to provoke a response from the woman.

"You must be pleased for your brother, Miss Bingley," said Mr. Gardiner, drawing her attention to him. "He is a good man, one my Bennet relations have come to esteem. I hope you understand the good fortune he has obtained because of his sterling character."

Lady Margaret was engrossed in speaking to Mr. Bingley, and Lord Arundel was intent upon whatever the gentleman's mother was saying, so Elizabeth thought only those near her heard the exchange. Miss Bingley, however, behaved with precise correctness, as if the prince regent himself were present.

"Charles is an excellent brother; it pleases me you all recognize his exceptional qualities. Although my father passed away early to our misfortune, Charles has had good examples of other admirable men to guide him in becoming his own man."

It was, perhaps, an unsubtle reminder of Mr. Bingley's continued friendship with the Darcys, and the way Mr. Gardiner looked at her, he was not unaware of it himself. As she did not wish her mother's table to become a battleground, Elizabeth was quick to interject.

"It is clear your father raised you all properly, Miss Bingley," said Elizabeth, drawing the attention of both Miss Bingley and Uncle Gardiner. "All any of us could ask for is good parents to help us weather our most trying years, and while your brother was so blessed, I would also assert his character is naturally good."

"Yes, I can agree with that, Lizzy," said Uncle Gardiner. "I have always been easy with his interest in Jane, for there has never been any question of his character."

"I thank you," said Miss Bingley. By virtue of her short answer, with no further comment, Elizabeth understood Miss Bingley decided it was not in her best interest to elaborate any further.

"Might I assume the Bingley family has received an invitation to the ball at Lucas Lodge?" asked Elizabeth, determined to avoid any other potentially explosive topics.

Miss Bingley seemed grateful for the change of subject. "We have.

I expect a fine evening in fine company, for Lady Charlotte's efforts last year yielded such an elegant affair."

"Though we were not present last year," said Elizabeth, "the year before it was excellent. Lady Charlotte is a talented hostess and an exceptional woman. Jane and I appreciate her friendship."

"I have also been friendly with Lady Charlotte," replied Miss Bingley. The woman paused and eyed Elizabeth, seeming to debate what to say next. Then she essayed to say: "Might I ask what you will wear to the ball? Perhaps we could compare notes."

Sensing a safe topic, it pleased Elizabeth to oblige, and they spent the rest of the meal conversating about fashion. Elizabeth had always known Miss Bingley possessed a keen eye for the best styles, but the woman surprised her when she offered a few suggestions which Elizabeth thought would enhance her own appearance.

Mr. Gardiner looked on them for a few moments after they began to speak, and after a time he winked at Elizabeth and turned to Mary, who was on his other side. In this fashion, the rest of the dinner passed pleasantly.

When the ladies separated from the gentlemen to return to the sitting-room, Elizabeth decided it was best to have a brief word with Miss Bingley. Though the woman had shown good manners, it was still clear to Elizabeth that she wished to be anywhere but at Longbourn that night. Though Miss Bingley had always been skilled at dealing with those higher than her in society, a wrong word to Lady Margaret or Lord Arundel would bring their condemnation down on her head, and Elizabeth did not wish that. When Lady Margaret and Mrs. Bingley drew Jane into a discussion, Elizabeth saw her chance and approached the younger Bingley woman.

"Miss Bingley," said she, "I wish to thank you for your suggestions. I believe I shall incorporate them into my dress on the night of the ball. I hope it shall be to my benefit."

"It was an enjoyable conversation," replied Miss Bingley. It seemed the woman had relaxed to a certain extent, which would make Elizabeth's designs easier to accomplish.

"Yes, it was," agreed Elizabeth. "If you will allow me, I wish to inform you of something, and I ask you do not take offense, for I intend none."

Curious, Miss Bingley agreed there was no offense, to which Elizabeth said: "In the matter of the divide between my family and the Darcy family, I would urge you to take no sides."

A furrow appeared on Miss Bingley's brow and she opened her

mouth to speak. Then she seemed to think better of it, paused in thought for a moment before exhaling and fixing Elizabeth with a sheepish look.

"I had thought I hid my dissatisfaction well."

"It was not noticeable to anyone who did not look for it," replied Elizabeth. "There is nothing I can say in criticism of your behavior tonight, for you have conducted yourself with perfect civility."

"I would have you know," began Miss Bingley, her words halting, "that I bear no ill will toward your sister, nor am I so foolish as to consider her unfit for my brother."

"And I did not think it of you," replied Elizabeth. "It is clear your family has long associated with the Darcy family, and thus your allegiance was toward them. That is understandable.

"As my father has suggested, it will be the younger generation who will resolve the difficulties between our families, and your brother's engagement to Jane is the first step on the road to reconciliation. Perhaps Lord Arundel and Mr. Darcy will never be easy with each other, but most of the rest of us have little antipathy for the Darcys."

It was an oblique sidestepping of the issue, for Elizabeth was well aware that Miss Bingley's opposition had spawned from *her* desire to marry the man Elizabeth herself had already come to love. The woman took the lifeline Elizabeth offered, however, and did not contradict her words.

"I believe that would be best for the neighborhood. The disharmony between your families has existed for too long."

"In that, you have my fervent agreement," replied Elizabeth.

The sudden thought struck her that though their discourse was cordial at present, should Miss Bingley know of the state of affairs between Elizabeth and Mr. Darcy, she would loathe Elizabeth above all other women. The urge to laugh at the thought was strong, but Elizabeth resisted it, intent upon neutralizing Miss Bingley's venom.

"And it is not so terrible, you know," said Elizabeth with a grin. "Though you may have had your own ideas about who would suit your brother as a marriage partner, the connection to a baron is not an inconsequential matter, is it?"

"No, it is not," said Miss Bingley, as if she had not thought of it in those terms before. Elizabeth thought it probable she had not.

Her point made, Elizabeth fell silent, allowing Miss Bingley to speak if she desired it. The woman, however, remained thoughtful for some time, until their mother released Jane from whatever discussion she had thought necessary. Then Miss Bingley approached her and they sat together, their conversation becoming easier and warmer as the evening passed. Pleased with herself for assisting Miss Bingley to acceptance, Elizabeth turned her attention to her sisters.

When the gentlemen rejoined them, Elizabeth noted her father and Mr. Gardiner watching Miss Bingley as Mr. Bingley went straight to the two women and joined them. Soon all three were speaking and laughing together.

"It seems Miss Bingley has grown more accepting since the ladies returned to the sitting-room," observed Mr. Gardiner when Elizabeth came close.

"Yes, well, she remembered the benefit to her family of being connected to a baron," said Elizabeth. "And she is not a *bad* woman, after all; she is nothing more than one who attempted to remain loyal to friends of longstanding."

Lord Arundel and Uncle Gardiner seemed to understand that Elizabeth's words were an overreach, but neither commented. Instead, Lord Arundel nodded his approval.

"It was good of you to help her remember that fact, Lizzy. Though her behavior has not been egregious, it was clear when she arrived that she was not happy. Miss Bingley has occasionally spoken out of turn; I would not wish to reprimand her if she should say something without adequate forethought."

At that moment, Miss Bingley and Jane laughed at something Mr. Bingley said. Elizabeth regarded them, pleased, and turned back to the men of her family.

"It appears all is resolved. There is no need to worry."

With a nod, Lord Arundel turned away and joined his wife, leaving Uncle Gardiner with Elizabeth. The gentleman took her hand with affection and said: "Your role as a peacemaker suits you well, Lizzy. I think you are the only one of your family who possesses the ruthlessness required to fulfill the position in the manner it must be occupied."

Then he turned away himself, leaving Elizabeth to bask in the approbation of the men she cared about most. There was one more gentleman whose opinion mattered as much—or more than anyone else. Elizabeth had no more notion that her father and uncle would accept Mr. Darcy. But these small steps to improve matters would bear fruit—of this, Elizabeth was certain.

CHAPTER XIX

$\mathcal{B}$alls were always an occasion for young ladies to anticipate. Whether for a special young gentleman's benefit or just a time when a woman could be admired for her youthful beauty, it was a time for primping and preening, exquisite gowns and elaborate hairstyles. Given these considerations, it was difficult to prepare for an evening in company when a young brother of ten years insisted on keeping a young woman company.

"You will be the most beautiful lady at the ball tonight, Lizzy," said Thomas for perhaps the third time. Seated as he was on the edge of Elizabeth's bed, feet dangling over the side, swinging at times, the boy was enraptured by Elizabeth's preparations for the evening's entertainment, though she had learned he had no desire to attend himself.

"Thank you, Thomas," said Elizabeth, gazing at the boy with affection in the mirror, while Lucy worked on pinning her unruly locks just so. "But I rather think Jane will lay title to that claim, and several other ladies are just as pretty as I."

"Jane is a pretty young woman, but you will outshine them all," averred Thomas, his tone filled with the confidence of absolute surety.

There was nothing to say to that, so Elizabeth contented herself with a softly spoken thanks and turned her attention back to Lucy's efforts. Her maid had taken her hair back and piled it in an elegant knot on the back of her head, lending her a certain sophistication she most often eschewed in favor of a simpler style. Elizabeth rather liked the effects.

Though Jane was preparing with Mr. Bingley in mind and Mary with Mr. Collins, Elizabeth was not doing so to impress anyone in particular. At least, no one would see her preparations as a compliment to a particular man. Mr. Darcy had suggested they might dance the supper set together, but in reality, Elizabeth thought it unlikely. While she had seen a thawing of the opinions of some members of her family toward the Darcys, it was not enough for such an open statement. No, she was certain no Darcy would dance with a Bennet that evening.

"I do not believe I should like to dance."

Thomas's voice interrupted Elizabeth's thoughts and her eyes once again found his in the mirror, a question inherent in her look. The little scamp was only too happy to oblige.

"Why, it would mean being close to a girl. I prefer boys, for girls do not know how to have fun."

Lucy snorted her laughter, and Elizabeth was no less amused. "Oh, am *I* also afflicted by this lack of knowledge you attribute to all girls?"

"You are an exception," replied Thomas. "Other than Lydia, none of my other sisters like to have fun, and even she can be a bore. Most other girls are the same."

"I believe you will have a different perspective when you become older, Thomas," said Elizabeth.

While her brother gazed at her with open skepticism, he asked: "Why do you say that?"

"Because you have said nothing different from almost every young boy since the dawn of time," said Elizabeth.

Lucy spoke to say she was finished, and Elizabeth admired herself in the mirror before thanking her maid and rising. Then she went to the bed and caught her young brother up in an embrace.

"Trust me, my dear Thomas. One day, you will realize that ladies are nice, and you will find one you cannot live without. Just like Jane, who once told me she would never marry because boys were such disgusting creatures, you will discover the value in members of the other sex."

"If you say so, Lizzy," replied Thomas.

"I do. Now, off with you, for I must dress."

When Thomas scampered from the room, Elizabeth watched him with fondness, before turning a raised eyebrow on her maid. Lucy grinned and said:

"I have three younger brothers myself, Miss Elizabeth. They are all the same."

Elizabeth laughed. "It is difficult for me to keep up with *one*—I should not like to have *three!*"

"And are sisters much different?"

Shaking her head, Elizabeth said: "I believe you have caught me there, Lucy. Sometimes Lydia has been as difficult as any brother could be."

Lucy smiled and helped Elizabeth into her ballgown, making a final few touches to her appearance before Elizabeth dismissed her maid for the night, assuring her that she would not require her services when she returned home. The mirror in her vanity provided Elizabeth one last look at her gown, and she found herself pleased, for the ivory gown clung to her slender form, accentuated by the bits of soft green ribbon Lucy had woven into her hair. Elbow-length gloves of the same hue as her gown covered her hands and arms, and Lucy had painted her cheeks with just the slightest hint of rouge. Though Elizabeth knew Jane would outshine every other lady in the room, she was pleased with her appearance.

In the manor's entryway, the ladies gathered to don their pelisses and ready themselves. No departure could be complete without Lady Margaret inspecting her daughters' appearances, adjusting the way a dress hung here or smoothing an unruly curl there. No daughter received as much attention as Elizabeth, and it was all for her untamable hair, which had long been the bane of her existence.

"It appears Lucy has done wonders with your mane, Lizzy, though I suspect it will be a fright by the end of the evening."

"Do not allow Lucy to hear you say that, Mama," replied Elizabeth, "for she would feel offense at your lack of faith in her abilities. I believe she considers her efforts this night to be a masterpiece."

Lady Margaret patted her daughter's cheek with amused affection. "The effect of her efforts is stupendous, my dear. You shall be the talk of the room, for you will draw every eye to you. If you play your cards right, an eligible young man might even take a fancy to you."

"Thank you, Mama," said Elizabeth. "But I believe I am in no rush to follow in Jane's footsteps."

"Nor should you be. But when you find a young man without whom you cannot live, you must act to secure him. Do not let love slip from your grasp, should it present itself."

The effect of this comment on Elizabeth was not as Lady Margaret had intended. Giving her a smile and her hand a pat, Lady Margaret moved to another of Elizabeth's sisters to examine her, leaving Elizabeth with her thoughts. No doubt Lady Margaret had thought to suggest Elizabeth could find a man to love, not knowing she already had. The longing for Mr. Darcy, for the acknowledgment and acceptance of both their families, filled Elizabeth, and she wondered if those who mattered most would ever allow their love.

"Ah, what visions of loveliness we see before us, Brother," a voice interrupted them. Uncle Gardiner had entered the room with their father and was gazing at them all with appreciation.

"Yes, it would seem to be so," replied their father. "I declare I have some of the loveliest daughters in the kingdom." Lord Arundel grinned and approached his wife, giving her cheek a kiss. "And you are as lovely as any of them my dear, for I believe you could pass as one of their sisters."

"Flatterer," said Lady Margaret, though she was not displeased with her husband's words.

"Perhaps," replied Lord Arundel with a wink. "But I think *I* shall be as envied as Bingley or Collins tonight, for I shall have the fairest lady of them all gracing my arm."

"Speaking of the aforementioned gentlemen," said Uncle Gardiner with a nod at Mr. Collins, who had entered with them and was regarding their interaction with great affection, "I believe that Bingley has Jane's first and Collins Mary's. Thus, I shall ask Elizabeth for your hand for the first sets."

"Of course I will dance with you," said Elizabeth, by this time accustomed to the ache of her situation with Mr. Darcy.

"Thank you, my lady," said Uncle Gardiner, bowing to kiss her hand. When he straightened again, he turned to Lydia and Kitty and winked. "I hope you do not hold my request to Elizabeth against me, my dears. It would make me happy if I could dance with all my fair nieces tonight."

"Of course not, Uncle," said Kitty. "Lizzy has precedence, after all—it is only right she should dance the first with you."

"Then shall we depart?"

To the general agreement of all, they gathered their wraps and reticules and followed the elder members of their party out into the moonlit night. Two carriages awaited them, Lord Arundel's largest carriage along with Uncle Gardiner's—it was his custom to travel to events with his relations. The arrangements were quickly made, the eldest three siblings and Mr. Collins to travel with Mr. Gardiner while the youngest two with the baron and baroness, and once the doors closed behind them they departed.

The journey was an easy distance, past the town of Lambton and to the north a little way, and the party was in good spirits as they traveled, with much laughter and jesting passing between them. Even Mary and Mr. Collins, who were of a more serious disposition than the others were quick to join in. The moonlight, which Elizabeth had noticed upon exiting the house, was bright, allowing the drivers to guide the carriage through the labyrinth of fine Derbyshire roads with little difficulty. Soon, the house at Lucas Manor rose before them, signaling the end of their journey.

When the carriage stopped in front of the entrance after a brief wait for the carriages before them, Mr. Gardiner and Mr. Collins stepped down, turned and assisted Jane and Mary, and Elizabeth in turn. They waited by the side for the Bennet carriage, and when they were all present, they turned to enter the house.

Lucas Manor was a grand old estate, large and imposing, with the finest ballroom in the district, though Elizabeth had heard that Pemberley's formal ballroom rivaled it in grandeur. The family, consisting of the earl and his only child, stood near the entrance greeting their guests. In this, Elizabeth was grateful the family was so small, for the line moved with swiftness, unlike it would have if one of the larger families had been hosting the event.

The baron greeted the earl and shared a few words with him, after which his family made their way down the line. Friends that they were, Lady Charlotte greeted both Jane and Elizabeth with some enthusiasm, congratulating Jane on her recent engagement, while welcoming Elizabeth in the manner of an old friend.

"Elizabeth," said the woman, "I hope you find the entertainment to your taste tonight."

Confused at the mysterious way in which her friend had spoken, Elizabeth was slow in replying. "You know I enjoy a ball, Charlotte."

"Yes, I am certain you do," said she. "Let this be a night you find special enjoyment. Who knows? Perhaps you will even find a man who can be to you what Mr. Bingley is to Jane."

It was so like what Lady Margaret had said before they departed that Elizabeth had no recourse but to laugh. "What should I make of this sudden desire to pair me with an eligible man?" asked Elizabeth. "Before we left, my mother also suggested I might find my future husband here."

Lady Charlotte grinned. "Your mother is wise, Elizabeth. I have no doubt tonight will be a memorable might for you. Enjoy yourself, my friend, for I believe it will be a magical time."

With a nod, Elizabeth moved away, mindful of the line of those waiting to greet their hosts for the evening. Accepting her uncle's arm, Elizabeth allowed him to lead her into the ballroom, where tasteful and artful arrangements coupled with the thoughtful placing of candles to minimize the dripping of wax on the revelers gave the impression of romance. In the center of the dance floor, Elizabeth noted the earl had commissioned a large representation of his crest in the customary chalk, elaborate designs flowing out from it to cover the whole floor. It was a work of art, though it was destined to be destroyed by many thousands of footsteps treading upon it that night. It was a wonderful display and so considerate of the earl, for his guests would not need to chalk their slippers against the smooth slickness of the floor.

The Bennets met their other relations there that evening, for not only were Mr. Edward and Mrs. Madeline Gardiner in attendance but Aunt Madeline's family — the Plumbers — were also present, alongside many more. When the greetings were offered and accepted, Aunt Madeline made her way to Elizabeth and greeted her with a soft embrace, then grasping Elizabeth's shoulders at arms' length.

"How have you been, Lizzy?"

"Very well, Aunt. It has been some time since we have come into Lambton. How are the children?"

"Oh, they are well and trying my nerves," replied Aunt Madeline with good humor. Then her manner turned serious. "Have there been any . . . developments of late, Lizzy?"

Elizabeth knew to what her aunt referred, and she colored, thinking there had been a great many developments. But she had already informed her aunt of too much of her doings — she would not say more in a crowded ballroom.

"Nothing of substance, Aunt."

When Aunt Madeline watched her, skepticism clear in her gaze, Elizabeth was quick to assert: "All is well, Aunt. Truly there is nothing the matter."

Before her aunt could respond, a sudden cessation of all talk in the room, though it lasted for only an instant, alerted Elizabeth to the arrival of the Darcy party. It had always been thus, for the neighborhood held its collective breath for the second of the warring parties to arrive.

Aunt Madeline looked at her with some concern, but Elizabeth would not allow herself to show how affected she knew she would be at the sight of Mr. Darcy. To prove her aunt there was nothing to worry herself over, Elizabeth gave her a smile. Then she turned to see the newcomers and looked into the eyes of Mr. Fitzwilliam Darcy.

At Pemberley, the Darcy party had partaken in a similar ritual of preparation for the evening's entertainment. Darcy had always thought it was easier for men than women, for after a bath, his valet would help him dress, and once his man had pulled a comb through his hair, he was ready to depart.

On that evening, anticipation had prompted him to prepare early, the result of which was his pacing in the entryway while he waited for the rest of the family to prepare themselves. Though Darcy knew his wish of dancing the supper set with Elizabeth was nothing more than fantasy, the ability to see her after being denied the past few days was a palpable longing in his heart. The trick would be to avoid making a scene by staring at her all night.

"It seems your brother is eager to depart," came the voice of his cousin. The note in his voice informed Darcy that Fitzwilliam was in a teasing mood, but then, when was he not? "Given how much he has always detested such activities, one might ask why he is so impatient to depart tonight."

"It must be Anne," said Alexander with a smirk. "Perhaps he is wavering and will fulfill Lady Catherine's fondest wish tonight."

Fitzwilliam laughed, Alexander joining in the mirth. Darcy did not waste the effort to glare at them, for he knew it would only induce their behavior to worsen. Even that decision did not prevent his cousin from continuing to speak.

"By your behavior, I might almost think you have a lady you wish to see, Darcy. Do you care to share the identity of the wondrous creature who fills your thoughts?"

"You are being ridiculous," snapped Darcy, sidestepping the subject. "If we must attend, I should like to get it over with. I doubt I will dance much tonight."

"Then you are missing a grand time," said Alexander. "There are some ladies of uncommon beauty who will be in attendance; one of them must be acceptable to your discriminating tastes."

"The Bennet sisters, for example." Darcy turned a confused eye on his brother, wondering if Alexander knew something of his meetings with Miss Elizabeth. "They are pretty enough to tempt any man.

Perhaps I shall ask one of them to dance tonight."

Fitzwilliam snorted. "If you did so, it might provoke a war. Now, if your brother did so . . . ."

"It would be better if you left your impudence at home, Alexander," said Darcy, ignoring his cousin. Inside he released the tension his companions' teasing had provoked, for it seemed like nothing more than their typical brand of carelessness. "I do not think the baron would appreciate a Darcy asking one of his daughters to dance."

"Could he speak against it?" demanded Alexander. "We all know the consequences for a young lady if she refuses a request to dance. And it *is* only a dance."

"I do not disagree," replied Darcy. "But I believe it would be best to avoid entertaining such foolish notions."

"If it is foolish, then I do not wish to be rational," snapped Alexander. "I care nothing for our stupid dispute, for there is little sense in it."

Alexander turned away and refused to speak again, leaving Fitzwilliam and Darcy looking at each other, wondering what he was about. In the end, Darcy decided there was little to concern himself. As far as he was aware, Alexander had not had contact with any Bennet sister other than the two outside the bookshop, and would not be acquainted with them, which would render any efforts to dance with them impossible. Fitzwilliam seemed to agree with Darcy, for he shrugged in response to Darcy's questioning look.

It was a few moments before the rest of the party joined them. Georgiana, who was still not out and did not attend every neighborhood function, was eager for her first ball, while Anne appeared willing to partake in the evening herself. Both were beautiful in their well-fitted ballgowns, Georgiana in a more girlish style, while Anne gave the impression of a sophisticated and wealthy young woman, which she was. Had Darcy not thought of her as a sister all these years, he might have been interested, for she was not only intelligent but attractive too.

Lady Catherine was watching Darcy, wondering if there would be anyone in attendance who should concern her, while Darcy's father appeared to be girding himself for an unpleasant task. Understanding his father's feelings—for it had been forever thus since the passing of Darcy's mother—he shot his father a sympathetic smile. Lady Anne had been a wonderful woman, and Darcy missed her almost as much as his father did.

In part to remove his thoughts from such a morbid subject, Darcy turned to Anne. "As my father will dance the first with my sister and Fitzwilliam will impose upon his intended, I should like to ask for your hand for the first sets if you will oblige me."

With a giggle, Anne accepted, though Fitzwilliam protested Darcy's mocking words. As he might have expected, Lady Catherine's look became positively gloating. It was certain she was anticipating a wedding due to his application for a single dance. Anne saw this and shook her head at her mother.

"It is only a dance," said she which set Lady Catherine to scowling. "Besides, it seems to me it is nothing more than Darcy's usual attempt to give no young lady precedence by asking for her first sets. By asking me, he does not raise a young lady's hopes, and can still dance the first."

"You say that as if Darcy *ever* wished to dance at all, let alone the first," said Fitzwilliam.

"Do not tease Darcy, Anthony," scolded Anne. "I understand his desire to avoid being the prize stallion at a horse market. In a similar way, I understand the feeling very well."

"It may be best if you held your tongue, Catherine," said Robert Darcy, and Darcy noted that his aunt's mouth snapped shut. "I suspect it would be best if we departed. Let us go now, for we shall be late if we do not."

The company agreed and after a final check of their attire, they were soon off. The Darcy's main carriage, followed by another family carriage, both gleamed in the light of a few torches along Pemberley's drive. They made their way to the conveyances to embark, and as they were doing so, Darcy found himself beside Anne.

"You should not tease Mother like that, Darcy," said Anne in a soft voice, careful to avoid being overheard by her mother who was walking ahead with Darcy's father. "You know she takes every interaction between us as proof we shall do as she wishes."

Though her admonishment tempted Darcy to respond, he contented himself with grinning. The gentlemen handed the ladies into the carriages—the Darcy family settled into one, while Fitzwilliam and the de Bourgh's used the other—and then they set off. There was not much conversation as they traveled, as each contemplated the night ahead. Considering the scene which had just occurred prior to their departure, Darcy knew he should feel some remorse for raising Lady Catherine's hopes, but he found he could not. The lady still clung to the hope they would marry, no matter how many times they denied it; and yet she persisted. It was all her own doing.

The distance was not great and soon the Darcy carriage pulled into the torchlit courtyard of the Lucas estate, where they disembarked. The company entered the house where they met the earl and his daughter, and Darcy was grateful to see there were few ahead of them in line and almost no one behind. It seemed they were one of the last families to arrive.

Darcy greeted the earl and his daughter, but his heart was not in it, for he knew every step, every moment brought him closer to once again being in Miss Elizabeth's presence. Though he knew he could not dance with her, could not approach her or speak with her or bask in the brilliance of her presence, being nearby would be enough. Gazing on perfection was sufficient. It must be.

In the distance, the light of the ballroom beckoned, and Darcy strode forward like one of Odysseus's sailors, drawn by the song of a siren. The décor of the ballroom he did not notice and the few greetings he offered to friends were little more than perfunctory obligations. The ballroom was already full to the brim of those of the neighborhood, scattered about in small groups, conversation a low buzz akin to an insect flitting about near one's ear. Darcy cared not for any of them; he cared only for the one woman he could not acknowledge.

The instant the Darcy party entered, there was a brief lull in the conversation, as if everyone in the room had stopped speaking at that precise moment. Then the mass of humanity seemed to part before him, like the Red Sea parting at Moses's command. And there, at the other end of the room, stood Miss Elizabeth, speaking with someone of her party—her aunt, with whom Darcy had exchanged many conversations.

Then she turned, and Darcy saw her for the first time that night.

CHAPTER XX

*D*arcy was transfixed. The vision who stood before him on the far side of the room was beautiful beyond any earthly notion of beauty. The ivory dress she wore seemed to illuminate her, provide her with some ethereal inner light that outshone every other woman in the room. And when her gaze found his, Darcy felt his heart soar, knowing he had found in her a woman precious as the costliest jewels, her heart as devoted to him as his was to her. It was a sublime moment, and for an instant, the urge to cross the room and sweep her up in his arms was nigh overpowering.

It was the woman by her side who caught Darcy's attention and prevented him from doing something rash. Mrs. Gardiner looked back and forth between Darcy and her niece. Darcy saw her lips curl in a smile, and at that moment Darcy knew their secret was not as much of a secret as he had thought. Far from regarding them with repugnance, the woman appeared to be enjoying their inability to move, though she put a hand on Miss Elizabeth's shoulder to pull her from her moment with Darcy.

At that moment, the conversation about them began again as a low murmur, which gained strength and rose to a roar. The intimacy between them broken, Darcy turned and attempted to gain better regulation over himself. That evening's festivities had become more daunting, an agony to be endured rather than an amusement to be savored. How Darcy could refrain from making himself a fool over her he did not know.

"It seems the Bennets have preceded us."

Darcy turned at the sound of his father's voice, noting the distaste with which he watched the other family, who, Darcy could see, were doing their best to ignore the Darcys in turn.

"Yes, well you did not expect the earl to slight the Bennets and invite us alone," said Darcy to his father.

His father's eyes found him, for a moment rigid as the hardest diamond. Then his manner softened and he nodded, albeit with an uncharacteristic curtness. "The earl may invite whomever he pleases to his ball."

"There is little to gain from attempting to stare holes in them," said Alexander, close by their father's side. "It is best to ignore them. We have done it many times."

Though Alexander's words were reasonable and his manner dismissive, Darcy noted his brother watching the Bennet family himself, his gaze open and unflinching. Curious, Darcy fixed his brother with a questioning look, but when he noticed, Alexander contented himself with an indifferent shrug.

"Yes, well there is nothing we can do, I suppose," said Mr. Darcy.

For the next fifteen minutes, the Darcy family involved themselves in greeting friends and speaking amongst themselves. Darcy attempted to put the angel from his mind, but he caught sight of her enough times that he wondered that no one had noticed his interest.

On one occasion, not long before the dancing started, Darcy noticed an exchange between Lady Catherine and Lord Arundel. The lady sniffed when she saw the baron's eyes on her, and it appeared Lord Arundel was nothing more than amused at her disdain, for he grinned and favored her with a mock bow. Lady Catherine's response was a haughty glare, after which she turned and ignored the gentleman.

The greeting she shared with Mr. Collins was perfunctory, though the gentleman appeared eager to resume their acquaintance. While he bowed and spoke with ease, Lady Catherine's responses were short and haughty. Darcy was not close enough to hear their exchange, but when Mr. Collins excused himself a short time later, Darcy was certain his aunt's former parson had been disabused of any friendship between them.

A short time later, the strains for the first dance of the evening wafted out over the assembled and they took their positions for the dance. Though Darcy was dancing with Anne, he noted Miss Elizabeth standing up with her uncle, the sound of her laughter rising over the company, imbuing Darcy with a sense of lightness and joy. Oh, to have that laughter directed at him every day, to hear her joy and immerse himself in it as a lover! What greater happiness could mortal man achieve?

"I know you are not interested in me as a wife, Cousin," Anne's amused voice penetrated Darcy's consciousness. "But I am astonished my feminine charms are not enough to hold your attention, even for the short period of a dance."

"I beg your pardon, Anne," said Darcy. "It seems I allowed myself to become distracted when I should have been attending."

Anne's laughter informed Darcy he had not offended her. "It is of no consequence, Darcy, though I will own I am curious who has caught your interest."

"No one in particular," replied Darcy, though certain he had not fooled Anne in the slightest.

"I might have thought it was one of the Bennet sisters," said Anne, fixing him with an amused grin. "But I know you Darcys detest all Bennets and will not fraternize with those you consider the enemy."

"I do not hate all Bennets," protested Darcy.

"If that is the truth, it pleases me to hear it. Then I will not offend you when I ask for introductions to them throughout the course of the evening."

"Not at all," replied Darcy, not having to feign his approval. "If you do so, however, you will need to contend with your mother, for she will not appreciate your actions."

"Yes, I am acquainted with my mother's opinions," replied Anne. "While I attempt to avoid provoking her anger, I think I shall not suffer a jot of concern tonight."

Amply distracted, Darcy conversed with his cousin for the rest of their time together, and while he still caught sight of Miss Elizabeth occasionally, and the dance drew them together once, he did not allow his attention to waver again. Anne was interested in what she was seeing, asking Darcy questions about those attending, and Darcy agreed to inform her of what he knew, pointing out some ladies with whom he thought she could form friendships. In this pleasant manner, the rest of their time together passed.

To Elizabeth's great surprise, Colonel Fitzwilliam approached her with Lady Charlotte in tow soon after the first sets to request an introduction and a dance.

"Are you certain it is wise?" asked Elizabeth, employing a hint of her teasing manner with the gentleman. "Will your relations not become so incensed with you that they will throw you from Pemberley in their anger?"

Colonel Fitzwilliam showed his genial nature when he guffawed at her jest, saying: "As I informed your sister's future husband, I respect my Darcy relations without hesitation, but I reserve the right to choose my own friends. I hardly think one of them could condemn me for choosing such a bright young lady as a partner for a single dance."

"Then I shall dance with you."

Lady Charlotte fixed them both with a bright smile. "I shall leave you to it, for I believe there are some matters I should see to."

The lady embraced Elizabeth and excused herself, and soon Colonel Fitzwilliam escorted Elizabeth to the dance floor. Though she noted a look of distaste from the elder Darcy, he said nothing in her hearing. The younger Darcy fixed her with an amused look and even dared to roll his eyes at his cousin, which required Elizabeth to stifle a giggle in response.

In fact, Elizabeth was well entertained by Colonel Fitzwilliam. The gentleman was an excellent conversationalist, his manners playful and engaging, and there was no want of conversation between them. The colonel entertained her with his shameless flirting and laughter and even made a few choice comments about members of his party. It was the mention of one of them in particular which sparked Elizabeth's interest.

"Lady Catherine wishes her daughter to marry Mr. Darcy?" asked Elizabeth, not having heard this information before.

"She claims it was an agreement between herself and Darcy's mother while they were in their cradles," said Colonel Fitzwilliam. "Given Darcy is more than three years Anne's elder, I doubt they were *both* in their cradles when this supposed agreement was being planned."

Elizabeth nodded, catching the amused tenor of Colonel Fitzwilliam's words, knowing there was no threat to her happiness from that quarter. "It seems to me the lady is not one to be gainsaid."

"In that you are correct," said Colonel Fitzwilliam with a laugh. "But Darcy is more than a match for her hard-headed insistence, and his father does not favor the match either. Had his father passed away rather than his mother, no doubt Lady Catherine would have been much more insistent, but Uncle will not tolerate her harangues on the matter, so she attempts subtlety."

The dance took them close together in that instant, and Colonel Fitzwilliam took the opportunity to whisper to her as if imparting a secret: "Of course, her attempts at delicacy are about as subtle as riding an unbroken horse."

Elizabeth could not help but chuckle at the picture he painted of his aunt. "I doubt she has given up hope."

"No, in that you are correct. Lady Catherine will not give up hope until Darcy signs the register at his own wedding."

"I thank you for this hint of the workings of the Darcy family, for I find it most amusing."

"Then you would not be averse to making the acquaintance of another of my family who does not bear the Darcy name?" Elizabeth regarded the man, and he saw her look for the question it was. "Anne has made it known she would like an acquaintance with you and your sisters."

"Would we not invite the wrath of your aunt?" asked Elizabeth.

"Perhaps we would," said Colonel Fitzwilliam, still shaking with suppressed laughter. "But Anne has more than enough spine to resist her mother's displeasure and has already informed her mother of her intentions; Lady Catherine will not like it, but she will not interfere."

"If that be the case, it would please me to make her acquaintance," replied Elizabeth.

When the sets had concluded, Colonel Fitzwilliam led her to where Miss de Bourgh's partner for the previous dance had escorted her and performed the formidable introductions. As the two women curtseyed to each other, Miss de Bourgh fixed a frank look on her.

"I must own to confusion, Miss Elizabeth. Might I inquire where you keep your horns and tail? For by my Darcy cousins' accounts, you are all succubae, intent on stealing the souls of men for your own nefarious purposes."

Elizabeth laughed, replying: "And we consider all Darcys to be horned devils who rule over their fife with an iron fist and a cruel indifference for lesser mortals."

The three laughed together, Elizabeth appreciative of the humor these two members of the Darcy family were able to summon. "I am happy to have made your acquaintance, Miss Elizabeth, Perhaps I could induce you to introduce me to the rest of your sisters over the course of the evening?"

"It would be my pleasure, Miss de Bourgh."

The looks Anne received from some of her party did not escape her attention, but she had little difficulty ignoring them. Her mother, Anne discounted without another thought, for her opinion derived from some grudge she held against the baron, coupled with a desire to improve her standing with Darcy's father. Mr. Darcy, Anne noted, allowed a little frown to escape his mouth when he saw Anne becoming friendly with the Bennet sisters, but said nothing. As for her cousins . . .

Anne found their reactions informative, for neither betrayed any hint of disgust. In fact, Alexander appeared more amused than anything, while Darcy's attention was on another quarter altogether. It was the behavior of her eldest Darcy cousin that interested Anne the most. Darcy had never been one to dance much at a ball — he was not the kind of man who enjoyed such activities. That he was often by the dance floor observing the dancers was not a surprise; that he observed one dancer in particular *was*. And given Fitzwilliam's testimony of Darcy's strange behavior of late, the possible reason for it began to percolate in Anne's mind.

The rest of the Bennet sisters were a mixed bag of characters; Anne did not think she had ever met such a disparate group so closely related to one another. Jane was sweet and angelic, Mary quiet and serious, Kitty shy yet exuberant, and Lydia bold and brash. Anne found that she liked them all very well.

"Well, Darcy," said Mr. Bingley a little later in the evening when he approached Darcy after a set had just ended. "I see you are set upon standing by the side in your usually stupid manner when you could be dancing."

It seemed to Anne, who had been speaking with Darcy, that the conversation had played out many times, for Darcy grinned at his friend. "Better to stand about than make a fool of myself on the dance floor as you have been doing, my friend."

Mr. Bingley replied with laughter. "So you always tell me." Turning to Anne, Mr. Bingley said: "Shall we find him a partner for the next sets, Miss de Bourgh? If I did not think it would stop the earth from turning, I might suggest Darcy dance with my fiancée."

"That would be a mistake," said Anne. "I think neither family is ready for such sacrilege."

"If that be sacrilege," said Anthony, striding up to them, "then I am already guilty of it, for I have danced with both Miss Bennet and Miss Elizabeth, and found them both lovely young ladies."

When Fitzwilliam's eyes flicked to where Miss Elizabeth was standing not far away—but behind Darcy where he could not see— Anne knew her cousin had some mischief in mind. "Though I have often heard it said that the Miss Bennets are great local beauties, I have never felt it so true as when Charlotte introduced me to them. Miss Elizabeth, in particular, is a bright and beautiful light, whose incandescence shines upon all us poor mortals."

"Methinks you are laying it on a little thick, Anthony," said Anne *sotto voce.*

"I have always thought Miss Elizabeth is an exceptional young woman," said Mr. Bingley. It seemed to Anne he had realized what Anthony was doing, but she did not think he had seen Miss Elizabeth standing nearby.

"Come now, man," said Anthony. "She is a beautiful woman, one whom any man would be fortunate should she deign to give him the slightest notice. What say you, Darcy?"

The grin with which Miss Elizabeth regarded Anthony's flowery words suggested she understood his jesting tone. Anne locked eyes with the other woman, and they shared a looked heavenward, each almost bursting into giggles at the hilarity of the situation.

Darcy, it appeared, was growing more uncomfortable as the moments passed, and as Anne had learned in the past, a flustered Darcy was a thoughtless Darcy. He proved it with his reply.

"There is nothing exceptional about Miss Elizabeth." Darcy's tone was haughty and dismissive. "If she was not the daughter of a baron, I doubt any man would pay her any attention at all."

In response to Darcy's uncharitable words, Anthony fixed him with an even look, which reminded Darcy he had spoken out of turn. Bingley shook his head and shared an exasperated glance with Anthony. More to Anne's interest, however, was Miss Elizabeth's reaction. The way her frown fixed on Darcy suggested she was uncertain what to make of his words, and instead of marching over and informing him of his blunder, she stood quietly contemplating him.

"If you think that," said Anthony, "I must assume you are a simpleton, Darcy. "There are no words which contain less truth than the ones you just spoke, and if you had any honesty at all, you would own that they are false at once."

Anthony gave his cousin a glare and stalked away, and Bingley, though not as angry, slapped Darcy on the shoulder and departed himself. In a moment of inspiration, Anne knew what to do to provoke

Darcy to confirm what her eyes had informed her was happening all night.

"Darcy," said Anne, speaking in a whisper so Miss Elizabeth could not overhear, "the woman you just insulted was standing near enough to overhear."

In an instant, Darcy turned as white as a sheet, his eyes darting about before they fixed on Miss Elizabeth. Anne moved away from her cousin, though she thought he would not have heard her had she marched away riding an elephant. But Anne kept her eye on him, watching him, wondering what he would do.

A moment later, Darcy's eyes darted about the room, and seeing there was no one paying any attention to him, he moved close to Miss Elizabeth and said a few words to her, and while she did not reply, she nodded, though the action was almost imperceptible. A moment later, he stepped away, but the damage had already been done. There was something happening between Darcy and Miss Elizabeth, for they were better acquainted than Anne thought possible. What it portended she could not say. The matter intrigued her, however, and she could not help but wish to know more.

Though he had danced the first with Elizabeth, David Gardiner kept himself aloof from the dancing for the rest of the evening. While gentlemen were encouraged to ask young ladies to dance at a ball—it was even a duty, some claimed—Gardiner had little liking for dancing. Furthermore, Gardiner did not like to leave his nieces unattended, especially with the Darcys present—and one Darcy in particular. Thus, he walked about the perimeter of the dance floor attempting to watch all his nieces at once.

"I believe your vigilance is for naught, Mr. Gardiner," a voice interrupted him after some time of this.

Turning, Gardiner noticed a young woman nearby watching, a woman he had seen but to whom he had never received an introduction. She was petite but pretty, her dark hair intertwined with a string of pearls and ribbons, her dress a lovely shade of light green. While she was not beautiful, her face was round and pretty, and the light of intelligence shone from her dark eyes.

"To what do you attribute my vigilance, Miss?" asked he, knowing he should not be talking to her without a formal introduction.

"To the sincere desire to protect your nieces, I would suppose." The woman turned to watch Alexander Darcy, who was dancing with a young woman of the neighborhood, following his form for a moment before her attention returned to Gardiner. "My cousin is many things—a flirt, a little too free with his money, not to mention far too careless about life itself. But he will not hurt your nieces. He is not a bad man, Mr. Gardiner."

"You are Miss de Bourgh, correct?" asked Gardiner.

"I am," replied she with a small curtsey. "It occurs to me that we are not yet known to each other. Then again, ballroom etiquette is far too stuffy. Would you not agree?"

Gardiner laughed in spite of himself. "Oh, aye. I could have one of my nieces introduce us, for I have not missed how friendly you have been to them all this evening."

"Where would we obtain the excitement of illicit acts if we did that?"

Again, Gardiner released his mirth. "Yes, where, indeed." For a moment, he turned back to the younger Darcy and eyed him as he laughed with his partner. "There is little enough to condemn in his behavior tonight; that is true."

"I believe, Mr. Gardiner, you have little to fear. Even should Alexander forget himself enough to ask one of your nieces for her hand for a set, he would do so without a hint of impropriety."

Gardiner snorted at the notion. "I think matters are a little too frosty between our families to contemplate such a notion."

"And yet, if there was one who *would* contemplate it, that man would be Alexander."

"You are visiting your Darcy relations at present?" asked Gardiner.

"Yes. Lady Anne Darcy was my mother's sister, you see. Though my mother delights in requiring our family to wait on us in Kent, this year I determined I wished to come here."

"Is there any particular reason?"

"Only the desire to leave Kent for a time," replied Miss de Bourgh. "My mother seldom wishes to leave home, and since she considers me all but engaged to my cousin, she sees little reason to attend the season."

That bit of new information pricked Gardiner's interest. "Then she does not consider the importance of alliances and maintaining a presence among one's peers. Excuse me, but you are engaged to one of your cousins?"

"If you listen to my mother, you would believe it to be so. But neither William nor I have ever taken mother's assertions seriously, and William's father is less inclined to it than we. But one does not contradict my mother."

So Gardiner had heard if the rumors were to be believed. Gardiner snorted with amusement, noting the woman by his side gazing across the room at her mother, a hint of wryness hovering about her. Lady Catherine, it seemed, knew of her daughter's present position, and did not like what she saw. It was also clear that Miss de Bourgh did not much care for her mother's displeasure, for while she was looking at the elder woman, her eyebrow arched in challenge. While Lady Catherine's countenance darkened at the sight, she made no move to separate them.

"It appears you are correct, Miss de Bourgh." Gardiner paused and showed her a wolfish grin. "Does the possibility of contamination from associating with one of the detested Bennet clan not concern you? Though my surname is not the same, my sister is the present baroness, so I am close to the family."

Miss de Bourgh returned his grin with equal amusement. "No more concerned than you are for one of the detested Darcy family. I am close to them too, for my mother is the late mistress's sister."

Mirth burst out between them, and Gardiner reflected that he had quite enjoyed this banter with Miss de Bourgh. There was something about her, some wry or ironic sense of the absurd which appealed to him. It was with this understanding he turned to give her more of his attention, and his interest in the dancing waned as a result.

They spoke for some time, canvassing subjects of interest to them both, and Gardiner found he had never been so entertained in a ballroom. The music ceased and the dance ended, and they hardly noticed when the next dance began and a new set of dancers took to the floor. Another five minutes into the next sets and Gardiner began to wonder about the relative benefits of asking this woman to dance.

Then he saw it. Nothing had prompted his glance out onto the dance floor, for it had been a reflex and nothing more. What he saw there filled him first with disbelief, then with anger. He flexed and unflexed his fists as his attention turned on the dancers to the exclusion of all else.

A gasp by his side alerted him to the fact that Miss de Bourgh had seen what he had seen, though he could not spare her a glance. Gardiner was turning toward the dancers when he felt a small hand grasp his arm and hold him back.

"Gently, Mr. Gardiner," said she, her tone warning. "Nothing good will come of making a scene."

"I will not allow this to continue, Miss de Bourgh," said Gardiner. Though he was not in the mood for humor, a sudden thought made itself known, and he shot her a grin as sickly as the weak burst of dark amusement which had filled his breast. "It seems you were correct, Miss de Bourgh. He *has* summoned the audacity."

Then with Miss de Bourgh following close behind, Gardiner moved to intercept the dancers.

CHAPTER XXI

*W*hen the commotion began, Elizabeth was standing on the side of the ballroom immersed in conversation with a friend. While she had not been solicited for every dance, Elizabeth had been active, though the one man with whom she wished to stand up was denied her. Still, she thought with some hope for the future, coming to know Anne de Bourgh was another bridge built between the two families, as was her uncle's current position of easy conversation with the same woman.

Then the general noise of voices in the room rose to a crescendo and confusion reigned among the dancers as a commotion interrupted their movements. Elizabeth, uncertain what was happening, cast her gaze across the room, finding the tall form of her uncle at once, as he stood confronting a pair of revelers.

Her uncle's harsh baritone rang out over the gathering, silencing the music and all conversation as he demanded: "What are you doing with my niece?"

Following his gaze and the eyes of every onlooker in the room, Elizabeth gasped when she saw Mr. Alexander Darcy. Across from him in the line, stood Lydia.

As the scene began to play out before her, Elizabeth hurried toward the hostilities, noting several others doing the same from other directions. Elizabeth could not reach them, however, before she heard Mr. Darcy's response.

"Surely you cannot misunderstand our activity, Gardiner, for we are dancing."

The insolence with which he retorted sent shivers up Elizabeth's spine as she reached the combatants, the first of the family to do so. Unfortunately, however, she could not prevent Lydia's equally impudent response.

"Upon my word, Uncle, you need not be so protective. What does one do at a ball other than dance?"

One glare from Uncle Gardiner silenced Lydia, though her defiance did not dim a jot. Before he could say another word, however, Lord Arundel, stepped forward and captured his daughter's arm, even as the elder Mr. Darcy reached his son.

"Come away, Lydia," said Lord Arundel. "You should not be dancing with Mr. Darcy, for there is no telling what mischief he might be contemplating."

"Perhaps, Arundel," said Mr. Darcy, his voice cracking like a whip, "you should concern yourself with your shameless daughter."

"If you will excuse my saying so," said Lord Arundel, "it is not my daughter who is reputed to be a rake. You will excuse me if I consider the possibility of mischief as being more likely to come from *your* son."

Mr. Darcy's countenance darkened. "That is the second time you have insulted Alexander. I have half a mind to call you out."

"If you had any more than half a mind," spat Lord Arundel, "you would use it to rein in your son!"

Elizabeth did not miss the rising sound of the whispers growing in volume around them. In desperation, she cast her eyes toward her love, beseeching him to interfere and defuse the situation. It seemed Mr. Fitzwilliam Darcy had come to the same conclusion himself when their salvation approached from another source.

"That is enough!"

As one, the adversaries turned to see the earl standing nearby, glaring at them all. He was not pleased.

"Arundel, Darcy, I had thought the bounds of polite behavior would induce you both to leave your ridiculous quarrel behind when attending an event at my house. It seems I was mistaken."

Both patriarchs wished to respond, and from the way they glared at each other, it was clear where each wished to lay the blame. It was fortunate that both mustered some well of discretion and refrained from open accusations.

"I will not have any more of this from any of you," continued the earl, his gaze sweeping over them all. "My daughter has organized this event for all our neighbors. I will not have it ruined by the actions of a few malcontents." Lord Chesterfield looked about and motioned to the musicians. "Let us begin the dancing again. Darcy, Arundel, I would have a word with you."

Looking for all the world like naughty schoolboys caught in some prank, the two men followed the earl to the side of the room where he began to speak with them. The assorted Darcys and Bennets who had approached at the sound of the confrontation drifted off the floor, though Elizabeth noted her Uncle Edward coaxing his brother away from the scene. The music resumed, and the dancers began to move. Then the next crisis made itself known.

"I shall not allow this to continue," snarled Uncle Gardiner as Lydia and Mr. Darcy continued their dance as if nothing had happened. No one misunderstood the hint of defiance in their postures.

"It would be best to let them be," said Uncle Edward, holding his brother back.

"She should not be dancing with him!" hissed Uncle Gardiner.

To Elizabeth's surprise, it was Miss de Bourgh who seemed the most effective in holding her uncle back. She joined Uncle Edward, touching Uncle Gardiner's arm and drawing his attention to her.

"Let us watch them from here, Mr. Gardiner, for there is nothing else we can do. None of us wish to draw the earl's ire yet again."

The man Miss de Bourgh had referenced was still berating the two gentlemen, neither of whom appreciated being called out by their social superior. But Elizabeth noticed that neither was protesting their treatment either.

"They can get up to no mischief on the dance floor, and when the sets end, we may separate them. Come, Mr. Gardiner, it is for the best."

At last, her uncle subsided, though Elizabeth noted he did not take his eyes from the couple for the rest of the dance. Kitty and Jane had been dancing the same set and Elizabeth did not think they had been close enough to understand what was happening. Mary stood by the side of the dance floor speaking to Mr. Collins in low tones, though Elizabeth could not understand what they were saying. It seemed the crisis had been averted for the moment, allowing Elizabeth to release a sigh of relief.

"It seems our families have provided ample fuel for the gossips tonight."

Though startled by the voice, Elizabeth kept her composure, a glance to her right informing her Mr. Darcy had stepped next to her. As he was not looking at her, instead watching her sister and his brother with as much intensity as Mr. Gardiner, Elizabeth decided it was best to avoid drawing attention. Inside, however, she longed for him to take her into his arms and assure her all would be well.

"It seems we have, Mr. Darcy," said Elizabeth, though modulating her voice so only he could hear. "And for what? This is a dance at a ball given by persons of great standing and high character."

"I agree with you," said Mr. Darcy, "though if I am honest, I believe my brother might have shown better judgment."

This time Elizabeth turned to look at the gentleman, her gaze searching. Mr. Darcy did not delay in answering.

"Considering a few choice words my father had for your family upon our arrival, he should have known Father would not appreciate such actions as this. It seems your uncle was in agreement."

"But it is all so senseless! What harm can come to my sister in a ballroom? What harm could your brother come to dancing with the daughter of a baron?"

"Again, I do not disagree with you, Miss Elizabeth. In fact, ending this conflict is growing more urgent in my mind, before someone says or does something that truly sets us against each other."

"I will never go against you," said Elizabeth, hoping he could hear the fervency in her voice. She thought Mr. Darcy understood it, for he fixed her with a tender look, though understated to avoid drawing attention to them.

"And I promise I will love you forever."

It was the first time either had raised the subject of love between them. A mist entered Elizabeth's eyes, blurring her vision, a sob lodged itself in her throat, threatening to overwhelm her composure.

"I return my love with my whole heart," Elizabeth managed to say.

The gentleman did not respond with words. Reaching out with one hand as unobtrusively as possible, he captured hers in his own and squeezed once before releasing it again. Overcome with emotion as she was, Elizabeth could not help the single tear which emerged from one eye and rolled down her cheek. As casually as she could, she reached up to wipe it away, determined to avoid giving anyone any sign of anything amiss.

While her heart was bursting with love for this man, she wondered if it would break apart into pieces. As events that night had demonstrated, no one in either family would accept their feelings for what they were. Was there any possibility of a future between them, or would this infernal feud continue to separate them, to pull them apart in fire and destruction? Elizabeth could see no hint of hope for the future, no possibility of resolution. What exquisite torture this was!

"It seems his lordship has had his say," said Mr. Darcy, an imperceptible motion of his head drawing her attention to the side of the room.

In this, he appeared correct, for while Lord Chesterfield was nowhere in evidence, Mr. Darcy and Lord Arundel were standing near to each other, but clearly alone. Both men were stiff with anger and neither would look at the other though she thought each was so aware of the other's presence that they might have been standing nose to nose. It was a sign of the circumstances between the two families, and a further testament to the hopelessness of the situation.

"Do not agonize over it, Miss Elizabeth," said Mr. Darcy, seeming to sense her thoughts. "Do not lose heart. Come what may, I have faith we shall conquer all obstacles."

"It warms my heart that you have such confidence, Mr. Darcy," said Elizabeth. "I confess, I have little myself."

"Then you must trust in our love, Miss Elizabeth," said Mr. Darcy, turning to her for the first time. "Believe in *us*. I will allow nothing to come between us—of that I assure you."

Elizabeth searched his eyes for several moments before releasing a shuddering sigh of pent up emotion. "I do believe you, Mr. Darcy. I hope you can see some way forward, for I must confess I cannot."

"Lizzy!" the stern voice of her father interrupted her tête-à-tête with Mr. Darcy. "Come away at once, Daughter, for I believe it is best we keep our distance."

As surreptitiously as she could, Elizabeth cast Mr. Darcy an apologetic look before she joined her father. What she had not predicted was Mr. Darcy's bow to her father.

"Of course, Lord Arundel. I cannot agree more. Let me, however, apologize for my brother's impulsive behavior. Please know that I shall speak with him about it in the sternest possible fashion."

While Lord Arundel peered at Mr. Darcy, attempting to see whether he was in earnest, at last, he gave a curt nod and turned to lead Elizabeth away. Elizabeth fixed the gentleman with one more look in appreciation before she lost sight of him.

A few moments later, the music faded away, and Mr. Gardiner stepped forward at once to take his youngest niece in hand. In doing so, he stepped close to Mr. Alexander Darcy and hissed something to him, which prompted a harsh glare and a retort from the younger gentleman. Uncle Gardiner paid him no heed, however, as he guided Lydia back to where the family had all gathered together.

"Oh, Lydia," clucked Lady Margaret as she inspected her youngest as if she feared to find some damage. "Are you well, Daughter?"

"It was only a dance, Mama," replied Lydia. "Mr. Darcy was a perfect gentleman—how could I have been in any danger on a dance floor?"

Elizabeth agreed with her sister, but the eldest members of the party were not impressed. Lady Margaret pursed her lips and frowned, but Uncle Gardiner was not about to remain silent.

"You are as aware of the history between our families as the rest of us," said he. "It would be best if you exercised discretion, Lydia, for there is no telling what may happen."

"And *I* saw you speaking with Miss Anne de Bourgh," accused Lydia. "Should we not also take you to task for such misbehavior?"

"That is enough, Lydia," interjected Lord Arundel. "Not only is your uncle an adult, but the de Bourghs are much further removed from this situation."

"But they are still related to the Darcy family," insisted Lydia.

"Papa," said Elizabeth, "I must find I agree with Lydia. There is no danger in a ballroom. Is it not time for this silly dispute to end?"

"You may be correct," replied Lord Arundel, "but this is not the fashion in which we should end it. There is too much opportunity for misunderstanding."

"Would you have me refuse an offer to dance?" asked Lydia, petulance overflowing in her voice. "Then I must sit out for the rest of the evening."

"I would ask you to avoid putting yourself in a situation where you must refuse," snapped Lord Arundel. Lydia's mutinous glare did not relent, but neither did her father's.

"Lydia," interjected Uncle Gardiner, "you must know of Mr. Darcy's reputation in the district. Is that the kind of man with whom you wish to be connected?"

"I can see nothing of it, Uncle. Mr. Darcy was both proper and solicitous as to my comfort. Your experiences with him have jaded you."

Uncle Gardiner's countenance darkened in anger, but Lord Arundel silenced all arguments and fixed them all—in particular his youngest daughter—with a pointed gaze which allowed for no disagreement.

"For the rest of this evening, there will be no further contact between Bennets and Darcys, and that applies to the extended Darcy family."

"But Papa!" said Jane, perhaps the least likely to protest, "Anne de Bourgh has been friendly to us all this evening."

"That is my decision," said Lord Arundel. He looked around to all his family and added: "Yes, I understand some members of that family are welcoming but let us avoid any further possibility of discord. Unless I am very much mistaken, I believe Mr. Darcy is giving the same instructions to his family at this very moment, so there should be no further problems."

It seemed her father was correct, for Mr. Darcy had gathered his family about him and was speaking to them, his demeanor as stern as that of Lord Arundel. Elizabeth caught *her* Mr. Darcy's eyes and was forced to stifle a giggle at his look skyward. There seemed to be little more appetite in Mr. Darcy's family for his instructions as there was for Lord Arundel's, for the younger Mr. Darcy was leaning against the wall with complete indifference, while the other members of the family appeared to be showing varying degrees of irritation.

While Elizabeth was watching, she noted when Colonel Fitzwilliam said something harsh to his uncle and turned to stalk away. The elder Mr. Darcy watched him as he left, before turning back to his family and saying a few more words, punctuated with rapid hand gestures before he dismissed them.

"Am I very clear?"

Her father's voice returned her attention to her own party, and she realized she had heard nothing he said while she had been distracted. The rest of her family gave their assent, though some with great reluctance, all except for Lydia, who stood ramrod straight, her lips forming an angry line. Knowing the girl was about to say something which would provoke her father to greater anger, Elizabeth stepped forward and grasped Lydia's arm, fixing her father with a weak smile.

"I shall speak with Lydia, Papa."

"It is all so unfair, Lizzy!" exclaimed Lydia as Elizabeth led her away.

For a moment Elizabeth saw red, her mouth opened with a retort to tell her sister *how* unfair it all was. Discretion, however, came to Elizabeth's rescue and she swallowed the words she so wished to say.

"Perhaps it is, Lydia," said Elizabeth instead. "There is no choice but to obey Papa. It would be best to let the anger cool for there is no call to continue to argue."

Lydia shot her a sour look, but she did not respond. Taking her aside, Elizabeth situated herself by her sister, allowing Lydia's anger to drain away. As Mr. Darcy had inferred, there was a swell of voices, as the story flew throughout the room on wings of gossip by who had witnessed the exchange to those who had missed it. Being the highest members of society in the district, other than the Lucas family, Elizabeth had no worry about it being to her family's detriment; the longstanding nature of the affair meant it was often discussed regardless. That did not appease her to any great extent, for she did not appreciate being the target of the neighborhood's gossips.

"How did you come to be dancing with Mr. Darcy?" asked Elizabeth after a few moments.

"The usual method," responded Lydia, her anger fueling her continued shortness. "Our coming close to each other was an accident. He made a comment, I teased him in reply, and he asked me to dance. There was nothing improper about it."

"I do not accuse you of impropriety," said Elizabeth, though she reflected that had she possessed Lydia's fearlessness, she might have been the first to draw their family's ire by dancing with Mr. Darcy. In some ways, she wished she *had* danced with him. "There was nothing more than curiosity in my question."

Lydia grunted and no further words passed between them. It was not long before Elizabeth realized that the incident had other consequences that were not so readily apparent. For one, though the Bennet sisters were among the most popular dance partners at most events, none of the sisters danced very much again that evening. Whether there was some concern over offending one or the other of the families, none of them enjoyed themselves, for neither Darcy brother danced again, though Colonel Fitzwilliam continued to be his jolly self. Mr. Bingley also engaged with Jane on the dance floor again, though otherwise he ignored the activity after that and stayed by her side.

This did not mean the end of the hostilities between the Darcy and Bennet families, however, and if Elizabeth had thought on the matter at all, she would have understood it was inevitable. Though no open disagreements erupted between them, and the earl, standing as stern watch over them all warned against any misbehavior, little digs occurred with regularity. Elizabeth found herself near enough on one occasion to overhear Lady Catherine referring to her as an "outspoken girl, rattling on about things she knew nothing at all." That was not the worst of the little snide comments, but they did not bother her at all.

Kitty, being much more sensitive, was brought to tears when Lady Catherine made a similar comment in her hearing. It was the pattern that suggested Lady Catherine was attempting to make her sentiments known, for the possibility of multiple instances of another overhearing were beyond belief.

"Do not concern yourself, Kitty," said Elizabeth when her sister approached her with tears in her eyes. "She is an overbearing, conceited, ignorant sort of woman. We need not care for her opinion."

As Lady Catherine was nearby and Elizabeth had made her comments with the intention of her overhearing them, she was not surprised when the lady whirled on them, her eyes blazing with anger.

"What are the Bennets but a jumped-up house far too proud for their own good? I knew your father when he was a young man—it seems to me the weakness of character traits in him are manifest in his daughters."

"And I have also heard of the insolent harpy intent upon pushing her opinion upon all and sundry," snapped Elizabeth in return. "Your opinions mean nothing, Lady Catherine, and I would appreciate it if you would refrain from sharing them and insulting my sister who has done you no harm."

The lady's face took on the hue of a ripened tomato. Had Mr. Darcy not arrived to coax his aunt away from them, Elizabeth might have thought the woman's shrieking voice might carry throughout the hall. The apologetic look he shot her told Elizabeth he had heard everything his aunt had said, and Elizabeth nodded in response, informing him she did not hold him at fault.

The misbehavior did not exclude the Bennets, however, for Elizabeth witnessed more than one instance of sniping back and forth between the families. After dinner Lady Charlotte led the way to the pianoforte, performed for the company, and then invited others to display their own talents. Some few ladies did before Mary took to the instrument.

Mary was proficient, but if she exchanged some of her technical skill for more feeling, her playing would be more enjoyable. But she acquitted herself well, blushing from the applause which greeted her performance. When she stepped away from the pianoforte, however, a single voice rose in disdainful commentary.

"If Lord Arundel has paid a substantial amount of money for his master, he should fire the man, for Miss Mary does not have the taste Anne possesses. My niece, Georgiana is skilled, so we are in for a treat. Of course, had I ever learned, I should be the most talented performer

218 *&* Jann Rowland

in the company!"

It was clear to Elizabeth that Lady Catherine's words had offended Lady Margaret so much that she seethed during Miss Darcy's performance. So fixed was her attention on the performer, she did not notice when the earl stepped up to Lady Catherine and informed her, in a voice harsh and carrying, that he would have her removed if she persisted. Lady Catherine did not like the set down she received, but Elizabeth noticed she made no further comments.

When Georgiana completed her piece, Elizabeth applauded along with the rest of the company. Unfortunately, her mother, not to be outdone by Lady Catherine, sneered at the young girl and said in a loud voice: "Miss Darcy's playing is adequate, I suppose. But it is not beautiful enough to tempt me to applaud." Lady Margaret turned to Elizabeth and gestured toward the instrument. "You should perform, Lizzy. Then we would all hear the true measure of talent and skill."

By this time the disgust Elizabeth felt for them all was so great, nothing would induce her to perform for such unworthy people. Lady Margaret, it seemed, did not repine the lack of her performance, for she patted Elizabeth's hand.

"I understand, my dear. It is to your credit you do not wish to outshine them all, for you are such a good and modest girl. Perhaps, instead, I may ask Kitty to perform."

At that moment, Lady Charlotte called for a return to the ballroom, diffusing the situation. The whispers and glances her family, along with the Darcys, were receiving as those present exited the dining room, informed Elizabeth that they had given them all more about which to gossip. The entire night was a disaster for them all, in Elizabeth's opinion, for they had shown themselves to be unruly school children rather than families of standing and wealth.

"Lady Charlotte," said Elizabeth, as she approached her friend later that evening, showing her deference with a low curtsey. "You have my apologies for the behavior of us all. I should think you wish to be rid of the lot of us, for none have acquitted ourselves well tonight."

"Dearest Lizzy," said Lady Charlotte, engulfing Elizabeth in a warm embrace. "Please do not take the misbehavior of others upon your head. This evening has turned out more . . . interesting than I might have expected or wished. But I do not believe any of it is your fault."

Elizabeth gave her friend a weak laugh. "Perhaps it is not. But I feel the shame of it, nonetheless."

"It will turn out well, I dare say," said Lady Charlotte. "You need to have faith."

Faith, however, was a commodity in short supply at present. Despite her friend's encouraging words, Elizabeth could not feel other than that her family had been proud, ridiculous, absurd, and mortifying that evening. And given their behavior, the gulf between Darcy and Bennet was wider than it had ever been before. How could they recover; how could she obtain her happiness after events such as these?

CHAPTER XXII

*G*iven the evening that had just occurred, Darcy found he could not find sleep that night. In fact, he did not even make the attempt. Thoughts of the ball, the behavior of his family together with that of the Bennets plagued him when he returned to his home, and the most he could accomplish was to throw his jacket over a chair before the fireplace while he sank into its mate to stare with moody annoyance at the smoldering embers in the bottom of the grate. There was not even enough motivation in him to add a log or stir the embers to provide more heat.

After his family's performance, Darcy wondered that Miss Elizabeth still thought well of him. That her family had behaved little better Darcy knew, but considering his desire for the woman of his heart to think well of him, he pushed all thought of the other Bennets from his mind. In particular, Lady Catherine's incessant comments designed to insult after the earl had already made his wishes known galled Darcy, for not only had the woman stated her ridiculous opinions incessantly, but she had insulted Elizabeth herself on no less than three occasions that Darcy had overheard. Had he possessed less discretion, he might have cheered when Miss Elizabeth set her down, calling her an insolent harpy. It was nothing less than the truth.

The final indignity, however, had come when they entered the family home, for his father had reiterated his words at the ball. Anyone associated with the Darcys were to avoid the Bennets at all costs; he would tolerate no objections. Well, his father had received more than he had bargained, for one of those in attendance was not in the mood to listen.

"Much though I respect you, Uncle," Fitzwilliam had said, glaring at the elder Darcy, "I am not your son, nor will I endure being ordered to comply with your commands."

"You are a guest at my house," replied Mr. Darcy. "Thus, you will obey my rules."

"If you wish me to leave because of my defiance, that is your prerogative. But you shall not coerce me into behaving in a manner which I consider ridiculous. My future wife is not only close to the Bennet sisters, but I consider this entire matter to be nothing less than a farce. I am a Fitzwilliam, and I will do as I see fit."

The Darcy patriarch glared at Fitzwilliam, but he was not intimidated. When they had attempted to stare each other down for several moments, Fitzwilliam shook his head and stood to retreat from the room.

"If you wish me gone, please inform me in the morning," said Fitzwilliam. "I have other friends in the neighborhood with whom I can stay if need be. For now, I shall bid you all good night."

The bow Fitzwilliam offered upon departing the room was as curt as it was perfunctory, surprising to many in the party who could not think of their relation as anything other than a genial man. To Darcy, however, Fitzwilliam's refusal was not unexpected, for he knew his cousin better than any other man and knew of Fitzwilliam's will of iron. And Darcy could not be more in agreement.

"You may as well let him have it, Father," said Alexander. Upon entering the room, his brother had thrown himself into a chair with little elegance, seeming bored with the proceedings. His words bordered on insolent. "I agree with him. This dispute is beyond silly."

"I would have you hold your tongue, Alexander," growled his father. "It was your actions that led to much of the hostility this evening."

"Yes, yes, it was all my fault," said Alexander, springing to his feet. "I am sure the kingdom will go to war because I danced with Miss Lydia Bennet, a young woman who does not deserve to be treated with disdain by anyone in this family. She is sixteen! What manner of lunacy is this that we treat such people as less than the dirt on our boots?"

"That is enough!" bellowed their father. "Though Fitzwilliam may defy me if he chooses, you are my son and you *will* obey." Mr. Darcy's harsh gaze found Georgiana and the de Bourghs, and he stated in a voice which allowed for no disagreement: "That goes for anyone who lives in my house. There will be no more contact with any member of the Bennet family. If you cannot obey my dictates, you may depart."

Cowed by her father's implacable tone, Georgiana nodded with vigorous agreement. Alexander shrugged, while Darcy avoided saying anything. It was Lady Catherine whose words ended the night in further acrimony.

"The Bennets are nothing more than ruffians," huffed Lady Catherine. "Be assured that Anne and I have little desire for congress with them."

The elder Darcy nodded, though Darcy saw what he did not—Anne rolled her eyes. Those eyes contained a hint of a mutinous glint, one Darcy thought was much more in alignment with Alexander and Fitzwilliam's opinions. Lady Catherine, however, was not finished speaking.

"Given the events of the evening and the artfulness of the Bennet family, I believe the time has come to solemnize Darcy's engagement with Anne."

"Be silent, Lady Catherine!" hissed Darcy, much to his aunt's shock. "The Bennets can have nothing to do with your insistence on promoting this fantasy of yours. I will not marry Anne and she will not have me. Do not speak on this subject again!"

Lady Catherine's countenance darkened and she opened her mouth to retort, but Darcy cut her off. "Of all of those who were to blame for this evening's debacle, I consider *you* to be the worst! Not only did you take every opportunity to belittle and insult, even after the earl instructed us all to desist, but you would not stop though you were told several more times to do so. It is my opinion that Miss Elizabeth's accusation concerning your character could not be more correct!"

Turning on his heel, Darcy stalked from the room to the sound of his aunt's shouted protests. Darcy did not listen, though he thought he heard his father silencing his aunt as he departed. With any luck, his father would order her from the house. Lady Catherine was too much to endure at the best of times, and this was far from the best!

The memory of those events provoked Darcy's ire once again, and he rose to stalk about his room, his pacing akin to the caged lion he had seen at the London menagerie. Darcy had always considered himself to be a dutiful son. The respect he held for his father was unshakable, and he had always followed his father's instructions to the letter.

Obedience was not possible — not now. How was he to convince himself to avoid Miss Elizabeth? *He could not!* It was in every way unfathomable. Darcy could no more shun the woman who held his heart than he could forget his name. He would not do it.

For a moment, Darcy toyed with the notion of informing his father of his actions and declaring his intention to marry Miss Elizabeth, for he had tired of hiding it and feeling more than a little guilty. That he had not yet spoken of the matter with Elizabeth stayed his hand; his father's present mood firmed his conviction that now would be a poor time to make such an announcement. Lady Catherine would only further the pandemonium, should she learn once and for all of the failure of her schemes.

On a sudden impulse, Darcy grasped his jacket from the chair and slung it over his shoulders again. Walking to the door, Darcy opened it with great care, peering both directions down the hall for any sign of activity. There was none — not a soul moved in the house. Moving back into his room, Darcy went to his dressing room and found a pair of knee-high boots — they did not match his evening ball attire, but at this point Darcy cared little for his fashionable appearance.

A few moments later Darcy left his room, crept down the stairs and out of the house, making his way toward the stables. Zeus, his horse, eyed him when he entered the stall, the animal's eyes blinking away sleep. In no time, Darcy had gathered a saddle and slung it over the beast, tightening the cinch underneath before taking the bit and bridle and preparing for departure. Then he led the horse from the stables, along the length of the house toward a path leading south.

Pemberley house sat tall and proud near the northern end of the long valley in which the estate sat, further from the southern boundaries than from the north. It was toward the longer path he directed Zeus, mounting once he judged he was far enough away from the house to avoid being heard. Then with a softly spoken command and a tightening of his knees and heels, he urged the animal forward, flying through the still empty fields toward the Bennet estate in the distance, eschewing any paths to minimize any chance of discovery.

When he reached the low hill between the properties, Darcy slowed, examining the fence between, wondering if he should risk jumping it. If the sun was up, he would have done it, for the fence would be no match for a stallion of Zeus's abilities. In the dark, however, he risked injuring himself and his mount, and while he might have assumed that risk for himself, he would not put another creature in that situation.

Dismounting, Darcy tied his horse to a post, whispering soft words to him. The animal eyed him with what Darcy took to be a look of reproach and soon hung his head. Darcy knew Zeus would be well until he returned, so he patted the animal's head and vaulted the fence, making his way forward on foot. Though he had little knowledge of the Bennets' lands, he thought Elizabeth had once told him that the manor was not far distant from the northern border, which gave him hope he would reach it before long.

What Darcy had hoped to accomplish by intruding upon Longbourn in the dead of the night he could not even discern for himself. All he knew was that the need to be near Miss Elizabeth was akin to a physical ache emanating from his very bones. But luck, it seemed, was with him that night, for as the stately bulk of her home rose before him, Darcy saw the woman herself.

Though it was not cold, it was for a woman dressed in naught but a nightgown and a dressing gown, yet Miss Elizabeth seemed to take no notice. The moon was bright and full that night, illuminating all below in a soft, white eldritch glow. Miss Elizabeth was standing on the balcony outside what he guessed was her room, leaning against the balustrade, and it seemed to Darcy's eyes a glow, far brighter and more glorious than the pale light of the moon was emanating from her head like some heavenly halo, for she was as precious as an angel to him. For a moment Darcy paused and drank in the sight of her; perversely, the words he had spoken at the assembly concerning this glorious creature returned to taunt him. How blind he must have been to consider her flawed, for she was perfection itself!

A sense of mischief came over Darcy, and he stepped forward, calling out to her as loud as he dared: "But, soft! what light through yonder window breaks? It is the east, and Elizabeth is the sun. Arise, fair sun, and kill the envious moon, who is already sick and pale with grief, that thou her maid art far more fair than she!"

Though she started upon hearing his voice, his Elizabeth—*his Elizabeth!*—caught his reference at once and was quick to respond.

"'O Fitzwilliam, Fitzwilliam! wherefore art thou Fitzwilliam? Deny thy father and refuse thy name; or, if thou wilt not, be but sworn my love, and I'll no longer be a Bennet.'"

With a grin, Darcy stepped forward, seeing nothing but the face of this beautiful woman before him. "'I take thee at thy word: call me but love, and I'll be new baptized; henceforth I never will be Fitzwilliam.'"

"'What man art thou that thus bescreen'd in night so stumblest on my counsel?"

"'By a name I know not how to tell thee who I am: my name, dear saint, is hateful to myself, because it is an enemy to thee; had I it written, I would tear the word.'"

"'How camest thou hither, tell me, and wherefore?'"

"To see you, my dearest love," said Darcy, his heart full of adoration for this woman. "I could not stay away."

Miss Elizabeth looked down on him, her love for him radiating from her in waves, bathing him in the beauty and wonder of its intensity. For a moment she peered at him, then she commanded: "Wait there, for I shall come down."

"Nay, fair maiden, for I shall come to thee," said Darcy. He spied a trellis running up the side of the house, growths of ivy intertwined around it. One look informed him it would support his weight, and he began to climb, ignoring the gasp of the woman above him.

"Mr. Darcy!" hissed she. "I do not think this is a good idea!"

"Nothing shall keep me from thee, beloved Elizabeth."

The climb was a few short moments of effort, as the trellis was sturdy and fastened tight to the wall. Within moments he had attained her balcony and reached for the balustrade, swinging one leg over to sit on the edge, grinning at her. Miss Elizabeth was not amused, though the sentiment warred with delight at seeing him here.

"'With love's light wings did I o'er-perch these walls; for stony limits cannot hold love out.'"

"It seems they cannot," said Elizabeth, amused anew at his daring. "So tell me, Mr. Darcy, shall we end our tragic love right here, fling ourselves to our deaths on the ground below and thereby heal the division which lies between our families?"

"I should rather have you for a lifetime than measure our love in hours or minutes, dearest, loveliest Elizabeth." Darcy swung his other leg over the banister and caught her hands between his. "I have no desire to end like those star-crossed lovers of old. Instead, I would give you all I have and all that I am, if you would only consent to be my wife."

"Oh, Mr. Darcy," said Elizabeth, melting like putty before him.

Darcy pulled her close, reveling for the first time in the closeness of her body to his, the scent of her hair and the lavender water she used, a hint of which still hovered about her. She clung tightly to him, a sentiment Darcy was eager to return, to never let go. Would that they could stay like this for an eternity.

"Please call me William, my dear, for I would have nothing, not even the formality of address between us."

Elizabeth pulled back from him, her face alight with amusement. "Is your full name a little too stuffy, even for a Darcy?"

With a delighted grin, Darcy leaned down and kissed her nose. "Stuffy, perhaps, but too much of a mouthful for everyday use. Everyone in my family who does not refer to me as Darcy calls me William, though Lady Catherine prefers to stick to formality. She considers it a distinguished old name, one which should not be altered."

"That does not surprise me," said Elizabeth, wrinkling her nose with disgust at the mention of Lady Catherine. "Not to offend, but your Fitzwilliam relations have not held their title as long as my forbears have held ours."

"I am not offended at all, for it is the truth," said Darcy. "Lady Catherine is the only member of the family who gives herself airs, for the rest of the Fitzwilliam clan are quite the humble bunch. You have met my cousin—his family is much like him in essentials."

"Colonel Fitzwilliam, at least, provides proof of your assertion."

Elizabeth paused and nibbled at her lower lip, an action Darcy found adorable. Maddening too, for it filled him with the wild desire to kiss her.

"Well, Elizabeth?" asked Darcy after a moment. "What say you? I offer you my heart, the soul of a man deeply in love with you, an organ that will never love another. One word from you and we may be together forever. If you wish me to end in the manner of which you spoke only moments ago, you need only reject me, for, without you, no life is worth living."

Miss Elizabeth gazed on him with adoring eyes. "If you will have me, William, I am yours."

His heart soaring at her acceptance of his love, Darcy leaned down and for the first time kissed her with all the passion he possessed. One might have thought a young woman, sheltered and untutored in such activities might have become frightened at the pure need in his kiss, but nothing could be further from the truth. How long they stood there engaged in a duel of tongues, a blending of hearts and minds, Darcy would never know. It seemed like a lifetime, and yet it was not enough—not by half.

As all things must, however, soon the demands of the situation took precedence. Darcy pulled back from her amid pecks on her lips, eyes, everywhere on her face he could, while she shivered with delight at his attentions. The passion subsided, though the need burned as hot as it ever had, and soon he leaned his head against hers, caressing her silky cheek with one of his fingers.

"Though I would stay with you like this forever, I believe we must discuss what lies before us."

With a sigh and a nod of acknowledgment, Elizabeth took his hand and led him to a chair on her balcony, and though it was fashioned for one, Darcy sat in it and pulled her onto his lap. Elizabeth allowed it without question, putting her arms around his neck and pulling him close. Once again, she chewed on her lip as she often did when deep in thought, and after a moment, she turned and met his eyes in the dim light of the moon.

"I do not think we have much time, William. It would not do if anyone found you here when the sun rises. The house will begin to stir before long."

"Though I would very much like to brave all your father's displeasure, at present I can do naught but agree. The question is, can we reconcile our families?"

Grimacing, Elizabeth shook her head, saying: "If there is a way, I do not see it—not after our mutual performance tonight. Might I assume your father warned you all against associating with any Bennets?"

"He did," replied Darcy, "though he did not receive the obedience he had expected. Lady Catherine was his faithful parrot, but Fitzwilliam flatly refused, saying he would not behave in so reprehensible a manner, and offering to leave if he is unwelcome because of it."

A sadness entered Elizabeth's eyes and she said: "Ah, the poor colonel. Lady Charlotte is my closest friend, you understand—I would not wish for any strain to be placed on their shoulders in this season of joy."

"And I would agree with you." Darcy paused and sighed. "To be honest, I doubt my father will press the point. But Fitzwilliam was not the only one to rebel, as Alexander was no more interested in my father's decrees than Fitzwilliam. And Anne, though she remained silent, did not appear impressed. Did your father give you all similar instructions?"

"Yes, he did," replied Elizabeth. "Lydia was as mutinous as ever, but the rest of my sisters kept their own counsel. Papa knows that Jane will come into contact with your family by virtue of her marriage to

Mr. Bingley, but Papa wishes to lessen the tension between our families by insisting we keep to ourselves."

"That is unfortunate," murmured Darcy.

"How can we work on them?" asked Elizabeth, tears standing in the corners of her eyes.

Dismayed by the sight, for no woman so glorious as she should ever be so distressed, Darcy drew her closer, giving all the comfort he could impart. "I will own I do not know. But it will not change my mind, Elizabeth. I mean to make you my wife; I shall allow nothing to come between us."

While her lips curled up, the storms raging in the depths of her eyes did not give way to calmness. "Would that I could believe it will be that easy, William. But I fear it shall not. I cannot see how my father would allow it. Do you think yours would?"

Darcy paused and considered the matter, and said: "I confess, I do not know if he would. It is possible."

"Then how can we marry? How could we support ourselves without our families?"

"I have an estate that might serve," said Darcy. "Blackfish Bay is near the coast in Lincolnshire. It is not a large property, as its income is only two thousand pounds, but I inherited it from a distant relation, so it is mine alone. If our families should continue in this manner and reach no détente, we could marry and live there."

Darcy searched her eyes. "Would you find contentment living in such reduced circumstances?"

"As long as I am with you, I cannot fail to find happiness," said Elizabeth, love shining in her eyes. "I do not require riches, William. Relationships bring happiness, not great fortune."

"That is an interesting position for the daughter of a wealthy peer, a woman who has been raised amid great privilege."

Elizabeth caught the irony and humor in his voice and replied in like fashion. "What of you, who was reared in a lavish house amongst servants to see to your every need? Would you a simple life in Lincolnshire suit you?"

"If we are together, I will be content," said Darcy, punctuating his statement with a kiss.

Then a thought occurred to him. "I apologize, Elizabeth, but might I ask if you are of age?"

It was a critical question, and the answer was destined to disappoint him. "I am not," said she. "My birthday is in July—until then, I am only twenty."

The thought of waiting until the summer to be united with this woman was not palatable to Darcy in the slightest. There was a possible solution to the problem but given how much he had already asked of her Darcy hesitated to suggest it. Better to keep it in the back of his mind and offer it up should the situation become untenable than to frighten her with it now.

"It seems to me," continued Miss Elizabeth, "we have little choice but to wait and watch, to hope our families come to their senses. Perhaps through careful guidance, we might induce them to reason."

Though Elizabeth's words projected confidence, Darcy knew she was as little convinced as he was of the success of their efforts. Still, for the present, there was nothing to do but to make the attempt. Some miracle or pathway forward might present itself should they only have faith and stay to their course.

Few words passed between them after that, for the two lovers contented themselves in sitting together in silence, enjoying the company of the other. Darcy refused to depart until the last moment in which he thought he could make his escape with success. He might have judged better and left earlier to avoid tempting fate, but he could not pull himself away.

It was the sense that Elizabeth was falling asleep in his arms which roused Darcy to leave her, allowing her to seek her bed. A few more kisses and promises of everlasting devotion were exchanged until he climbed down the trellis again. As he trudged toward the trees on the northern end of the glade in which the house stood, he stopped and turned to gaze at her, noting she was watching him as he departed. She kissed her palm and blew it to him, and for a moment, he fancied a helpful wind had born it on wings of air to him. Then she turned and entered the house.

With a sigh, Darcy began to trudge away toward the border fence and Zeus, trying to ignore the gaping hole in his breast. For Fitzwilliam Darcy had left his heart behind that night. He would never again feel whole until they were united forever.

CHAPTER XXIII

$\mathcal{G}$iven her late night, first at the ball, then contemplating all that happened there on her balcony, then the subsequent time stealing a few forbidden moments with William, Elizabeth might have thought she would awake exhausted the following morning. While she found a few hours of precious rest after William's departure, she woke far sooner than she might have wished, her heart and mind alive with memories of the gentleman's proposal. Knowing she would sleep no longer, Elizabeth arose and had her mount saddled, leaving Longbourn before anyone else in the family stirred from their rest.

Setting out at a quick pace, Elizabeth made her way toward the meadow she shared with William, hoping against hope she would find him there. To her utter delight, William's thoughts had mirrored her own, for she found him seated on their rock, enjoying the morning.

Spurring her mount forward, Elizabeth approached at a gallop, eager to be in his arms again. When she pulled Midnight to a halt and slid down from the saddle, he granted her wish with a searing kiss, which informed her without the possibility of misinterpretation how much he had missed her.

"One would think we had not seen each other for a month or more, William," said Elizabeth, giving him a playful grin.

"It seems like a lifetime to me," said William, leading her to sit beside him. "Every moment appears that way to me."

Elizabeth could not disagree with him. They spent some time sitting on that rock, speaking of many things, and Elizabeth found herself telling him secrets she had kept her whole life, some of which she had not even told Jane! They were not together long, for Elizabeth knew if she stayed all morning she would be missed and her family would become suspicious. But she treasured her time with the man she loved and wished they could meet without fear of causing a crisis. Perhaps someday . . .

While it was Elizabeth's intention to avoid provoking suspicion, she was not entirely successful. When they parted and Elizabeth turned her mount's steps back toward Longbourn, she found another making his way there, her presence surprising him.

"Elizabeth," hailed her Uncle Gardiner as she allowed her horse to walk down the road which led to the estate. Her uncle regarded her with some interest as he cantered up to her, taking in her appearance, seeming to inspect her, perhaps to see if she had ridden Midnight hard. The slow pace of the return to Longbourn was a benefit, for Midnight showed no signs of ill use.

"I might have thought you would not be eager for exercise after the late night at the earl's home."

"And yet, you know I never miss the opportunity to be out of doors," said Elizabeth with a laugh, attempting levity. "Mayhap I will sleep this afternoon for a time, but I never rest much past daybreak."

Uncle Gardiner regarded her for several moments before turning toward Longbourn again, motioning her to ride alongside him. "Then since you were on your way home, let us go together."

They rode side by side, exchanging few words between them, though when her uncle did speak to her, Elizabeth thought it was with a sense of probing. What he suspected she could not say, and he did not ask open questions. But Elizabeth's heart was disquieted, the sense that he was not taking her words at face value whispering therein. She began to wonder if her secret was in danger of being discovered.

Tired of it all though she was, Elizabeth refrained from giving her uncle any further reason to suspect her. Inside, however, she felt sick at heart. When would this situation end? There was no help for it, for her feelings would not allow her to pull away from Mr. Darcy. There would come a time, however, when it all became too much, and Elizabeth feared that time was quickly approaching.

When they arrived at the house, Elizabeth thought to make her escape, but it was not to be. Uncle Gardiner waited for her while she saw to Midnight's stabling, and then accompanied her into the house, where they met her father.

"Gardiner," greeted the baron before directing a questioning look at Elizabeth.

"I came upon Elizabeth on the road to the house," said Uncle Gardiner in response to his unspoken question.

"Yes, Mr. Hill informed me of her departure this morning," replied her father. He smiled at her before adding: "Apparently she left at an hour later than is usual for her. It appears the late night affected even *you*, Lizzy."

"Not so much that I did not wish to feel the wind on my face."

Lord Arundel grinned and then turned to his brother. Uncle Gardiner observed her with care, and when he noted them both looking at him, he was quick to respond.

"It may be best to limit Elizabeth's propensity to ride or walk all over the neighborhood, Brother. We would not wish her to succumb to any entanglements."

"To what do you refer?" asked her father with a frown.

In a placating gesture, Uncle Gardiner put out his hand in surrender. "It is not my wish to imply I do not trust Elizabeth."

"I should hope not!" exclaimed Lord Arundel. "Lizzy is my most sensible daughter."

"And yet, you have always allowed her the freedom to wander as she wishes," replied Uncle Gardiner.

"Uncle!" protested Elizabeth, even as her father regarded him, a hint of annoyance playing about his manner.

"Many young ladies ride out when they wish, Gardiner," said the baron. "Elizabeth has never given me a hint of concern about her judgment."

"And I do not wish to question it," replied Uncle Gardiner. "But let us face the facts, Brother: you are more apt to allow your daughters to do as they will than provide protection. In the present circumstance, the disagreement with the Darcy family has once again become a festering problem, I think it would be best to keep your daughters closer to home."

"Are you suggesting the Darcy family means us harm?" demanded Elizabeth, offended on Mr. Darcy's behalf. "It is a grave state of affairs, indeed, if the Bennets believe the Darcy family are capable of assaulting gentlewomen regardless of their feelings for them."

"Do not exaggerate!" snapped Uncle Gardiner, his own irritation beginning to show. "No, the Darcys would not attempt to harm you. On the other hand, the younger son, in particular, has such a reputation as to render me suspicious of what mischief he might contemplate."

Elizabeth did not know Mr. Alexander Darcy as well as she knew his brother, but William had told her something of him, had informed her the rumors were overstated—Elizabeth trusted William to be candid with her. Elizabeth knew, however, it would be best to hold her tongue, for Uncle Gardiner was in such a mood that to provoke him was unwise.

"Then you need not worry, Uncle," said Elizabeth. "I have neither seen the younger Mr. Darcy on my rides nor do I imagine he would approach me if I did. Your worries are unfounded."

With those final words, Elizabeth excused herself to return to her room. What her uncle meant by his innuendo Elizabeth could not say. It was clear she would need to be more careful, for her uncle appeared watchful.

"Tell me, Brother, what was the delightful Miss Elizabeth Bennet saying to you at the ball last night?"

Darcy turned and regarded Alexander, wondering what his question presaged. It was apparent his brother saw his hesitance, for he shook his head.

"I accuse you of no improprieties, William. But I saw you standing by the dance floor after the confrontation and wondered if she was flaying you with the sharp edge of her tongue."

"No, she was not," replied Darcy, irritated by his brother's words but unwilling to allow him to see it. "We did not stand together long, but her comments dwelt on the events that provided much grist for the gossips and how the continued argument between us was pointless."

"With that, I must agree with her," said Alexander.

Darcy turned to his brother. "As do I. However, I must wonder why you asked Miss Lydia to dance, in particular after your meeting with the girl on the street and the subsequent argument with her uncle. You must have known it could not pass without controversy."

"That is what I wish to know."

The brothers turned as one to see their father standing in the door. The elder man watched them, his manner intense and interested, more for his brother than for Darcy himself. For the first time, Darcy was struck with the similarity of their situations: though Alexander's disobedience had been *overt*, Darcy was no less engaged in rebellion

than his brother. It could be argued that his was for a greater cause —
he loved Miss Elizabeth like no other, whereas Alexander was his
usual wild self. But the sudden realization did not sit well with Darcy.
A solution must be found for their predicament, for he did not wish to
sneak about the countryside meeting with Miss Elizabeth, putting her
reputation at risk.

"Well?" demanded their father when neither brother spoke. "Why
did you dance with Miss Lydia, of all people?"

"Because, Father," replied Alexander, for once no hint of
nonchalance staining his voice, "I found her intriguing. Moreover, I
consider this feud to be silly — if we cannot even dance with the Bennet
girls in front of the neighborhood, how can we ever hope to put the
disagreement to rest?"

Mr. Darcy grunted. "The disagreement shall rest when the Bennets
show they are worthy of trust. From this day forward, I expect you to
exercise more judgment. There are many acceptable young ladies in
the neighborhood; there is no need for you to solicit the hands of those
chits in particular."

"Those 'chits,' as you call them," said Alexander, his temper rising,
"are the daughters of a baron."

"I know who and what they are," snapped his father. "They are off-
limits at balls, parties, or even if you meet them on the street. Am I
clear?"

Though Alexander gave his agreement, it was little more than a curt
nod. Mr. Darcy seemed to accept it, for he did not make any further
demands. Instead, he turned the conversation to the confrontation on
the dance floor.

"What did Gardiner say to you?"

"Very little," said Alexander, his manner still brusque. "He asked
me what I was doing with his niece, I replied I was dancing, and she
said that dancing is what one does at a ball. After that, you and the
baron came to separate us and engage in your own spat."

Mr. Darcy grunted. "That is well then. I must own that Gardiner
makes me wary, for it seems his temper is unstable. You should not
provoke him, for there is no telling what he might do."

The grunt from Alexander served as his agreement, for he said
nothing more. The subject might have rested there, had they not soon
joined the rest of the company for luncheon, for there was one among
their number who had never held her opinion about anything. Though
Darcy wished his brother would hold his tongue, he could well
understand why Lady Catherine annoyed him enough to provoke a

response.

"I hope my brother has reminded you of the foolishness of your actions," said Lady Catherine when they were all seated to luncheon.

"Yes, Catherine, I did," replied Mr. Darcy, shooting his sister-in-law a quelling glare. "There is no more reason to belabor the point."

Lady Catherine did not listen—then again, she never did. "I hope you will take our advice and leave the Bennet sisters alone. You would not wish to run afoul of them, for we cannot trust them."

"In fact, Aunt," replied Alexander, his glare at his aunt revealing his waning patience, "I found in Lydia Bennet a pleasant girl and an excellent dancer. There was nothing objectionable in her—this whole situation has become a farce. I would prefer to leave the subject alone."

"She is a *Bennet!*" snapped Lady Catherine. "Dishonor is in their very blood."

"Miss Lydia Bennet is a young woman, like any other," rasped Alexander, the sound of his chair sliding away as he rose to punctuate his statement. "Once again, the great Lady Catherine de Bourgh is intent upon having her say, even when the rest of the company wish she would be silent."

Alexander turned and strode toward the door, his father's voice interrupting him before he could leave. "Where are you going?"

"It seems I have lost my appetite, Father," said Alexander, fixing Lady Catherine with a contemptuous glare. "If you will excuse me."

Then Alexander left before anyone could say another word, leaving silence in his wake. It did not last long, of course, as Lady Catherine was not a woman to allow such a slight to pass without comment. It was fortunate his father did not sit still for her diatribe, or Darcy might have followed his brother's example.

"Catherine, if you cannot be silent about the Bennets, please keep to yourself." When Lady Catherine turned an outraged look on him, Darcy's father returned her anger to an equal degree. "Not one more word! If you cannot behave yourself, I will ask you to return to Kent."

The glance Lady Catherine gave Darcy left no one in any doubt of why that option was unpalatable but it resulted in Lady Catherine huffing and falling silent. Darcy shared a look with Anne, who shook her head in amusement at her mother before focusing again on her meal. The rest of the family's time together was spent in silence.

"Father," said Darcy as they left the room a little later, prompting his father to stop and wait for him. "Given the situation, it may be best to send Alexander away again. Perhaps it would be best if he were to go to Thorndell to inspect his estate. That would remove him from any possibility of trouble with the Bennets."

Though his father eyed him for several moments, deep in thought, Darcy never thought he would agree. His supposition was proven correct when his father said: "I will not always have my family running from the Bennets."

"That is not what this is about, Father," said Darcy. "Sending Alexander to Thorndell would remove the most likely member of our family to cause a problem from consideration, and it is time he looked in on his holdings regardless."

With a grunt, Mr. Darcy shook his head. "I have just had my son returned to me and I would prefer not to give up his company again. If the situation becomes worse we can consider your suggestion further, but at present, I wish Alexander to remain."

The decision made, his father took his leave, refusing to speak of the situation any further. Given recent events, Darcy thought it better if Alexander departed, and perhaps if Darcy went with him, that would give tensions a time to recede. Darcy had no wish to be away from Elizabeth, but he could not help but wonder if greater trials were destined to come their way.

While Darcy worried for the future, the weather over the next few days rendered his immediate concerns moot, for the very next day the rain began to fall. While Darcy might have welcomed a light, cleansing shower to wash away all his worries, what ensued was nothing less than a downpour. Lightning crashed, illuminating the landscape outside the house, while the winds howled and the rain fell, lashing the house and drenching everything in its path. The outside world was not fit for man nor beast, and on the few occasions Darcy had ventured out of the house, it seemed the rain was driving sideways.

The benefit of this inclement weather was, however, the cessation of any ability for tensions to rise between the two families. While it also deprived Darcy of Elizabeth's company, the strain on the relations within Darcy's family began to ease, and comments of the Bennets, ubiquitous in the outset, trailed off as tempers began to cool. Though he could not be certain, Darcy thought the baron was of a temperament which did not hold grudges, though what Mr. Gardiner thought was beyond his understanding. Given Elizabeth's testimony of the gentleman, Darcy hoped he too would allow the matter to rest.

While the rain allowed the families a respite from each other and from other society, it was not all beneficial, a fact which soon became clear. Spring had come in fits and starts that year, the weather warm at times while cooler at others, and while the snow had melted, there was still enough in the peaks to cause problems should the rain continue unabated. It was during one of the infrequent lulls in the rain that the family received word of trouble on the estate.

"Let us ride out to the McGregor farm," said Mr. Darcy after the messenger had departed.

"Is there a problem?" asked Darcy, noting his brother entering the room.

"It is possible," replied his father, "though at present it seems like it is only the threat of trouble. I would like you both to come and offer your opinions. It will be educational for you, Alexander."

Making no comment, Alexander agreed with a nod, and the three men returned to their rooms to make the appropriate changes to their attire. When they met in the stable a short time later, the three set out, as their horses were already saddled and waiting for them.

The ride was unpleasant, which was saying something, as one of Darcy's favorite activities was riding over the fields of Pemberley. The warmer weather, which had carried the promise of spring only a few days before, was now a distant memory, leaving the air chilled enough that the men and horses left a trail of mist every time they exhaled into the cool morning air. While the constant rain had dwindled to little more than a fine mist at the moment, it settled into their bones and set them to shivering, which they combated by drawing their greatcoats around them like shields. When the rain began to fall again, as Darcy knew it would, what was uncomfortable would become unbearable.

Mr. McGregor's farm was a plot of land toward the southwestern side of the estate, adjacent to the small river which ran through the valley and the middle of Pemberley's lands. The McGregors had farmed the land for several generations and were among the most dependable of Pemberley's tenants, known for their stolid soberness and ability to coax the most out of the fields they farmed.

"All this rain has caused us a spot of trouble, Mr. Darcy," said Mr. McGregor when he greeted them. "A bit of the hill along the edge of the valley gave away under the heavy rains."

"Did it cause any damage?" asked Mr. Darcy as he motioned for the farmer to lead the way.

"Some," said the tenant. "The house is far enough away to have escaped, but one of my barns is a little too close; the flow of mud undermined its foundation."

The gentlemen inspected the damage and, as Mr. McGregor had said, it was light. Still, the area would need to be dug out once the ground was a little firmer, and the base of the building reinforced before it deteriorated further, otherwise, they would lose the barn. The damage, however, was not the worst of the farmer's concerns.

"The river is running high," explained the farmer as he led them toward the ribbon of water bordering his fields. "If we get too much more rain, I am worried it will overrun its banks."

"Which would disrupt our planting," said the elder Darcy. "As I recall, we built a large berm here a few years ago."

"Aye, the lands I farm have always been among the most flood-prone," agreed Mr. McGregor. "At present, the berm is holding the water away. But if we get much more rain, it will put the barrier to the test."

"Have the waters risen, that quickly?" asked Alexander.

Mr. McGregor turned a kindly eye on Darcy's brother. "It was a harsh winter, young master, at least until the weather broke. There was more snow than usual, which meant more water entering the streams. The excess of snow *here* means the snow in the peaks was also heavier, and much of that snow has yet to melt. The rivers have been running high all spring—the recent rains have made it worse. I was speaking to old man Gallagher on Longbourn's land last week, and he reported the same problem there."

Though Mr. Darcy shot his tenant a look Darcy could not define, he said nothing in response. It was common knowledge the tenants cared nothing for the disputes between families; cooperation between the various families, regardless of their masters, was beneficial for all.

The berm, as Mr. McGregor had informed them, was holding and did not look to be in any danger from the swirling waters it had been built to hold. The river, little more than a large stream, bubbled and boiled as it made its way through the landscape, nothing like the placid waterway in which Darcy had often fished as a boy. As they stood to survey the land, Darcy noted the way the muck oozed under his feet, how a boot would slip out from under the unwary. The situation was worse than he had ever seen.

With a few more words, Mr. Darcy promised Mr. McGregor the help required to repair his building and instructed him to keep them apprised of the situation. Then they made their way back to the horses and began the frigid journey back to the manor. As a final insult, the rain began to fall again as soon as they mounted their horses.

"William," called his father when they had been riding for some minutes. "Have you heard from the steward at Thorndell of late?"

"His last letter arrived earlier this week," replied Darcy, noting his brother moving closer, listening with interest. "It was before the rain began, so I am uncertain if matters have changed in the interim, but he did not report any difficulties."

Mr. Darcy grunted. "It would be best if you wrote to him again and inquired. None of the other satellite estates are a concern at present, but Thorndell's proximity to the peaks means we should be watchful."

"I should prefer to be involved," said Alexander. "It is time I began to take more control over the place. It is my estate."

"Then let us write it together," said Darcy, pleased with his brother's diligence.

By the time they arrived back at the estate, all three were cold and miserable, as the rain had thickened to a steady fall once again. The worst part of it, in Darcy's estimation, was the way it prevented him from meeting with Elizabeth again. The situation at Longbourn would be similar to what Pemberley was experiencing, which meant there would be similar inspections happening there. It all led to the inescapable fact that Elizabeth would find it more difficult to slip away from her family undetected.

Not for the first time, Darcy wondered if they would be best served to steal away and elope. Gretna Green was not so very far away—should they depart with no one the wiser, no one could stop them before they reached their destination.

The dutiful son in Darcy, however, would not allow such actions, for his father needed his help. But when the situation allowed it, Darcy was determined to allow nothing to separate them.

CHAPTER XXIV

*F*or days while the rain continued to fall, the Bennet family found themselves confined to the estate. For Elizabeth, her inability to meet with William was hard, though she succeeded in convincing everyone in her family her discontent resulted from being denied the outdoors.

"Do not concern yourself, Lizzy," said Lady Margaret when she noted her daughter wandering the room on the fourth day of her captivity. "The rain will end soon, and when it does, I am certain you will once again be traipsing and riding all over the countryside."

Elizabeth gave her mother a slight smile. "Do not concern yourself for me, Mama. This is not the first time circumstances have denied me the outdoors, and it shall not be the last."

With a nod, Lady Margaret went back to her needlework, emulating her eldest daughter. Jane fixed Elizabeth with a grin before she too looked away, leaving Elizabeth to her restlessness. Her mind was miles away, focused on whatever room William inhabited at Pemberley, a place she had never laid eyes upon.

Of surprise to Elizabeth was Lydia's behavior, for her youngest sister appeared as restive as Elizabeth felt herself. Lydia, though not a sedentary girl, had never shown a similar interest in nature, but the girl fidgeted even more than Elizabeth.

"What is it, Lydia?" asked Elizabeth later that day. "I have never known a little rain to bother you."

"It is not a little rain," replied Lydia with a scowl. "Can we not have one day of sunshine, or are we to forever be subjected to this dull weather? I long to go into Lambton, to get out of this dreary house for a time. I have half a mind to order the carriage now and brave the weather if it will remove me from this place."

"The carriage is not available for your use," interjected Lord Arundel. "I will not subject our drivers or footmen to a deluge to satisfy your wanderlust, Lydia—do not even ask."

With a scowl and a pout, Lydia replied: "I would not require it of them, Papa. It is just so boring that I long to be free!"

"That is understandable, Lydia. No inclement weather can last forever—you must be patient."

Though Elizabeth could not know of the exact situation at Pemberley, it was no stretch to guess it was like that at Longbourn. Though different rivers ran through their lands, Elizabeth could not imagine the rain was not as much a concern to the master of Pemberley as it was to her father. There were no incidents among Longbourn's tenants, but the situation of the weather worried them all, and Elizabeth overheard her father speaking with his steward on the matter more than once.

When the rain ceased at last and the sun climbed out from behind the massive clouds the next day, the family all breathed a sigh of relief. The landscape was still sodden and would be for some days, but at least the windows now admitted a hint of cheery light, and while the sun hung weak and pale in the sky, it was better than no sun at all. That was when the other member of the family who had spent too long indoors began to make his opinion known to them all.

"Can we not go on a picnic again, Lizzy?" asked Thomas. "Would you not like to feel the sun on your face?"

"I would appreciate it very much," replied Elizabeth. "But the ground is yet too wet for such activities. We had best wait until it dries."

The boy released such a put-upon sigh that Elizabeth could not help but laugh. "If we cannot picnic today, perhaps we could, instead, go to Lambton for a time."

"And visit the sweet shop?" asked Thomas, his sudden excitement showing his eagerness.

"Your penchant for sweets far exceeds what is good for you," observed their mother.

Thomas directed a pout at his mother and moped, but when Elizabeth caught her eyes, Lady Margaret winked at her. Then she turned back to her son.

"Well, I suppose this one time might be acceptable."

With a whoop, Thomas threw himself into his mother's arms. "But let this not be a habit," she warned, "for I think you sneak more sweets from the kitchen than you require."

"Yes, Mama," said Thomas, a serious promise Elizabeth knew he would forget the moment it was convenient.

The rest of the sisters were also eager to escape the house—other than Mary, who instead went outside to walk along the paths of the back gardens with Mr. Collins. When they applied to Lord Arundel, he only waved them away, his mind on other matters. As there would be no danger for the drivers in the cool but dry air, they ordered the carriage and were soon off.

The visit to Lambton was more eventful than any of them had a right to expect. The first stop was the confectioners where Elizabeth purchased the promise sugar stick for Thomas, which he eagerly accepted along with the admonishment to avoid getting himself all sticky. Then the party separated their own ways to visit those locations which appealed to them. Thomas went along with Kitty, who wished to purchase some sheet music for the pianoforte, and though Elizabeth thought to accompany them to the bookshop, she never reached it.

"Elizabeth!" a hissed voice caught her attention.

Seeing the tall form of Mr. Darcy between two of the shops, Elizabeth looked about, and seeing no one in the immediate vicinity, darted into the dim space there. It was, indeed, Mr. Darcy, and it appeared to her the man was as relieved to see her as she was him.

"How are you, Elizabeth?" asked he. His hand rose of its own accord, though he stopped it and rested it at his side again, though he had been about to touch her face. Though Elizabeth longed for his touch, she knew anyone could come upon them at any moment—seeing him at all was taking a large risk, one which would be made immeasurably worse should someone discover them in an embrace, or even just touching.

"Annoyed with all this rain and desperate to see you," replied Elizabeth.

The man gave her a beaming smile. "Then we are of like mind, dearest Elizabeth. I might have braved all the rain in the world, had I thought I had an opportunity to see you."

The words filled Elizabeth with contentment, but at the same time with concern, for they evoked the memory of what had happened the last time she had seen him. With a quick glance at the alley's entrance, Elizabeth, satisfied they would not be interrupted for at least a few more moments, turned back to the man she loved.

"There may be a problem, for my uncle came upon me after we last met."

William frowned. "He did not see you leaving the meadow, did he? Unless he was in the trees watching us, he could not have seen me."

"No, he found me as I was returning to Longbourn, some time after I left you."

Elizabeth proceeded to inform William of her discussion with her uncle, including her impressions of his feelings. Uncle Gardiner becoming ever more watchful over his nieces would make it much more difficult for her to meet with William. It was clear in his expression as he listened to her that he understood the challenge himself.

"Elizabeth," said he, stepping forward and catching her hands in his own, heedless of how someone might find them, "the situation is becoming untenable. That I am disobeying my father's express wishes weighs on me, and I cannot look upon my behavior with satisfaction. I am certain your father has given you similar instructions."

"Yes, he has," replied Elizabeth, her heart filling with trepidation, thinking he was building up to informing her they should not meet again.

"It is my belief," continued William, "that it would be best if we announced our engagement to our families."

Gasping, Elizabeth stared at him. "How will that make the situation any better?" asked she. "Can you imagine either of our fathers would allow us to see each other again?"

"I have no answers," said William. "But the situation cannot be any worse. If we announce our engagement, that will at least allow us to deal with our fathers with honesty. Perhaps it might also lead to reconciliation."

"I can see no result other than our fathers being angry with us," replied Elizabeth. "What if they do as I fear and forbid us to see each other again?"

"Then we decide what to do should that come to pass."

"I . . . I do not know, William," replied Elizabeth.

The moment was lost when the sound of a commotion not far from their alley reached their ears. When the voices, loud enough for

Elizabeth to identify as those of Mr. Gardiner and Lydia told them something was amiss, they looked at each other and hurried from their place of concealment.

"Lydia!"

Alexander Darcy ducked behind a carriage stopped in front of the mercantile, noting the coachman watching him with some curiosity. The man was of no consequence, however, and Alexander ignored him, focused on the young woman he had seen walking down the street.

Seeing when she stopped and turned to look in his direction, Alexander cast a quick glance about, and noting no one nearby, he stepped forward. Miss Lydia was watching him, the half-smirk she often wore adorning her face. Alexander grinned. Her spirit and sense of adventure was the attribute he liked most in her.

"Calling me in the middle of a street in Lambton, Mr. Darcy," said she, her voice colored with a hint of playful teasing. She made a clucking sound with her tongue. "You are incorrigible, sir, for should our relations discover us in such circumstances, the tumult will be dreadful."

Another glance about revealed no one, so Alexander fixed his attention upon the young woman. "We should be safe for a moment or two. Have you considered my suggestion from the last time we met?"

Miss Lydia did not reply at once. When she did, it was with a hint of hesitance. "That is a wide chasm to leap, sir."

"Are there any other choices that you can see?" asked Alexander. "This incessant fighting between our families will never allow us the freedom to do otherwise."

"I think," said Lydia, "that a little time will improve matters. If it does not, we can consider the situation further at a later time."

"Lydia," said Alexander, stepping close to her. "I tire of this clandestine manner of our meetings, and I know you do too. This disagreement between our families has been ongoing for many years now—how can you say that it will improve in a manner of weeks? Our stratagem at the ball was an abject failure; I can see no way forward except that which I proposed."

"We have time," said Lydia, though he could see she was wavering. "I am not yet seventeen."

"Yes, I am well aware of your age. As I told you before, I care little for it. "If your father will not give his blessing, I am prepared to do what I must to ensure I have you in my life."

For a moment, Lydia regarded him, though saying nothing, and Alexander thought she might agree with him. The moment passed, however, lost as a loud voice interrupted their interlude, prompting Alexander to spin around to confront the owner of the voice.

"Lydia, what are you doing?"

It was Mr. Gardiner, Lydia's uncle. Alexander winced—there was no worse time for the man's interruption than the present. He had been so close.

"Nothing, Uncle," said Lydia, stepping in front of Alexander to confront her irate uncle. "Upon my word, I think this silly feud has begun to addle the wits of all caught under its spell. I am in the middle of a busy street—how can you think I will come to harm in such circumstances I cannot imagine!"

"That is enough from you, Lydia," commanded Mr. Gardiner. He grasped her arm in a gentle but firm grip and pulled her toward him, moving forward himself to take her place and confront Alexander.

"It seems to me, young Mr. Darcy, that you have a fascination for my youngest niece. That you are often in her company is contrary to her father's decree, and—I might add—what I suspect your father has also instructed. What do you have to say for yourself?"

"Uncle—" Lydia tried again, but a severe look from her uncle silenced her, though Alexander could see she was not pleased.

Then Mr. Gardiner's hard gaze once again rested on him, and for one of the few times in his life, Alexander Darcy did not know what to say. How could he explain to this man the regard which had been building in him for the youngest Bennet? If Alexander made any mention of their frequent meetings of late, the situation would become so difficult he doubted he would see her again.

"It seems your glib tongue has deserted you, sir."

"I mean no harm to your niece, Mr. Gardiner," said Alexander.

As he might have expected, his protest did not sway the other man in the slightest. "And yet it seems you are harming her—or her reputation at least."

"How can I be harming her reputation?" asked Alexander with a snort, his voice returning to him. "Men and women speak on the street many times. There is nothing improper about it."

Mr. Gardiner's eyes burned, and when he spoke, his voice was akin to gravel rolling down a hill. "It seems you do not understand, so let me enlighten you. Lydia is sixteen, and she is not formally out in society. Furthermore, you are a Darcy and she a Bennet, and the relative situation between your two families is such that you should not be speaking to her for *any* reason!"

"Mr. Gardiner—"

"Silence!" roared the man.

Though Alexander felt the force of Mr. Gardiner's glare upon him, consuming most of his attention, he possessed enough presence of mind to note his brother hurrying toward them with Miss Elizabeth following some distance behind. William's presence was a boon, for his calm ability to control any situation would be welcome at present. It was a skill that Alexander had never owned himself.

"I will hear no more, Mr. Darcy," growled Mr. Gardiner. "My brother has made it clear his children are not to have any congress with your family. Even if you have no care for your father's decrees, I would ask you to respect the instructions the baron has given to his daughters. Do not approach them again!"

"Let us speak of this rationally, Mr. Gardiner," said William as he strode to them and inserted himself between. "I am certain there is no reason to make a scene in the middle of the street."

"No, there you are correct, Mr. Darcy." Mr. Gardiner turned and began to shepherd his nieces, including two more who had arrived in the interim, away. "Talk some sense into your brother, sir, for this continued disobedience is straining matters between our families."

Then Mr. Gardiner turned and a moment later, the Bennets had disappeared. William watched them, then he turned around to regard Alexander. But Alexander was not about to stay and listen to his brother's lecture.

"I do not wish to hear it, Brother," hissed he.

Then he turned and stalked away, making his way toward his horse. Swinging himself into the saddle, he kicked his mount into motion and made his way out of town. As soon as he reached the outskirts of Lambton, Alexander kicked his horse into a gallop, hoping to relieve some of the excess energy and stress. Curse this stupid situation with the Bennet family!

When the Bennet carriage carrying the siblings began to roll out of town, Anne de Bourgh stepped toward the gentleman who stood watching it leave, deep in thought. As a newcomer, though one who was connected to one of the combatant parties, Anne thought she was in a perfect position to offer her own thoughts on the situation. If only Mr. Gardiner was of a mind to listen.

"It seems there has been more excitement between our families, sir."

So caught up in his thoughts was Mr. Gardiner that he jumped at Anne's words. When he noticed her, however, his reaction was not what she might have expected, given the implacable determination with which he had just castigated Anne's cousin. Then again, given how he had spoken with her at the ball, Anne did not expect he would act the brute with her.

"Once again centered on the same players, Miss de Bourgh," said he, his eyes turning to once again follow the progress of his niece's carriage leaving town. "Given this latest incident, I wonder if there is something else happening between your cousin and my niece."

"And this is a matter of concern?"

The man's hard gaze fell on Anne, though she was not at all put off by his ire. "If the memory of the situation between the two families is not enough to render any contact between them unwise, I would remind you of Lydia's youth. She is but sixteen years of age, Miss de Bourgh."

"Yes, that is a concern," agreed Anne. "However, I do not think they could come to mischief on a street in Lambton."

"It is not Lambton that concerns me," replied Mr. Gardiner. "As I said, I wonder if they are better known to each other than any of us knows. There is also your cousin's reputation to consider."

"Alexander is not the blackguard you make him out to be," said Anne. Though she supposed she might have felt the insult of his words concerning her cousin, in reality, Anne knew it was Alexander's own fault. His own behavior had made others mistrust him, so he could not complain now. While Alexander had sometimes been uncaring, cavalier, and prone to behavior which was not laudable, however, he was not a man so depraved as to trifle with a young woman's heart — particularly a young woman who was the daughter of a peer.

"You have my apologies if you believe I consider your cousin in such a light, Miss de Bourgh," said Mr. Gardiner with a short bow. "It was never my intention to say anything of him which is unwarranted."

Anne smiled at Mr. Gardiner's obvious obfuscation. "Oh, well done, sir. But I have understood what you did not say. There is no need to deny it, for I am well aware of the reputation my cousin has gained of his own volition, and I do not deny it is deserved to a certain extent.

"I would also aver that my cousin has changed these past months, for he differs from what I remember when I saw him last."

"How so?" asked Mr. Gardiner, seeming curious in spite of himself.

"There is a more serious air about him," replied Anne. She paused and grinned, adding: "Oh, he will never be as grave as his elder brother, but there is something about him which suggests he has left the greater part of his insouciance behind."

Mr. Gardiner frowned and considered the matter. "This sudden change in him concerns me."

"Truly?" asked Anne, confused by Mr. Gardiner's sudden statement. "I cannot imagine why—I should think better behavior is worth celebrating."

"Yes, that is true," replied Mr. Gardiner. "Please do not construe my words as censure of your cousin. I am concerned for what has provoked such a change."

"In truth, I cannot say." Anne paused and considered the gentleman. "It may be nothing more than the weight of greater experience and maturity that has led him to alter his behavior. It also may be the looming prospect of responsibility—he returned at his father's bidding and desire that he take on the management of his own estate, as I understand."

"And yet some who begin as libertines, gamesters, and the like never change their ways."

"That is true," agreed Anne. "With such excellent examples as his elder brother and father, however, I would hope he would not forever be beyond the reach of amendment."

Though the mention of the other Darcys caused a certain tightness about Mr. Gardiner's eyes, the gentleman did not reply. It seemed he was capable of understanding the goodness in her relations, despite his family's persistent troubles with them. After a moment more of thought, Mr. Gardiner sighed, then turned his attention back to Anne, a slight smile playing about the corners of his mouth.

"If there were cooler tempers at hand more often," said he, "it is possible this feud may be settled."

"Are you referring to your own temper?" asked Anne, amused by his openness.

Mr. Gardiner laughed. "I have not been blessed with the evenest disposition, Miss de Bourgh. It is no secret I am protective of my nieces, and when provoked, my anger tends to burn hot, though it is also extinguished quickly."

"In that case," said Anne, "I shall attempt to be available more often, for none have accused me of being quick to anger."

"But then your mother must also be close by," said Mr. Gardiner, his amusement plain, "and *she* most certainly possesses that reputation!"

They laughed together, Anne exclaiming: "You have the right of it, sir."

When their mirth had run its course, Anne could not help but observe: "If only all our family could get on as well as we do, the troubles between us would come to naught." Then Anne fixed him with a look of mock sternness. "Of course, by your standards, we should not be speaking with each other, for we are both embroiled in our families' troubles, are we not?"

"Part of my reason for interjecting with my nieces," replied Mr. Gardiner, "is because their father has made his wishes known. Part of it is also because Lydia can be headstrong and set on having her own way. With you, Miss de Bourgh, while I sense you can also possess determination to a large degree, you are also a woman, not a young girl. Your last name is not Darcy, and mine is not Bennet—what we do with our time is our own concern."

Anne looked at him, unable to hide the speculation she felt at his declaration. Mr. Gardiner, she decided, was a good man, one she would like to know better. Anne well knew her mother would not appreciate her defection, as she would see it, but as Anne had no intention of ever marrying her cousin, perhaps there was another who might suit.

"Are you suggesting something further, sir?" asked she, attempting to convey a playful attitude, though the question was far more serious than she let on.

"This is only our second meeting," said Mr. Gardiner.

"Indeed, it is," murmured Anne.

"Having said that," said he, "it *has* occurred to me that perhaps there are other ways to heal this breach between Bennet and Darcy. Since it is too much to ask that *they* do it for themselves, it may be best to look to other possibilities. An alliance between close relations would go a long way toward restoring peace."

As much as she had anticipated what he might say, Anne could not help the surprise which rolled through her. "It . . . This is a little . . . precipitous, is it not?"

"Now then, Miss de Bourgh," said he, fixing her with a grin, "it is not as if I have proposed, is it? I do not think acknowledging potential future *intention* is tantamount to a *declaration*."

"Then," said Anne, after thinking on it for a moment, "I believe you may proceed, as long as you do not do so with all speed. Let us become accustomed to this, Mr. Gardiner. Let us ensure our families become accustomed to it."

Mr. Gardiner nodded and grinned. "Shall your lady mother call me out, do you think?"

The laugh which comprised Anne's response bubbled up of its own accord. "Do not concern yourself, Mr. Gardiner—should she do so, I shall insist on being your second."

They laughed together again, and to Anne it felt right, as if warmth was shining on her from above, informing her that all would be well. When she approached Mr. Gardiner that day, she had no notion it would have prompted such a response. But perhaps there was something there, something she had not known was possible. Anne de Bourgh was eager to learn what lay in her future, for Mr. Gardiner, she decided, was a good man.

CHAPTER XXV

" *D* amn and blast! What can he be thinking?"
Darcy wished to discover what Alexander was thinking himself, for it was putting needless strain on the relations between the families. That it was like Darcy's own situation with Elizabeth he dismissed without another thought—Darcy was in love with *his* Bennet sister, but he doubted Alexander felt such depth of emotion for the youngest. No, it was Alexander's continued flouting of propriety and his father's commands at play here.

As his father paced the study where Darcy had informed him of the events in Lambton, he could feel a hint of shame for thinking as he had about his brother. Regardless of whatever Alexander was thinking when he approached the youngest Bennet, he had no notion of his brother having a motive injurious to the young woman. Even at his most dissipative, Darcy had never known his brother to be careless with a woman's reputation. Would he be so now with the wellbeing of the daughter of a baron?

"Where is your brother now?" asked his father, drawing Darcy's attention back to him.

"After the confrontation," replied Darcy, "Alexander rode off. I had assumed he was headed for Pemberley, but it seems I was mistaken."

The elder man shook his head with disgust. "Your brother has improved of late, I had thought, but his actions speak of a return of his thoughtless attitude. When he returns home, I shall have many things to say to him, for his actions regarding this girl are not what they should be."

While Darcy could agree with his father's assessment, he was uncertain, for Alexander's behavior confounded him. Mr. Darcy paused, considering the matter, then turned to address his son again.

"I cannot say I know anything of Arundel's daughters, but the youngest girl, Miss . . ."

"Lydia," supplied Darcy.

"Yes, that is the one. Does she not seem a little . . . flirtatious to you?"

"I will own I do not know her well enough to judge her," said Darcy, thinking of what Elizabeth had told him of each of her sisters. "There is little harm in her, I think, but I believe she may be a little bold for her age. But I have never seen her behave in a manner I find improper."

The elder man grunted as if annoyed his son denied an avenue of exonerating his son. "I suppose you are correct. For all that I do not hold with Arundel and his family, I cannot say he does not know how to raise his children."

"Given some of Alexander's behavior," said Darcy, his comment pointed, "I do not think anyone of our family is in a position to cast shade on another. Alexander has improved, but there still remains about him a rash insouciance which cannot be rationalized away. Though I know my brother does not intend to hurt her, Lord Arundel does not have that luxury—he is correct to be concerned. That concern must also extend to Miss Lydia's uncle, who, as I understand, is protective of the girls."

"Yes, I well understand my son's character," replied his father. "However, I still dislike this Mr. Gardiner's insinuation about him, and I would not wish the Bennets to spread their vitriol far and wide."

"Do you think they would?" asked Darcy. "I cannot think they wish to bear tales. It seems to me they would far prefer to ignore us, as much as we wish to avoid thinking of them. There is also the matter of their daughter's reputation to consider—if they spread tales of Alexander, it would affect Miss Lydia."

"You may be correct," acknowledged Mr. Darcy.

As his father continued to think on the matter, Darcy watched him, heartened that his mien was turning from anger to deep thought. While his father was a good man, one thoughtful and sober, Mr. Darcy also tended toward sudden anger toward any perceived slights against the respectability of his family.

"As I recall, you suggested I should send Alexander to Thorndell." The mention of their previous conversation caught Darcy by surprise. "I still believe it would be beneficial."

A slow nod was his father's response, which he followed by saying: "At present, I still wish him nearby. But you are correct—it *would* help diffuse the situation if Alexander was not in the neighborhood. I would have you go with him to assist him in taking control of the estate."

"Yes, I can see where that would be desirable," said Darcy. Though little wishing to be away from Elizabeth, at present it would be too risky to see her. If he journeyed to Thorndell with his brother, there would be no temptation.

"Then you will go with him?" pressed his father.

"If you wish it, I will go," said Darcy.

"Thank you, Son," said his father, clasping his shoulder. "I appreciate that I have always been able to rely on your support."

"It is no trouble, Father."

Mr. Darcy nodded and squared his shoulders. "I suppose I should visit Longbourn and speak with Arundel."

Surprised, Darcy queried: "Go to Longbourn?"

"It would be for the best," replied his father, though a moue of distaste hovered about his mouth. "Though I have little desire to endure the man's ill-conceived humor, this business of Alexander and his daughter must be as concerning to him as it is to me. As you suggested, he must wish to protect his daughter's reputation as much as I do Alexander's."

"A sensible plan," replied Darcy. Though he said nothing, this evidence of his father's belief in a possible rapprochement heartened him. Only a few months ago, Darcy was certain his father would not even have considered visiting Longbourn.

"Do you wish me to accompany you?"

While he thought about it for a moment his father shook his head. "It is best not to for the present. I expect a civil conversation, but *no more* than civil. I shall discuss the situation with him and return at once. Should your brother return, keep him at Pemberley. I hope he will not force me to order him to Thorndell, but I shall if I must."

With a nod, his father walked from the room, leaving Darcy alone with his thoughts. What would come of this meeting? Darcy had some hope it would begin building a bridge between families. What he was not was confident, for they still had much to overcome.

The larger concern in Darcy's mind at the moment was his impending journey to Thorndell. Darcy did not know how long he would be away, but to go with no word to Elizabeth, leaving her wondering if he was abandoning her could not be contemplated. The question was, how he could inform her of his departure and the reason for it.

A smile crept over Darcy's face as he thought of a way to let her know. With determination in his step, Darcy moved to his father's desk and took a sheet of paper from the drawer in which he knew his father kept his stationery, and sitting at the desk, he began to write.

The visit of a Darcy to Longbourn had not taken place within living memory, and the reverse for likely much longer. When the butler appeared in Arundel's study to inform him of Mr. Darcy's presence, he was inclined to think it a great joke. Why would a man as stiff-necked and proud as Mr. Robert Darcy come to confront the enemy on his own ground?

Then the thought of what his brother had informed him sobered Arundel and he informed Mr. Hill to lead him hither, for it seemed it was now time to discuss the problem as rational gentlemen. Lydia, he had already confined to her room in anticipation of a discussion he knew would come later. The girl was far too confident for her own good, did not understand the ways of men as she ought. Perhaps it had been a mistake to allow her to attend local events at such a young age. Arundel made a mental note to discuss the matter with Margaret later.

When the elder Darcy appeared in his room, Arundel noted his pinched expression and knew how he must detest this necessity as much as Arundel did. The image of the proud gentleman approaching him with hat in hand welled up in Arundel's mind, a hint of glee rose within him. This visit served well to remind the arrogant Darcys of their actual place in society, never mind the connections about which they never failed to boast.

"Lord Arundel," said Mr. Darcy with a slight incline of his head, shattering the image in Arundel's mind. Though Mr. Darcy might have come to Longbourn, it was clear his pride had not suffered because of the indignity.

"*Mr.* Darcy," replied Arundel, noting from the scowl that the gentleman had noted his emphasis on the title. "What may I do for you today?"

"It seems to me we should speak concerning our children," replied Mr. Darcy, a shortness in his tone Arundel might have expected. "This latest incident in Lambton suggests a greater problem. It would behoove us to resolve it at once."

"You are correct," replied Lord Arundel. He motioned his guest to a chair and leaned forward, resting his forearms and elbows on the desk between them. "It seems to me I have often seen and heard of your son mentioned in the same breath as my youngest daughter. To what can I attribute this close . . . proximity?"

"Just what are you insinuating?" demanded Mr. Darcy. Though he had perched himself in the indicated chair, he was ill at ease, sitting on the edge, his gaze focused on Arundel.

"I insinuate nothing, I assure you," replied Arundel. "I wish to understand what is happening between our children. You must understand your son's reputation, and I am a concerned father. My daughter is, after all, only sixteen years of age."

"If I could answer that question, I would be very well pleased," replied Mr. Darcy.

"Have you not asked your son?" demanded Arundel, feeling more than a little disdain for this man well up within him. Arundel would have thought Robert Darcy better able to control his brood than he was showing himself capable.

"Alexander has not returned home yet," was Mr. Darcy's short reply. "When he appears, you may be assured I will require he account for his behavior."

Arundel snorted. "Yes, that would be for the best. In the meantime, I shall act as any other father of a young daughter and see to her protection."

"Are you suggesting my son is a danger to her?" spat Mr. Darcy.

"I suggest nothing more than that she is but sixteen years of age and appears to have been importuned repeatedly by a man of five and twenty!"

"Do you not think your flirt of a daughter has attempted to draw him in?"

An icy chill settled about Arundel's heart. "If I thought you were suggesting my daughter is a scarlet woman, I would call you out for the insult, sir."

The two gentlemen glared at each other, neither giving an inch. It was well, Arundel thought with a grim sense of amusement, that the desk lay between them, for his anger was such that he considered throttling the other man where he sat. It was fortunate Mr. Darcy made no more accusations, for Arundel knew he would not be responsible for his actions if he did.

"If it was not already obvious," said Mr. Darcy, "our distrust for each other runs deep, provoking both of us to say words we would not otherwise think of uttering."

"In that, you are correct," grunted Arundel, feeling the oppressive atmosphere in the room ease, if only a little. "For what it is worth, I thank you for your conciliatory words, sir, for I believe we were on the verge of coming to blows."

Mr. Darcy nodded, though he did not respond to Arundel's assertion. "Then what do we do to resolve the situation?"

Sitting back in his chair, Arundel regarded the man in his study. The Bennet family, it was true, had disliked and distrusted the Darcy family out of principle, long after the original insult had been forgotten. Though it galled some part of him to allow any good quality in this man, he could confess that this Mr. Darcy seemed to be a man of integrity. In the past, there had been some conflict of an active nature, and Arundel had little interest in returning to such times.

"It seems we must attempt to control our children, sir," said Arundel at length. He snorted a mirthless laugh and added: "Though I will not presume to judge your son, my daughter, though she is a good girl at heart, is headstrong. Though I see little in her behavior other than thoughtlessness, inducing her to desist will be a difficult endeavor."

Mr. Darcy barked a laugh. "Stubbornness is a trait, it seems, our families share in abundance." After a short pause, Mr. Darcy leaned forward and said: "Why do you suppose they have been insistent upon speaking to each other?"

"If I knew that," said Arundel, "I might have some hope of curbing Lydia's behavior. It seems to me there might be some interest in each other, perhaps some lure of the forbidden."

"Interest?" asked Mr. Darcy, his brow furrowing in surprise. "Do you suggest there is some attraction between them?"

"It is possible there is some understated interest," replied Arundel. "But I do not think they have been together enough for it to have developed into anything more. Mayhap, when the time comes, we should allow it to flourish if there is anything there."

The surprise with which Mr. Darcy regarded him was enough to provoke Arundel's amusement. "Do you suggest we encourage them to marry?"

"At present, Lydia is too young," replied Arundel. "However, if you think about it, history is littered with conflicts resolved by means of a strategic marriage."

"That is true," replied Mr. Darcy. Though he was clearly thinking of the matter, he shook his head a moment later. "But you are correct—now is not the time. At present, it would be best if we stepped back and allowed the tension to ease."

"I agree."

"There is one more matter," said Mr. Darcy. "That of your brother."

"Do not concern yourself for Gardiner," said Arundel. "He considers it his duty to be a protector to my daughters, but he is a good man. As long as we can separate our children and he does not think your son is importuning my daughter, he will desist. I shall speak with him and inform him of our resolution."

Though Mr. Darcy stared at Arundel, wondering if his words were a slight against his son, he came to the correct conclusion. Then he stood and offered his hand, which Arundel took with only the barest hesitation.

"Then we agree."

"It seems we do."

With a bow, Mr. Darcy departed, leaving Bennet to his thoughts. In some ways, the conversation had been a surprise, for while the insults and ill feelings had simmered under the surface, that they had come to an agreement about their children was not an insignificant achievement.

At length, Arundel sighed and rose to his feet. Lydia, he knew, would rail against the unfairness of his instructions, for no other reason than it would curb her activities. The girl was obstinate and little enjoyed receiving instructions from anyone. It would not be an easy discussion.

No one in the family had known of Mr. Darcy's visit to Longbourn. Thus, when Lord Arundel gathered them in the sitting-room after the fact, going so far as to summon their uncles to an impromptu meeting of the family, the surprise they all felt was unmistakable. Or at least it was in most of them—Lydia, it seemed, had taken it into her head to be angry, and with her father most of all.

"Lydia," said he for what seemed like the tenth time, "what has been happening between you and the youngest Mr. Darcy? And before you attempt to dissemble," warned her father as she opened her mouth to speak, "remember we have found you in his company three times now, and I know not if there have been more occasions outside of those instances of which we know."

Lydia's response was a mulish glare; Elizabeth shook her head, knowing the girl's willful defiance would not serve her well, though she was too pigheaded to see it. The girl folded her arms and directed a cross glare about the room, daring any of them to ask her any further questions. When she did not respond, her father again questioned her.

"Has Mr. Darcy importuned you or has this been a willful bit of disobedience on your part?"

"Upon my word, you are eager to convict him!" cried Lydia. "There is nothing the matter with Mr. Darcy, for he has been nothing other than friendly and respectful to me."

"That is good to hear, Lydia," said Lord Arundel. "Of issue, however, is the tension it is creating between the families and your willful disobedience in the face of my express wishes. What have you to say for yourself?"

"There would not be any tension between us if we all let go of this ridiculous dispute."

"You may be correct," said Lord Arundel, his voice rising in sharpness. "At present, however, the situation is what it is. I can foresee a hint of softening in our relations, Lydia, but these things take time. Your intractable insistence on pushing matters will only make it worse—you must see this!"

Though it was clear to see Lydia wished to protest further, she remained silent, her mouth a thin, straight line of displeasure. When her father realized she would not speak again, he sighed and shook his head.

"Though I must wonder if you are hearing anything I say, I must repeat myself, it seems. From this point forward, you will not speak with Mr. Darcy again, is that clear?"

Lydia did not reply, keeping her silence. "I said, am I clear?"

"Of course, Papa," said Lydia in a simpering voice laced with disdain. "I shall sharpen my sword and run it through Mr. Darcy's black and shriveled heart should he have the temerity to glance at me again."

"That is enough!"

The thundered voice was unlike her father, for Lord Arundel did not often raise it to that extent. One might be excused in thinking it would cow a young girl of Lydia's age, but it did not affect her defiant glare or posture in the slightest. It was worth noting, however, that she did not contradict him again, though Elizabeth had no expectation of the girl's compliance.

"I will have your obedience, Lydia," continued Lord Arundel. "Willing or no. It occurs to me that we have been a little lax in monitoring your activities of late. You are not yet seventeen, and while you might not credit it at present, you are *not* yet out."

Lydia shot to her feet, her fury a living entity. "Then you will confine me to my room, bar me from society and anything in which I find pleasure?"

"If you behave like a child, then you shall be treated so!" rejoined Lord Arundel, rising to his feet to face his daughter. "The decision is yours, Lydia. You may behave yourself or I will curtail your activities until you do. At present, I require you to tend to your studies to prepare for your eventual coming out and keep your distance from Alexander Darcy. Can I trust your compliance? If so, there is no need to further restrict you. Know that I will if I must."

"It seems I have little choice," spat Lydia. Then she turned and stalked from the room, her voice floating back to them, an acidic: "If anyone wishes to see me, I shall be in my room studying to become an accomplished woman."

The remaining family glanced at each other, stunned at the confrontation, while Lord Arundel sank again into his chair, resting his head in his hand. "That child will be the death of me," muttered he, though his words were audible to everyone in the room.

"There, there, Husband," said Lady Margaret, patting his hand. "She is an intractable child but I dare say it shall turn out well. I shall be certain to give her more of my attention and guidance, and I dare say we shall curb this recklessness which has crept into her character."

Lord Arundel responded to his wife in like fashion before turning his attention to Mr. Gardiner, who had watched the bit of drama, impassive to what was occurring before him. Upon realizing his brother was watching him, Mr. Gardiner, unconcerned, raised an eyebrow.

"It is time for you to pull back, Brother," said Lord Arundel.

"Do you truly suppose you have clipped Lydia's wings?"

"No, I do not suppose it. But I also do not believe that this insanity between Lydia and the youngest Mr. Darcy to be his fault alone. It seems my daughter has had an active part in it."

"And that is the problem," replied Mr. Gardiner. "I have every confidence Mr. Darcy wishes to settle the rising tensions and commend him for it. The son, however, is a bird of another feather, and Lydia's imprudence is a match for his."

Lord Arundel fixed a steady look on his brother. "Do you suspect something more than we know?"

"I am uncertain. It seems likely they have met more often than the three occasions which have caused all the commotion, but for what purpose I cannot divine. Yes, I agree we should endeavor to ensure the situation does not worsen. Letting down my guard, however, would be unwise at present. I shall continue to practice vigilance."

"That would be for the best," replied Lord Arundel. "I shall do the same. But tread lightly. Let us allow the tension between our houses to dissipate before something worse erupts between us."

By the time his father had returned to Pemberley, not only had Alexander arrived, his hair sticking every which way out from his head, his mount blowing as if he had been riding it hard, but Fitzwilliam had also returned. Regardless of his father's edict to them all to avoid the Bennets, he had not required Fitzwilliam to leave Pemberley, not that Darcy had expected he would. Fitzwilliam had been largely silent and watchful when among them since that day, but Darcy did not miss the hint of sardonic amusement with which he regarded them—in particular, the revelation of Alexander's continued interest in Miss Lydia.

"Well, Alexander," said Fitzwilliam upon seeing Alexander stride into the house, "it seems you have kicked the hornet's nest."

"Enough, Cousin," said Alexander. "I have little desire to hear about how imprudent I have been from you too."

"On the contrary," said Fitzwilliam, "I have no such purpose. In fact, if you are as tired of this situation as I have become, you are to be commended." Fitzwilliam's eyes caught Darcy's and he added: "It seems to me the younger generation have become more aware of the silliness of what is happening than their elders can see."

Curious though he was why his cousin would look at him, Darcy was distracted when Fitzwilliam laughed and added: "When I was returning from Lucas Manor, I chanced to come upon Mr. Gardiner and our lovely cousin, Anne, speaking in the street. There seemed to be little discord between them, I might add, for they were speaking with perfect civility."

Darcy shot a glance toward the sitting-room, where he knew his aunt and cousin were visiting with his sister, and turned back to Fitzwilliam. "It may be best to refrain from speaking of such subjects, for it would not do to alert Lady Catherine to her daughter's actions."

"Had I any notion her mother's displeasure would affect Anne in any way I might agree. Our Anne, however, has grown something of independence, though I suspect she always possessed it, carefully hidden from her mother."

"You may be correct," replied Darcy. "But let us refrain from adding to the discord swirling about us.

Fitzwilliam gazed at Darcy, making him feel uncomfortable. "Yes, Cousin, it would be best to avoid further dispute, for we would not wish to become the focus of such dissension, now would we?"

The frown Darcy leveled at his cousin did not alter his expression a jot, and for a moment Darcy wondered if he was speaking of something specific. The memory of the initial days of his interest in Elizabeth arose in his mind, and he recalled some pointed remarks Fitzwilliam had made to him. Had he somehow discovered Darcy's secret?

"Do not concern yourself for me," said Alexander, breaking the tension between cousins. "As I have said, I have heard it from you all and prefer not to hear it any further. If you will excuse me, I believe I shall return to my room and change."

"One moment, Son."

The sound of their father's voice drew the brothers' attention, turning them as one to see him framed in the doorway. Fitzwilliam seemed already to know of his uncle's presence, for he betrayed no surprise at seeing him there.

As their father advanced, Darcy could hear his brother mutter, "Oh, Lord!" under his breath. Darcy fixed him with a glare, which he ignored, while Fitzwilliam snorted his amusement. Their father, it seemed, had not heard.

"I have just come from Longbourn."

The announcement caught both Alexander and Fitzwilliam's attention, though in different ways. Fitzwilliam appeared interested while Alexander was hopeful; Darcy, who had known of the visit made no response.

"It seems Lord Arundel suspects my son of ulterior motives. When considering the matter from his perspective, I cannot blame him."

"There is nothing for you or his lordship to concern yourselves," replied Alexander in a manner at once dismissive and careless. "I am only having a bit of fun, and I know Miss Bennet is the same."

"And that is why we must concern ourselves," retorted Mr. Darcy, glaring at his younger son. "In case you have forgotten, I shall remind you that Miss Lydia is the daughter of a baron; it would be unwise to behave toward her with anything other than the utmost in propriety.

This cavalier attitude of yours must cease."

"I assure you, Father," replied Alexander, his manner everything serious, "that I have never treated her so."

Mr. Darcy nodded, though he was not finished issuing instructions. "Though I am loath to give up your company, I think it would be best if you were to go to Thorndell for a time to allow tempers to cool."

"You wish me to go to Thorndell?" Alexander's response was not what Darcy might have expected. In fact, he had thought his brother would become irate at being banished once again to his estate. However, Alexander seemed more thoughtful and curious than anything else.

"I do not *wish* you to leave at all," repeated their father. "For the good of us all, however, I believe that it would be best if you did."

When Alexander did not respond at once, Mr. Darcy continued, saying: "I have achieved a détente with the baron, but at present, it is new and will not continue if you are caught found in the girl's company. If we are ever to have peace with the Bennet family, we must take slow steps, learn to trust each other. That cannot happen if you continue to importune the baron's youngest daughter, and that is why I believe it is best you depart."

"Must it be my fault, Father?" asked Alexander.

"No, I would not accuse you of it. It seems to me the girl has been a willing conspirator in your recent meetings." Mr. Darcy paused and eyed his son. "Tell me, Alexander, Mr. Gardiner has seen you speaking with Miss Lydia in Lambton twice, besides the infamous dance at Lucas Manor. Have you met with the girl on other occasions?"

"Would it matter if I had?" asked Alexander.

For a moment his father watched him, and Darcy thought he might pursue the subject further, but he seemed to decide Alexander was in the right. He shook his head.

"Perhaps it does not matter. Whatever has happened between you, however, must stop now. Will you go to Thorndell as I ask?"

"I shall accompany you," added Darcy, drawing his brother's gaze to himself. "If only to acquaint you with matters at the estate and help you settle in."

"Do you mean to be my minder?" Alexander's tone was unfriendly.

"Is a minder necessary?" asked Darcy, his pointed glare falling on his brother.

"No, it is not."

"That is well, for I am not your guardian."

"Very well," said Alexander, his manner everything that was short.

"Now, if you will allow it, I shall return to my rooms."

Without waiting for an answer, Alexander turned and bounded up the stairs three at a time, eager to leave them behind. A moment later, they heard his door closing behind him. Though Darcy would not accuse his brother of childish behavior, he might have thought he would have closed the door with more force.

"What do you think of his reaction?" asked Mr. Darcy, turning back to his remaining son.

"It is obvious he little likes being directed," deflected Darcy. In truth, he had no notion of his brother's thoughts at the moment.

"Your sons are obdurate, Uncle," said Fitzwilliam.

"While I rejoice that I have raised confident men," replied Darcy's father, "at this moment, I would prefer more tractability." Then he turned to Darcy. "Please watch out for your brother. If he can settle in at Thorndell for even a month or two, that would improve the situation."

With those words, his father turned to depart. Darcy could not consider the matter any further, for his cousin's teasing made itself known.

"Yes, Darcy," said Fitzwilliam, the mocking in his voice easy to hear, "you had best watch your brother, for he might do something rash if left to his own devices."

Before Darcy could call his cousin on his words, Fitzwilliam turned and departed, leaving Darcy wondering as to his meaning. It was becoming clear Fitzwilliam suspected him at the very least. Though the thought of not seeing Elizabeth at all did not sit well with him, perhaps going to Thorndell was best.

CHAPTER XXVI

ﾟﾍﾞﾙﾟﾍﾞﾟﾍﾞﾟﾍ

*M*uch though Darcy had always considered Lambton to be one of the most charming towns in existence, that morning he saw none of it. The hour was still early and the streets bare of traffic which would appear at a later hour, but as he was scheduled to depart with his brother for Thorndell in only an hour, there was no help for it. Making his way down the narrow cobbled street on Zeus, Darcy ignored the shopkeepers readying their wares for the day's business in favor of his destination, the church.

The building, situated on the center of Lambton's central hill, stood on one of the only flat places in the town not far from the smithy and the green where the town gathered for festivals and other amusements. It was a beautiful, large building, able to accommodate those of the neighborhood, the white boards comprising its walls gleaming bright and pure in the morning sun.

Upon catching sight of the church, Darcy reined his horse to a stop, wondering how to proceed. Though it was true he had spoken to Mrs. Gardiner on several occasions, those meetings had always been by chance—never by design. Speaking with the woman did not concern Darcy, but he wished to avoid any notice of his actions.

Luck, it appeared, was with Darcy that morning, for the woman herself stepped from the cottage situated just a short distance away and walked toward the church. Taking it as a sign he should proceed and with a mutter of appreciation, Darcy dismounted and tied Zeus to a nearby post. Then he stepped forward, knowing there was little time to accomplish what he must.

"Mrs. Gardiner!" called he as he approached.

The woman straightened from what she had been doing and put a hand over her eyes to shade them from the morning sun. While in the past she had greeted him with a smile and a few softly spoken words of welcome, on this occasion her gaze was appraising, firming Darcy's belief she was aware to some degree of what had passed between himself and her niece.

"How do you do this morning, Mrs. Gardiner?" asked Darcy as he bowed to her.

"Very well, sir," replied Mrs. Gardiner, dropping into a curtsey.

"I hoped I would see you this morning." There was little reason to prevaricate and time was of the essence. "Forgive me if I speak out of turn and know I am well aware I might reveal something I ought not, but am I correct in apprehending that you know something of the situation between your niece and me?"

Mrs. Gardiner gazed on him for a moment, her expression unreadable, before she responded in the affirmative. "I am, Mr. Darcy. Elizabeth informed me of it several weeks ago, though she betrayed the matter in a moment of thoughtlessness. As we have always been close, she informed me of the truth when I pressed her."

Darcy had not been conscious of the breath he had been holding, waiting for her answer. A sigh of relief passed through him and he attempted to give the woman a smile.

"Thank you for confirming that, Mrs. Gardiner. Please know that I would not ask under better circumstances, but I must leave the neighborhood for a few days, and I would not have her misunderstand the reason for my departure."

"You must leave?" asked Mrs. Gardiner, cocking her head to the side.

"After the last incident between Miss Lydia and my brother, my father has decided it is best that he retire to his estate which is some thirty miles distant. I go with him because I have been managing it in his stead for some years—though I expect I will be absent only a few days, Elizabeth may not understand why I am gone, since I expect it will be spoken of in the neighborhood."

"Yes, I can understand why that would be of concern," murmured

Mrs. Gardiner. The woman turned a questioning look on him. "Then you wish me to inform Elizabeth of the reasons for your departure?"

"If you please," said Darcy, drawing the letter he had written the previous day from his pocket. "I know it is not proper, but I have written her a short letter explaining the matter. If you are not comfortable passing my letter to her, informing her of the reason for my absence would be sufficient."

Mrs. Gardiner glanced at the folded paper in his hand, but she made no move to accept it. Instead, Darcy found himself the subject of her scrutiny, as if he was being tested, weighed, examined to ensure he was good enough for her precious niece. After a moment, Mrs. Gardiner spoke:

"Sending a letter to a young woman who is not a relation or fiancée *is* improper."

"Then you need not concern yourself, Mrs. Gardiner," said Darcy, a slow smile stealing over his face. "I proposed to Elizabeth after the ball and she accepted. Though our fathers have not given their blessings, I consider myself engaged to your niece, and I know she feels likewise."

"It seems to me there is a story of which I am not aware in your words, sir," replied Mrs. Gardiner. "Your confession implies you love her."

"More than anything in the world."

"Then I shall do as you ask," said Mrs. Gardiner, returning his smile, though hers was wistful, misted over by powerful emotion. "I wish for nothing more than this for Elizabeth — for all my nieces. Please know that I am your supporter, for I believe in her happiness with you if you can surmount the barriers that stand in your way."

"Thank you, Mrs. Gardiner," said Darcy, his heart full in response to the trust she extended to him. "If I might also, should there be a need, please inform me at this address." Darcy handed her a small card on which he had written the direction to Thorndell. "I do not ask that you breach propriety, but if there is anything for which Miss Elizabeth must contact me, I wish you to know how I may be contacted."

"Very well," said Mrs. Gardiner. "Then Godspeed, Mr. Darcy."

With those final words, Mrs. Gardiner took the envelop he still held out to her and curtseyed before returning to the house. Darcy took himself away to his horse, swinging into the saddle and making his way back toward Pemberley, confident Elizabeth would not misunderstand his reason for departing.

While the atmosphere at Longbourn roiled with ill feelings and tension, Elizabeth felt little of it. The center of the discord was Lydia to no one's surprise, who, though she did not rant and storm and carry on about it as she might have when she was a young girl, was still unhappy and not afraid to display her displeasure to them all. Not knowing just what her sister was playing at—and Lydia refused to elucidate—Elizabeth could not stifle the annoyance welling up within her.

Whatever her sister was about, she could not imagine it was anything other than Lydia's willful disobedience, and the fact was that it curtailed Elizabeth's own activities. Had it been nothing more than being denied the freedom to walk or ride alone, Elizabeth might have accepted it with philosophy and waited until matters settled. The consequences, however, manifest themselves in Elizabeth's inability to see Mr. Darcy, and as she now found herself quite in love with that man, being denied his company was akin to physical pain.

"You seem to be much in evidence of late," said Jane one morning only a few days later. Mr. Gardiner was, as usual, visiting, and though Elizabeth appreciated his attempts to lighten the mood, she was ill inclined to allow her pique to be mollified.

"Perhaps I am," replied Uncle Gardiner. His gaze found Lydia sitting with Kitty across the room, whispering, though Elizabeth was certain her youngest sister knew of their conversation. "Shall I not visit my favorite relations?"

Uncle Edward, who was visiting that morning as well, snorted his amusement, while his wife looked at them all with concern. In particular, Aunt Madeline watched Elizabeth, and being the only person who knew of her meetings with Mr. Darcy other than Elizabeth and the man himself, she knew her aunt was concerned for her.

"Lizzy," said Aunt Madeline after a few moments of watching her, "might I interest you in a walk in the gardens? There is something of which I would speak to you."

Suspicious though she was of why her aunt would wish to speak with her alone, no one else noted anything out of the ordinary; Elizabeth and Aunt Madeline were very close, meaning such private conversations were not at all out of the ordinary. Even her Uncle Edward, at whom Elizabeth looked as she rose, seemed to have no apprehension of the likely subject of Aunt Madeline's wish to speak with her, for he smiled at his wife and turned back to his brother.

When they reached the paths in the gardens after donning their outerwear, Aunt Madeline lost little time in opening the conversation.

"Lizzy, how are you feeling?"

Attempting to put a brave face on her annoyance, Elizabeth said: "I am well, Aunt."

Aunt Madeline fixed Elizabeth with a stern look. "It seems you have not been . . . wandering the countryside much of late, my dear."

"With the rain and my uncle's scrutiny I have had little opportunity to do so."

"Which means you have not seen your young man of late."

It occurred to Elizabeth to wonder what her aunt knew of her recent contact with Mr. Darcy. Her aunt seemed to understand her interest, for Aunt Madeline was quick to speak again.

"Yesterday morning Mr. Darcy paid me a visit, much to my surprise."

"Mr. Darcy visited you?" asked Elizabeth, her focus now on her aunt to the exclusion of all else. "He did not see you in the street and stop to speak with you?"

"No, Lizzy," said Aunt Madeline. "The gentleman came to the parsonage and spoke with me as I was outside. His purpose was to give me this letter, which he asked me to carry to you."

Elizabeth gasped and took the folded paper with trembling hands, while her aunt continued to speak.

"Though I have not read it, I know what it contains, for the gentleman entreated me to convey his message if I was not uncomfortable carrying a letter to you. Please keep it private, Lizzy, for I am uneasy about this situation without even considering the impropriety of passing you a letter from a gentleman."

With a nod, Elizabeth secured the letter in a pocket, mindful of the need to ensure no one else knew of its existence. Then she tore her attention away from it, already feeling as if it was burning a hole in her dress and regarded her aunt.

"What provoked Mr. Darcy to take this extraordinary step?"

"It would be best," said Aunt Madeline, "if you were to read his words and discover it for yourself."

With a murmured assent, Elizabeth walked on with her aunt, but now her attention was fixed on the letter in her pocket to the exclusion of all else. She longed to be in her room to read William's words but did not wish to offend her aunt by cutting their walk short.

A moment later her aunt's tinkling laughter interrupted Elizabeth's thoughts. "Of course, you wish to read your letter, Lizzy, and I shall not keep you from it. Before you go, however, there is one thing I wish to say."

Elizabeth stopped along with her aunt, noting the woman's serious countenance, and her mirth faded like mist on a bright August day. "Lizzy, I must own that I am . . . uncomfortable about this situation. I have kept your secret for you, even from my own husband, though I suspect Edward would support my decision."

"Thank you for your support, Aunt," replied Elizabeth quietly. "It has meant much to me."

"You know it was my pleasure to offer it. If there is anything I can do for you, you know I will do it, and that includes sending word to Mr. Darcy should it be required."

Elizabeth fixed her aunt with a sharp look, to which she clarified: "Yes, Lizzy, he gave me directions to reach him should it be necessary. I will not give it to you, for I would not wish you to be tempted; but I have his directions."

"Of course not," murmured Elizabeth. "I should never dream of asking you."

"That is good to hear." Aunt Madeline paused for a moment before she continued to speak, saying: "Though my willingness to assist is given freely, that does not change the fact that I believe you have not considered exactly what you are doing. You are withholding this from your father and disobeying his instructions, and that does not sit well with me. If you consider it with honesty, clear of any self-interest, you are engaged in the same behavior as your sister Lydia, and to a greater extent, for I know you have met Mr. Darcy many times."

"I am not Lydia," said Elizabeth, frowning at her aunt. "Though I do not know what she is thinking, *I* have more in mind than mild flirtation."

"Are you different?" demanded Aunt Madeline, her gaze piercing through Elizabeth's defenses. "I will own, Lizzy, that I do not know what your sister is thinking. But whatever your motivation, you are not as different as you would like to think. It is not right to cast shade on your sister's character when your actions have been the same. 'He that is without sin among you, let him first cast a stone . . .' Are you clean of any wrongdoing, Lizzy?"

Stricken, Elizabeth gazed at her aunt. Aunt Madeline saw her consternation, her gaze softened and she looked at Elizabeth with clear affection, taking her hand and patting it, a soothing gesture.

"Please do not misunderstand me, for I have only the highest regard for you, and despite my words, I do *not* believe you are the same as your sister. But I must confess I the secrets you are keeping weigh down on me, and I suspect if you looked within yourself, you would feel the same."

"William and I have both long been uncomfortable with our disobedience," whispered Elizabeth. "But I fear what my father will do if he learns of it. Will he forbid me from seeing William again? I do not believe I could endure it."

"You are one and twenty in July, are you not?" asked Mrs. Gardiner with a smile. "When you reach your birthday you may do as you like."

A hesitant smile stretched Elizabeth's lips, prompting her aunt to pat her hand again. "You may also find your father more predisposed to pity your plight, Lizzy. Regardless of his reaction, however, I think you would be easier with your actions if you were to tell him the truth. Please consider it—that is all I ask."

Having made her case, Mrs. Gardiner led them back to the house where they rejoined the family. It was not much longer before the younger Gardiners excused themselves and departed, and her elder Uncle Gardiner followed them soon after. Though it was only a few moments, to Elizabeth it felt like a lifetime, for the impulse to go to her room to read her letter was nigh overpowering.

Freed at last, Elizabeth excused herself and went to her room, opening the letter with trembling hands, admiring the neatness of the masculine handwriting as she did so. When the pages fell open to her eager eyes, she read the short missive, learning that William was to be absent at his brother's estate. While unhappiness coursed through her when learning of their pending separation, accompanied by resentment toward her youngest sister, Elizabeth appreciated the lengths to which he had gone to inform her of his departure. If she had learned of his absence by other means, Elizabeth knew she would have agonized over the reason for his absence!

When the first emotions of reading his letter passed, Elizabeth fell into pensive thought, considering the letter before her, her aunt's words, and all that had passed before. William's departure, she decided after some thought—which involved a time spent working through her frustration—was a virtue. At present, Uncle Gardiner's vigilance rendered any meeting William an endeavor fraught with the danger of discovery.

Elizabeth soon found her discomfort with the situation increasing tenfold. The longer this charade with William continued, the greater the chances of discovery grew. Would her father not be more disappointed with her if the matter came to his attention because of a chance discovery than if she informed him of the truth? Though fearful of being forbidden from seeing William at all, the thought of ending the weeks of sneaking about disobeying her father held some appeal. Elizabeth knew it was what she should do.

With a sigh, Elizabeth lay back on her bed. The next days, she knew would be laden with indecision and deep thought.

"Did you know my cousins have both left Pemberley?"

That bit of information seemed unknown to Mr. Gardiner, for his ears seemed to perk up like a dog hearing its master's call. "They have departed from Pemberley?"

"Yes," replied Anne, urging him to continue walking. "Two days ago their father ordered them to Alexander's estate." Anne paused and laughed. "To be more accurate, I suppose he ordered *Alexander* to Thorndell, but he *requested* William accompany him. My mother claims it was to keep him from mischief, but my uncle has refuted her view, saying he wished William, who has been managing the estate, to assist Alexander with assuming the role as the estate's master."

"It seems to me," said Mr. Gardiner, "your uncle sent him away to relieve tensions."

"That was the primary reason," agreed Anne. "It is also true that Alexander is at an age where he must manage his own affairs. I believe Uncle saw this as an opportunity to bring that to pass and remove him from the neighborhood at the same time."

Mr. Gardiner nodded still caught in the grips of introspection. When he did not speak up for a long moment, Anne felt a hint of mischief fill her mind and she stopped, pulling the surprised man with her.

"Are you not concerned William's absence will prompt my mother to conclude there is no reason for us to stay in Derbyshire?"

It seemed Mr. Gardiner caught the teasing note in her voice, for he grinned. "If she does, will you allow her to drag you back to Kent?"

"Would it distress you if I did?"

Laughter was the gentleman's response. "Yes, it would, Miss de Bourgh. While we have only met on a few occasions, I respect your opinions and enjoy your company. I believe it would distress me very much if you were to depart."

"Then you do not need to concern yourself, Mr. Gardiner," said Anne, a lightness entering her heart. "Despite my mother's wishes, I have no desire to return to Kent, and I know my Darcy relations will continue to host me if I ask them."

"That is welcome news, Miss de Bourgh," said Mr. Gardiner, clasping her hand to his arm and continuing their walk down

Lambton's street. "It would distress me to lose your company at present, for I believe our association is doing us both much good."

While Anne agreed with Mr. Gardiner's statement without reserve, her own assertion was put to the test as soon as she returned to Pemberley. The two gentlemen remaining in residence, both of whom appeared rather grim, waylaid her as she entered the house.

"Anne, will you join me in my study for a moment?"

"Of course, Uncle," said Anne.

It was clear her secret—which she had never considered to be a secret—had become known to him, so there was no point denying him his opinion on the matter. In truth, thought Anne with a chuckle to herself, she had no interest in denying it, and would not allow her uncle to dictate to her—in this, she fancied herself as resolute as Fitzwilliam, who was trailing them to the study. To her surprise, it was Fitzwilliam who spoke up when they had reached the room.

"You have my apologies, Anne," said he, "but I saw you with Mr. Gardiner in Lambton for the second time today."

"Of more importance to the current situation," said Uncle Darcy, "was that I saw you, and your mother was within a hair's breadth of seeing you too."

"If my mother should know of my association with Mr. Gardiner," said Anne, "it would not cause me a hint of concern."

Uncle Darcy peered at Anne as if trying to understand her. Unwilling to allow his somber scrutiny to persist, Anne released an amused laugh. "Are you surprised, Uncle? Should I attempt to portray the cowed daughter, obedient to my mother's every nonsensical whim?"

"You know I have never seen you that way, Anne," said Uncle Darcy.

"I do and I thank you for it." Anne paused, a thought coming to her. "There is one matter which I find curious, however—how did my mother come to be in Lambton when she has always disdained going there?"

"The fault was yours, Anne," said Fitzwilliam. "Though I know you—all of us—like to think your mother is only able to see what she wishes, she has noted your frequent journeys thither of late and wished to discover your purpose."

"As Fitzwilliam says," interjected Uncle Darcy, "he knew of your meetings with Mr. Gardiner, but I did not. When Lady Catherine insisted on following you to Lambton this morning, he informed me of the matter and we determined to ensure she did not become aware of your actions to the best of our abilities."

"Then you might not have bothered, Uncle," said Anne. "I am not afraid of my mother."

"And how do you think she would have acted, the presence of others notwithstanding? The family has been the target of enough gossip of late; I would not wish to add your mother's behavior to the ledger."

"Anne," added Anthony, "I believe there are too many secrets afoot of late. There is this business of Alexander's, your meetings with Mr. Gardiner . . ."

For a moment Anne thought he might add to that list, though his voice trailed off. Suspicious as she was about William's activities, she wondered again about any knowledge Anthony might possess concerning Darcy's activities.

"You are both correct," said Anne. "I would not have wished my mother to make herself foolish in front of everyone in the town."

Uncle Darcy gave her a tight nod.

"It seems you succeeded in diverting her, then."

"We did," said Uncle Darcy. "Fitzwilliam interested her in some wares displayed in the dressmakers."

Anthony laughed. "I believe she will subject you to a discourse of the lovely fabric she found for your wedding dress, though she must have it fashioned by the most skilled modiste in London."

"I would have expected nothing less!" exclaimed Anne, joining him in his mirth.

"Yes, well, let us come to the point," said Uncle Darcy after a few moments of indulging them. "I wish to know, Anne, that you understand what you are doing."

"What I am doing, Uncle," said Anne, giving him a pointed glare, "is following my heart. Mr. Gardiner, I have found, is intelligent, interesting, gentlemanly, and not lacking in pleasing physical attributes."

"He is also connected to the Bennet family," said he. Though Anne searched for it, there was no hint of rancor in his statement—it was a statement, and nothing more.

"Why that should affect me, I cannot say," said Anne. Uncle Darcy did not speak, so Anne continued, saying: "I am not affected by this dispute of yours, Uncle. As Mr. Gardiner has said himself, if the Bennet and Darcy families are incapable of resolving the conflict themselves, then perhaps it falls to others to do it for them. If I was to marry Mr. Gardiner, could you continue this silliness with the Bennets?"

"Are you thinking of marriage already?" asked Anthony, raised eyebrows showing his surprise.

"Not yet," said Anne. "At present, I still do not know the gentleman well enough to know if I wish to marry him. However, we have spoken of the possibility, and it is not onerous to either of us."

"And what of your mother?" asked Uncle Darcy.

"Let me deal with my mother," said Anne. "In keeping her away this morning, you performed a welcome service, for you are correct: it would not have been a pretty scene had she seen me. I shall inform her of the truth of the matter, but I ask you to allow me to do it in my own time and in my own way."

Uncle Darcy and Anthony shared a look, then turned back to her. "Very well, Anne," said Uncle Darcy. "We shall trust you in this matter. Please do not allow your mother to discover the truth by chance, for I do not believe any of us would emerge from such an experience unscathed."

"In that, I agree with you, Uncle," said Anne. "I shall do so when the time is right."

"Very well. Then I shall leave it to you."

With a nod, Anne let herself from the study, soon noting that Anthony had followed her from the room. Though Anne fixed him with a curious look, she knew asking him if he suspected William of some intrigue would be fruitless. Claiming a matter of business, Anthony excused himself and climbed the stairs toward his room.

Anne put him from her mind, turning to the task before her. Lady Catherine was sitting with Georgiana at the moment, and she would not make her young cousin uncomfortable. Anne knew she would need to make the communication soon, but years of handling her mother had informed her an opportunity would present itself. Patience was required, as it would minimize her mother's eruption when she learned of the matter.

CHAPTER XXVII

*A*fter the delay of a full day spent in deep thought, Elizabeth lost no more time in acting on her decision. Rather, she acted in a manner that would free her from any obligation to continue to keep her secret. As she was not the only one involved, Elizabeth rationalized she should not decide without consulting the other principal in the matter.

It was, she knew, something of an excuse to delay informing her father as she was now convinced she must do, for William had already stated his opinion. That Elizabeth had been the one to urge continued secrecy was now a matter of shame—an honest woman, Elizabeth had always prided herself in her integrity, honor which she felt had tarnished by her recent behavior. An excuse it may be—and she confessed it to herself—but she remained uncomfortable about going to her father without William's concurrence. Thus, her present errand.

"Where are you bound, Lizzy?" asked Uncle Gardiner when he witnessed her preparations to depart that morning.

"To Lambton to visit Aunt Madeline," replied Elizabeth.

When her uncle fixed her with a look of contemplation, Elizabeth laughed and said: "You may ask her later if you wish, but I promise I will do nothing more than ride to Lambton, visit with her for a time, and then return home."

A slight smile was his response. "I hope you do not find my recent actions officious, Lizzy. It is nothing more than a sincere desire to protect you all."

"I understand," replied Elizabeth, giving him an affectionate kiss on the cheek.

"Lizzy has your trust, yet I do not," came Lydia's petulant voice.

The girl had shown little improvement since being taken to task by her father, though the news of Mr. Alexander Darcy's departure from Pemberley had allowed Lord Arundel to relax some of the strictures on her movements. Lydia was calmer now, though they were all still subjected to petulant outbursts from time to time. Uncle Gardiner looked heavenward and turned to his youngest niece.

"When you can prove yourself worthy of being trusted, we will trust you."

"Come, Lydia," said Lady Margaret, cutting off an argument before it could begin, "let us speak of happier subjects."

Lydia acquiesced, seeming to care little. Elizabeth took the opportunity to flee. The past day of reflection had not been kind to Elizabeth's perception of herself and her behavior these months. In particular, Elizabeth was feeling the effects of hypocrisy, of engaging in the same behavior for which she had disparaged Lydia, and to a much greater extent! It was Elizabeth's hope that Mr. Darcy would respond in a timely manner, leaving her free to speak with her father.

The ride to Lambton was much the same as it always was, though on this day she saw little of the scenes which so often delighted her. She thought the journey took much longer to complete than usual, plagued as she was by thoughts of how absurd she had been. When the church and parsonage came into sight, Elizabeth found herself relieved.

"Lizzy," said Aunt Madeline when she entered the room. "I am surprised to see you today."

"It astonishes me to hear it, Aunt," exclaimed Elizabeth, a storm of emotions welling up within her breast. "Your persuasions were of such a forceful variety that I would have thought you would expect me on your doorstep at first light, begging your forgiveness."

Seeing Elizabeth was on the verge of tears, Aunt Madeline gathered her close and led her to a nearby sofa, all the while clucking to her in soothing tones. When Aunt Madeline had Elizabeth seated by her side, her eyes found Elizabeth's, searching for answers which the younger woman was all too willing to provide.

"I have thought of nothing other than your words since you departed yesterday; while the process of understanding myself was painful, I have come to understand you are correct. Informing my father is long overdue, something I ought to have done long ago. However, there remains an obstacle to making my communication."

"Mr. Darcy?" asked Aunt Madeline with a knowing smile.

"Yes," said Elizabeth. "As this matter involves Mr. Darcy, I cannot speak to my father without first obtaining his consent."

"I believe," said Aunt Madeline, "Mr. Darcy would understand and approve of your determination, my dear, especially if he loves you as much as he claims."

"While I would not dispute your assertion," said Elizabeth, "I do not feel comfortable informing Papa without Mr. Darcy knowing. Please indulge me in this, Aunt—I would not feel right unless he has offered his explicit consent."

"Which is why you have come to me," said Aunt Madeline, displaying her understanding of the situation. "You would have me send a letter to Mr. Darcy?"

"Yes," said Elizabeth, handing her a single sheet of paper folded and addressed to her love. "In this, I have explained my reasons for wishing to speak to my father. If Mr. Darcy agrees, I have asked him to tell you so you may inform me."

Aunt Madeline reached out and accepted the letter, though not without hesitation. For a moment she looked at it as if attempting to see through the paper to the words contained within. Should she ask, Elizabeth would give her consent to her aunt reading the missive. Aunt Madeline did no such thing, however, her eyes rising to Elizabeth filled with compassion.

"I will send Mr. Darcy this letter, Lizzy. However, I wish to inform my husband of the matter with your blessing." Elizabeth felt a hint of panic, which her aunt acted to relieve. "Your uncle, as you know, believes this dispute must end, Lizzy. Though knowledge of your actions will surprise and disappoint him with his aid we can carry word to Mr. Darcy more quickly. In particular, Edward could engage someone in the village or our manservant to ride to Mr. Darcy's estate and return with an answer. If I send it post, there is no telling how long it will be before we receive a response."

"If you think that is for the best," said Elizabeth, noting that while her words portrayed bravery, the fear of her uncle's response settled in her stomach, inducing it to roil and turn over in anxiety.

"I do," said Aunt Madeline. "Please wait, Lizzy, for your uncle is in his study researching for this week's sermon. I shall summon him."

While she had feared for her uncle's disappointment, the matter proceeded as her aunt had suggested it would. The few moments her aunt was absent from the room were awful to Elizabeth's nerves, the minutes passing like hours while she waited and fretted. Her uncle's return saw him greet her with much less than his usual heartiness, as he either sensed something was amiss or his wife had told him something of the situation.

It was to Elizabeth's great relief that Aunt Madeline related the details of the matter as she knew them to Uncle Edward while he listened, a gravity about him he reserved for when he was acting in his official capacity. When Aunt Madeline had the matter before him, he asked a few questions of Elizabeth. He focused on Elizabeth's regard for Mr. Darcy, and the matter of him asking her to marry him. Then, when he had asked all his questions, he sat back in his chair and sighed.

"There is no need for me to take you to task for your behavior, for I believe you already feel it. I have one further question for you, Elizabeth—is there any particular and . . . *pressing* need for you to wed Mr. Darcy?"

For a moment Elizabeth did not understand. Then her uncle's meaning bloomed in her mind, and while she could not see herself, her cheeks were hot enough that she thought she must resemble a ripe apple.

"No, uncle," said she, resisting the urge to protest with more vigor. It was a logical question for him to ask. "Not only have we met out of doors in conditions and seasons not conducive to such . . . activities, but I would never act in such a way, and neither would Mr. Darcy."

"Very well," said Uncle Edward. "I hope you understand why I needed to ask the question."

"I do," was Elizabeth's simple reply.

"By all rights," said Mr. Gardiner, "I should speak with your father about this. But I shall not if you promise me you will do so yourself."

"That is the purpose of my letter to Mr. Darcy, Uncle. I believe he will agree with my decision, for he has suggested it in the past."

To Elizabeth's relief, Uncle Edward seemed to realize Elizabeth required this assurance from her lover.

"Then we shall send the message to Mr. Darcy. As your aunt has suggested, I believe it would be best to see to it with all haste. If I engage our manservant, we may have an answer from Mr. Darcy by tomorrow. I shall not allow him to return your letter and will make that stipulation plain in my letter to him. But I will pass any answer he gives to you."

"Thank you, Uncle," said Elizabeth, tears again welling in her eyes. Then she turned to her aunt and said: "I apologize for bringing you into this situation, Aunt Madeline. It was not my intention to foment discord or put you in a difficult position."

"It was no trouble, Lizzy," said Aunt Madeline. "If there is any assistance I may offer to you, it is my pleasure to do so at any time, for you are so very dear to me."

"Do not concern yourself," added Uncle Edward with a grin. "While I might prefer your aunt had come to me sooner, I believe she has acted with the appropriate measure of guidance and thought given the situation."

Uncle Edward rose and approached Elizabeth, sitting beside her and catching her up in an embrace. "This has been hard for you and your young man, my dear, but I believe this is the correct step. Please know we will support you, come what may."

"Thank you," whispered Elizabeth.

"You have become distraught," said Aunt Madeline, putting her own arm around Elizabeth's shoulders. "Shall you not rest in Abigail's room for a time? In fact, I think I should like you to stay the night with us. We can send word to your family that we persuaded you to stay and ask for some of your clothing. Then you will be on hand when Mr. Darcy's response arrives on the morrow."

"I would like that very much, Aunt," said Elizabeth with a smile.

Soon she was resting in her cousin's room, as her aunt had suggested, drifting into a deep sleep her thoughts had denied her the night before. As she slipped into oblivion, the final thought she had was an image of William's beloved face. It would not, she hoped, be long before they were reunited, never again to be sundered.

Thorndell was a picturesque estate. Situated close to the Peak District, those majestic spires of rock which presented a ghosted image across the horizon on a clear day from Pemberley rose tall and strong from Thorndell.

Given the beauty of the Peaks, the gently undulating land, combined with groves of trees and massive spurs of rock jutting up in various locations, one might consider Thorndell among the most beautiful places in England. Many considered it even superior to Pemberley.

Darcy was not one of them, for Pemberley, to him, was the most beautiful place on earth. Thorndell had been in the family for several generations, purchased by a Darcy master in excess of fifty years before. At first, it had been a small satellite estate purchased as an extension of the Darcy holdings. Darcy's great grandfather had purchased a neighboring estate for his second son and combined them. That second son had then built a new house to replace the poorer of the two houses, which had resulted in a modern manor of the time, a building about the same size as Bingley's manor house at Netherfield.

As the second son had passed on without issue, the estate had reverted to Darcy's grandfather and had been part of the family holdings ever since, as Darcy's father had had no siblings to inherit. It was a good bit of land, fertile for all manner of crops throughout, producing sheep in the rockier areas, and a large stable which could be used for breeding horses.

"It is a pretty prospect, is it not?" said Alexander one day as they were riding the estate. "It is fair enough," said Darcy. "The Peaks in the distance make the view that much more pleasing."

Alexander nodded and kicked his horse into motion, leading the way back toward the house. They had ridden out that morning to meet with a tenant, a Mr. Travers by name, and in Darcy's experience, the most difficult man at the estate. It was fortunate this visit had been nothing more than an opportunity to introduce Alexander again, as they had been doing since they arrived. Darcy had the sense that the tenants were relieved there was a master in residence once more, though he suspected most thought Alexander would not stay long.

As he rode, Darcy watched his brother, noting his quietude, his almost careless negligence with which he held the reins and guided the horse. Since their arrival at Thorndell, Darcy had attempted to induce his brother to speak of the matter of Lydia Bennet, but his Alexander had remained introspective. It was uncharacteristic of his irrepressible brother, and it worried Darcy, for he was still unable to say what Alexander had been about.

Darcy's mind was also full of thoughts and reflections, matters which he could not share with his brother. A letter had arrived from Fitzwilliam the previous day, informing Darcy of his cousin's knowledge of his activities with Elizabeth, and urging him to speak to his father on the matter. A grim amusement settled over Darcy as he had read the letter — it seemed his suspicions of his cousin had not been as unfounded as he thought. The question was, what he should do about it. Darcy had thought for some time now it would be best to inform his father, but Elizabeth's fear for their families' reactions had stayed his hand. Perhaps it was time to convince her of the wisdom of his conviction.

When they rode their horses into the yard by the stables, Alexander dismounted and threw the reins to a waiting groom, turning to march into the house. Though Darcy preferred to see to his animal's disposition himself, on this occasion he followed his brother instead. With a quick word informing Darcy he would join him after changing, Alexander climbed the stairs two at a time and entered the master's suite, leaving Darcy looking after him, bemused. As he had promised, however, he soon joined Darcy in the study and set his mind to the books, from which Darcy had been educating him since his return to Derbyshire.

"It seems to me the income is stable at about four thousand a year," said Alexander some time later.

"There has been little fluctuation these past three years at least," agreed Darcy. "If you oversee the estate personally, I am confident you will increase that number. There is only so much one can do when managing it from a distance, even as near as Pemberley."

Alexander glanced at Darcy and shook his head. "Perhaps if my talents were at your level I could raise my income, but I have not the abilities you possess. I will endeavor to do what I can, but I suspect four thousand a year is all my future wife can expect."

His interest aroused at his brother's words, Darcy said: "Have you thought of taking a wife?"

"Who in our position has not?" asked Alexander.

"I could name some," said Darcy, considering several ne'er-do-wells, among the many who populated the circles in which they moved.

Alexander shook his head. "Yes, there are many who care for nothing but gratifying their own desires. I hope I have never been among their number, though I will own there was a time when I did not consider my responsibilities as much as I should. In answer to your question, yes, I have considered taking a wife."

"And what has brought about this change?" asked Darcy.

"Our father calling me back to Pemberley," replied Alexander with a shrug. "It is obvious why he wished me to return; while I tried to tell myself I was content in London and did not wish to return home, I had become tired of everything in town. The prospect of staying at Thorndell alone, however, seems like a daunting proposition. A wife to keep me company would be just the thing."

"What of local society?" asked Darcy. "There must be others your age in the neighborhood."

"That is possible," conceded Alexander. "But I am unknown to them, and though I am not incapable of making friends, one cannot always be with one's friends."

"I suppose that is true," murmured Darcy. The image of a dark-haired beauty with laughing eyes entered his mind, reminding Darcy with whom he would like to be at this very moment.

"Do you then have a candidate in mind?" said Darcy, tearing his thoughts away from the memory of Elizabeth to his brother.

"Do you?" asked Alexander, directing a pointed look at Darcy. "You are the elder brother and the heir to the Darcy name and most of its holdings. Should you not be considering who the future Mrs. Darcy will be?"

The hairs on the back of Darcy's neck stood up at this bit of avoidance. Considering his brother's odd mood, Darcy thought it would be unwise to allow his brother's question to go unanswered. But if Alexander thought Darcy would release him from the obligation to respond, he was to be disappointed.

"I have given the matter some thought," said Darcy, "and I shall select a woman when the time comes."

Alexander snorted with amusement. "That sounds rather clinical, Brother. 'Selecting a wife' is not the same as purchasing a horse at an auction. It is expected that a man will woo a woman before making her an offer, though I suppose you could ask Father to negotiate a contract with one of our acquaintances and spare yourself the bother."

"Thank you for that advice, Alexander," said Darcy, "but I believe I understand the process. Now, you did not answer my question—do *you* have a candidate in mind?"

"Like you," said Alexander, "I imagine I shall choose a woman when the time comes. At present, there is nothing more to say."

They remained in the study for some more minutes, speaking of various matters of the estate, but Darcy had little attention to give to such matters. His brother's glibness, the way he had avoided the question and answered in a manner mirroring Darcy's spoke to intentions Darcy was uncertain he wished to consider. Was Alexander's connection with Miss Lydia Bennet greater than anyone believed? If so, what did it mean?

"Well," said his brother after a time of this, "I believe that is enough for today. If you will excuse me, I shall retire to my room until it is time for dinner."

Dinner was a dull affair, even after one considered the afternoon

Darcy spent alternating between reading and napping. Alexander, it seemed, had lost none of his introspection, for their conversation during the meal was desultory. It seemed the brother he knew before his departure for London had been slowly disappearing, especially since their arrival at Thorndell. After a time, Darcy began to long to return to Pemberley, for at least there he would have his cousins, his father and sister, and even his aunt, difficult though she was.

Just after they stood up from dinner, a break in the monotony announced itself when a rider bearing a message arrived at the manor. The butler alerted them to the newcomer, prompting Darcy and Alexander to go to the door in curiosity. There was a man waiting on the step, a young fellow perhaps a few years younger than Darcy himself, wearing no discernable livery, and looking fatigued, as if he had spent the entire day in the saddle. Behind him stood a horse, head down in weariness who matched him in every respect.

"Mr. Fitzwilliam Darcy?" asked the man when the brothers drew near.

"I am Fitzwilliam Darcy," said Darcy.

"Then I have a letter for you, sir," said the man, handing the missive to a startled Darcy. "I was instructed to wait for a response."

"Of course," said Darcy. "Is it urgent?"

"I am sorry, sir, but I was only instructed to wait."

Darcy acknowledged the man, looking to his brother.

Alexander nodded and gestured to the butler. "Please see his mount is stabled and provide him with a room in the servant's quarters."

"I shall have a letter ready for your departure in the morning," said Darcy, thanking the rider for his diligence.

"If it is serious, I can return tonight. But I will require a mount."

"That should not be necessary, but I shall inform you if it is."

The man nodded and allowed the butler to lead him away to the servant's quarters. Darcy was already turning the letter over in his hand. There was no indication as to the sender, for the paper was plain and utilitarian rather than fine, the letters of his name written in a strong, flowing hand, one which Darcy did not recognize.

"Who sent it?" asked Alexander, pulling Darcy from his inspection.

"I do not know," replied Darcy with an absence of mind.

A momentary thought struck him, that it might be a missive from Mrs. Gardiner concerning her niece, but Darcy did not think the woman wrote in what he took to be a masculine hand. Still, Darcy did not feel confident opening the letter in front of his brother since he did not know what it contained. Thus, he looked up to find Alexander peering at him as if attempting to puzzle him out.

"If you do not mind," said Darcy, "I believe I shall retire to deal with this."

Alexander gave him a slow nod. "If you wish. Then I shall see you again in the morning. For myself, I shall also retire."

The brothers parted at Darcy's door, Alexander's rooms being further down the hall. As was his custom in his own rooms, Darcy shed his jacket and untied his cravat, throwing them both over an armchair, knowing Snell would deal with them in the morning. After a moment more turning the letter over in his hands, Darcy chided himself for delaying and broke the seal, to find a short note on the inside of the paper, with another letter enclosed.

Astonished to see it was from the parson, Edward Gardiner, Darcy read through the missive, noting the secret of his clandestine meetings with Elizabeth was becoming more widely known. Mr. Gardiner, it seemed, had learned of their meetings and engagement, and had allowed Elizabeth to persuade him to send him her letter, though he admonished he would not allow it again, promising to inform Elizabeth of Darcy's answer.

Once he had finished reading the parson's words, Darcy broke the seal on the second letter eagerly, feeling warmth at reading Elizabeth's words in her own letter. It too was short, but instructive, asking his permission to inform her father of their recent meetings. When Darcy finished reading the letter, it was the work of a moment to consider her request and respond in the affirmative—it would be better if they were open with their families. Darcy was certain of it.

"Elizabeth," he breathed, holding the letter close, catching a hint of the scent Darcy had come to associate with his beloved. "How I long to see you, my love."

Without further hesitation, Darcy moved to the desk in the room and pulled out a piece of paper. Mindful of Mr. Gardiner's restrictions, he addressed the letter to the parson, rather than the man's niece, instructing him to tell Elizabeth that he supported her in her decision. Darcy also abjured the man to inform his niece that Darcy would return at once to support her, for Darcy was determined they would face their families together. There was an important communication he must make to his own father, the same message Elizabeth would take to hers. The time for hiding had passed.

CHAPTER XXVIII

"*Y*ou mean to return to Pemberley?"

The disbelieving note in his brother's voice caught Darcy's attention. The impromptu announcement at the breakfast table would be no less than a surprise, mused Darcy. There was nothing to be done, however, so Darcy bent his mind toward placating his brother.

"I do," replied Darcy. "There is some business I must see to which requires my presence. Little more remains for me to inform you. Full control of the estate is already yours and you are aware of what must be done, so there is no reason for me to stay longer."

"It was my understanding you would stay for at least a week, maybe two."

"I offer my apologies, Alexander, but that has now become impossible. Tomorrow morning, at the latest, I shall return to Pemberley. Let us cover those final few subjects before I go—if you require anything, you may write to me."

Alexander peered at him, his manner faintly suspicious. "Is your sudden need to depart due to the letter you received last night? Did you not dispatch the rider with a response at first light?"

"Yes, I did," replied Darcy.

"And what is this matter concerning?"

"It is a private matter," said Darcy, beginning to become annoyed with his brother's questioning. "It is an issue which is mine alone and does not concern anyone else. Again, I offer my apologies for my need to depart before planned, but it cannot be helped."

Pursing his lips, Alexander gazed at him. Though Darcy thought his brother might protest further, he seemed to determine there was little need to do so.

"Very well, if you must go, I cannot keep you. There is some correspondence I would like to attend to this morning—perhaps we should meet in the study in an hour to discuss whatever subjects you feel my knowledge is inadequate?"

"It is not a matter of inadequacy, Alexander," said Darcy. "There is nothing lacking in your capabilities—of that I have little doubt. If there are further questions you wish to ask me, then I am at your disposal."

"Then let us meet in an hour."

"Very well," said Darcy. "As I have already instructed my man to prepare, I shall depart for a short ride and attend you in the study."

With those words, Darcy rose, never noting his brother's intense look at he strode from the room. Darcy was, instead, considering the journey the following day, mulling over what he would say to his father. Darcy knew his letter to Elizabeth would reach her some time that afternoon in the hours preceding dinner. When she informed her father of their activities, Darcy thought it a possibility the baron would speak to his father. Given the expected timeline, it would be best if Darcy could leave for Pemberley that day, but he would not abandon his brother without ensuring he was armed with everything he needed to manage his estate. In the meantime, a short ride would help him work off excess energy and prevent him from rushing off to Pemberley.

Though knowing word could not come earlier, Elizabeth waited with bated breath the following day for William's response. Aunt Madeline, who watched her with some amusement throughout that day, seemed content to leave her alone, though she pressed Elizabeth to play with the children whenever Elizabeth's patience seemed to be at an end. As it distracted her from waiting at the window, Elizabeth consented.

When, at length, the rider appeared, Elizabeth used every bit of restraint to refrain from confronting him and demanding the letter. Her aunt did not miss her eagerness.

"Edward will inform you of the contents, Lizzy," said she, her voice colored with amusement. "I had not thought my favorite niece was so lacking in patience—this day has been educational."

Elizabeth managed a sickly smile at her aunt's quip, which set Aunt Madeline to further laughter. It was not mean-spirited, but still, Elizabeth chafed at the delay, worried for what William would say to her. When her uncle entered the room, she jumped to her feet, her anticipation not allowing her to sit still.

"It seems you have noted Peter's return," said her uncle, his dry tone setting his wife to laughter.

"If she has been away from the window for two minutes all afternoon I have not seen it," said she, throwing a fond smile at Elizabeth.

"Yes, I can imagine your eagerness to hear from your lover." Uncle Edward paused and fixed Elizabeth with a look more serious than his previous jovial tone. "Mr. Darcy has returned our joint letter. In it, he gives his full consent to your plan to inform your father, and asks me to further relate that he will return at once."

"At once?" asked Elizabeth. "Then why did he not come here and inform you himself?"

"Do you think I understand the working of the minds of these great men?" asked her uncle, a hint of amusement again appearing in his tone. "If I were to guess, Mr. Darcy considers it his duty to ensure his brother knows what he is about at his estate. I can also conjecture his thoughts are bent toward his own father and how *your* father might inform *him* when you tell him of your recent activities."

Elizabeth had not considered this possibility, and she wrung her hands in dismay. "Perhaps I should wait for his return, then. I would not wish to make matters difficult with his father."

"Lizzy," said Uncle Edward, interrupting her fretting. "It is my advice to you to return to Longbourn and inform Lord Arundel as per your previous plan. Let Mr. Darcy worry about his father—if you wish, you might even ask Lord Arundel to delay before informing him."

"Yes, I suppose that is best," said Elizabeth.

"Then you should return to Longbourn, my dear," said Aunt Madeline. "I had your horse readied as soon as I spied the rider, so you should be ready to go in minutes."

"Thank you, Aunt Madeline," said Elizabeth, embracing her aunt, an affectionate action which Mrs. Gardiner returned tenfold. "And you, Uncle Edward. I cannot begin to express my appreciation for all you have done to assist."

"There is no price on our aid," said Uncle Edward. "If you wish to repay us, please do so in speaking the truth to your father and finding happiness with your young man."

"Thank you," whispered Elizabeth. "I shall do my utmost to follow your wise instruction."

When Darcy walked into the study at the appointed time, it was to the sight of a stony-faced brother, one who was glaring at him as he had not since they were boys caught in some fisticuffs. Pausing as he entered, Darcy wondered what might have angered his brother. Then he caught sight of a familiar piece of folded paper on the desk to Alexander's right.

Darcy stalked forward and snatched the paper from the desk. His brother rose to face him, his manner even unfriendlier than it had been before, and Darcy noted the flexing of his hand into a fist, a sure sign Alexander was angry.

"What right do you have to peer into my private affairs?" demanded Darcy.

"The right of a brother who has endured attacks from one engaged in nothing less than the same behavior."

"The same behavior," said Darcy, his reply laced with contempt. "Though I cannot say just what manner of silliness has provoked your actions, I cannot think it was anything like mine."

"Oh? Then please, illuminate my understanding, since I am so unworthy and unintelligent as to misunderstand. Given the missive you received last night, it seems to me you have been meeting with a woman—the sister of the woman I have been accused of misusing, no less. These meetings, I might add, have been so frequent as to lead you to the belief you are in love with her, sufficient to result in a proposal. How can you say that your behavior has differed from mine?"

Alexander's chest was heaving as if caught in the grip of some great emotion, his indignation bringing him to greater heights of fury. The accusing glare and continued flexing of his hand suggested he was on the verge of physical violence. It was this, more than any thought of his own culpability — which Darcy possessed — that led him to attempt a more conciliatory tone.

"Do you love Miss Lydia, Alexander?"

"You think I do not."

"I have seen no evidence of it, but I will not pass judgment. Yes, I confess to meeting with Elizabeth in secret, but I also declare that my heart has been engaged from almost the first."

"And yet you saw fit to castigate me for the same behavior as that in which you engaged," spat Alexander.

"If you recall," said Darcy, "the only comments I made were concerning the visible nature of your actions. I took great care to avoid sullying Miss Elizabeth's reputation, but I could not turn away from her when she held my heart."

"A fine distinction," said Alexander, turning away and shaking his head. "There is a word that describes your behavior of late, Brother, and that word is hypocrite."

"Perhaps you may see it that way, and I cannot gainsay you," said Darcy. "But I will have Miss Elizabeth for a wife, Alexander—I am determined. If we had not thought our fathers would force us apart, we would have formalized a courtship long ago."

Alexander turned back to Darcy, coldness clear in his blank stare. "And you thought I was any different?"

"Your treatment of women has always been more than a little careless, Alexander," said Darcy, fixing his brother with a sharp glare. "Do you love Miss Lydia? Have you met with her enough to form an attachment? Prove me wrong, Brother, for it seems to me our situations are not equal at all. Should another discover me with Elizabeth and the demands of propriety force us to wed, I would go to the altar happily, eagerly. Can you say the same about Miss Lydia?"

For a moment, Darcy thought his brother might answer him, for he gazed at Darcy, his eyes searching. Then the moment passed, and a hardness came over Alexander's countenance again.

"It seems you have already convicted me of indifference for her."

"As I said, Alexander, I am more than willing to be proven wrong. Can you not speak something of what has motivated your behavior of late? I will remind you, Brother, that while you provoked a scene at the earl's ball by brazenly dancing with a young girl, not even a woman, when you knew there were several people in the room who would object. *I* refrained from making that same scene, though I would have danced with no one other than Miss Elizabeth the entire night. Has anything other than selfishness and insouciance motivated your actions?"

When Alexander refused to respond, Darcy shook his head and said: "As you no doubt read in the letter, Miss Elizabeth has decided it is time to inform her father and was writing for my opinion on the matter. My response expressed my wholehearted agreement. *That* is why I must return home, as I have the same communication to make to our father."

"And do you think he will support you?"

It was an incongruous question; Darcy did not know why his brother cared. "In truth," said Darcy, "I cannot predict Father's response. The events of recent weeks have hardened our positions against the Bennets, but in some ways, I sense Father has also softened toward them. But I will not relent."

"Then it is best you depart," said Alexander. "Do not let me keep you, for I have matters well in hand here."

Taken aback, Darcy said: "Shall we not discuss those final few matters?"

"You misunderstand me, Brother," said Alexander, his gaze falling on Darcy like an icy gale. "Please leave at once, for I have no further need of your hypocritical and sanctimonious drivel, nor do I wish you to lecture me about the estate or any other matter. I would be much more at ease if you would just leave."

"If that is what you wish, I shall depart," said Darcy. Before he left, he could not but make one more comment. "Know this, Alexander: if you have some interest in Miss Lydia, I suggest you treat her as the lady she is. The girl is yet too young to marry. If I can somehow effect a reconciliation between families, your pathway will clear, but *only* if you begin to be the man our father raised you to be."

Bowing, Darcy turned and exited the room. Within a few short minutes, he had changed to his riding clothes and instructed Snell, his man, to pack his few remaining items and set out in the carriage for Pemberley. Darcy meant to go on ahead on horseback. It was later in the day than he would wish to depart, but if he set a good pace, he should arrive at Pemberley that evening.

Upon Elizabeth's return to Longbourn to her family's welcome, she lost no time in asking her father for a moment of his time. Though Elizabeth could feel her mother's eyes on her, she ignored Lady Margaret in favor of her father. Lord Arundel gave his consent and led Elizabeth to the study, seeing her comfortably seated in one of his armchairs before he sat in the other. As was his wont, he injected a little humor into the situation.

"I will own to a little trepidation, Lizzy, for I know of no young woman who *wishes* to speak with her father. Will the content of this interview force me to call out some blackguard who has misused you?"

The notion of her father demanding satisfaction both filled Elizabeth with dread and calmed her, for she knew her father, though he was eager to joke, would never call out a man much younger than he. It was this humor, she thought, that allowed her to proceed with little hesitation or quaver in her voice.

"I should not think so, Papa. But there are matters of which you are unaware, and I must inform you of them at once."

"Then please, let me know what they are. I find you have piqued my curiosity."

Whatever her father might have thought, being informed of his daughter's recent activities with a Darcy was not what he had expected. Though nervous, Elizabeth forced herself to continue, to explain the entirety of her history with Mr. Darcy, acknowledging that she had disobeyed his instructions, but emphasizing the state of her feelings for the gentleman. When she had completed her recitation, his response was surprising.

"You have been meeting with Mr. Darcy? Then what of his defiance and insistence on meeting Lydia?"

At once Elizabeth realized her mistake, and she could not help the bubble of hysterical laughter which welled up from her breast.

"Mr. Fitzwilliam Darcy, Papa. Not Mr. Alexander Darcy. I know not what Lydia has been doing with the younger brother; I was speaking of the elder."

Lord Arundel regarded her for a moment in disbelief and shook his head. "It seems all my daughters are determined to defy me."

"You are not angry?" asked Elizabeth, confused over his response.

"Perhaps I should be," said her father, a wry note in his answer. "You are the second daughter who has flouted my express instructions. So much has happened in recent days that I do not know whether I should laugh or rail in fury."

For a moment her father watched her as if he did not know her, then he asked: "May I know why you have been meeting with him?"

"Because I love him, Papa," said Elizabeth without hesitation. "I would have thought that would have been clear from my account."

If her father thought she would say more, she disappointed him, for Elizabeth thought her answer was sufficient to state her case. Thus, when she said nothing more, Lord Arundel laughed, a rueful response.

"Perhaps you do, my dear. If it were Lydia or Kitty I might press you to ensure you know what you are about, but as you are the most sensible of my daughters, I shall not treat you as if you do not know your own mind. I also do not know how this came about, but I shall not ask, as I doubt I will like the answer.

"However, I have one question." The way her father peered at her

Elizabeth could see his usual sardonic amusement was absent in favor of seriousness. "Might I assume that you have attained your meeting of minds with this Mr. Darcy of your own volition? And before you answer," said he, cutting Elizabeth's words off before she could speak them, "know that I do not accuse your young man. I wish to know that your feelings are true."

"They are, Papa," said Elizabeth. "Though acrimony characterized our initial meetings, rancor quickly gave way to a meeting of minds and hearts." Elizabeth paused, remembering the stolen hours she had spent in Mr. Darcy's company and she flushed a little when the recollection of being held in his arms swept over her. "Mr. Darcy," continued she after a moment, not seeing companion, "is the best man I have ever known."

"Thank you for speaking clearly, Lizzy," said her father after a moment — Elizabeth had no notion of how long she had considered Mr. Darcy's perfections. "I need not tell you, I hope, of the many obstacles set in your path."

"No, you do not," replied Elizabeth, uncertain if her father could hear her for the softness of her voice.

"Then let us have no more of this." Lord Arundel paused and laughed. "I suppose I should take you to task as I have Lydia, but as I sense your interest in Mr. Darcy is of a more mature variety than Lydia's, I shall content myself with a warning: these clandestine meetings must cease."

Elizabeth gazed at her father, a protest poised on her lips, though she did not think it would do her any good. His raised hand silenced her.

"Yes, Elizabeth, I understand your frustration. But you must recall that not only have you disobeyed me repeatedly, tensions are high between our families at present. If there is to be any entente between us, we must take care to bridge the distance in a measured and rational manner."

"Then you are not dismissing the notion out of hand?" clarified Elizabeth.

Lord Arundel sighed. "If I did, I suppose you would steal off in the night with him, would you not?"

Elizabeth looked away, which her father took for confirmation, though Elizabeth had not considered it and did not know what she would do until confronted with the choice.

"My heart is not hardened against your plight, Daughter," continued her father. "At present, however, I must insist upon patience.

"Now, must I confine you to the house with your sister, or will you obey me in this?"

"You will assign a footman to me if I do not," said Elizabeth with a sigh.

"As I recall," replied her father with some amusement, "I tasked John with your protection when you were younger. He is capable of resuming that duty, should you prove difficult."

"There is no need for that, Papa."

"Good girl," replied her father. "Then I will allow you to go about your day, while I consider this matter further."

Elizabeth whispered her assent and kissed her father's cheek as she left. The last sight she had of him was a man deep in thought, but not angry as she might have expected. Perhaps there was some hope for them — had Elizabeth not thought there was any hope, she would not have come forward under any circumstances. She was honest enough with herself to know that much

Upon returning to the rest of her family, it was unsurprising they subjected her to account for her failure to return the previous evening. Elizabeth did her best to answer those pertaining to Uncle Edward and Aunt Madeline, but she was steadfast in refusing to say anything of her conversation with her father. Though it would become known in time, and Elizabeth was certain he would inform her mother at the first opportunity, it would be his decision whether to reveal it to the rest of them. The matter was the last thing she wished to discuss with her family at present.

"You now tell me you were cavorting with that Bennet girl for months and yet you criticized your brother for the selfsame behavior?"

Mr. Darcy's eyes burned with a cold fury, but it was not his anger which provoked Darcy's own; it was the way he had branded Darcy's association with Elizabeth as if she was some woman of the night. Given Darcy knew he *had* disregarded his father's instructions, he knew he deserved whatever anger his father saw fit to direct at him. But nothing would induce him to allow anyone to say anything against Elizabeth.

"Yes, Father," said Darcy, his own voice and countenance stony, "I will own that I have met with Elizabeth in defiance of your instructions. But if you must be angry, direct your rage at *me* and not at *her*."

A snort of contempt was his father's reply, accompanied by a sharply snapped: "It seems these Bennet girls have slipped their father's leash. Or perhaps Catherine is correct about their lack of training for the strictures of polite society."

"Though we have met together," said Darcy, clenching his teeth to refrain from snapping at his father, "nothing untoward happened between us. The Honorable Miss Elizabeth Bennet is just that—an honorable and good woman, who deserves none of your censure.

"In addition," added Darcy, "while I know nothing of Alexander's connection to Miss Lydia, I will remind you that Elizabeth is a woman who will be of age in only three more months. Her sister is naught but a girl of sixteen. I cannot speak for her or for Alexander, but I will inform you here and now that I love Elizabeth—I have proposed to her and she has accepted. Whether you or her father accept it, we are now engaged. I will have her for a wife."

In cold silence, Darcy's father peered at him, his gaze searching as if he was attempting to determine the extent of his resolve. Darcy had never been more certain of anything in his life, a fact he attempted to inject into his demeanor. He must have found success, for his father scowled.

"Perhaps I should take Catherine up on her desire to wed her daughter to you. That would resolve matters to everyone's satisfaction."

"Not in my opinion, and not in Anne's," replied Darcy. "I am of age, Father. You cannot force me to marry where I do not wish."

"I can prevent you from inheriting Pemberley," spat his father.

Darcy laughed, a cold, harsh expression of disdain. "To whom will you leave it? Alexander? If you have forgotten, I shall remind you he has engaged in his own intrigues with another Bennet sister, and for much less reason than I have."

"Georgiana may inherit. Do you wish me to pass you over for your sister and leave you with nothing?"

"It seems you have neglected to recall that Blackfish Bay is *mine*, and not part of the Darcy family holdings. You may withhold Thorndell from Alexander if you desire, but you have no control over Blackfish Bay. Should you disinherit me, it will only firm my resolve to wed Elizabeth—we may then retire to Lincolnshire and put this idiocy of our families behind us."

Mr. Darcy sighed and shook his head. "I might have expected this defiance from Alexander, but never from you."

"If you consider it defiance, I apologize. In actuality, it is nothing more than my determination to follow my heart."

A slow nod was his father's response. "No, I had not forgotten your other inheritance, nor did I neglect to consider the possibility you might defy me and do as you like. Your circumstances would be much reduced, but Blackfish would support you and your wife."

"In some ways, it might be a relief," said Darcy. "As you know, I am not fond of society."

Mr. Darcy barked a laugh. "Yes, in that you are much the same as I. Since it seems I cannot deny you your lady, I shall not make the attempt. However, I must ask you to do nothing rash for the present." Darcy could not misunderstand the stern glare with which his father regarded him. "As I informed your brother, the situation between our families is delicate at present. Do nothing to upset matters any further."

"Very well, Father," said Darcy. "If you would avoid speaking of the matter with Aunt Catherine, I—and I suspect Anne—would very much appreciate it."

"I have little more desire to hear Catherine's harangues than you do," grunted Mr. Darcy. His father peered at him for a moment before saying: "Were you aware that Anne has also been meeting with a Bennet? Or a Bennet relation, to be exact, for she has become entangled with Mr. Gardiner."

This was a piece of news Darcy had not yet heard. "Entangled?" asked Darcy, seeking clarification.

"It is, perhaps, not the best word to use," said his father with a snort, "but there are so many of these of late that it has become difficult to remember we have been at odds for generations. Fitzwilliam saw them together several times, and the last time we spoke with her concerning it. Though she would not declare her intentions, she suggested it may be up to her and Mr. Gardiner to resolve the impasse between our families, as we could not do so ourselves."

Darcy chuckled. "Anne has shown she has more determination than her mother thought or hoped. Might I assume Lady Catherine knows nothing of it as yet?"

"You are correct," said his father. "Anne informed us she would tell Lady Catherine herself, but at a time of her own choosing."

"Then I wish Anne luck. That discussion will be more difficult than ours has been."

Mr. Darcy nodded, though he paused before speaking. "I suppose you mean to continue to meet with your young woman?"

"There is little desire in me to be separated for months," said Darcy. "We shall be circumspect, but I shall also endeavor to avoid meeting with her in secret."

A grunt was Mr. Darcy's response. "Secrecy will protect you from Catherine's wrath; circumspection will do nothing more than delay the inevitable. Your aunt will discover this matter soon. Heaven help us all when she does. With that and Anne's bit of defiance, there may not remain two stones of Pemberley's walls standing when she learns of it."

"I shall handle Lady Catherine," said Darcy. "Leave that matter to me."

"Very well. Please leave me be."

Darcy's unscheduled reappearance surprised the rest of the family, and he suspected Lady Catherine considered it a compliment to her daughter. Darcy did not care to disabuse the lady, and as Anne looked at him with amusement, he decided she was not injured by her mother's speculation.

It was Fitzwilliam whom Darcy wished to see. When confronted, he had confessed to seeing Darcy with Elizabeth soon after his arrival, not to mention his hope that bringing them together at the ball would be beneficial for their future. This last assertion had caused Darcy's dark amusement.

"You were incorrect about that, were you not?"

"If you see it that way," said Fitzwilliam with a shrug. "I will suggest that had it been *you* and *Miss Elizabeth* dancing, the outcome might have been very different."

"In essentials, I must disagree with you," said Darcy, "though it is possible the reaction might have been muted."

"You have informed your father?"

"I have," said Darcy. "It has been on my mind for some time that it would be for the best, but Elizabeth was fearful of being separated."

"Which fear was not unwarranted," noted Fitzwilliam.

"Indeed. Her uncle forwarded a letter from her yesterday, in which she declared her resolve to speak to the baron, asking for my consent. I gave it and returned to inform my father of the same." Darcy paused and sighed. "Alexander became suspicious and discovered the letter."

The wince with which Fitzwilliam met that bit of intelligence summed up how Darcy felt himself. "He did not take it well?"

"Called me a hypocrite," said Darcy. "On a certain level, I can well understand his feelings. Had he any affection for the youngest girl, his arguments might have moved me, but he would not declare any such feelings."

"I hope he does nothing stupid," muttered Fitzwilliam.

It was a possibility Darcy had not considered. As part of his communication with his father, he had revealed Alexander's discovery and reaction to the news, an opinion with which his father had not disagreed. Any further action Darcy thought was best to leave to his father, for Darcy had never had success in controlling his brother.

"For what it is worth," said Fitzwilliam, clasping Darcy's shoulder, "I believe you have done the right thing, even if your father did not take it well."

Darcy snorted. "I had to remind him of Blackfish Bay."

A laugh was Fitzwilliam's response. "Perhaps not the most tactful thing to do, but it will inform him you are determined."

"Of that, he is now in no doubt."

Fitzwilliam did not respond with anything other than a slap on the back. That evening Darcy did his best to ignore Lady Catherine's antics, keeping to Fitzwilliam's society and speaking in low tones.

When a message arrived for his father late that evening, Darcy suspected it was from Lord Arundel. Though he had no notion of what it contained, Darcy noted his father remained thoughtful until he retired.

CHAPTER XXIX

*H*ad her family left Elizabeth to herself she might have thought her continued separation from William would dominate her thoughts, filling her with the overwhelming longing to be in his company. For some time, Elizabeth found herself caught in the depths of that despair, for all of her father's words notwithstanding, the prospect of being denied William's company was hard to bear.

Thomas, however, would not allow Elizabeth to wallow, though she suspected he would not have understood the situation even if he had known anything of it. His youthful exuberance was such that Elizabeth could not remain dejected, often being drawn into his games. Though he was at an age when his lessons often intruded—in his opinion—into his ability to have fun, Elizabeth waited until the tutor released him from his studies, for his presence would cheer her, and his requests to play would induce her to forget her troubles. On one subject, in particular, Thomas was insistent.

"Lizzy," said he, the day after Mr. Gardiner had discovered Elizabeth in William's company, "you promised we would go out on a picnic. The rain has stopped, so I expect you to keep your promise."

With a laugh, Elizabeth caressed her brother's cheek, fixing him with a smile. "I did make that promise, did I not?"

"You did," was the boy's solemn reply. "It would be a great scandal if my sister was proven untrustworthy."

Elizabeth laughed again and pulled the boy into an embrace. "Only a scandal to a young boy intent upon having his own way. But a promise is a promise, and I am willing to keep my engagements."

The boy whooped, and Elizabeth moved to once again rein him in. "The ground, Thomas, is still muddy, so we shall need to wait until it has firmed enough that we will not return covered with mud."

When Thomas pouted, Elizabeth was quick to reassure him. "I believe another day or two should do the trick, dear brother. And as we must wait, perhaps another locale would be desirable for our outing? Longbourn is well known to us. Would you like to visit a place you have never seen?"

"Where?" asked Thomas, his eagerness causing him to fidget.

"There is an old ruin north of Pemberley," suggested Mr. Bingley, who had been watching the interaction between siblings. "There is enough room there for us to have a picnic and games, and perhaps even indulge in a little fishing."

"That sounds like an excellent plan, Mr. Bingley," said Elizabeth, showing the gentleman her appreciation with a grin.

When her father heard of their intentions, his first reaction was to give Elizabeth a long and steady look. Knowing he was about to say something and misconstrue the reason for the location of their intended outing, Elizabeth was quick to reassure him.

"It was Mr. Bingley's suggestion, Papa. As you are aware, I have not even been out these past days, and have no way to contact Mr. Darcy. I have no expectation of seeing him there, and do not mean to seek him out."

That seemed to mollify her father, for he grasped her shoulder and squeezed. "Thank you, Lizzy, for indulging me. Then I shall leave you in Bingley and my cousin's capable hands for your outing." Lord Arundel paused and then he enfolded her in an affectionate embrace. "Patience, Lizzy. We cannot rush this matter of you and Mr. Darcy. I am inclined to allow your desires to come to fruition, and I believe the elder Mr. Darcy is coming around to my way of thinking."

Those words heartened Elizabeth, and though she still did not see William, she hoped it would not be long before she would. They soon decided among them that Mr. Collins and Mr. Bingley would accompany the siblings, but there was one who expressed contempt for their chosen amusement.

"Why should *I* wish to picnic in such conditions as this?"

demanded Lydia when they put the suggestion to her. "I should spend my time much better in studying to be an *accomplished young woman.*"

Lydia had repeated that phrase many times in the past days, and to Elizabeth, Lydia's attitude was becoming tiresome. Elizabeth had been denied her love, which was a much larger matter than Lydia being kept from her flirtations. But Lydia did not see it that way, for she seemed determined to cause as much trouble and draw as much attention to herself as she could. That their father had not further censured her was a testament to her good behavior — as far as anyone in the family could tell — though she insisted on making a commotion. Lord Arundel had not even assigned a footman to her when she left the house, not that she had been out these past few days.

Elizabeth decided Lydia was just being the same headstrong and slightly spoiled girl she had often been. Lady Margaret stepped in to speak to her youngest, and guided her away, whispering to her, to which Lydia nodded, seeming to settle a little. If Lydia wished to pout and refuse to take part in their outings, it was of little consequence to Elizabeth, so she put her sister from her mind.

The only thing marring Darcy's return to Pemberley was his inability to see Elizabeth. Though he wished to see her again and rejoice in how close they were approaching to their families accepting their desire to be together, there was no way to contact her. While Darcy knew she had informed her father of their history, he did not think calling at Longbourn would be acceptable at this time. It was fortunate, therefore, that a solution presented itself.

"Darcy!" exclaimed Bingley when Bingley arrived for a visit one morning. "I see your sojourn at Thorndell was of a short duration."

"It was," said Darcy, accepting his friend's hand in his own. "There were matters here that required my attention, and I returned to see to them."

"Matters such as Miss Elizabeth Bennet?" asked his friend with a grin.

Nonplussed, Darcy stared at Bingley. "What do you know of it? I would not have thought the baron would announce it to his family."

"He has not," said Bingley. "But Miss Elizabeth told her closest sister, who, if you will recall, is my betrothed. Jane then shared her intelligence with me, though I will own I had wondered if there might be some partiality between you."

"My friend Bingley, who notices nothing when his lady is nearby, suspected me of holding Miss Elizabeth in affection?"

Bingley laughed. "You make me sound thoughtless, my friend."

"No, Bingley," said Darcy, "just single-minded when it concerns your lady. Now, perhaps you should explain to me how you saw through us."

"Saw through you is overstating the matter," said Bingley, sitting in a nearby chair Darcy. "I saw you speaking together after the incident with your brother and Miss Lydia, and I noted how you seemed to watch her during that incident in the bookshop."

"But that was some time before we began meeting," protested Darcy.

"Perhaps it was," said Bingley. "I would wager, however, that you had already begun to think of her in warm terms before that incident. Can you deny it?"

"I have no wish to deny it," said Darcy. In his mind's eye, he thought of those days, of his ever-increasing attraction to the charms of Miss Elizabeth Bennet. In this, Bingley was correct—while Darcy had tried to deny how she affected him, it had been impossible to do so and maintain any pretense of honesty.

"Now I feel like I am looking at myself," said Bingley with a laugh, pulling Darcy back to the awareness of his friend's presence. "If that is how I looked those many times you called me out for contemplating a pretty face, I wonder that you did not burst out laughing every time."

"You are not incorrect, my friend," said Darcy, fixing him with a rueful grin. "We have not been together enough since you began your courtship of Miss Bennet, but I imagine the occurrence of that expression has increased tenfold."

Bingley responded with a laugh of hearty amusement, not offended by his friend's characterization of his distraction. "I will own to it without reserve, for there is so much perfection to consider when thinking of my betrothed!

"However, I must insist you share your history with Miss Elizabeth with me, Darcy," continued Bingley. "Jane did not know all the details, though she informed me she would further interrogate her sister when the opportunity presented itself. Can you not assuage my curiosity?"

As it happened, Darcy was not at all averse to sharing his story with his friend. They sat for some time together, Darcy sharing his history with Elizabeth. While Bingley had owned to idle thoughts of Darcy's interest, it was clear from the exclamations of surprise that he had known nothing of the truth of the matter. Then again, no one—not even Fitzwilliam, who had observed them together once—knew of the fullness of the matter. Darcy was determined no one ever would hear of certain events. The night on her balcony after Lord Chesterfield's ball, for example, was precious to him and meant to remain between Elizabeth and Darcy. It was possible they might share the story with their children one day, but at present it was a treasured memory he shared with her alone.

"It is possible you have already heard it from others," said Bingley when Darcy finished telling his tale, "but I am astonished the ever-proper Fitzwilliam Darcy went so far as to meet with a young woman in secret, enough to have proposed to her. How can you account for such a blatant breach of propriety?"

As he knew his friend was jesting, Darcy took no offense because he knew it was nothing less than the truth. "You are correct," replied Darcy, feeling a hint of chagrin. "There is only one way I can justify my behavior—that Miss Elizabeth caught me in her web and induced me to be in love with her before I knew what was happening. I could have withstood her allure no more than I could walk on water."

"That, my friend, is more evidence of your besotted state than anything else you have said today. Now you have firsthand knowledge of how I feel!"

"That I do, Bingley," replied Darcy quietly. "That I do."

Darcy turned to his friend and noted his grin, but desperate as he was to hear of Elizabeth, he ignored. "Have you any news of Elizabeth?"

"Missing her, are you?" asked Bingley, no little sympathy in his voice.

"More than you can know," said Darcy. "Though I have spoken with my father and she with hers and we both consider ourselves engaged, I cannot visit Longbourn at present and have no way of asking her to meet me elsewhere. I have been to the places we met before but have seen no sign of her."

Bingley nodded in commiseration, and Darcy reflected that his friend likely knew what he was experiencing. "Elizabeth is well, as far as I can see, though perhaps a little out of spirits. It seems to me she is missing you as much as you are missing her. While I do not think her father has prohibited her from seeing you, I understand he has asked for her patience."

While he nodded, Darcy could not have felt more dispirited. How he was to endure the days and weeks if Lord Arundel did not relent, he did not know.

"But all is not lost," said Bingley with some cheer in his voice. Darcy looked up to see his friend grinning. "Should she leave Longbourn for any reason, why, I think your path would be clear."

"And do you know of such an excursion?" asked Darcy.

"I might," said Bingley. "You did not hear this from me, you understand, but it is possible that the Bennet siblings *might* consider picnicking near the old ruin on Pemberley's northern border tomorrow. If they should do so, Mr. Collins and I will likely accompany them, but we will be so caught up in admiration for our own ladies, I am certain our vigilance shall lapse long enough for a certain lady to walk, and if you were in the vicinity, you may come across her."

With a grin, Darcy grasped his friend's hand. "I will be there, Bingley. What time do you expect to arrive?"

"A little before luncheon, perhaps," said Bingley. "And you need not concern yourself for Collins. The man knows nothing of these matters and does not agree with the difficulties between Pemberley and Longbourn regardless."

"Thank you, Bingley. You may have saved my sanity."

"It is my pleasure to be of service. Perhaps we may discover some way to resolve this situation."

"It is my fervent hope we shall," said Darcy.

Anticipation coursed through Darcy the next morning as he prepared to depart from Pemberley. It had been a week since he had last seen Elizabeth, and the longing to be in her company again was almost a physical ache. The prospect of holding her in his arms again set Darcy to greater introspection than was his wont, the eagerness so great, he tried to occupy himself as a means to prevent saddling his horse hours before he needed to.

As the time approached, however, he felt ready to depart, and while the hour meant he would wait there for her to appear longer than he might wish, he could no longer delay. That was when another distraction presented itself in the person of his cousin.

"Darcy," said Anne as she met him in the hall outside the family wing. "Might I ask for your indulgence for a moment?"

Though eager to leave, Darcy knew there was no rush, and as such he allowed his curiosity to guide his response. "Of course, Anne. How may I be of service?"

Anne made a shushing motion, holding her finger to her lips, motioning Darcy to follow her. Intrigued, Darcy did so, finding himself in a smaller parlor toward the back of Pemberley's main floor. When Anne entered, Darcy followed her, knowing that if it had been her mother, it may well have been an attempt to compromise them together.

When she had ensured the door was closed behind them, she turned to Darcy and fixed him with a raised eyebrow. Darcy, understanding she was waiting for his protest, laughed.

"I shall assume your mother will not arrive to find us alone, Anne."

The grin with which she responded told Darcy he had guessed correctly. "No, but I wished to speak to you in private. The matters I wish to discuss will become known to my mother before long, but I believe we should present them to her with a united front."

"In that, I assume you speak of your association with Mr. Gardiner," said Darcy.

"As much that as your own secret," replied Anne, her eyes never leaving his. "Or am I mistaken?"

"No, though I am interested to learn how much you know of it."

"I know nothing of it other than what I have observed. Anthony, I suspect, knows more."

"Yes, I am already aware of what Anthony knows," replied Darcy. "As it will not remain a secret much longer, please know you will not endure your mother's raptures on the subject of our engagement much longer, as I am now engaged to Miss Elizabeth Bennet."

The confession did not surprise Anne as much as Darcy might have thought, for Anne only nodded. "I suspected something of that nature. That is the reason I wished to speak to you this morning. The time has come to inform my mother and disabuse her of the notion of our engagement once and for all."

Darcy regarded Anne, his thoughts on her mother, wondering why she would suggest this now. Anne, it seemed, understood his curiosity, for she was quick to continue.

"As you said, your secret will not remain so for much longer. Mine also, for my mother has already suspected my activities."

"Therefore, you wish to inform her of our secrets together."

"Yes," affirmed Anne.

"Then shall we?" asked Darcy, offering his arm.

Anne laughed as she accepted his arm. "I had thought you might be less eager, Cousin, though I am not surprised at your willingness to brave the lion in her den."

"If it rids me of one more complication in the quest to ensure the family accepts Miss Elizabeth as my wife, I cannot meet the prospect with anything less than enthusiasm."

"Then let us proceed."

A moment later they walked into the sitting-room, and it surprised Darcy to see almost the entire family in residence gathered there, for it seemed they had caught wind that something significant was in the offing. Georgiana was absent, for which Darcy muttered a prayer of thanks, while Fitzwilliam, true to his character, regarded them with open amusement. The elder Darcy watched them with pensive resignation.

Lady Catherine, by contrast, noted Anne's hand on Darcy's arm and nodded to herself with satisfaction. Had she kept her thoughts to herself Darcy might have pitied her. But the lady had never been known to keep her own counsel.

"Have you come to your senses at last?" demanded she in a haughty tone, as if she alone had known all along. "I must commend you, for it has been obvious to me all this time."

Though Darcy had not discussed how to handle this with Anne, a look shared between them settled the matter. As Darcy was the one Lady Catherine considered the greater impediment to her designs, the greater burden of her displeasure must fall upon him.

"In fact, I believe we *have* come to our senses, Lady Catherine," said Darcy, disengaging Anne's hand and seeing her seated on a nearby chair, then turning to face his aunt. "You may congratulate me, Aunt Catherine, for I am engaged to be married to Miss Elizabeth Bennet."

Darcy's father groaned at the manner in which he had just stated his intentions regarding the daughter of his greatest enemy, but Darcy did not spare him a glance. It was time this matter was wholly out in the open, and Darcy would not shirk when Anne's own happiness was also at stake.

"Engaged to Miss Elizabeth Bennet?" gasped Lady Catherine. "That cannot be!"

"I assure you it is," replied Darcy, unruffled by his aunt's shock. Meanwhile, Anne sat near her mother appearing the demur and dutiful daughter to a casual viewer, which was, of course, nothing close to the truth. Fitzwilliam was laughing without disguise.

"It cannot," was Lady Catherine's forceful reply. It seemed the lady was regaining her balance after having it upset. "You know you are not available to engage yourself to Miss Elizabeth, for you are already engaged to Anne."

The reactions of all were predictable, though his annoyance with his aunt swallowed any amusement Darcy might have otherwise felt. Of importance to the present situation was Anne, whose reaction could be termed nothing other than a glare, though Lady Catherine did not deign to notice, and his father's shaken head, which seemed to indicate to Darcy that his father would do nothing to deal with the irascible woman—Darcy would need to make his case himself.

"And again I will inform you," said Darcy, "that as you do not have mine or my father's signatures on a contract, as Anne and I both do not wish to marry the other, and as I have not proposed, let alone been accepted, there is no engagement."

Lady Catherine opened her mouth again, but before she could speak, Darcy growled: "Do you wish for a break in the family, Lady Catherine? The earl will not support you, as you know, and my father does not oppose the match. I will not give way in this, and as you have no standing on which to protest, the only thing you will do is provoke an estrangement between us. Thus, I will ask you again: do you wish this family to be broken asunder because of your inability to accept this dream of yours was never a possibility?"

A sour look at his father was Lady Catherine's response. "Have you betrayed me in this matter, Robert? Do you not know what your wife wished?"

"There has been no betrayal," replied Mr. Darcy shortly. "It is only that you have never accepted it, though everyone else in the family has. Desist, Catherine, I beg of you,"

For a moment, Darcy thought Lady Catherine would continue her protests, for the mutinous glare she directed at her brother was not at all accepting. Then she looked around at all in attendance, noted their amusement, disgust, or whatever they felt on the matter, and saw their resolve. It seemed, at last, she understood, for she huffed her annoyance and slumped back in her chair, regarding then with moody petulance.

"This will be your undoing, Darcy," said she. "These Bennets are all for what they can get, and it seems, against all probability, they have gotten you."

"Perhaps they are," said Anne, breaking her silence. "But I, for one, applaud Darcy for seeing the merit in Miss Elizabeth, for she is a wonderful woman."

As Lady Catherine gasped in outrage at her daughter's betrayal, Darcy could not help the laugh which escaped at her ridiculous statement. "What could the Bennets possibly gain from entrapping me?"

"Wealth!" snapped Lady Catherine. "The Darcys are wealthier than the Bennets, and by a wide margin."

"Not so wide as you would believe," replied Darcy's father,

"though you are correct in essence."

"And they are nobility," said Darcy. "One might even laud them, for they are allowing all three elder daughters to marry gentlemen who are lower than they in society. I understand the third daughter is on the verge of an understanding with her cousin."

"A cousin who was nothing more than a parson less than two years ago," sneered Lady Catherine. "It is just like that family to dilute their blood in such a fashion."

"Do you considering marrying my son to be diluting their blood further?" demanded Darcy's father. Lady Catherine seemed to realize she had spoken out of turn for she refused to respond. "Your own sister married *me*, Catherine, for if she had not, you would not be here in all your displeasure."

"You know of what I speak," snapped Lady Catherine. "Mr. Collins is nothing more than a simpering, sorry excuse for a parson, let alone the master of an estate."

"And yet he is a cousin to the current Baron of Arundel," said Darcy. "If the Bennet sisters *are* attempting to raise themselves in society or gain wealth to themselves, they are going about it poorly — I am the only one of three suitors for their daughters who is wealthier than they, and even that is future wealth as Father owns it all now."

"Do you mean to allow this?" Lady Catherine once again turned on Darcy's father, this time her tone more pleading than domineering. "Were you not counseling strict separation from these Bennets only a week ago?"

It was apparent to Darcy his father was uncomfortable, for it seemed his time with the baron had not softened his mind toward them to any great degree. It heartened Darcy when he endeavored to respond, for he knew how difficult it must be for his father.

"It seems there is little I can do, Catherine. I will own I am not comfortable with the new state of affairs. But it seems I cannot compel my son, nor do I wish to curb his independence. If I must, I shall accept his Bennet bride and allow the difficulties of the past to remain in the past."

"There is one more matter of which you must be aware, Mother," said Anne. "Even if Darcy had not engaged himself to Miss Elizabeth, I still would not wish to wed him, as I have told you many times."

"You would do as you are told," spat Lady Catherine.

"In that, you are incorrect, as usual." Anne, though sitting with her hands clasped in her lap, was ramrod straight, no hint of compromise in her manner or posture. "I have never desired marriage to Darcy, any more than he wishes to marry me. In fact, I have another man that I am considering for a husband."

"Another man?" echoed Lady Catherine clearly confused. "Of what are you speaking, Anne. There has been no one else in evidence, no one who could suit as a future husband. Are your wits addled?"

"My mind is clear, as are my wishes, Mother. Though I have not spoken of my intentions, I, like William, believe the time for secrecy is past. While I do not yet know if I wish to marry him, I intend to allow Mr. Gardiner a courtship to learn if we are compatible."

If any of them thought Lady Catherine was angry before, it was nothing compared to her display upon hearing Anne's declaration. Her countenance turned almost purple in her anger, and for a moment she could say nothing, so incensed had she become. That did not last long, however, to their detriment, for she soon found her voice.

"No! I absolutely forbid it! Heaven and earth, Anne, think of what you are saying. Would you pollute the noble line of de Bourgh by capering about with such an unsuitable man as Mr. Gardiner? What are you thinking?"

Standing, Anne glared down at her mother. "I am thinking of my happiness, not your overbearing designs. I am my own woman, Mother, and may do what I please—I would also remind of what you seem to have forgotten; my father was a knight, yes, but a knight is not noble. It is your decision, Mother, whether you accept my wishes in this matter. But even if you do not, I will have you know I will not relent."

Then Anne turned and departed from the room, leaving silence in her wake. Knowing this was not an opportunity he should miss, Darcy also bowed to the company to excuse himself.

"Please know that I support Anne in every particular, Lady Catherine. Now I shall bid you a good day."

With a quick stride, Darcy followed his cousin from the room, turning toward the front doors and his horse waiting there. An appointment with the woman he loved awaited and Darcy would not miss it for all the world.

CHAPTER XXX

When the day of the picnic arrived, the assorted Bennets and their suitors made their way toward their proposed picnic site in a pair of carriages. The ruin to which Mr. Bingley had referred was little more than a stone foundation set into the turf, with little of walls and nothing of roof remaining. It was a spot well-loved by those of the neighborhood, for it was calm and peaceful, there was a wide field perfect for gatherings, and a river ran to one side.

"Was this a castle?" asked Thomas, wide-eyed as they inspected the few low walls remaining.

"It seems to me it was much too small to be something so grand as a castle," said Mr. Bingley, indulging the boy's questions. "Given some of the layout, it is possible it was a small fort."

Thomas seemed to consider this, a hint of disappointment hovering about him. "You do not know?"

"I am not a font of all knowledge," replied Mr. Bingley with a laugh. "This location is mentioned in none of the histories of which I am aware, and thus, we can only guess about the purpose of this place based on what we can observe."

"Where have all the walls gone?" asked Thomas with a nod, peering about with interest, his active young mind likely full of glorious battles and desperate last stands.

"The stones have been taken for use in other buildings, I should think," replied Mr. Bingley. "Such is often the fate of abandoned structures. Some of the stones which made up the walls of this place may reside now in one of the neighborhood estate houses, perhaps even Pemberley or Longbourn."

That seemed to catch Thomas's imagination, for he exclaimed and pulled Mr. Bingley along to investigate further. Mr. Bingley went along willingly, with Mr. Collins following them and adding his own observations to the other gentleman's. The sisters began to remove their hampers of food and set up their picnic while the gentlemen were thus engaged.

Another sight drew Elizabeth's attention, for the days of rain they had endured had made the river run higher and faster than she had ever seen it. Leaving her sisters to the task, she approached the river, noting how it was several feet above its usual level, the way a small branch caught in its course bobbed along with its current, racing past Elizabeth's position quicker than she might have thought possible. At various locations in the river, rocks at the bottom caused the water to splash over them, creating large waves that boiled and pitched in the restless water. There was little to be done that day other than to stay clear of it.

"There will be no fishing today, Thomas," said she to her brother when the gentlemen returned. "The water is running swift and high; it would not be safe to stray near. Please take care and do not approach the river."

Thomas appeared put out by Elizabeth's declaration, but Mr. Bingley nodded. "I suspected it might be so." Seeing the boy's annoyance, Mr. Bingley laughed and ruffled his hair. "We can return some other time, Thomas, when the water level is lower. Perhaps we might even fish in the stream at Longbourn."

"And catch frogs?" asked Thomas, gazing up at Elizabeth.

"Of course," replied Elizabeth with a laugh. "We must catch frogs, for it has become one of your great ambitions in life, has it not?"

The boy gave her an eager nod and sat on the blanket. The rest of the party smiled at their youngest member and they all sat together to partake of the repast the Bennet sisters had set out for them. For some time, all was laughter and good cheer, the warmth of the day and the excellent fare bringing out the best of their moods in response.

After lunch, the company stayed in that attitude for some time in conversation, and to Elizabeth's relief, no one said anything of recent events or the Darcy family. Thomas, though she knew he would become active again soon, dozed in the sun's light, his belly sated, his happiness complete, having achieved his desire to be out of doors. As her sisters talked and laughed with the gentlemen, Elizabeth allowed her attention to wander, reflecting upon the simple pleasures of life, content with her lot for the moment. These past weeks when all her focus had been on William, she had forgotten something of the wonder of nature; she welcomed this reminder of how wonderful was the location in which she made her home.

It was to no one's surprise that Thomas woke soon after and began clamoring for activity. They indulged him, and soon the company was engaged in playing games of his own devising. Then Elizabeth, seeing her brother occupied by his other sisters, decided a short walk about the area would be just the thing, and informed her sisters of this desire.

"Do not wander too far, Lizzy," said Jane, though with an amused grin. "You never know when highwaymen might be about, lying in wait for unaccompanied and unwary baron's daughters."

Elizabeth thought it was an odd comment and was even more confused when Mr. Bingley chuckled in response to Jane's tease. Her surroundings were calling to her, however, so Elizabeth avoided pursuing any question of her sister's jest and departed.

Had Elizabeth been considering the matter properly, she might have known what was afoot. But as she would concede later, there was nothing in her mind other than the desire to walk a little among the soothing calm of nature. Thus, when a man appeared before her, Elizabeth was so shocked, she almost released a surprised shriek.

"I had not thought my presence would distress you, my dear," said William, fixing her with a satisfied smirk.

Seeing him for the first time in days suppressed Elizabeth's inhibitions, and she darted forward, throwing her arms around his neck and pressing her lips against his. Within moments their embrace became impassioned, for William's arms snaked around her back, gliding over the soft planes of her form while she entangled her fingers in his hair and did her best to meld herself into his embrace. And then it changed again, as the need evinced in their initial embrace cooled into one more affectionate and at once more satisfying. Elizabeth reveled in his attentions, the little nipping kisses he pressed against her eyelids, her neck, and it seemed like every inch of her face.

At length Elizabeth sighed with contentment and pressed her cheek against his broad chest, feeling loved and protected in the circle of his arms. How long they stood in this attitude, Elizabeth could not say with any certainty, though she wished to continue it indefinitely.

"How I have missed you, Elizabeth," murmured Mr. Darcy.

"I had not expected to see you here," said she, unable to summon more than a whisper. "How did you know?"

"Bingley mentioned it to me yesterday and *suggested* it was likely you would wish to walk during your picnic."

Gasping, Elizabeth pulled away from him. "Mr. Bingley informed you?"

"Yes," replied William, his eyes dancing with merriment. "It seems we are gathering supporters to us, Elizabeth, for he was eager to be of service."

"Jane must have known too," said Elizabeth, "considering her words to me when I departed." Elizabeth paused and frowned. "My father has instructed me to avoid seeking you out, and I have disobeyed him again."

"But if you recall, *you* did not seek *me* out," replied William, a hint of laughter in his voice. "This meeting was all my doing, with some judicious help on the part of my closest friend. None of it can be attributed to you."

"Perhaps not," said Elizabeth. "But that is nothing more than casuistry, and you know it."

"Mayhap I do," replied William. "Then shall I go away? I should not wish to do anything to make you uncomfortable."

"You are aware I wish for little other than your company," replied Elizabeth.

"As I wish for nothing more than to be in yours." William paused and his manner became more serious. "What happened when you informed your father of our situation?"

Elizabeth sighed, wishing they could avoid the subject, yet knowing it was important. "Papa was more understanding than I expected. At the same time, he does not believe our union may be accomplished quickly. He spoke of moving slowly, so as to allow the situation to settle."

William snorted. "That was more than my father offered."

When Elizabeth looked at him in question, William explained his own conversation with his father. Though it heartened Elizabeth to hear that Mr. Darcy had backed off his threat of disinheriting his son, his continued opposition threatened to overwhelm whatever hope she had gained during this brief interlude.

"You do not suppose your father will attempt to carry through his threat to force you to marry Miss de Bourgh?"

William shook his head. "I cannot imagine it, for my father knows very well that neither Anne nor I wish it. Anne would no more fall in with my father's schemes than would I." Then he paused and grinned. "Besides, it seems Anne has a mind of her own and is involved with her own intrigues."

"Anne?" asked Elizabeth.

"Yes," said William. "It seems Anne has found someone of her own to admire, one who is close to your family."

At that moment it fell into place. "Uncle Gardiner?" William nodded with delight. "I saw them speaking at the ball, but I had not thought it would lead to this."

"This morning Anne informed her mother after I informed her of our engagement."

"That cannot have gone well," said Elizabeth with a wince.

"From Lady Catherine's perspective, it did not go well at all," replied William, not holding a wide smirk in check. "I have no doubt she will continue to bluster, but there is nothing she may do to persuade us. Lady Catherine believes she commands her daughter but Anne is of age and her father's heir. Lady Catherine has no more control over her than she has over me."

"That is good news," said Elizabeth. I had worried about Lady Catherine's actions, for her opposition would continue to muddy the waters if nothing else. However, I believe you have activated Lady Catherine's desperation by informing her, so it would be prudent for you to take care."

"I shall," said William. "Neither Lady Catherine nor anyone else will cheat me from heart's desire."

"Then I suppose there is no choice but to wait until matters improve," said Elizabeth with a sigh.

"There is one other possibility," said William.

Elizabeth shot him a searching look, which William took as an invitation to explain. "Come away with me, Elizabeth. Let us go to Gretna this very afternoon and we shall be wed. Then your father and mine must accept it or we will retire to Blackfish Bay."

"Elope?" gasped Elizabeth. "Can you imagine the scandal if a daughter of the Arundel barony and the eldest son of the Darcy family were to flout all propriety and steal away to Scotland?"

"I care nothing for their gossip or their disapproval," declared William. "*We* shall achieve our happiness; that is all that matters."

It was tempting—oh, so tempting. The thought of being bound to William without the possibility of anyone ever separating them again was the fondest wish of Elizabeth's dreams, and she came near to accepting at once.

But the thought of her father's disappointment, her brother's bewilderment, her family's disapproval all gave her pause. Jane, in particular, would be affected by her actions, as would Mary, both of whom were engaged to good men. Could she throw the relationships with all her family away in so selfish a manner? Elizabeth could not fathom it. There must be some other way to have what her heart desired without putting herself before the needs and desires of so many.

"Nothing would please me so much as to be your wife forever," said Elizabeth, gazing up into his well-loved face. "But I cannot do this to all my family — at least until we have exhausted all other options."

William chuckled. "It was my suspicion you might say that. Though Bingley suggested it would be agreeable to *him* to have me as a brother, I suppose he must wait."

It was impossible for Elizabeth to avoid laughing at this characterization of Mr. Bingley. "It seems my sister's suitor is turning into quite the wolf in sheep's clothing. What would my father say if he should learn of his future son-in-law's betrayal?"

"Bingley does not consider it a betrayal," replied William. "And I think it would not cause him an instant of distress. As the engagement is public and, from what I understand, the articles already signed, there is nothing your father could do other than allow the wedding to go forward. Given what I know of the baron, I think he might find it a great joke."

"In that, you may be correct," said Elizabeth with a laugh. "My father's sense of humor is enough that he would see the ridiculousness in it once his offense had dimmed."

"Let me inform you, Elizabeth," said William, as he leaned forward to kiss her forehead, "I wish for nothing more than to give you everything in the world, including a wedding without equal in all recorded history. But if I have no other choice, I should rather have you for a wife through the auspices of the blacksmith in Gretna Green than to live without you."

"I feel the same," whispered Elizabeth, overcome with emotion. Trying to keep the happy tears at bay, Elizabeth willed her emotions to allow her to speak again, and when they did, she managed to say: "But I should prefer not to take that step unless there is no other option. Let us give our families time, William — with recent events, I think they will come to accept us."

"I shall abide by your wishes," replied William. "Know, however, that you have only to say the word and I shall whisk you away to Gretna and ensure nothing will ever separate us again."

Having resolved that question between them, they stayed in that attitude for several moments longer, enjoying each other's company. Elizabeth, though she was loath to confess it, was storing up the memory of his presence to sustain her through the expected long days without his company. The mere thought almost prompted her to agree to his proposal then and there, but in some manner, she prevented herself from speaking. When they separated, it was with great reluctance on both their parts. Perhaps Mr. Bingley would continue to be a willing intermediary, for even the occasional letter would be preferable to the loss of all contact.

When Elizabeth pried herself away from Mr. Darcy's company, she thought to wander a little longer, preparing herself to meet her party again. As she had been with the gentleman for some time, however, she decided instead to make her way back to their picnic site.

As she stepped into the clearing, Elizabeth shook her head clear of thoughts of Mr. Darcy. Then she heard the sound of a large splash, mixed with the roar of the river, along with the scream of her most beloved sister. The horror would haunt her dreams for days and weeks after.

"Thomas!"

Casting about wildly, Elizabeth noted her sister running toward the river. In an instant, she followed Jane to see a horrifying sight: Thomas's dark jacket bobbing in the river as the boy struggled to keep his head above water. Elizabeth moved forward, intent upon jumping into the water after her brother.

Then the most wondrous sight she had ever beheld presented itself before her eyes. From the woods further on down the river, Mr. Darcy burst from the foliage and jumped into the water. As the boy swept past him, he reached out and caught hold of Thomas's jacket and held fast.

The water was high and strong, pushing against the gentleman, darkening Mr. Darcy's jacket up to his chest, even along the edge of the river, and as he struggled to maintain his footing, Elizabeth could see him slip more than once on the slick rocks on the riverbed. Then Mr. Bingley, who had been further from the edge of the river, along with Mr. Collins, rushed down along the edge of the bank, throwing themselves in the water when they reached William, and the three men, using each other to maintain their balance and footing, forced their way to the bank.

"That is it," said Mr. Bingley, panting but grasping the nearby branch of a tree to steady himself. "Out you go, Master Thomas."

Elizabeth had moved to the point along the stream where the gentlemen were attempting to climb from the river, Mary appearing by her side with a picnic blanket held in one hand. And the gentlemen passed one soaked and bedraggled little boy up to the waiting arms of the ladies.

When he was safe within their grasp, the four sisters hovered around him, drying him with the blanket as much as they could. Though warm for spring, the weather was still cold when one was soaked through, as evidenced by Thomas's uncontrollable shivering.

"Let us get him out of these wet clothes," said Elizabeth, beginning to strip off his jacket.

While the gentlemen pulled themselves from the frigid water, the sisters undressed their brother, leaving him in his smallclothes, but wrapping him in a second blanket. At length, Thomas's shivering lessened and he settled. The men seemed affected in the same manner as the young boy, but as they were not wet from head to toe, it appeared they were better able to withstand the effects of their impromptu swim.

"Thank you, Mr. Darcy," whispered Elizabeth to the man she loved, every bit of her heart contained within her eyes. "You have saved my brother, and for that, I can never repay you."

"This is Mr. Darcy?" demanded Thomas, gazing at the gentleman with such a look of wonder that it set them all to chuckling. "He does not appear to be a scoundrel like our father says."

This time open laughter met his declaration, though Mr. Darcy contented himself with stepping forward and clasping the boy's hand.

"Fitzwilliam Darcy, at your service, Master Bennet. I have never considered myself a scoundrel, though I suppose those who do not know me might disagree."

"What are you doing here?" asked Thomas.

Though William's eyes flicked to Elizabeth for a brief instant, she thought most of the rest of the party did not see it. "It seems fortunate that I was nearby, Thomas, for I was in the perfect position to reach you when you fell into the river. Now, will you give me your promise you will take great care around rivers from this time forward?"

Thomas gave him a solemn nod. "I shall. I have no desire to be swept away, never to see my sisters again."

"Excellent!" said William. "Now, perhaps it would be for the best if you returned home and acquired dry clothing. It would be best if I did the same."

The company all agreed they had seen enough excitement for one day, and Elizabeth's sisters began to make their way back toward the carriages. Mr. Collins, seeing the difficulty Thomas had in walking, swept him up in his arms and carried him, while Mr. Bingley shook William's hand, offering his own thanks. Elizabeth saw all of this only peripherally, for her focus was on William to the exclusion of all others.

When Mr. Bingley turned and made his way back himself, Elizabeth even ignored the wink with which he favored her. Once alone, Elizabeth burrowed herself into his breast heedless of his wet state, wondering at having attracted this wonderful man's affection.

"Though I think the image will be fetching," said he, a rumbling chuckle in his breast, "I believe you should return too, Elizabeth, for your dress is wet. The picture you present is not one I would wish any man to see, and I would not have you catch your death of cold."

"Thank you, William," said Elizabeth, pulling away and sharing a watery smile with him. "A can never repay what you have done here today in saving my brother."

"Repayment is not what I desire. The only thing I desire is *you*."

"And you shall have me before long," replied Elizabeth with a grin. "I shall make sure of it."

Then she curtseyed and turned to join her family, her heart full of love. Never had she been so certain of her choice as she was now.

CHAPTER XXXI

𝓗 enry Bennet, Baron of Arundel was a man not given much to introspection. While a quiet man, one who enjoyed books and port in equal measure, he also did not second-guess himself much, being, at heart, confident in his position, his intelligence, and his sense. Arundel well understood his own foibles; more apt to laugh at those about him and tend to his own affairs, he also possessed a streak of pride in his family name and history and possessed little patience for the foolish.

At present, however, Arundel was feeling more than a little foolish himself. For weeks, his cousin, his most intelligent daughter, and even other members of society including the earl in their community had been urging him to mend fences with the Darcy family and allow the difficulties between them to rest. But the familiar was a comfortable place to be, and there was little more familiar to the Bennet family than that the Darcy family were proud and disagreeable, untrustworthy and false. And yet the Darcy family's eldest son had saved Arundel's own heir from injury if not death.

Thomas seemed to be none the worse for wear despite his experience. Once outfitted in dry clothes, his heir had been more than eager to recite the story of his rescuer's bravery, the tale becoming more embellished with every telling, than to take to his bed or submit to his mother's worried ministrations. Ah, for the resiliency of youth! Arundel could do with a bit of Thomas's youthful vigor, when he felt nothing like a respected baron, more like a foolish old man.

When matters had settled an hour after luncheon and the boy was sent to bed — for the excitement gave way to exhaustion after a time of repeating his tale — Arundel sent for Elizabeth. There was a certain task he knew he needed to perform, but he was loath to do it until he had spoken with Elizabeth and heard her account of the events of the morning.

"Well, Lizzy," said he when his daughter was seated in his study, "it seems you have had some excitement this morning."

"Yes, we have," was Elizabeth's quiet reply.

"My gratitude for Mr. Darcy's presence is beyond what I can express, though I will confess I cannot account for it. One might think a most beloved daughter, whom I instructed with no possibility of misunderstanding to avoid a certain gentleman, somehow found a way to ignore her father's strictures."

When Elizabeth opened her mouth to protest, Arundel raised a hand and chuckled. "Do not concern yourself, Daughter, for I have no intention of accusing you of any wrongdoing. Given the few pointed words Bingley spoke to me after your return, I suspect *he* was the author of Mr. Darcy's presence. I must give Bingley credit, for he has proven himself to be more a lion than the puppy I made him out to be, or at least he is when he feels he has good cause. Given his actions — and those of his friend — have resulted in the continued good health of my son, it would seem ungrateful to me to take him to task, would it not?"

"I am also grateful Mr. Darcy was there," replied Elizabeth. "His actions relieved me of the need to follow my brother into the river, for there was no one else close enough to assist and Jane cannot swim."

"Then I am doubly grateful to the gentleman." Arundel paused and fixed his daughter with a look, though of some nonchalance. "Might I also assume you saw and spoke to Mr. Darcy before Thomas's adventure?"

Elizabeth's blush told Arundel all he needed to know, though she attempted to explain: "I had no notion of seeing him there. When he presented himself as I walked, I could not refuse to acknowledge him."

With a laugh, Arundel allowed it to be so. "No, I suppose you could not at that. I know little of these Darcys as individuals, and I will confess I have been proven shortsighted, given the events of the morning, but it seems your Mr. Darcy is a man of honor."

"Mr. Darcy is among the most honorable men I know, Papa," replied Elizabeth. "If Mr. Bingley is a good man—and he is—do you not think he would choose to surround himself with other good men as friends?"

Again, Arundel chuckled at the continued evidence of his daughter's intelligence. "That is not an aspect I considered, though I must submit to your good sense. I hope the elder Darcy is the man his son has established himself to be, for your sake, Lizzy."

Arundel could see the hope well up in Elizabeth even as she said: "What do you mean, Papa?"

"It is my thought, Lizzy, that the older we grow, the more obstinate, stubborn, and set in our ways we become. I am more than willing to own to my fair share of these traits myself. Thus, the most likely obstacle to your union with Mr. Darcy is the man's father."

Tears welled up in his beloved daughter's eyes. "You mean to support us?"

"Of course, I do." Arundel grasped Elizabeth's hand. "How could I not? It is clear that you love the young man and will not live without him. Logic, therefore, dictates that I must give way, or lose you, for I doubt you will be content to continue on this course for long. And if that sounds like an old man selfishly refusing to give up the company of his daughter, then I will own to it without disguise."

"Oh, Papa," said Elizabeth through happy tears.

"I want nothing more than your happiness, my dear. Please forgive a foolish old man for only remembering this after so serious an event as that which happened this morning."

"There is nothing to forgive, Papa," said Elizabeth.

"Forgiveness is required, I think, and I thank you for offering it without reserve." Arundel paused, his thoughts going down another path which might not be so easy. "This, however, depends on Mr. Darcy, Lizzy, for if he takes it into his head to oppose your union with his son, matters will still be difficult."

"Mr. Darcy—Fitzwilliam Darcy that is—possesses his own estate which he did not inherit through his father," ventured Elizabeth.

"Your discussions have proceeded to that point, have they?" asked Lord Arundel, giving his daughter a smile. When she confirmed it, he said: "Then that removes the problem of the gentleman being unable to support you. Might I suppose the estate is not a large one?"

"It is not, Papa, but we shall be well enough if it comes to that."

With a nod, Arundel replied: "With your dowry added, you will be comfortable, though it will not be the Darcy legacy. Then again, if what I suspect of your young man is true, it is very possible he will simply create a *new* Darcy legacy."

"I believe, Papa, we will set our minds and create a new family situation for ourselves if we must. Then again, I imagine we would do that at Pemberley too, should his father accept me."

"True," replied Arundel. "Then I would ask you to leave it to me, Elizabeth. I shall do what I can to persuade your future father-in-law of the inevitable. Know, regardless, that you have my permission and blessing."

Elizabeth rose and with great affection embraced him, which Arundel returned without hesitation. Seeing her so happy after she had been so despondent these last days — and had hidden it so well for the sake of her family — was a balm to his old heart.

"Thank you, Papa."

"It is the least I can do, Elizabeth. Now, get along with you, for I have a call I must make."

When Elizabeth departed, Arundel squared his shoulders and set about his task. There was little point in delaying, and every reason to act as soon as may be. It seemed his daughter's happiness depended on his ability to convince his neighbor to reconcile.

Robert Darcy was a man who was feeling far too much glee at the prospect of his old nemesis visiting Pemberley, though the situation had been reversed only a few short days ago. His son, Fitzwilliam Darcy, who sat by his father in his study, waiting for the baron to attend them, watched his father for signs of the pride which afflicted every member of the Darcy family — in this, the Bennets were not incorrect. His father would remember his manners soon enough, but it may not be before he offended the baron, an incident Darcy intended to prevent if he could.

"Why have you come here in all this state?" his father had asked when Darcy had returned to the estate, wet to his chest after his encounter with Thomas Bennet in the river.

"I happened to be of assistance to the Bennet family this morning, Father," Darcy had replied, much to his father's bewilderment. "The children were picnicking at the old ruin to the north when the Bennets' only son fell into the river. As I had been in the area and was able to help, I entered the water and caught him before he was carried away by the waters."

"You saved the future baron?" asked the elder Mr. Darcy, shock flowing from him.

"It was nothing, Father," said Darcy, eager to avoid any mention of heroics or the like. To assist was the mark of a gentleman, and to do so when able was the mark of any man of good moral fiber. "I was in a fortunate position which allowed me to fetch the boy from the water — anyone else would do the same."

His father's eyes narrowed in suspicion. "And why were you nearby?"

"I have already informed you of my intentions regarding the baron's daughter," replied Darcy, not giving an inch. "Bingley informed me of their plans and I went intending to see the woman I love. I am sorry if you do not appreciate my actions, but I will not apologize for them."

Mr. Darcy grunted, but then his manner turned introspective. Having changed — and fended off questions from his Aunt Catherine about the reason for his sodden state — Darcy spent the rest of the morning in his father's company, noting how the elder man remained distracted. Darcy knew the approximate length of time it would take for the Bennets to return to their home, and calculating that time, along with explanations and other such activities, he judged it likely the baron would grace their home by about the second hour after noon. It was obvious to Darcy that his father had made the same calculations and came to the same conclusion. The thought of the baron waiting on *him* was appealing to his father.

When the man in question entered the room, his erect bearing did nothing to promote the image of a humbled supplicant with hat in hand. As his eyes fell on Darcy, however, his gratitude was clear to see. Darcy did not mean to make him pay for that gratitude by humiliating him, nor would he allow his father to do likewise.

"Lord Arundel," said Mr. Darcy, rising to greet their guest. "Welcome to Pemberley."

"Thank you, Mr. Darcy," said Lord Arundel.

The lower-ranked gentleman did not offer his hand, and the higher did not appear to notice that lack. At once, Lord Arundel approached Darcy and offered his own hand, which Darcy did not hesitate to take.

"I wish to thank you, sir, from the bottom of my heart, for the succor you rendered my heir this morning in the river. Your quick actions showed great courage and selflessness, and I cannot express my gratitude for the nobility of character which prompted you to put aside the enmity between our houses and extend your helping hand to my distressed son."

"Lord Arundel," said Darcy, "please do not consider the matter any further. I believe that *any* man of any integrity would have acted the same way. The river is not deep, and even in its heightened state, I do not think I was in any danger. It was my pleasure to assist."

The baron chuckled. "I should take greater care in heeding my daughter's judgment, for she has informed me of your honorable nature. Now that I have seen it for myself, I can only be ashamed I allowed the situation between us to blind me.

"Though you do not know it, I believe you were of greater assistance than you know; Elizabeth informed me herself she was on the edge of following her brother into the river to attempt to retrieve him."

Darcy stared at the man in shock, not having known of Elizabeth's intentions. It was clear he should have suspected her capable of such an action, for there was no more fearless lady in the district. The baron had seen his shock and consternation, for he chuckled and squeezed Darcy's hand, which he still held.

"I see you had not known that, young man; it seems you do not know my daughter as well as you thought. Let me tell you here and now that my Elizabeth would jump into the depths of the sea to help another if she thought it necessary. In the future, I would recommend you keep her away from swiftly flowing rivers."

The mention of his future association with the baron's daughter heartened Darcy enough to provoke a grin. The baron returned it in every particular—for the first time it seemed they saw each other without prejudice marring their sight. Darcy felt that having this man for a father-in-law would be a desirable circumstance!

"I shall be certain to remember that, sir," said Darcy. "If there is any need to enter a river to save some unfortunate, I shall ensure that person is myself."

"An excellent notion."

"Thank you for coming here today," said Mr. Darcy, interrupting their greeting. Darcy turned to his father along with the baron and noted the elder man regarding him with some pride. The pleasant nature of their greeting, however, seemed to have removed the gloating from his father's mood, for he displayed none of it now.

"It was the least I could do, to thank my son's benefactor," said Lord Arundel. Then he turned to Darcy and added: "You should prepare to receive a certain measure of hero-worship from my son, sir, for he is certain you must be the equal of Hercules, at the very least."

Darcy laughed. "I shall endure it, sir, though I hope he will come to see me as an elder brother as we become better acquainted."

"Shall we sit down to a glass of brandy?" asked Darcy's father, once again taking their attention.

"That would be welcome, sir, for there is one other matter I have come to discuss. I suspect it would be more easily accomplished if we had some fortification."

Both father and son understood the baron's meaning, though the subject was more palatable to the son than the father. But his father said nothing, contenting himself with pouring a finger's width of the amber liquid into three glasses, and handing one to each of Darcy and the baron. When they sat around the desk, his father sipped his drink and made his opinion known.

"I believe it would be premature to accede to what I believe you are suggesting, Lord Arundel."

"I disagree," was the baron's firm but polite response. "The evidence of my daughter's feelings for your son has become unmistakable, and I cannot doubt his in return. It seems to me this is a perfect time and means of repairing the divide between us."

Mr. Darcy once again sipped from his glass, his manner introspective. "Yes, I understand the historical advantage of a strategic marriage. But if you will forgive my saying so, it seems to me my son's actions in assisting your heir have skewed your judgment."

"Influenced my judgment," corrected Lord Arundel. "I do not dispute your assertion, Mr. Darcy. However, I would say that rather than having skewed my judgment, as you say, it has caused me to reevaluate what I believe to be important. My daughter's happiness is of paramount importance to me. If we can help repair our relations through our children's happiness, then it seems we need not consider the matter further."

Nodding slowly, Mr. Darcy turned to his son. "I understand you have offered for Lord Arundel's daughter."

"I have, Father. In our eyes, we are engaged, though we have not been so fortunate as to gain the blessings of our fathers."

"I gave my blessing to my daughter before I departed Longbourn," said Lord Arundel. Then he grinned at Darcy and added: "Do not think, however, that removes the necessity to come to me to ask for her hand. It is the duty of every father to make the man his daughter means to marry sweat a little."

Darcy laughed along with the baron. "Have you not had your fill of it? Has Bingley not already sued for your eldest daughter's hand?"

"You have my apologies, sir, but it is tradition. We cannot go against tradition, can we?"

"No, I suppose not," replied Darcy with a chuckle.

The way his father was watching them, it seemed to Darcy he had come to some understanding of the man Lord Arundel was and found it intriguing. The elder man, much like Darcy was himself, was a man of soberness and duty, but that did not mean he did not know how to laugh. If they allowed themselves to come to know each other, Darcy could not but suppose they would each like what they saw and become firm friends.

"Tradition it may be," interjected Darcy's father, "but I wonder if it would not be better to take our time rather than rushing into a wedding."

"What do you mean?" asked Lord Arundel.

"Only that it may be best if we proceeded slowly. To the neighborhood and society at large, the Bennets and Darcys are still the bitterest of enemies. Perhaps a courtship would be advisable? Then society may become accustomed to seeing our children together."

"The prospect of further gossip concerns you?" asked Lord Arundel.

"Yes," replied Mr. Darcy. "We Darcys do not appreciate being the target of the wagging tongues of society, though I must confess the state of matters between our families has provided much fodder over the years. If we announce a sudden engagement between our offspring, there is no telling what others will say of them."

The notion of delaying his union with Elizabeth was not one which was palatable to Darcy, for he thought he had waited long enough. Then the thought of having Elizabeth as his wife, despite the rancor, despite decades of distrust and hostility filled him, and Darcy knew that to wait for a short time would be a small price to pay to achieve the desire of his heart. The other two gentlemen were watching him, Lord Arundel with amusement written upon his brow, while his father's look was more pleading. Darcy made the only decision he could.

"To prevent gossip, I will accept," said he. "But I will not wait for long. I should think a courtship of three months, followed by an engagement of another three should be enough to quell the worst tendencies of the gossips."

"Very well," said his father, though Darcy was certain he might have wished for more time. "If Lord Arundel will agree, then I will concur."

"That sounds reasonable to me, gentlemen," said Lord Arundel, raising his glass.

So decided, they spent a few moments speaking in a desultory fashion, and if their conversation was marked by a certain hesitation, Darcy was heartened to see the two elder gentlemen making the attempt. Nothing of any substance was said for the most part, but the first few tentative steps were taken between them. Then the baron raised a matter of importance to them all.

"What of Lady Catherine?" asked Lord Arundel, though his grin suggested he already knew of the situation. "It was my understanding that she wished your son to become her own. Shall she not cause trouble?"

"Anne and I both told her, in language which she could not misunderstand, that we would not fall in with her schemes." Darcy paused and laughed. "For that matter, do you know of Mr. Gardiner's association with my cousin, Anne de Bourgh?"

"Is there more fraternizing between our families of which I was not aware?" asked Lord Arundel.

The baron seemed inured to surprise by this time, though his words proved he was not aware of the connection between Anne and Mr. Gardiner. In as brief a manner as possible, Darcy explained what he had learned from Anne, and recounted the confrontation with Lady Catherine that very morning. The baron chuckled throughout his recitation, shaking his head in wonder.

"It seems our families are intent upon ensuring our spat is ended, sir," said he, raising his glass to Darcy's father. "I say there is no reason to attempt to deny them any longer."

"Yes, it appears to be so." Mr. Darcy paused and then said: "Lady Catherine will do as she will, and there is little anyone can do to prevent her. If she becomes too unruly, I shall send her home to Rosings. She may complain there as much as she likes, and it shall not concern me a jot."

"We may be buried by a flurry of letters expressing her displeasure," said Darcy.

Lord Arundel laughed. "From what I know of the lady, you may be correct."

"Is it not still early enough in the year to warm our rooms with our hearths?" asked Mr. Darcy in a wry tone. "If she bends enough of her attention to letter writing, it will relieve us from the burden of cutting wood for our fireplaces."

The three gentlemen laughed, but at that moment they became aware of a disturbance outside the room. It surprised Darcy to hear

Bingley's voice demanding to be shown to the study and was about to rise to investigate the commotion when the door swung open. Bingley appeared agitated, for he looked at them all, a hint of wildness in his eyes.

"Lord Arundel!" said he urgently. "I have just come from Longbourn. Your lady wife has discovered a note in Miss Lydia's room announcing she has left in Alexander's company for Gretna. They have eloped!"

CHAPTER XXXII

*F*or a moment no one spoke, the gentlemen in the room because they were too surprised, while Bingley was engaged in catching his breath. It was unsurprising to Darcy when his father provided the means of response.

"Alexander? Eloped with Miss Lydia Bennet? Impossible!"

In Darcy's mind's eye, however, he was considering Alexander's demeanor when he had ordered Darcy from Thorndell. Though he had not considered it at the time, there had been an air of determination about his brother—perhaps it was correct to say he *had* seen it but had not considered it anything other than Alexander's wish for him to leave. Could Alexander have eloped with the youngest Bennet? Darcy was forced to acknowledge it was possible—more than possible, in fact.

"Send word to Thorndell at once!" said Mr. Darcy, speaking through the door to the butler. "Send a footman asking Alexander to return to Pemberley."

"Of course, Mr. Darcy," said Mr. Parker, their butler, in a voice of much diffidence, after which he bowed and turned away, and Darcy's father stepped back into the study, confusion on his countenance. As the man who bore the tidings of the supposed elopement, the two elder gentlemen turned to Bingley while Darcy watched.

"What did my wife find, Bingley?" asked Lord Arundel.

"Your daughter did not appear when your son returned to the estate, but in the excitement no one noticed," replied Bingley. "Then, after Thomas was sent to bed and you departed, Lady Margaret became concerned that Lydia had not appeared today."

"Which is when she discovered Lydia's note," said Lord Arundel with a nod. "Did she speak with Lydia's maid?"

"Miss Lydia dismissed the maid when she retired yesterday evening and informed her she did not wish to be disturbed."

Lord Arundel shook his head and turned to his host. "It seems they planned this in advance, through what means I cannot say. There have been times when Lydia has stayed abed until late morning, so her absence early in the day would not have excited suspicion."

"Is this something of which you consider your daughter capable?"

When Lord Arundel did not answer at once and regarded Darcy's father with a pointed glance, Darcy reflected that not all had been put aside between the two families. There was still opportunity for misunderstanding and conflict if they did not take care to speak clearly. Fortunately, the Darcy patriarch seemed to understand how his words could be understood and hastened to clarify.

"If it seems like I was attempting to heap the blame on your daughter, I apologize. My son, I know, must bear a large measure of the responsibility if they have gone off together. It was not my attention to accuse."

"Do not concern yourself, Darcy," said Lord Arundel, waving him off. "It seems we must take care to avoid taking offense at everything one of us says. Regarding my daughter, I must say that she can be willful she feels she is justified. I have always said Lydia possesses far too much courage; unfortunate though it may be, that daring is not always checked by good sense. What of your son?"

Mr. Darcy considered the matter for a moment and grimaced. "Yes, I can see Alexander running off with your daughter. Though his reputation in the district is embellished, he, too, is accustomed to leaping where fool's fear to tread."

"I offer my apologies in advance," said Lord Arundel "but I must ask this question. Can your son be trusted to take her to Gretna?"

"I cannot see Alexander attempting anything untoward with your daughter," interjected Darcy.

"Yes, I must concur," said his father. "If he has taken her away, I must assume his purpose is marriage."

Lord Arundel spoke again. "It seems this event has given us new insight into the relationship between our progeny, and given what has happened, I cannot but suppose they have met far more often than we were led to believe." Lord Arundel's eyes found Darcy and he smirked. "It appears you are not the only Darcy son to be meeting with a Bennet daughter away from the eyes of society."

"That must be so," replied Mr. Darcy. "If we leave now, we may still reach them before they arrive at Gretna?"

"I must disagree with you, sir," said Lord Arundel when Mr. Darcy began to rise. At Mr. Darcy's frown he said: "They have had most of the day to put as much distance between themselves and Derbyshire as they can, and if your son is at all sensible, he will press on, stopping late and leaving early. Under those circumstances, they can reach Gretna Green within about three days' time. As they have almost a full day of travel, if they left early enough, it seems unlikely we could catch them before they arrive."

Mr. Darcy nodded, though his unhappiness could not be mistaken. When he rose and began pacing the room in his agitation, Darcy knew his father was considering going after them regardless.

"I should not wish my family name to be on the tongue of every gossip in Derbyshire and beyond," said he. "A marriage now must be inevitable, but should we not bring them back and force them to marry in the proper manner?"

"The family name has already been on more than one tongue these many years," was Lord Arundel's reply. In Darcy's mind, Lord Arundel seemed rather indolent now, for he was resting back in his chair, his eyes following Mr. Darcy's pacing with amusement. "I dare say an elopement—if they were both sensible enough to avoid . . . consummating their relationship until after the wedding—is much less serious than many other transgressions might be. When we put out news of the future marriage between your eldest and my second child, I believe that will become the main topic of gossip. I should think now that Alexander and Lydia have forced the issue, it would be best to announce the engagement, rather than waiting as you suggested."

The way his father's lips contorted suggested to Darcy that he had thought to use the time of the courtship to attempt to convince Darcy against Elizabeth. Whether his conjecture was true Darcy did not know, but he decided against pursuing the matter. There had never been any chance of success, and now events had proceeded too far to be recalled, regardless.

"I suppose you must be correct," said Mr. Darcy at length, ceasing his pacing by throwing himself into his chair. "When Alexander gets back, I shall give him a piece of my mind, and see if he possesses the stomach for it."

"Darcy, my friend," said Lord Arundel, still displaying that measure of jollity Darcy had noticed before, "I believe you are not considering the implications of these events."

Though his father frowned at the baron's use of the term "friend," he appeared intrigued by his words. "What do you mean?"

"Why, that this business between our families has been settled with very little effort on our parts. We cannot continue to be at odds if there are two marriages between our families."

"Perhaps three," interjected Darcy. When the elder men looked at him, he shrugged and said: "Remember the matter of Anne and Mr. Gardiner."

Three months ago it could not have been contemplated, but on that morning the two gentlemen looked at each other and laughed, Lord Arundel exclaiming: "Yes, this matter of Gardiner and Miss de Bourgh is intriguing! Since he has always considered himself to be my daughters' protector, I can only conjecture he thought to resolve our conflict himself.

"In that case, there is only one thing we can do—let us celebrate the end of our feud with a drink or two. And should you run out of brandy I have a fine French vintage at Longbourn waiting for us."

Again Mr. Darcy laughed and rose to his feet, going to the decanter. "You do not think my cellars are so poorly stocked, do you? I must own that I am scandalized—a peer of the realm in possession of illegal French brandy?"

"One of the perks of the position," said Lord Arundel with a dismissive wave of his hand. "I have a very good man of business who gets me a case occasionally."

"Then let us toast to our future," said Darcy's father, pouring brandy into the three glasses, while producing a fourth for Bingley.

Darcy, while he was feeling ebullient at the direction matters had proceeded, was not eager to stay with his father and his future father-in-law while they became soused on French brandy. It seemed Bingley was of like mind. Thus, after a single drink, the two younger men excused themselves, leaving the elder to their revelries, the intake of spirits and the shocking news having lowered their inhibitions toward each other.

"Shall we go to Longbourn, Darcy?" asked Bingley when they had exited the room. "I am eager to see my betrothed, and I cannot but suppose you are impatient to see your own."

Correct though Bingley was, Darcy had a sudden notion that Longbourn was not the most probable place to find Elizabeth. "You go on ahead, my friend," said Darcy. "Before I may depart, I believe I should like to have a word with my sister."

Whether Bingley understood his meaning Darcy was uncertain, but he was not about to delay. After a quick farewell and a hearty slap on Darcy's back, his friend made his way to the door with a spring in his step. Though Miss Bingley would not appreciate the upcoming acknowledgment of his engagement to Elizabeth, Bingley, it seemed, was eager to have him for a brother. Darcy was scarcely less eager himself.

It was a merciful bit of serendipity that Darcy found his sister together with his cousin; Lady Catherine nowhere in evidence. There was little doubt in Darcy's mind that the lady had sequestered herself to invent some stratagem to realize her wishes. Anne regarded him as he entered, her slight smirk suggesting she knew something of what had occurred, while Georgiana looked at him with curiosity for his cheerful state.

"You appear like the cat who has gotten into the cream, Cousin," said Anne. "As my mother has retired to her room for the afternoon, there is no reason for circumspection."

"What do you know of the matter?" asked Darcy, a mild amusement welling up within him.

"Only that Mr. Bingley arrived a short time ago appearing like a pack of wolves were nipping his heels," replied Anne. "Now, what has you in this uncharacteristic mood?"

"We have just learned of an event of some significance," said Darcy, as he proceeded to explain what Bingley told them. Georgiana, it appeared, was shocked, though all he could see in Anne's reaction was mirth. Then he explained their conjecture and the reason they had decided not to pursue the illicit lovers and informed them of his father and Lord Arundel's situation in his father's study.

"That leaves the field clear for you to marry your own Miss Bennet," said Anne with a grin.

"And leaves the field open for you and your Bennet relation," rejoined Darcy.

"That is yet premature, Darcy," said Anne with an airy wave.

"Bennet relation?" squeaked Georgiana. "Of what are you talking?"

"It is my understanding," said Darcy, winking at Anne, "that Anne has become comfortable with Mr. Gardiner of late."

"And yet we are not even courting yet," said Anne.

Darcy laughed. "Yes, for that to happen, I suspect we must send your mother back to Kent with all haste."

"And you mean to marry Miss Elizabeth?" asked Georgiana.

"We have already been engaged for some days," replied Darcy. "Now, having no other choice, our fathers have agreed to sanction our marriage."

"I am happy for you, Brother," said Georgiana. A shy smile came over her and she added: "When we met Miss Elizabeth, I liked her very well. I shall like to have her for a sister."

"Not to mention Miss Lydia," said Anne. "And there are three other sisters, too."

"Do not concern yourself, Georgiana," said Darcy, amused by his sister's sudden trepidation. "I suspect they will welcome you with open arms."

At that moment, the housekeeper arrived with a visitor in tow, a woman Darcy wished to see as little as he did his aunt—it was, perhaps, late for a social visit, but that had never stopped her before. Miss Bingley, sensing the good cheer in the air, glided toward them as if she suspected she was the subject of their ebullience. Then Anne, who had become Darcy's favorite cousin, took pity on him and addressed Miss Bingley in his stead.

"Thank you for visiting us, Miss Bingley. Come and sit with Georgiana and me, for I believe my cousin has an urgent errand to which he must attend at present."

"Yes, I do," replied Darcy, favoring his cousin with a grateful smile. "I believe I must be about it at once."

Miss Bingley, it seemed, was not willing to give up his company. "Mr. Darcy, I hurried here at once when I learned of your heroic actions to save young Master Bennet from certain death! Of course, I would have expected nothing else from a man of your quality. The circumstances which led to your presence there are a mystery, but I commend you for your actions."

The searching quality in her question was not lost on Darcy, but he was not about to allow her visit to keep him there against his will. "It is nothing more than any man of conscience would do, Miss Bingley," said Darcy, ignoring her comments about his presence there. "I would act the same in any such situation. Now, if you will excuse me, I must depart."

Though Miss Bingley opened her mouth, Darcy turned to stride from the room. As he departed, he heard Anne's voice addressing Miss

Bingley:

"Come, Miss Bingley," said she. "It appears there are a few matters we must discuss, for it has been an eventful day."

Darcy made himself a mental note to be Anne's most fervent supporter whatever she decided with respect to Mr. Gardiner. Taking upon herself the duty of informing Miss Bingley of his engagement to Elizabeth was a bit of kindness for which Darcy would always be grateful to her.

Now was not a time for such thoughts. There was a young woman Darcy was certain was waiting for them in their personal bit of heaven, and Darcy meant to join her as soon as may be.

To Elizabeth's great delight, she had predicted William's actions with perfection. As soon as they discovered her sister's flight and Mr. Bingley departed to inform her father, Elizabeth knew there could be no further impediment against her own marriage, regardless of how obstinate their fathers chose to be. It was a simple leap from that realization to expect William to depart from Pemberley hoping to meet her, and she was certain he would check the meadow before proceeding to Longbourn.

When he came charging toward her on his tall stallion, Elizabeth's heart skipped a beat at the sight of him. Soon she found herself in his arms, reveling in the freedom they would now have to express their affection, the future which had seemed denied to them now released. After their usual greeting, which consumed several long moments, they sat on their usual rock to speak of the matter.

"I suppose it would be customary to express regret for the actions of my imprudent sister," said Elizabeth.

"What of *my* imprudent brother?" asked William, to which they both laughed.

"Yes, I suppose his part in this is a match for my sister's," replied Elizabeth. "But even though I am a little vexed with Lydia for acting with such precipitous rashness, I cannot but be pleased with the result."

"It makes our own situation that much easier," agreed William. "Even my father is not so set against us now, though I should not have concerned myself with his opposition if he was."

Elizabeth turned to regard William, curious as to his father's behavior. "He still protests against me?"

"It is a little more complicated than that, I believe," replied William.

He proceeded to inform her of what had happened at Pemberley that day, the discussions before and after Mr. Bingley's arrival with the shocking news. Elizabeth laughed when he informed her of their state as he had left them alone and opined that her father would return to Longbourn a trifle disguised. Perhaps they were on their way toward friendly relations—she hoped so, for she wished to be cordial with her future father-in-law at the very least.

"I believe there must have been some cooperation from Lydia's maid," said Elizabeth as they spoke of how their siblings had kept in contact. "Hettie has often been a friend to Lydia as much as a servant. It is possible she was tasked with carrying messages to and from her mistress. My mother might have suspected it, but she will say nothing. Now that Lydia is to be married, I suspect Hettie will go with Lydia to her new home."

"That is likely for the best," agreed William. He paused, appearing pensive, and then said: "I can only hope that they will do well together."

"Lydia and Alexander?"

"Yes," replied William. "Alexander has often been unserious; forgive me if I am speaking out of turn, but your sister seems rather immature."

"You are not incorrect," said Elizabeth with a sigh. "Perhaps they will learn responsibility together, though I cannot imagine they will manage it without some effort."

"I have noted Alexander's improvement since he returned home," mused William. "It may be the demands of a wife and the care of managing his own estate will provoke him to become a better man."

"That is my hope," replied Elizabeth. Then she turned to him and said: "Now, enough of our siblings, for I had much rather speak of our future. Do you believe your father will still require us to wait six months before we can marry?"

William laughed and kissed her. "Given your father's opinion that an immediate announcement would be best to take the focus of the gossip away from our siblings, I cannot imagine he will not see sense."

"Good," said Elizabeth. "For I would not wish to defy him and create a greater scandal by setting off for Gretna Green this very afternoon."

With a delighted laugh, William exclaimed: "Yes, that would be unfortunate, would it not?"

"Unfortunate in the extreme! But I should not hesitate if they proved intractable."

"The question is, how to manage all these weddings," said William.

"Unless I am mistaken, I believe two of your sisters are already engaged, are they not?"

Elizabeth confirmed his words by saying: "Mr. Collins plucked up the courage this morning while the rest of us were picnicking."

"I should not wish to wait until your other sisters marry before taking you to the altar."

"Then we shall have a multiple wedding," said Elizabeth, shrugging as the matter was of no consequence. "Mary and Jane will, I am certain, be happy to share their wedding day with me. Jane and I have often spoken of how wonderful it would be if we married in the same ceremony."

"Bingley would not protest," replied William, "though I have no notion of how Mr. Collins would react."

"Mr. Collins would agree," assured Elizabeth. "In fact, I believe he would consider it a great honor."

"Then it is settled," replied William. "If your sisters are agreeable, we shall marry together."

For some time after, the couple sat and spoke in soft tones, the blanket Elizabeth had set underneath them providing comfort. While she could not like the way it had come about—and determined to press Lydia and new husband to account for their behavior when they returned—Elizabeth was grateful the last vestiges of resistance to their union were at an end. Their conversation was thus characterized by those little confidences shared between lovers. Not that there was no serious conversation between them.

"Uncle Gardiner and Miss de Bourgh," said Elizabeth when William spoke the possibility another marriage between the families. "I had heard nothing of a connection between them."

"It is ironic, is it not?" said William. "With three connections between our families through marriage, there will be no choice but to allow the matter between us to rest."

Elizabeth considered the matter for a moment before saying: "Yes, I suppose that must be."

"I hope they find happiness together," said William. "I was surprised how resolute Anne was against her mother's anger, and she will still need to face the prospect of enduring Lady Catherine's complains, for the lady will not give in without a fight. If Anne is determined to have Mr. Gardiner, that will prevent Lady Catherine from using her to arrange a stupendous marriage to spite me."

"While I would prefer to suppose you are jesting," said Elizabeth with a sigh, "I can imagine your aunt doing so given what I have heard of her."

"Oh, yes," replied William. "Lady Catherine is capable of that and much more."

"Is that not what landed our families in this predicament in the first place?" Mr. Darcy turned a questioning glance on her. "It seems to me," said Elizabeth by way of explanation, "much might have been avoided had this grudge not been passed down through generations. Perhaps our troubles began with a similar situation, a lover jilted or the interference of a domineering relation. You have my apologies if I am speaking out of turn, but I would rather those such as Lady Catherine mind their own concerns rather than cause trouble for all about them."

Mr. Darcy appeared amused. "Some might say that her daughter's future prospects *are* Lady Catherine's concern, the lady foremost among them."

"Perhaps they are. However, it strikes me that Lady Catherine's motivations are selfish."

"In that, you are correct, though I will not suggest you are sagacious for seeing it. The lady is nothing if not transparent."

With a grin, Elizabeth turned a playful look on William. "In the future, I hope you will check me, should I behave in so unreasonable a manner with our children."

"I assure you, my lovely future wife," said William, murmuring around a kiss he planted on her lips, "that I shall be your conscience and your best advocate."

Elizabeth might have responded, but at the moment she was much more agreeably engaged. It was some time before either said anything again.

Three days later a man stood in Gretna Green, watching the ebb and flow of humanity as they moved throughout the small town. It was a comely place, he supposed, though he did not see much of it, as his focus was on something else. Gretna's infamous blacksmith lay across the street, squat and dependable in the center of the town.

The trail had led to this place, over three days of travel, which might have been covered more quickly had the weather cooperated. The trail had been growing warmer as he traveled, so much so that his inquiries in the last town on the English side of the border informed him that his quarry had passed through less than an hour before. A quick pace set by the driver had given rise to the hope that he would be in time to catch them, but when Gretna had arisen on the horizon with no sign of them, he knew he was too late.

As he waited for them to emerge, David Gardiner considered the events which had led him here. A visit to his sister's home the afternoon of the event had revealed it to be in uproar because of the missing daughter, and while he might have awaited their return as he was certain Lord Arundel had done, something in Gardiner's character would not allow it. Lydia had never been his favorite niece, though he was fond of the girl—a part of him did not trust the younger Darcy, which had led to this long pursuit across the country. If he had set out even an hour earlier, he might have caught them . . . .

Now there was nothing to do but wait until they emerge and confront them. Even if he had succeeded in retrieving them before they eloped, he supposed it would not have stopped the inevitable. All he wished now was to determine if Lydia had done this of her own accord, with no undue influence by her paramour. If Alexander Darcy had pressured her, there would be a reckoning—this Gardiner pledged.

A few moments later, when the door to the establishment opened and the pair stepped out, Gardiner studied them, knowing they had not seen him yet. Lydia was, it seemed, so happy as to be almost incandescent, and her companion seemed scarcely less pleased. The sight was heartening, even while it annoyed him, knowing the worry and heartache these two had caused their families. It was that final thought which spurred him forward to confront them.

"Lydia," growled Gardiner, bringing the girl's fearful eyes snapping to him and startling Darcy. "What have you done?"

CHAPTER XXXIII

꘏꘎

onfronted as he was by the irate person of Mr. David Gardiner, the man with whom Alexander Darcy had shared public disagreements in the past, he did not know how to respond.

"Oh, my father will not chase after us," Lydia had said only moments after their departure three days earlier, "if we are gone long enough that he sees the futility."

"And what of your uncle?" Alexander had asked in return.

It was clear Lydia was not so certain of her uncle's actions, but she attempted to show a brave face regardless. "Uncle is not so fearsome as you believe."

"I am more concerned with whether he will pursue us with the purpose of preventing our marriage."

"It is possible," conceded Lydia. "If so, it would behoove us to proceed with all haste, would it not?"

To that Alexander could offer no rebuttal and had instructed his driver accordingly. While they had seen no sign of the man or any others who would stop them, Alexander had not relaxed until they stood within the blacksmith's, listening to the burly man perform the ceremony. That completed, none could separate Alexander again from the woman he loved.

To now be confronted by the person of Mr. Gardiner, the insecurities which had plagued him on the journey to Gretna returned with the force of a stampeding horse. Alexander had never had any illusions as to their families' opinion about their flight, a thought in the back of his mind leading him to propose to Lydia they retire to Thorndell rather than Pemberley and Longbourn, at least until tempers had calmed. The appearance of a belligerent member of her family was unwelcome after the joy of being joined together.

"Well?" demanded Mr. Gardiner when neither newlywed possessed the ability to respond. "I ask again: what have you done?"

As the young woman's new husband, Alexander felt it his responsibility to reply in her stead, prompting him to step forward and put himself in front of her. "I love your niece, Mr. Gardiner. As it was obvious our fathers would never accept our wishes, we decided there was no other choice but to elope."

"There is always a choice, young man," said Mr. Gardiner. The man's glare, which had heretofore focused on Lydia more than himself now beat down on Alexander, causing a nervousness to well up within him. Alexander had always thought Mr. Gardiner capable of implacable resentment and violence—it seemed this confrontation was about to prove those suppositions.

"Uncle," said Lydia, pushing her way forward and confronting Mr. Gardiner, her stance akimbo, one foot tapping with impatience. "I should think it is obvious what we have done. We have refused to allow the madness between our families and *your* efforts to separate us."

For a moment, Mr. Gardiner did not reply, his expression unreadable. Then he glanced away from his niece at Alexander, his gaze searching before he addressed Lydia again.

"I require you to answer me one question, Lydia. Can you please tell me if this mad escapade in which you have engaged was of your own volition? Or has this man persuaded you with the use of beguiling words and seduction?"

"There was no seduction involved, Uncle," exclaimed Lydia. Alexander could almost hear the rolling of her eyes in her head. "Can you imagine *me* enduring such disgraceful behavior? Not only did I travel here of my free will and judgment, but nothing improper has happened between us. I am yet a maiden—do you think I would allow liberties from any man without the protection of marriage?"

An odd look came over Mr. Gardiner's face as Lydia spoke, and he shook his head. "That, my dear niece, was a piece of information that, while comforting, I am not sure I needed to hear. No man who dandled a little girl on his knee wishes to be reminded that she is now a woman."

"I should think looking at me would inform you well enough," said Lydia with a huff.

"Perhaps you do. But any man wishes to continue to believe that his daughter—or young niece—remains as pure as the driven snow, even when she is in her dotage." Mr. Gardiner turned his gaze to Alexander and added: "Should you have a daughter of your own someday, you will understand."

Alexander surprised himself by grinning, a feeling of relief blooming in his breast—it seemed there was to be no further unpleasantness that day. "And yet, *you* are not a father, sir."

"At present, you are correct. But I have been much involved with my nieces and have some idea of my brother's feelings."

The reminder of the baron was not welcome at all. Mr. Gardiner, it seemed, noted this, for he gave them what Alexander thought was a rather vicious grin.

"No, I do not think your fathers will be at all pleased with this impulsive bit of defiance between you. My brother tends to be accepting, and other than the obligatory bit of threatening concerning his daughter's wellbeing, he will relent. As for your father, young man, though I cannot say I know him well, I suspect he will be harsher than the baron."

Even Lydia, by this time, appeared a little nervous, which Gardiner seemed to notice, as he barked a laugh. Alexander shared a look with his new bride and knew she was thinking the same as he was, though he had not yet mentioned his notion to her.

"It was my thought," said Alexander, voicing his opinion for both of them, "it would be better to retire to my estate at Thorndell for a time to allow tempers to cool."

Mr. Gardiner chortled. "It is no surprise you wish to avoid your families for the moment. However, I believe it would be better should you meet your fate sooner rather than later. There are many members of your respective families awaiting word of your return. You would not wish to cause further worry refusing to face them, would you?"

Alexander would *much* rather inform them all by way of a letter of their wellbeing. It was clear, however, that Mr. Gardiner was not about to allow it, and while Alexander was not averse to choosing his own path—as he had proven by stealing away with a baron's daughter— now was not the time to assert such independence.

"Do not concern yourself too much," said Mr. Gardiner with an entirely unwarranted level of amusement, in Alexander's opinion. "I doubt it will be uncomfortable for long. As I said, proving you will care for his daughter will placate the baron, and I have no doubt you will deal with your father in a similar manner." Mr. Gardiner turned a hard glare on Alexander. "You *do* promise to treat her like the priceless gift she is, do you not?"

"Of course," was Alexander's quick reply. "Lydia's happiness will always be foremost in my thoughts."

"Excellent! Now, it would be best if we departed for Derbyshire. I have already spent the better part of three days chasing you. The comfort of my home is calling me, and I have no desire to keep her waiting."

"Uncle," said Lydia in a diffident voice, "we had thought to stay in Gretna tonight before returning tomorrow."

"Nonsense!" was her uncle's jovial response. "We shall use my carriage — yours may follow along behind. There is much of which you are not aware, for your opinion regarding your union never receiving acceptance is not as accurate as you expected."

Alexander started and wondered what had happened — had William convinced their fathers to relent? Given no time to think on the matter further, for Mr. Gardiner led them toward his carriage and chivvied them inside, Alexander pushed thoughts of William and Miss Elizabeth to the side.

"Do not worry I shall keep you with me all the way to Derbyshire. I know young lovers wish to be alone in each other's company, and I shall not keep you for long. But for the present, there are certain matters about which you must be informed. Once that is complete, you may ride in your own carriage, while I follow you in mine."

Soon they were on their way, traveling most of the remaining hours until night began to fall. The revelations Lydia's uncle made to them as they traveled were no less surprising to Alexander than his bride, but they provided him with the hope that matters would not be as difficult as he had expected upon returning to their families. Though Mr. Gardiner had no intelligence of their fathers' reactions to the news of their siblings' connection, surely he could not continue to be so hardhearted when confronted with their union.

"I must own that I am surprised with you, Lizzy," said Lady Margaret. "As your father has said, I would have expected your youngest sister's defiance, but not yours."

This was not the first time in the previous days her mother had made such a statement; in fact, it had been a common refrain since Lydia left and her own engagement had become known.

"I am vexed with my youngest," continued Lady Margaret, repeating the refrain they had all heard several times already. "For she did not afford me the opportunity of planning her wedding."

"That is so," said Lady Charlotte, who was visiting them that morning, "but now you have Jane and Lizzy's weddings to plan, and I am certain you shall make up that lack with them."

"And do not forget Mary," said Elizabeth with a fond look at her sister. Mary beamed back at her.

"Oh, that is all very well," said Lady Margaret. "But whoever heard of a triple wedding? I had much rather plan a separate wedding for each of my girls as they deserve."

"And yet, Mr. Collins and I do not wish to wait a year to marry," said Mary, to Elizabeth's enthusiastic agreement. "We are more than content to share our wedding day, Mama."

"It is best to allow them their way, is it not?" asked Lady Charlotte. "Planning for a wedding is a large endeavor—only doing it once for three daughters is much easier than planning three separate fetes."

"I suppose it is if you put it that way." Lady Margaret regarded her progeny, seeming to attempt to determine how set upon this course they were. Elizabeth fancied she could detect the exact moment when her mother decided there was no arguing them from their positions, for she smiled and said: "Then I suppose we shall have to ensure it is a special occasion, one befitting all my daughters. And perhaps we can include Lydia in some part of the celebrations."

"And I am the only remaining unattached Bennet daughter," grumbled Kitty.

"Do not concern yourself, Kitty by dear," said Lady Margaret, diverted from her earlier thoughts, as Elizabeth thought was Kitty's purpose for speaking. "When you come out in London next year, we shall ensure you are the toast of society. Just think of how it will be— you alone of all your sisters will be out and single and will command the attention of a bevy of young gentleman suitors. Why, you shall have the pick of the lot!"

"Never mind all the *other* young ladies who will come out into society," said Elizabeth *sotto voce*.

As her mother was busy fussing over her second youngest and speaking of what they would expect, she had not overheard Elizabeth's comment. Jane and Lady Charlotte, who were close by, both laughed into their hands in delighted merriment. Kitty, Elizabeth knew, was not feeling left behind or unhappy at her status, and she thought the girl was eager to be in society without her sisters' vying for suitors' attention. As for her mother, Lady Margaret had the heart of an actress and had always desired to plan elaborate celebrations for her daughters' marriages. In the future, Elizabeth was certain she would look back on this time with gratitude they had accomplished three of them at once.

"Though I may echo your mother's words," said Lady Charlotte, "I must own that I am surprised with you, Lizzy."

Elizabeth raised an eyebrow at her friend. "I have it on good authority—from you yourself—that you knew of my meetings with Mr. Darcy."

"That is not it," said Lady Charlotte, a hint of laughter in her eyes and tone. "What surprises me is you did not inform me, your greatest friend, of your actions. I had thought we confided everything in each other!"

"Lizzy did not inform me either," said Jane, following along with Lady Charlotte's jesting.

"It seemed best to keep it to myself," replied Elizabeth. "I did not wish my two closest friends and sisters to ostracize me for the crime of loving a Darcy."

Jane and Lady Charlotte both laughed. "Oh, Lizzy!" exclaimed Jane. "Do you suppose that *I* of all people, would think ill of you?"

"Of course not," said Lady Charlotte. "Any more than I would think ill of her, considering my own dear Colonel Fitzwilliam is cousin to Mr. Darcy!"

"I also wonder how you could have overcome the acrimony between you," said Jane. "As I recall, did you not exchange terse words at the assembly in February?"

"Yes, we did," replied Elizabeth. "To own it, I have no notion of how it came about, for I was in the middle before I knew I had begun. Thinking back on it, I must assume Mr. Darcy had some interest in me, for the first time we spoke with any civility, he came upon me reading near the border between Longbourn and Pemberley, where we picnicked under the oak tree."

Jane and Lady Charlotte shared a look and a laugh. "That is certainly the way to our Lizzy's heart!" exclaimed Lady Charlotte with glee.

"Oh, yes," added Jane. "Mr. Darcy asked after her book and quoted verses to her, leaving her putty in his hands."

"I will have you know he did no such thing!" exclaimed Elizabeth. "Poetry, as you know, can never fan the flames of *impending* love. Mr. Darcy has never quoted verses to me."

"Then perhaps you should correct this lapse in him," said Lady Charlotte. "For there is nothing so wonderful as a man speaking words of the poets to you, for it feels as if the words were written for you alone."

"I should much rather a man quote Psalms to me," said Mary, "for it shows his devotion to me and to the Lord at once."

The statement was so like Mary that Elizabeth almost burst out into laughter. Unable to determine why a woman would wish to hear words of devotion as spoken by the Psalmist—hearing them on Sunday was another matter—Elizabeth gave her sister a smile.

"Mr. Collins will oblige you whenever you wish, dearest Mary."

"Indeed, I shall," said Mr. Collins, looking on his own Bennet sister with unfeigned devotion. Mary blushed at the sight while Elizabeth looked on with happiness for her sister.

"It has all ended well then," said Lady Charlotte. "Even though Lizzy's actions have been, by some calculations, imprudent—to say nothing of Lydia's—everything I have heard informs me our neighbors are happy the dispute has ended."

"That has been my sense too," said Elizabeth.

The entrance of several others interrupted their conversation. Georgiana had insisted on waiting on Elizabeth at once when she learned of the engagement, and in the intervening days, she had become a fast friend. While the elder Mr. Darcy remained aloof, the ladies of the family were eager to welcome their new relations, and visits were often exchanged between them.

All except for one of their number. As Georgiana and Anne, followed by William and Colonel Fitzwilliam, entered the room to greet the family, the brooding and unhappy presence of Lady Catherine followed behind. Seeing her with the group, Lady Margaret attempted to welcome Lady Catherine in particular, though her efforts to improve the woman's mood were nothing less than a failure. The rest of the company chatted away, and while Lady Catherine had as yet said nothing to Elizabeth of her disappointment, Elizabeth was certain it would not be long in coming.

"So, you have not thought better yet of marrying my dour cousin Elizabeth?" asked Anne in her teasing voice. Lady Catherine perked up at the notion, but Elizabeth dashed her hopes before she could even consider them.

"I am sorry to disappoint you, Anne. It seems you must endure me as a relation, for I am determined to have him."

"Well, I have done my best to dissuade you," replied Anne in a mournful tone. "I fear you have no notion what you are taking on."

"If you have not noticed, Anne," said William, "my manners have improved with Elizabeth's help. Now I have something about which to smile."

"It occurs to me to wonder if that is a jab at me, Cousin," said Anne with a mock glare. "The only other young woman to whom you have ever been connected in such a way was *me*."

"No one could repine the prospect of having you as a wife," exclaimed Lady Catherine, unable to remain quiet. "If your cousin has not chosen to exercise the privilege of having you as a wife, it is *his* loss alone. We shall ensure a stupendous match for you, the likes of which will fill all with envy."

The way Anne rolled her eyes Elizabeth thought she could guess the contents of her new friend's thoughts. It seemed Lady Catherine had discounted the notion of Anne and Mr. Gardiner out of hand. When the lady turned her attention to Elizabeth herself, the premonition of the lady saying something impolitic fell over Elizabeth. It appeared no one else in the room would have taken that wager, for the lady's character had become intimately known to them all.

"If this young lady had had any shame at all, she would not have intruded upon your already settled engagement."

"Settled, Aunt?" asked Darcy, the mildness of his tone belying his pointed look. Though Elizabeth knew he would defend her against anyone, his aunt prompted amusement and exasperation; it seemed he did not think it necessary to leap in when it came to Lady Catherine's ubiquitous complaints.

"It was the fondest wish of your mother and hers!" snapped Lady Catherine. "Though you have defied duty and common decency, I should think you would at least have the grace to understand that our plans have been thwarted by the upstart pretensions of a young woman without shame. You could have had so much better!"

"Is that so?" asked Lord Arundel. The way he looked at Lady Catherine showed the same mixture of amusement and aggravation they all possessed, though it seemed to Elizabeth her father tended more toward annoyance. "Elizabeth *is* the daughter of a baron. Though Darcy's father *did* marry the daughter of an earl, I should not think my daughter to be a less brilliant match for him."

"You know I was saying nothing of her standing," said Lady

Catherine.

"And yet, you have made it sound like Elizabeth is the lowliest scullery maid in all Derbyshire."

It was ever thus when Lord Arundel and Lady Catherine were in the same room together. Lord Arundel seemed to think the lady was crass, intrusive, and an unrepentant busybody, and Lady Catherine thought he was unserious, sardonic, and poor excuse for a peer.

"In fact," said William, interrupting their argument, "I am certain there could be no better match for me than Elizabeth. Not only is she the daughter of a baron," Mr. Darcy fixed his aunt with a pointed look, "but in terms of compatibility, I have found my perfect wife. There is nothing anyone could do to improve her, nor could I find someone better if I searched my whole life."

"Well said, sir," replied Lord Arundel, his challenging glare at Lady Catherine daring her to speak.

It was a challenge destined to remain unmet, for Lady Catherine fell into brooding and said little for the rest of their time together. Elizabeth did not miss the lady's poor attitude and biting comments, and she knew the rest of the company did not either.

A short time later, the company was treated to the long-awaited return of the newlyweds flown to Gretna. That was not without its own surprises, for when Uncle Gardiner led them into the room, Elizabeth saw she was not the only one who had not known of his involvement.

"Gardiner," said Lord Arundel, though his gaze did not leave his youngest daughter. "It is now clear why you ignored my letter asking you to come to Longbourn and take counsel with me."

"Indeed, Brother, I apologize," was Mr. Gardiner's reply. "When I discovered Lydia's disappearance, I followed them to attempt to prevent their precipitous match."

"I thank you for the attempt, though it seems like you were unsuccessful."

Mr. Gardiner grunted in reply. "I was less than an hour late, else I should have stopped them."

The focus of the party's interest turned to Mr. Darcy and the new Mrs. Darcy, who stood behind, relieved that Mr. Gardiner had been the first to speak. Lady Catherine scowled at them, as if they were the reason for her disappointment, while Lady Margaret stood and approached her daughter, placing a kiss on Lydia's cheek. To everyone's surprise, Lydia sobbed and buried her face in her mother's shoulder.

"I hope I can conclude these are tears of happiness, Mr. Darcy," said Lady Margaret, a hint of steel underlying her words.

The way Mr. Darcy regarded her mother told Elizabeth the gentleman had not expected the baroness to confront him instead of the baron. A darted glance at the aforementioned peer informed him he had best answer the question at once. Mr. Gardiner seemed disinclined to assist.

"Lady Margaret," said Mr. Darcy, with only a hint of a quaver in his voice, "it is my privilege to call your daughter my wife now, and while the manner in which it was accomplished is regrettable, I have no reason to believe Lydia is unhappy."

"Of course not," said a sniffling Lydia, pulling away from her mother. "Our departure was as much my doing as Mr. Darcy's. I am pleased to be Mrs. Darcy."

"They appear to be happy," drawled Uncle Gardiner. "Disgustingly so, in fact. It seems to me if they can rein in their impetuosity, they will do very well together."

"Lydia's happiness will always be my first priority," said Mr. Darcy.

"That is good to hear," said Lady Margaret. "But we are all afire with curiosity about how it happened and eager to hear your story. Do not think you are freed from the necessity of accounting for yourselves."

"And remember," said Mr. Gardiner, "once you have satisfied my family, you must go to Pemberley and see Mr. Darcy."

That task appeared more daunting to the newlywed couple than coming to Longbourn had been. Soon they took their places among the company to tell their story, Mr. Gardiner, Elizabeth noted, choosing to sit with Anne. The tale was similar in many respects to that Elizabeth and her Mr. Darcy had told only a few days before. The major difference was that Lydia and Mr. Darcy had conducted most of their illicit activities in or near Lambton, which made it all that much more amazing that they remained undetected as long as they had.

"I understand you have a similar story, Lizzy," said Lydia. "I hope you will not think less of me, considering how you were facing the same difficulties with which I contended."

"No, Lydia," said Elizabeth with affection. "Blame is not mine to apportion. Had matters continued as they were, I might have contemplated a similar solution."

"Please, no more elopements!" exclaimed Lord Arundel. "One in the family is enough. It is fortunate that most of society does not seem to concern themselves with your actions, though I do not suppose you will escape scrutiny the next time you venture into society."

"I believe I may safely promise you I have no intention of eloping, Papa," said Elizabeth.

"Unless relations once again turn sour," said William with a laugh. "If that happened, I will not be responsible for my actions."

Lord Arundel laughed. "Considering the way you dote on my second eldest, I am not surprised, sir."

"I find it ironic," said William's younger brother. "Having endured all of your lectures concerning proper behavior, I should not have thought you would meet a young lady in such an improper manner."

"As I informed you at Thorndell," said Darcy, "I had little to say about your tendency to seek out your wife. I was uncertain what I thought, but I did not think you possessed the level of affection for your wife you obviously do. For that, I apologize for misjudging you, Brother."

"Well, all is well that ends well," said Colonel Fitzwilliam. "I, for one, am grateful this ridiculous fighting between your families has ended. Had it gone on much longer, I might have taken to knocking some heads together."

Though Colonel Fitzwilliam delivered his final comment with some humor and the company obliged him by laughing, no one could disagree. It was nothing less than the truth.

CHAPTER XXXIV

❧⟨✤⟩❧

While the rest of Hertfordshire breathed a sigh of relief at the end of the hostilities between the two families, there was one who did not appreciate it. Then again, Elizabeth knew Lady Catherine did not dislike the warming of relations between the two families, notwithstanding her disinclination for the baron. To be more accurate, it was a matter which did not concern her, so she did not think about it at all. But the circumstances of that change concerned her, and she was not hesitant about sharing her opinions.

It would have taken the sudden loss of her sight for Elizabeth to misunderstand Lady Catherine's feelings toward her. The lady's glare upon catching sight of her when she entered the room at Pemberley during a morning visit would have rendered any lingering question of how Mr. Darcy's aunt had taken the news obvious had Elizabeth not already known of it. The only mitigating factor was how Lady Catherine remained silent and brooding in the face of the Bennet family's invasion of Pemberley that morning.

Upon seeing the woman, Elizabeth's thoughts turned to another woman, wondering how Miss Bingley, the other surely to resent her felt on hearing of the engagement. The thought passed swiftly, for it did not bear considering, in Elizabeth's opinion. She would become aware of it at some time or another, she supposed.

The other inhabitants of the house welcomed them, though the elder Mr. Darcy remained reserved as she might have expected. The Bennet sisters greeted their youngest sibling with affection, and soon it seemed like nothing had changed, for Lydia sat with Kitty nearby, whispering between themselves, giggles punctuating their discourse. That Lady Catherine was a frequent target of whatever comments were passing between them was not lost on anyone, least of all by the lady herself.

Elizabeth was more than happy to put the bitter woman out of her mind and give her attention to her betrothed, and William no less happy to receive it. In this manner, they passed half the allotted time for a morning visit. It was in the latter part of their visit that the interesting events took place.

It seemed Lady Margaret had taken a liking to Georgiana Darcy, for she sat by the girl asking her questions about herself, to which Georgiana responded with a certain measure of diffidence. This did not deter Lady Margaret, for her kindly attempts to come to know the girl better did not cease, and soon Georgiana was speaking with more, if not perfect, composure.

"It seems I must plan a wedding for three of my girls," observed Lady Margaret, "for they have determined that they wish to marry together."

This finally broke through Lady Catherine's moody silence. "A triple wedding! Whoever heard of such a thing?"

Lady Margaret, who had not been insensible to Lady Catherine's unhappiness, ignored the other woman. "I will, of course, wish to solicit your opinion, Miss Darcy, for you must know your brother's preferences. As his nearest female relation, your assistance would be invaluable."

"I am eager to help in any way I can," said Miss Darcy, to the sound of Lady Catherine's disdainful snort.

"Thank you, my dear," said Lady Margaret. "You should visit Longbourn next week so we may discuss the details."

"It seems I am the only Bennet daughter who has remained unattached," complained Kitty, by now a familiar refrain. "It is most unfair, for Lydia is younger than I."

"I will take you to the season next year, Kitty," said Lydia, squeezing her sister's hand in support. "We shall be very merry together, I am sure."

"Do not concern yourself, Kitty," said Lady Margaret, her reply also one which had been repeated many times. "Think what the next season shall bring: you shall experience your coming out and will not have your sisters to pull attention away from you. I think you will do very well next season and will have many admirers."

Lady Margaret turned and regarded Miss Darcy. "Perhaps you and Miss Darcy will enjoy the season together, for you are to come out next year also, are you not?"

The look with which Miss Darcy regarded her father set the man to chuckling. "I do not believe we have made that determination yet, but it seems as good a time as any."

"Then we shall plan Miss Darcy and Kitty's coming out together. A joint ball in London would be lovely."

"There is no need for you to put yourself out for my niece," said Lady Catherine, finally voicing her opinion. "I am her nearest relation and will have matters well in hand."

"Yet you live in Kent, Lady Catherine," said Mr. Darcy, "and Lady Margaret lives close by. In fact, I believe it would be beneficial to further show society that our difficulties are behind us by introducing our unmarried daughters together."

"Thank you, Mr. Darcy," said Lady Margaret, again ignoring Lady Catherine's annoyed huff. "Of course, I welcome the aid of all your relations in our planning. Perhaps we should include Lady Susan Fitzwilliam, for she has experience debuting her own daughters — I am certain Miss Darcy would welcome another friendly face."

"Susan has always spoken of assisting Georgiana," agreed Mr. Darcy.

"Then it is settled." Lady Margaret regarded Miss Darcy with a friendly, open smile, which the girl returned. "I hope you will come to consider us all your family, my dear, for you are gaining my daughters as sisters."

"I should like that, Lady Margaret," said Miss Darcy.

"There is nothing to be done, I suppose," said Lady Catherine, though her tone suggested she wished fervently there was something she could do to alter what was already decided. "Miss Elizabeth Bennet, come and sit with me for a time. Since there is no way to stop this . . . marriage from happening, I suppose I must work with what I have."

"You have my apologies, Lady Catherine, but I would ask you to clarify what you mean, for I do not understand you." Contrary to her assertion, Lady Margaret's harsh glare suggested she knew very well what the other woman meant and did not like it at all.

"Why," said Lady Catherine, her insolent tone deepening Lady Margaret's frown, "that if your daughter is to be my nephew's wife she must be trained to move with the proper decorum in society. I cannot have my brother's family disgraced by a young lady who does not know how to behave."

By her side, William shook his head, while Mr. Darcy appeared to be willing his sister to desist by the force of his eyes boring holes through her. Lady Margaret ignored the chuckles and shaken heads of the other members of the party to reply in a manner so frosty to Lady Catherine, that Elizabeth wondered why the other lady was not sporting icicles.

"Elizabeth is the daughter of a baron, Lady Catherine. There is no need to teach her how to move in society, as you say, for she not only possesses all the necessary ability but has been out in society for more than two years."

Lady Catherine's eyes raked over Elizabeth with contempt. "Considering how she was willing to meet in private with my nephew, not to mention your youngest daughter's infamous elopement with my other nephew, it seems to me your instructions have been deficient."

"Though I wish they had been more circumspect," said Lady Margaret, "I cannot argue with the results. In the end, no harm has been done, and my daughters have found their happiness."

"Of course, *you* would argue the ends justify the means when it benefits *your* family." Lady Catherine sniffed with disdain. "But we Fitzwilliams hold ourselves to a higher moral standard."

"And *your* nephews were not meeting with *my* daughters?" asked Lady Margaret. "Branding my daughters as improper when your nephews were engaged in the same behavior is more than a little hypocritical."

"I believe she has you there, Aunt," said Colonel Fitzwilliam with a chuckle and a shake of his head.

Lady Catherine did not deign to respond to her nephew, instead looking to William. "There is still time to extricate you from this entanglement, Darcy."

"It is time to drop the subject, Aunt," was William's even reply. "I have no interest in marrying Anne, and she will not have me. This fantasy you have perpetuated so long is at an end."

Though she regarded him with pursed lips, Lady Catherine was not ready to confess defeat. "If you are not to marry Anne, you should aim for at least the daughter of an earl, if nothing else than to honor your late mother."

"Could there be any greater honor to my mother than marrying a woman who will make an excellent mistress of Pemberley?" asked Darcy.

"You know to what I refer," spat Lady Catherine. "A marriage to the daughter of an earl would gain a useful connection. Marrying this . . . woman's daughter," Lady Catherine waved at an irate Lady Margaret, "gains you nothing, as your brother has already imprudently connected himself to the family. What of the Earl of Carlisle? It is my understanding he has several daughters, any of whom would do as a wife."

As Darcy shook his head in exasperation, Fitzwilliam spoke up, saying: "Carlisle is also an unmitigated ass. Father would disown Darcy if he married one of the man's daughters."

"There are many earldoms to which we do not possess a connection," rejoined Lady Catherine.

"And none of their daughters are Elizabeth Bennet," said Darcy, fixing his aunt with a pointed glare. "Before you say anything further, Lady Catherine, let me remind you I am my own man and care little for alliances and titles. I have chosen Miss Elizabeth because she suits me in every particular. I would ask you to cease your objections, for they will have no effect on me."

Mr. Darcy took up the argument, smiling, though faintly at Lady Margaret, saying: "I apologize for allowing you to be importuned so. I am old and the weight of change is difficult to bear; it appears it is doubly so for my sister by marriage.

"The point is," continued he, turning back to a seething Lady Catherine, "that the reconciliation between our families is a blessing, and I see no reason to deny my eldest son his happiness when my younger son has already married into the family. And before you say it, let me inform you I care as little about titles and connections as William. Why, half of those to whom we are connected I would not even greet if I had the choice!"

"Let me also be understood without any confusion, Aunt," said Alexander, speaking for the first time and fixing Lady Catherine with a withering glare, "I will tolerate no unkindness toward my wife. If you persist, we shall retire to Thorndell."

It seemed Lady Catherine had no reply for her brother and nephews' words, though her glare was hateful. How the argument might have proceeded Elizabeth did not know, but it was interrupted by the exclamation of one who had rarely held her tongue.

"Upon my word, Alexander," exclaimed Lydia, "I do not know how you withstood this harridan all these years."

While Lady Catherine purpled with rage, snickers burst forth from most of the rest of the room, and Lady Margaret looked on her rival with smugness. Seeing she was outnumbered, Lady Catherine decided retreat was the best option.

"It seems no one here wants my opinion."

"At last, she understands," muttered Lydia, to further tittering of the group.

Though Lady Catherine shot Lydia a hateful glare, she addressed her daughter. "Come, Anne, it seems there is nothing left for us in Derbyshire. We shall return to Kent to plan for your future. Since Darcy has spurned you, I see no reason we cannot capture an earl at the very least."

The lady turned and began to sweep from the room and was halfway through the door before she realized her daughter had not followed her. The confused glance she directed at Anne did not improve her image to those in attendance.

"Let us go to our rooms, Anne, for we have much to do to depart on the morrow."

"If you mean to depart, Mother," replied Miss de Bourgh, "then I wish you a pleasant journey. If Uncle will oblige me, I would much prefer to stay at Pemberley."

"Should he refuse," interjected Lady Margaret, "you may stay with us at Longbourn."

No one missed Lady Margaret's dig at Lady Catherine, least of all the lady herself. Mr. Darcy stepped in to defuse the situation.

"Of course, you may stay as long as you wish."

"This is not a matter for debate, Anne," said Lady Catherine, finally finding her voice. "Come with me at once. We will depart tomorrow."

"You may depart, but I will stay. As I have already informed you, I have entered a courtship with a good man; I wish to stay and discover if I wish to wed him."

"You will do as you are told!" screeched Lady Catherine. "I am your mother; you will obey me."

"I am of age and may do as I please," said Anne, remaining calm in the face of Lady Catherine's anger.

"Do you wish me to disown you?"

Anne snorted. "I am not a simpleton, Mother. I know very well that Papa left Rosings to *me*. Now that I am of age, the estate is mine, and nothing you say may affect his wishes. That I have continued to allow you to act as mistress shows my affection for you, but I will warn you now my patience is waning fast."

It seemed Miss de Bourgh's reply rendered Lady Catherine senseless, for she stood there, staring at her daughter for several moments. Then she did perhaps the most sensible thing Elizabeth had ever seen her do—she turned and walked from the room.

"Faugh!" said Lydia with clear disgust. "How you endure that woman is beyond my understanding, for she is the worst meddler I have ever seen in my life!"

Though Anne giggled at Lydia's words, Mr. Darcy turned a pointed look on her. "Catherine can be difficult, but a little decorum and restraint on your part would be welcome, Daughter."

"Lydia is yet young," said Lady Margaret, her gaze on her daughter a match for Mr. Darcy's. "A little maturity and experience will do wonders, though she has always been an outspoken child."

The gentleman and baroness exchanged glances which suggested they had reached an accord. Miss Darcy was soon pulled into Lydia and Kitty's orbit, and soon the three were speaking together in low tones, looking for all the world like three conspirators engaged in mischief. With Lady Catherine's exit, the group calmed, allowing Elizabeth to turn her attention back on her betrothed.

"Do you suppose Lady Catherine will subside?"

William's huff of disdain spoke to his feelings for his aunt. "Do not suppose Anne routing her in this skirmish will end the battle. I am certain she will return with greater force and attempt to browbeat her daughter into departing."

"Never would I have suggested such a thing!" exclaimed Elizabeth with a laugh. "It is clear she is a lady who little appreciates being gainsaid. Her daughter's defiance cannot have been palatable at all."

"And yet, she will not prevail over Anne's determination, I think. Though Lady Catherine has never deigned to see it, in many respects Anne's stubbornness is a match for her mother's."

"I am glad to hear it." Elizabeth paused and fixed William with a curious look. "What do you think of this matter of marrying in the same ceremony as my sisters? I hope you are not offended that our day together shall not be ours alone."

"My dearest, loveliest Elizabeth," said William, "I prefer to concern myself with nothing more than having you for my wife. If we should marry in a ceremony with fifty other couples it should not matter to me, as long as we say our vows together."

"Fifty!" exclaimed Elizabeth. "I have not the sisters for that, to say nothing of how tedious it would be to stand and listen to nine and forty other couples recite their vows."

William fixed her with an amused grin. "If we are among the first, we will be at leisure to depart and leave them to their own weddings."

"Then I shall leave you to supervise this epic endeavor, my dearest fiancé, for such a large wedding would be beyond my ability to endure."

"Then we shall have to content ourselves with three. As long as you are there, I shall not repine its simplicity."

For a moment, her mother shaking her head at them distracted Elizabeth, for it was clear Lady Margaret had overheard their irreverent conversation. When Elizabeth fixed a smile on her, Lady Margaret gazed skyward before directing a grin at her daughter, seeming to suggest she understood Elizabeth's proclivity for humor.

For the rest of their time together that day, Elizabeth was inseparable from her fiancé, having no time to give to anyone else. It seemed they had finally achieved that which they desired — a cessation of hostilities between their families, their blessings and their love. Nothing could be superior to this bliss.

EPILOGUE

$\mathcal{A}$s Elizabeth had speculated with her husband, Anne had stood strong against her mother's efforts to bend her to her will. When the lady departed the following day, it was with a sour expression and the expected recriminations. Since that day she had not appeared in Derbyshire. Today, however, the lady was to return.

"What do you think of this, Anne?" asked Elizabeth, gesturing to a sample they were perusing in anticipation of Anne's impending wedding.

"Oh, yes," said Lady Margaret, "that would be divine at your engagement ball."

"It is lovely," said Anne. She paused and laughed: "My mother might not appreciate it, for she does not like lavender. She calls it a weak, uncertain sort of color."

"All the more reason to have it," said Lydia with a sniff of disdain.

Elizabeth looked at her sister with a certain amount of exasperation. Though she had now been married more than a year, Lydia had not settled to any great degree. She was still fearless, at times loud, and invariably outspoken. The one thing Elizabeth could say with certainty was that Lydia was besotted with her husband, which sentiment Alexander returned. Fearing, as she had, for her sister's happiness when she had stolen away to elope the previous year, Elizabeth could confess a certain measure of relief it had turned out in that happy way.

"Perhaps it is not politic to suggest a choice because another would not appreciate it," said Lady Margaret, casting a quelling glance at her youngest. Elizabeth doubted it affected her sister to any great degree, but it did silence Lydia's comments for the moment.

It was amusing, Elizabeth thought, for Lydia had insisted on sitting in on the preparations, behavior which mirrored the planning for the wedding Elizabeth had shared with Mary and Jane. While the girl would not own to any such feelings, Elizabeth suspected she regretted her own hasty decision to elope and treated her sisters' wedding as her own vicariously. In Elizabeth's opinion, Lydia viewed Anne's wedding much the same as she had her elder sisters'. Cognizant though she was that Lydia's imprudence had allowed Elizabeth herself to marry more quickly, she felt a certain level of exasperation for her, for had she waited only a little longer, Lydia would have had a wedding of her own.

Matters had not been without difficulty between the two families, mused Elizabeth as the other ladies debated this fabric or that ribbon, discussed colors and combinations and flowers. Decades of enmity and distrust were not overcome in an instant, no matter how many marriages took place between the families. In particular, in accordance with her father's prediction, Mr. Darcy and Lord Arundel had almost come to blows on several occasions.

While it had been difficult and feelings had been offended more than once, the result was worth the effort. The two families were becoming more comfortable with each other, as this forthcoming wedding between Anne de Bourgh and Uncle Gardiner could attest. Elizabeth was amazed at the changes which had come over her uncle since he began courting Anne. A confirmed bachelor, the family had long thought the continuation of the family line would run through Uncle Edward and his sons. But Uncle Gardiner was reinvigorated by Miss de Bourgh as if he had shed a decade of careworn years in the space of a few months.

Watching them while they courted was a joy to behold, for it was obvious they were deeply in love. And with Anne's influence, Mr. Gardiner became less rigid, a more open sort of gentleman. And with her uncle's love and devotion, Anne had become less cynical and sardonic, and happier than she had seemed before. This was why the family was dreading the return of Lady Catherine, for if there was anyone who could inject division and argument into a harmonious condition, it was Lady Catherine de Bourgh.

"Lizzy, what do you think of this?" asked Georgiana, pulling Elizabeth's attention back to the discussion. "Anne is uncertain of this blue with the lavender, but I think they look beautiful together."

"It is not how well they complement each other," said Anne, gently contradicting her young cousin. "My dress will reflect some of these colors we choose, and I do not wear blues well."

"That is true," agreed Elizabeth, smiling at her sister-by-marriage. "Anne does appear to greater advantage in greens."

"Then what of this?" suggested Lady Margaret, holding up a sample of mint green.

As her companions began to once again debate the merits of colors and fabrics, Elizabeth's mind slipped back into her thoughts. Georgiana had blossomed under the combined tutelage of Elizabeth, Anne, and especially Lady Margaret. She and Kitty had made a wonderful debut, both cutting a swath through the hearts of gentlemen in society. Neither was interested in a quick attachment, which Elizabeth felt was for the best, but each had had suitors, and even one persistent young gentleman had made an offer for Georgiana. It had taken the combined power of the Darcy gentleman to convince the man she was not interested. Privately, Elizabeth suspected Colonel Fitzwilliam had offered to beat him to a pulp before he had finally desisted, though none of the gentlemen would speak of the matter.

In Elizabeth's opinion, the return from London had been accomplished at the perfect time. They had been in society for two months, the object of curiosity more often than not, for more than just those in Derbyshire knew of the rivalry between Bennet and Darcy. Anne's upcoming wedding had been a convenient excuse for them all to retreat, and Anne herself had been the subject of more interest than usual, now that William was off the market. That she had already been engaged by the time they went to London had meant little to some of them. Elizabeth's uncle had proven his reputation when he had disabused more than one young man eager to gain an estate that Miss de Bourgh would not be changing her mind.

"What of this one?"

The sound of the voice caught Elizabeth's attention, and she looked toward Miss Bingley, who was sitting beside Anne, engaged as any of the others in the debate. The woman had been a surprise to Elizabeth, for while she had been unhappy to learn of the engagement she had so desperately wanted, she had accepted it far sooner than Elizabeth might have expected. Though the woman remained unengaged herself, the rumors were that she had made the acquaintance a young man of a neighboring shire. Elizabeth had not heard more, for the woman remained reticent, but she wished Miss Bingley the best.

Mary and Mr. Collins were not present, though Elizabeth understood they hoped to attend the wedding. Unlike Jane, Elizabeth, or Lydia—none of whom had yet fallen with child—it seemed Mary had done so immediately, for she had given birth to a son almost two months earlier. He was a lusty child, from what Elizabeth had heard, and as he was also the first grandchild, Lady Margaret doted over him, proud of her middle and most unassuming daughter.

The ladies stayed in this attitude for some time after, Elizabeth becoming more involved with the discussion as it progressed. They had almost decided when there was a commotion in the corridor outside the room, and in walked the imperious figure of Lady Catherine.

Those in the room rose at the sight of the lady, while Elizabeth noted several others following her into the room, among them her husband. For a moment no one spoke.

"I see you have begun the preparations," observed Lady Catherine, surprising them all with her choice of greeting.

"Yes, Mother," said Anne, the intended recipient of Lady Catherine's comment. "The wedding is fast approaching. We would be unprepared if we had not already started."

Lady Catherine sniffed, but the action was surprising in its lack of clear disdain. "I hope you have not chosen lavender," said she, gesturing to the sample on the table near where Anne was sitting.

"As a matter of fact," said Anne, "we *had* considered it, but we rejected it in favor of light green."

"That is well, for you always looked wonderful in green."

"Thank you, Mother. I believe you are correct."

A pause ensued, and not a comfortable one. It seemed no one knew what to say. Behind Lady Catherine, Elizabeth noted her husband, and when William saw her regarding him, he shrugged his shoulders and looked at his aunt with exasperation. Elizabeth saw what was happening—Lady Catherine, having spent a year estranged from her daughter, wished to be admitted to her circle again, but was unwilling to debase herself to achieve it. Thus, Elizabeth made the first overture, for it was, in the lady's mind, Elizabeth's engagement that had led to the death of all her dreams.

"You must be exhausted from your travels, Lady Catherine," said

Elizabeth, gesturing toward the chair she had occupied. "Please come and sit while I call for tea. Or, if you prefer, you may seek your room to refresh yourself."

Though startled at being addressed, Lady Catherine's expression softened. "I am not fatigued at present, but I should change soon. First, I must . . . I should like very much to learn what you have accomplished, Anne."

"Of course, Mama," said Anne, throwing Elizabeth a grateful smile. "Come and sit with us, and we shall share what we have done. We would all appreciate your opinion."

Lady Catherine did as Elizabeth bid, while Elizabeth called Mrs. Reynolds to bring a tea service for her ladyship. With Lady Catherine in their midst, the discussion resumed, and if the lady stated her opinion with more volume and force than necessary, she did not direct and expect to be obeyed as she might have in the past. On one particular occasion in which the lady stated her opinion, Anne looked past her mother, caught Elizabeth's gaze, and rolled her eyes, requiring Elizabeth to stifle a giggle.

"Thank you, Elizabeth," said William quietly, stepping next to Elizabeth and pulling her close. "You have as much reason as any to resent Lady Catherine, and yet you have welcomed her into our midst with conciliatory words and gestures."

"It would be best if Lady Catherine reconciled with her daughter," replied Elizabeth. "I could see at once that she wished to be accepted — she simply did not know how to ask for it."

"Then it shows some greatness of mind to recognize her feelings for what they were," said William.

"I see it as the last vestige of our families' former troubles being put to rest. How can I not support such a worthy goal?"

"How, indeed?" asked William, pressing a kiss to her forehead. "It is my great happiness that I have you in my life, Mrs. Darcy, for there were times I wondered if it would all end in this happy manner."

"And yet, it is easy, in hindsight, to see how this end was inevitable," said Elizabeth. "It was that or open warfare."

William laughed. "Then we may be grateful it was not that second option. For if it had been, the only recourse would have been to emigrate to the New World."

"If it had come to that, my dear husband, I would have followed you there. I would have followed you anywhere."

Focused as they were on each other, neither Elizabeth nor William notice the look Lady Catherine was giving them. It was a wistful softness with none of the lady's rancor. But others noticed, and when Lady Catherine gave them a sad smile and turned back to the discussion with the rest of the ladies, they all knew the last bit of defiance in her had died. The conflict between the families was now dead, leaving a bright future in its wake.

The End

MORE GREAT TITLES FROM ONE GOOD SONNET PUBLISHING!

PRIDE AND PREJUDICE VARIATIONS

By Jann Rowland

Acting on Faith
A Life from the Ashes (Sequel to
Acting on Faith)
Open Your Eyes
Implacable Resentment
An Unlikely Friendship
Bound by Love
Cassandra
Obsession
Shadows Over Longbourn
The Mistress of Longbourn
My Brother's Keeper
Coincidence
The Angel of Longbourn
Chaos Comes to Kent
In the Wilds of Derbyshire

The Companion
Out of Obscurity
What Comes Between Cousins
A Tale of Two Courtships
Murder at Netherfield
Whispers of the Heart
A Gift for Elizabeth
Mr. Bennet Takes Charge
The Impulse of the Moment
The Challenge of Entail
A Matchmaking Mother
Another Proposal
With Love's Light Wings

By Lelia Eye

Netherfield's Secret

ALSO FROM ONE GOOD SONNET PUBLISHING
A COLLECTION OF COLLABORATIONS

PRIDE AND PREJUDICE VARIATIONS

By Jann Rowland & Lelia Eye

WAITING FOR AN ECHO

Waiting for an Echo Volume One: Words in the Darkness
Waiting for an Echo Volume Two: Echoes at Dawn

A Summer in Brighton
A Bevy of Suitors
Love and Laughter: A Pride and Prejudice Short Stories Anthology

By Jann Rowland, Lelia Eye, & Colin Rowland

Mistletoe and Mischief: A Pride and Prejudice Christmas Anthology

PRIDE AND PREJUDICE SERIES

By Jann Rowland

COURAGE ALWAYS RISES: THE BENNET SAGA

The Heir's Disgrace
Volume II Untitled*
Volume III Untitled*

OTHER GENRES BY
ONE GOOD SONNET PUBLISHING

FANTASY

By Jann Rowland & Lelia Eye

EARTH AND SKY SERIES

On Wings of Air
On Lonely Paths
*On Tides of Fate**

FAIRYTALE

By Lelia Eye

The Princes and the Peas: A Tale of Robin Hood

SMOTHERED ROSE TRILOGY

Thorny
Unsoiled
Roseblood

About the Author

Jann Rowland

Jann Rowland is a Canadian, born and bred. Other than a two-year span in which he lived in Japan, he has been a resident of the Great White North his entire life, though he professes to still hate the winters.

Though Jann did not start writing until his mid-twenties, writing has grown from a hobby to an all-consuming passion. His interests as a child were almost exclusively centered on the exotic fantasy worlds of Tolkien and Eddings, among a host of others. As an adult, his interests have grown to include historical fiction and romance, with a particular focus on the works of Jane Austen.

When Jann is not writing, he enjoys rooting for his favorite sports teams. He is also a master musician (in his own mind) who enjoys playing piano and singing as well as moonlighting as the choir director in his church's congregation.

Jann lives in Alberta with his wife of more than twenty years, two grown sons, and one young daughter. He is convinced that whatever hair he has left will be entirely gone by the time his little girl hits her teenage years. Sadly, though he has told his daughter repeatedly that she is not allowed to grow up, she continues to ignore him.

Please let him know what you think or sign up for their mailing list to learn about future publications:

Website: http://onegoodsonnet.com/
Facebook: https://facebook.com/OneGoodSonnetPublishing/
Twitter: @OneGoodSonnet
Mailing List: http://eepurl.com/bol2p9

Made in the USA
Columbia, SC
09 August 2020